GRIFFIN FARM

C.A. MacConnell

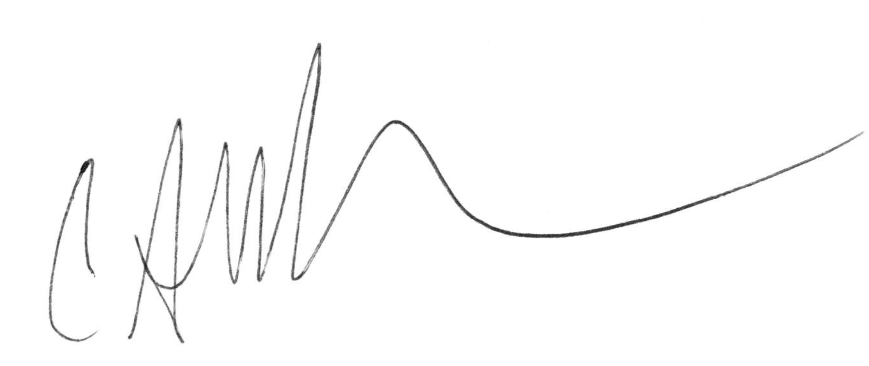

Acknowledgements

I would like to express my utmost gratitude to my higher power and to the following people, animals, and organizations: my loving family, Jess & Kel, Noah, Mardi Belfiore, Elise Allred, Jennie Smith-Parker, Alicia Rosselot, Adrienne Foster, Mary Sawyer, Kylin, all those who knew and loved Red Fox Stables, Star Attraction, Southern Accent, *CityBeat Magazine*, Larry Gross, Greg Flannery, John Fox, Mike Breen, The National Alliance on Mental Illness, Pat Brown, The Mercantile Library, Hawk, Carol Williams, Dan Smith, Big Mark, Railroad Ernie and his god named Fred, Jay Menard, Jay Malone, Portal, Rat, Ryan, 90s grunge music, the Virginia mountains, Jeanne Larsen, Rick Trethewey, Richard Dillard, and the entire English and Film Departments at Hollins University. Thank you all for the inspiration; you have all helped me turn this book into a reality. May you find peace and happiness. May love fill up your lives. – C.A. MacConnell

Dedicated to all those suffering from brain disorders

Part One. Captain Tomcat

The mountains of Scallycat. Press Play.

One.

His skin was all yellow. Then Grandpa hung himself. Margene, a.k.a. mother, only talked about it once when I was big enough to get it but still small enough so that Margene thought I didn't understand. One day, all casual, she told Dr. Dad about the hanging. She moved her hands around and everything. She described the day in detail – the sky colors, the blinding sunny weather, and the way she didn't scream when she found the body. Instead, she stared at it, shaking. Shaking and staring. Margene whispered out the story with a cool, shaky voice, like she was going to slap it down on her mile-long shopping list. Like this: *lite margarine, whole grain high fiber lite bread, and one more thing, Grandpa used a thick rope.*

Still wearing my pajamas, I asked Margene, "What kinda knot was it? Was it a pirate's hangman knot?" Thomas, my brother, had told me all about pirate knots.

Margene got all weird and started cleaning again.

Dr. Dad grabbed a beer from the fridge. Then he looked at me sideways. I could see his face scar worm its way down from his left eye to his lip, zigzagging across his cheek like face lightning, like a messed up skin zipper. Old car accident. Actually, not really an accident. Thomas told me that he heard Margene say that Dr. Dad was drunk driving and ran right into the side of a barn. Why he was out on the back roads, none of us had any idea.

Then Thomas rolled into the kitchen, yelling, "Geez, this is a serious crowd around here! What's going on?" He smiled big and goofy with his lips shut. When he didn't get any answers, he shook his head and yelled, "Shiver me timbers!"

I asked, "What does that mean, knucklehead?"

Thomas shrugged his skinny shoulders and said, "I dunno, Shorty. Sometimes you don't gotta know."

True. Sometimes, you don't gotta know. But sometimes you just do, even if you don't want to. Our Lochmore family no-no secrets leaked into the kitchen over time. Like thick water seeping into a crack on the ship's hull, a strange, slippery evil dripped out terribly slow. I was sure that bottom sucker fish were somewhere hiding in Margene's spotless kitchen, waiting for me, waiting to feed on my brain too. Thomas never told me I was fish food, but I worried. I worried about Grandpa's hanging, his "crazy." I worried I had his "crazy" too. I knew something was coming. Something bad.

Dr. Dad told me I even came out of Margene's belly wrong. Too soon. I was a screamer. I cried until they were about to give me the baby shake death, putting me out of my misery like a hard-up horse. See, they didn't get it. I was screaming for a reason. *Yo ho ho,* there was something wrong in my head too. Like Gramps. I guess I always knew, but Thomas told me that you should never tell a pirate secret, so I just shut up. But I knew. In my head. *Yo, ho, ho. Bad pirate.*

The Scallycat Mountains. They sat fat in the sky, watching over us, and when I looked up at them, I felt so safe. All the time, Thomas told me that the mountains had unicorns living in them. I only half-believed him on that one, because his eye twitched when he said it, and that was a dead giveaway that Thomas was full of it.

Our house was red brick and roomy. On a safe, dead end street of course. We were rich, but Thomas and I didn't have a clue that we were. The houses around were all creepy and old, but none of the paint was peeling. Set in a big bucks part of Scallycat, fresh houses were being dug daily; bulldozers emptied the valleys like magic. Everywhere, mud. But there were ancient fairy tale, tall trees, and some clean land was still untouched. We had a large, sloped backyard, and Margene made sure that the grass was always green. I swore that she ran out and spray painted it in the middle of the night while Dr. Dad was passed out. Maybe she did, who knows. She was always up to something weird.

At the top of the back hill, on the right side, there was a magic silver swing set where Thomas taught me how to hang upside down and stay there, holding my breath. The backyard was our hiding place, where Thomas and I ran away from The Big People.

Even better, straight behind the house, a weeping willow tree sat there as huge and shifty as some God crying all over us. Off of our property, the tree didn't really belong to the four of us Lochmores, but I told all the kids that the tree was mine anyhow, because I was a snob when it came to trees. Thomas agreed. It was ours. Daily, Thomas and I scampered up the hill to sit underneath the hair-like branches of our willow. I liked to study the branches, the patterns there.

I was five. Thomas was seven.

"Crazy Mary, your hair's so dirty, I bet you got bugs in there," he said. "Lice maybe, ha ha. Lemme look." He grabbed a chunk of my stringy hair, studied it and said, "Hmm, yep, there's some creatures in there all right, Shorty. Many, many creatures."

I jerked my head back, pointing at his nose. "And you got green snot hanging down. Everywhere, boogers," I said, laughing, using the branches to cover my face. "My hair's awesome clean. Shuddup, Tomcat." Margene called him that. Then we all did.

Thomas pulled on some branches, breaking off a few, braiding them together. Then he wrapped it around my arm like a bracelet, which was sort of cool.

"Pretty," I said, smiling. And I felt pretty. And I told him this.

He agreed. Thomas always agreed with everything. At the dinner table, when Dr. Dad said the food was good, Thomas agreed. When Dr. Dad drank and said the food sucked, Thomas agreed, not eating and getting all quiet. He was like a chameleon, blending in to whatever room was around him, melting into the people. That was Thomas. Not me. I stuck out like a Scallycat Mountain peak poking into any sky, messing with the whole scene, cloudy or clear.

There, under the willow, I wrote block letters. The stupid paper had my name at the top of it. Each page did. MARY LOCHMORE. Like I didn't remember my name or something. I knew it was kind of ridiculous, but Margene kept buying it for me every year for Christmas, so I had to use it otherwise she might freak out like she always did.

I wrote that I wanted black hair. Mine was dirty blonde then, and when I told Thomas I wanted mine black, he agreed.

"And I'd like to start smokin' a pipe," he said, sticking a willow branch in his mouth, showing some teeth. "And drink me some grog."

"What's that?" I asked.

"You know, rum, I think. Like that nasty stuff Dr. Dad drinks."

"Yeah." I laughed. "You'd look good with a pipe. Like a real man."

"A real man." Thomas puffed out his chest, acting like The Big People.

I scrawled some block letters carefully, slowly. I needed perfect letters; even my Q's were better than any Thomas could muster up. When I told him this, he agreed. But I still struggled to stay within the lines, as if some Big Person or Davy Jones' ghost was watching over my shoulder, someone who would stab me if I wrote outside the lines. I used a blue pen on the red lined paper. I thought about blood and bruises, just because.

Thomas crept up behind me, peeking over my shoulder, reading my words out loud: "CAPTAIN TOMCAT. HE RODE THE SEA. BUT NO ONE KNEW WHERE THAT SEA DOG MITE BE."

"Stop it," I said, folding the paper in half, hiding my name, hiding my words.

"But it's good, Shorty," he said, shrugging and spitting. Then he gave me a noogie. "I won't stop until you say it's good," he said, rubbing my head harder.

I laughed. "Stop it! I swear I'm gonna pee my pants," I said.

"Say your story's good, Shorty. Say it's good!" he said. By then, he had me in a headlock, and he was going after my armpits, tickling me.

"Okay, it's good," I finally said, still giggling.

Thomas let me go. Then he slipped on his eye patch, picked up his wooden sword, and started running.

I rolled my eyes. Sooner or later, I'd have to catch up with him. So I slipped my eye patch on too. Dr. Dad had bought us the gear at a costume shop. Thomas and I had spray-painted the swords to make them silver like the real thing. I watched Thomas, gripping my heavy, wooden, dull sword, but I didn't follow at first. I knew where he was going anyhow. There was no big rush, as long as I could still see his skinny butt.

He was going to the farmer's field behind our house to see the horses. Thomas was always running off. Out of breath, he stopped, turning around. "Come on Shorty, we got wild-eyed mustangs to catch!" he yelled after me, but I stayed under the willow for a while. Block letters and stories took time. Besides, we both liked suspense.

When Thomas left me, my writing changed, turning darker. I wrote, "BOTTLES, BROKEN GLASS ON THE BOAT. CAPTAIN BLACKEYE WAS CHASING HIM." Then I scratched them out, writing, "DIE, BAD, FAT CAPTAIN BLACKEYE. DEAD MEN TELL NO TAILS." Then I got scared. Thomas might find it. He might tell Margene or Dr. Dad, and I'd get grounded. Terrified of Captain Blackeye, I tore the words to shreds, making litter snow on the ground. If only I could *stop the bad head pirates.* See, there were many torn pages and many trips to the garage garbage cans when no one was looking.

Then I really hustled to catch up with Thomas in the field. While I ran, my shorts bunched up, and I had to yank the suckers down. Suddenly, my legs were getting too long for my clothes. And while I tugged at my shorts, I made up stories, creating characters in my mind; they came in color, speaking in whispers, until it became hard to tell the difference between my pirates and real people. I ran, but I felt tired, tired from all of the words, the thinking, the WORDS. They were so big in my head. I pulled my shirt down, covering my small belly. When I pulled my shirt, I heard this: *Why do you move? Margene and Dr. Dad would like you if you weren't so fat. You fat landlubber. Something bad.* I talked back to the words. *Shut up*, I whispered. *I'm busy.*

Thomas was lying on his belly, hiding in the tall grass on the inside of the farmer's fence.

I checked for horse poop, and then stretched out next to him. "I'm here," I said.

Thomas held a finger to his lips. "Shh, Shorty. The horses are coming closer."

And they were. They were huge, nudging their noses in the ground, grazing.

We waited, listening to the hooves push through the grass.

When the bigger, darker horse spotted Thomas, she sniffed him, nudged him with her nose, and kept right on grazing.

We laughed quietly.

"Someday, I'm gonna hop up there on her back," Thomas said, sticking his chin out, puffing up his chest, then sinking back down into the grass, hiding there.

"Like you could ever get up there," I said. "She's so big."

"Just you wait, I will. Hold yer breath, and I bet before you can even let it out, I'll be climbing up there riding that biggun. I am Captain Tomcat. I can do anything amazing," he stated, smiling. "And you know you can too."

I nodded. I believed him, because Thomas was seven, and he knew everything. "But I'm too fat to ride," I said.

He shook his head. "No, for real, you are one tiny pirate," he said. Then he looked at me straight in the eye. For a long time, he didn't blink. Out of the side of his mouth, he whispered, "You are my First Mate, Shorty. And I am Captain Tomcat. That makes you the most important person in this world, since you are my right hand man. Well, you're a girl really, but you're still my right hand man I guess, because I say so. And we're the most feared pirates in all of Scallycat. Don't ever forget that. Ever." He said this with a lisp. Thomas sometimes talked funny that year.

"I am your First Mate?" I asked him.

"Forever and ever," he said. "No matter what happens, nothing will change that, you hear me?"

I nodded slowly. "Forever and ever?" I asked.

Thomas agreed. "Hey, let's go get some grub from Margene. I bet she's cooking up some sea biscuits."

"What the hell are those?" I asked him, raising a brow.

"Ha, don't cuss, you're too little. Besides, Dr. Dad might hit you upside the head. I dunno what sea biscuits are, mate, but it sounds good to me. I'm so starving I could eat that horse right there. I mean, not really, that'd be mean."

I laughed. "So you really think you and me will be riders someday?"

Thomas agreed.

Two.

Margene rarely sat down. Ironing, cooking, cleaning, fixing her hair and makeup, she was always messing with something, never taking a break. So one afternoon, when she started resting on the white couch for days, Thomas and I tiptoed around her as if she had a big, bad wolf disease. Her eyes were watery, and her eyes were stuck open, as if she were lost on some deserted highway, scanning the road side for signs. She appeared to be smaller than normal, and her hair was strangely messed up with some wacky bedhead. The usual frosty orange lipstick was missing on her lips. Her mouth drooped in a thin, half-circle. She hugged at her middle, stroking her belly like she had the worst stomachache in the whole world.

I thought she was faking it, and I was bored. But then I looked at her closer, and it seemed like Margene was sick or hurt, like a lost baby bird, and her broken-up look made me want to have Dr. Dad put her whole body in a cast, especially her brain. I watched her rest. Then Thomas and I played around her, acting up. Even when we spilled soda on the white carpet, Margene didn't move. She gripped her middle, right by her belly button, creepily pressing it like it was her own personal alarm button. I thought she might turn into a koala bear, grow a pouch or something. But she didn't. She didn't eat, and her round stomach started shrinking into an empty bowl.

Then I heard Dr. Dad whisper to another Big Person that Margene was really losing it. Like Grandpa. I wasn't sure what exactly she was losing, but I knew it must've been something important. Like her brain. At least part of it anyway. Come on, Thomas and I hung out with horses a lot, but we weren't born in a barn. But Dr. Dad seemed so mellow and quiet when he phone-talked to his Doctor friends about "Margene's anxiety disorder." He had trouble getting the words out though. His scar twitched down from his eye to his lip. The usual slurring.

Thomas and I acted weird and shocked, like we were made of lightning; we went out to play and pretended nothing was new, except that there was thunder in our heads.

Actually, it was too sunny. It hurt my eyes.

When we came back inside, it was still sunny out, so we didn't know what we were doing because usually we stayed out, but Thomas and I went back in anyway. We were worried enough about Margene to majorly lose on a football game with the Bible Beater kids down the block, which was so sad. We never lost that bad. So we hung our heads like hungry horses and ran barefoot into the spotless kitchen to check on the scene.

I wore my lavender sweater, the one with flowers stitched near my heart. I had on tight, dark blue jeans, and I worried that the seams might bust. I swore everyone could see my stomach through the sweater. Tangle-free, my stringy, dirty long hair was center-parted, barely held back by two thin barrettes. I thought about taking the barrettes out. I wanted to cover up my cheeks. But then I stopped, snapping the barrettes back in place, because I was afraid to mess up my hair.

Thomas needed new school clothes. His sleeves came up short on his spindly arms. His yellow hair shot straight up from his wiry body; his clear blue eyes held a curious light.

Suddenly, Margene was somehow alive again. Furiously, she was up cooking. Sweating and sweating and cooking.

When we ate, everyone was quiet, except Thomas, who was slurping his noodles, being annoying. When no one was looking except me, he said, "They're really worms, Shorty," real quiet. "Mm, good worms." Then he smiled, noodles hanging down his chin.

Anxious, my stomach rumbled. I felt hungry, and I didn't want to feel hungry.

Margene broke the quiet. "Eat, Mary. It took me all night to make this. And you're going to turn into skin and bones."

I really didn't want to eat worms.

Thomas was slurping.

Dr. Dad was drinking. His plate was clean.

"I said, eat!" Margene said, slamming her fork into her plate. Her plate was full. She wasn't touching it.

One at a time, I started eating worms, choking them down, my face turning red. Somewhere inside me, something was boiling, churning. Anger rose inside my throat, resting there in between the worms. I stared hard at Margene and chewed. I took a drink, dropping the glass. It shattered across the floor.

"Mary! Be more careful," Margene yelled, heading to get a broom.

Across the table, Dr. Dad started nodding off.

Quickly, Thomas rose, grabbing my arm, pulling me up from my white chair. "Hey now, lets gather up these dishes, mate." And so we did. One plate, one bowl, one spoon at a time.

Margene cleaned the glass, layering on orange, frosty lipstick. Then she picked at the polish on her nails. Then she picked at the skin. After rewashing the dishes, making sure they squeaked, Margene started wiping the countertops shiny, no streaks. No crumbs were left on the floor. There was no trace of dinner left behind. She scrubbed hard, sweating and shaking, and she looked like she wanted to cry. Her eyes were watery, but they never spilled over. She wore orange, scrubbing hard. Her big hoops pulled and stretched her ears while she scrubbed. Her hands were red. Her hands were redder. She scrubbed. Her skin bled. She scrubbed. Her skin was raw meat. She scrubbed. Standing, sitting, she scrubbed. It had to be clean. On her knees, she scrubbed. Belly to the floor, she studied the cracks in the tiles, using her fingernails, digging at the dirt. She scraped. And scratched. Like a dog, I guess she was digging for dead things.

I studied her curves. I watched her twitch and shake to scrub. I scratched my head. It hurt. Then I found Thomas in the den. We fought over the remote.

Dr. Dad wandered in, giving us a "look of shame." When Dr. Dad gave us a look, his lips would disappear under his thick mustache, and we would become incredible shrinking people. Dr. Dad's looks were powerful enough to silence Margene, and "X" her words right out of her cheeks. One minute, Margene was about to talk, then Dr Dad would give her a look, and that scar on his face would bolt down from his left eye and shift around and seem to crack his skin in two, and poof, Margene's cheeks deflated like a sad balloon. Again and again, I saw Margene back down from Dr. Dad's looks. Like she was a scared stray cat. Then she scrubbed.

Thomas and I both shut up and watched Dr. Dad's crime show.

Dr. Dad passed out in his chair.

I got bored and went to watch Margene. She packed us healthy lunches after dinner. Then she started planning meals for the next day. Then she cleaned more. She ironed Dr. Dad's shirts and handkerchiefs. She pressed and pressed. She folded and pressed. She burned one shirt. She burned another one. She hid them in the bottom of the garage garbage cans. The burned ones were gone, gone, gone, without a trace.

I tried not to catch Margene's eye. I hated to help. I could never do it right. I wanted to tell her about the way the wind turned clouds into horses and unicorns. I thought about how the cloud horses' manes rose out from the blue sky dust, and then disappeared again, fading into cotton. Horses never scared me. How I wanted to have one, name him. I wanted to tell Margene about my ideas for names. I had a long list.

Big People were always so distracted or tired, sprawled out in lazy boys. No one but Thomas and me paid attention to the little, hidden worlds everywhere – inside clouds, wrinkles, stars. I wondered if I could blink and rest inside the white star on a horse's forehead. Die there.

I checked my dress for grass stains. My hair felt okay, and then it didn't. Margene always said she wished she had long hair like mine. Hers was thin, and sometimes, the ends broke. She said I had Dr. Dad's hair. Over and over, she said she was jealous.

Thomas wandered back into the kitchen. Gross, his ears were full of wax. He floated around, asking what was going on. Then he left like The Great Observer, wearing short shorts and tube socks, smiling a wicked smile, waving at me to follow him. Thomas was always saving me from The Big People.

Dr. Dad slept in the den that night.

Margene slept on the white living room couch.

Thomas and I slept in his room, in the bunk beds. He let me sleep with his stuffed monkey, because I was scared of worms still, and he felt bad, telling me he was only joking. The only time I saw Thomas cry was when he got scared at the movies. Monsters got to him. Not me. I couldn't care less about dangerous creatures that came from nowhere. I thought blood and guts were cool and told him he shouldn't worry. But a few times, Thomas walked out of theaters while I sat there, wondering if I was going to find my way out of the aisles alone. Or wondering if Margene would start cleaning her SUV and leave me there.

As I drifted off, I worried, thinking about the way Thomas liked to wander. Once, we lost him at the Scallycat Mall. Later, we found him in the parking lot, leaning against the car. All he said was, "Hi, where have you guys been? I've been so bored here, I nearly chewed off all my fingernails!" Actually, he was cracking up.

Margene was furious and frantic. Dr. Dad was red-faced, and I'm not sure if he'd been drinking, but he looked like he needed to be, or he needed to be drunker. Or maybe he was terrified, and I'd never seen Dr. Dad terrified. He slapped Thomas hard. Really, he punched him in the face hard enough that the skin turned pink, heading for a bruise.

Thomas felt his new cheek, the swollen one. Then he stared at Dr. Dad with big blue eyes. Like a curious seal. He didn't cry. Instead, he tilted his head to the side, confused, thinking, waiting, feeling his cheek. With his right hand, he made a fist. He raised his eyebrows. He looked at Dr. Dad, staring at him, scanning his size, measuring him from his lightning scar to his feet. Then his fist unfolded open. He grabbed my hand. He grabbed my hand harder. "Come on, Shorty," Thomas said. "Let's get in the car."

In the backseat together, Thomas and I stared out opposite windows. Then I looked over at him, studying his fingers, the way they were opening and closing, as if he was fighting against his own fists.

He looked over at me and mouthed, "Next time...he hits me...Captain Tomcat hits back." Then he grinned weirdly, like a snake. Suddenly, he looked older, and it creeped me out, because if he was older, then that meant I was older too. I didn't know if I was ready to be older yet. *Something bad. Big, bad pirate secret.*

I knew Thomas was serious. I nodded at him. I stared into his eyes, the lost blue. I could feel his hidden, deep, angry ocean that camped out behind his thousand smiles. My lips were stuck together in a tight, thin, anxious line. "I'm still your First Mate, right?"

"Forever and ever," he said. "You bet." And he blinked and blinked, shrugging. "We got to hunt for some treasure when we get home, big time. The seas are rough out there, but our ship, she's strong, aye?"

I smiled. My Thomas was back.

Then, silence. Silence in the car. The whole way home, silence.

Three.

Black soles and gutters. Deep gutters. Endless holes, like the ones in the Scallycat cul-de-sac where Thomas and me played with rocks; we made games out of our dead end. Thomas' eleven-year-old eyes were as blue and round as a cartoon owl. At dusk, when he looked up at the smoky Southern sky, watching the sun slide down, his eyes turned into thick, black flying saucers rimmed with electric blue. Like a space creature. It seemed that in the half-light of evening, those saucer eyes would beam out lasers, shooting a dark film across the world. And they did – when the sun blinked down, Thomas smiled at me, and I could only see the teeth. Then he'd say, "See, Shorty, I made the whole world black. I…am…Magic Man. Don't tell. It's our pirate secret." I believed him because Thomas was taller. Being the Big One meant being right all the time. Back then, Thomas' eyes were my world's one and only light switch.

By then, I was nine and "stretching out some" Dr. Dad said.

Because we were bored, we were hanging out more with the Bible Beaters down the block. Eyes shut in prayer, trying not to crack up, Thomas and I would read The Bible with them, acting like we were saved and full of The Holy Spirit and Jesus and angels and Big Old God. We were reading about stupid Jonah and the whale when Thomas got the giggles and had to cup a hand over his mouth to keep from really roaring. Some spit leaked through his fingers.

I rolled my eyes, saying, "I gotta go pee."

Thomas wiped his mouth, chuckled, and said, "Me too."

So we hopped up, escaping the Bible Beaters.

Back at the house, Thomas and I got greased up with sunscreen and headed out to the yard to goof off. I put on a dark, one-piece bathing suit, afraid I looked chubby. I set my towel out smoothly, no wrinkles. Before I was even warm, I was restless, sitting up, giving up on the sun, wishing it would rain, wondering when the thick heat would end. I reminded myself to breathe, thinking, *What if Dr. Dad's lightning scar came alive? What if thunder rose up out of this ground? Could the ground rumble and swallow me here? I'd be dead, but thinner, lighter, better.*

Thomas stretched out, sunning peacefully, only getting up to jump over the sprinkler every now and again. Then he stretched out flat for good, falling asleep. His wiry body was so long, I swear. Legs like green beans.

I studied his sweaty, white face, worried about his skin burning in the sun. I studied his large, shut lids. Margene always shook her head and said, "Tomcat could sleep through a war." But he woke pretty soon after, saying, "Look at the pictures in the clouds. Look close. There are so many creatures up there. Look."

I *was* a cloud. I told him this.

Thomas agreed. Then he made a face, pulling his eyelids back, making his eyes bug out. Wide-eyed and chuckling, Thomas stuck his tongue out at me, making faces.

Then we heard the first thunder. "We better go inside, Shorty," he said, scrambling through the grass.

But I stayed behind. I felt the thunder rumble inside me, churning. I thought of Margene. I knew she'd be worried, but I felt the power, then anger, wondering if I might burst. I thought that maybe that storm would be loud enough to crack the earth, and I could sink into it, thin and buried, touched by Dr. Dad's lightning scar. I heard the big, bad pirates fighting in the clouds. I felt the thunder inside. Deep inside me, something was way wrong.

I looked around, but Thomas was long gone.

For a while, I took my chances at being struck.

Back inside, stripping off my wet suit, when I looked in the mirror, my body looked wavy, blurry, wide, and thick, as if I were seeing myself in a wacky, circus mirror, and I was suddenly made of creepy, curved glass. *Something bad.*

Later, just after dusk, Thomas stole one of Dr. Dad's cigarettes right from his pocket, since Dr. Dad was passed out cold in his lazy boy again.

Out in the backyard, Thomas let me have a few drags.

Together, we coughed and smoked until Thomas got that look in his eye. "Time for trouble, Shorty," he said, putting the cigarette out. He ran inside. In a flash, he reappeared with some eggs and two bars of soap.

I tagged along while Thomas egged the Bible Beater's windows. "Pirate secret," Thomas said while we soaped their cars like little devils. Thomas' soap writing was all capitals: HI. I'M WATCHIN YOU. LUV GOD. Mine was big too: DEAD MEN TELL NO TALES. We smoked the rest of the butt and got head rushes and cracked up until I threw up on my overalls.

I was ten. Thomas was so close to thirteen that he claimed he already was. It was June, but our bodies were already cooked brown. School was out. It was getting late. Dusk. Our favorite time. But the days were growing longer, and the mountains hadn't swallowed the sun yet. It was Sunday. The Bible Beaters down the block were at church or Jesus study or one of those things.

Thomas' nose was shedding. We were so bored that he peeled off some dead skin and said, "Ahh, Shorty, my face is melting, ahhh," then stuck it on my shoulder, laughing.

Margene and Dr. Dad chuckled.

We were all in the spotless kitchen.

Margene's orange frosty lipstick cracked when she said, "Don't you and Tomcat run off 'til supper. It's almost ready, now." She crossed her arms on her big boobs.

From the table, Dr. Dad looked up from *The Scallycat Times.* Half-smiling through his scarred cheek, he ruffled the paper and said, "Margene, as long as these two got legs, we'll never keep track." His cheeks reddened when he short-laughed "ha, ha," then went back to the *Times.* With beer foam on his mustache, he was happy drunk that night.

I was so restless. It was me who talked Thomas into hunting. We put on our pirate eye patches, becoming Captain Tomcat and his First Mate, Shorty.

"Where are the swords?" I asked Thomas, rustling through the hall closet.

Thomas shrugged. "Let's go without them, matey, there's little time."

By then, Margene was scrubbing counters. Dr. Dad was drunk on the phone with Abraham, the Gutter Man. Our escape was easy.

We were true pirates that night, hunting for treasures hidden in the thick, Scallycat grass. We believed. We hurried to the farmer's field. But the rains hadn't come that year. The grass was parched. So yellow. Thomas and I had our faces trapped in kid squints, scanning the field, searching for horses. No luck.

"They must be tucked in the barn," I said, looking at Thomas through one eye.

Thomas agreed, staring back at me through one eye.

There, we studied skies. There were more hidden pictures in the clouds than we could even imagine. Backside to the ground, I sank into the tall grass.

And so did Thomas.

But we didn't stay down long. It was getting late. We were on a mission. Captain Tomcat and his First Mate, Shorty, needed to search the field for treasure.

It was me who led Thomas deep into the field. It was me who found the treasure. The black sole. The lost boot.

"Captain Tomcat! I spy a boot treasure up yonder!" I said. I tugged at the black sole. It was stuck, wedged under a log.

"Aye, aye, Mate Shorty!" Thomas yelled, huffing and puffing behind me. "Shiver me timbers! Ship ho! Captain Tomcat orders you to hold fire!" He was so slow.

With my thin arms, I heave-hoed on the boot. Hard. Because I wanted to be the first pirate to find treasure. I wanted to show him I had the magic, that I was big enough to make the world dark like Thomas, my Magic Man. Then the boot gave in. A little. When it moved, I pulled harder. Then it slipped from my fingers, and I jerked back, falling into the prickly grass. When I looked up, I found a live leg attached to the boot, a leg that grew into a living, strange being – a bad pirate hiding out in the field. Captain Blackeye. I remember his long, black beard, and a face made of sticks, stones, and muddy skin. A tic made his black eyes twitch, *one, two, three,* right before the bad pirate brought the boot down on my right wrist, shattering it. But I was small and quick. I knew how to weave and split.

But slow Thomas had the growing pains. He tripped. He tried to stand, but the grass was a slippery, yellow slide.

When Captain Blackeye's lost boot found Thomas' head, *one, two, three,* I was already running. To the house. My mouth was stuck open. Bugs went down my throat, but my lips stayed spread, gaping. I tried screaming. I prayed to Jesus or the Devil or God or the Sun for sound. But all I could do was swallow insects, hiccup, and run.

I heard a horse whinny. I heard hooves, the pounding of hooves, the thunder of it. I felt the thunder inside. I looked up. I thought I saw Dr. Dad's lightning scar. I saw it flash and flash and wriggle across his face. It was coming closer, the wormy scar. I saw it flash and flash. A skin zipper. I felt it burn my eyes. For many moments, I was blind.

Blue men. Black men. Guns. The Scallycat cops came. I strained to see Thomas' body, as if one glance, one smile, one touch from his First Mate, Shorty, would make him move. But the Blue-black Men blocked the whole yard with ribbons. I tried to break through to see, but I was blind behind The Big People. When I reached row one, the show was over, the body was gone, and I knew that Thomas' life had been left behind in our Scallycat field of treasure.

That night, Margene sat on the porch. She sat in her white rocker, whispering, "Supper's on, Tomcat. Time for supper." All night long, she layered on frosty lipstick, rocked, whispered, and waited. We all waited. For Captain Tomcat to come home.

At three in the morning, I still had my eye patch on. Dr. Dad tried to fix my wrecked wrist, but by then, it was crooked as all hell.

Four.

One year later

Margene forgot my eleventh birthday. She and Dr. Dad were still busy putting up posters, searching for Captain Blackeye, the murderous pirate. They looked. "They" = The Blue-black Men who had combed the fields. The Blue-black Men had brought out the dogs. The Blue-black Men had posted blue-black signs, but I had that eye patch on that day, so my one-eyed description was a little weak. Finally, The Blue-black Men gave up. So did Margene. So did Dr. Dad. The Lochmores gave up. All around Scallycat, there were whispers about The Lochmores giving up. All of us. Gave. Up.

Every Sunday, the Bible Beaters down the block sent us a casserole. Sometimes, Margene just sat in her porch rocker, calling Tomcat to dinner over and over. Then she'd snap out of it and brush the knots out of her fake blonde hair. Then she'd clean up the hairs that fell out. Piece by piece, hair by hair. She scanned the floors, picking up hairs and specks of dirt with her fingernails. Sundays, at dusk, she sure wasn't cooking.

Dr. Dad was always a quiet drunk. Then he became a quiet sea, waiting for the wind, waiting to burst into rapids. From a distance, I read his moods by studying his raised eyebrows and squints. When he bit the scarred side of his lip, I knew to stay away. Each night, when he came home from Chiron Hospital, he smoked, drank gin, ate, and passed out in his den lazy boy chair. Margene and I watched him, stayed quiet, and moved or didn't move, depending. Sometimes, really, we had to watch out for where his arms and legs might swing.

Then we went our separate ways.

I was suddenly growing, becoming pole-thin. My favorite dress was blue with red and yellow flowers sewn across my kid breasts. My favorite, not because of the color, but because I thought it made me look skinny. And to look thin was what I thought about, stretched out in the farmer's field, imagining a herd of horses surrounding me, welcoming me into their family. Even if they trampled me, I thought it'd be a good way to die. Then I blinked, and the clouds became wolves. Then deer. Then motorcycles, old men smoking pipes, a glass of milk, a child jumping rope, a snake, an apple, a chicken. I tried again, blinking hard enough to push out tears, looking deep into the white clouds, so deep that for a moment, everything faded, and I saw cloud people. Their faces were made of cotton. Their cheeks were puckered in kisses meant for me. I looked harder, hoping the clouds would lead me to someone real. In my silent world of clouds, I received secret messages. *Yo, ho, ho, it's Captain Blackeye in hideout here.* None of the voices were from Thomas.

I didn't tell Margene that I knew how she was feeling by the way she pulled the curling iron through the tail ends of her hair. Her hair had to be perfect. Big yellow curls meant she would be late. I could decipher Margene's mood from the slightest change in her fingers or skin. And when Dr. Dad nodded off, passing out on his desk, his study was off limits.

But something was burning in my chest. I wanted to feel rhythm, live with horses in a silent home, crawl inside the blacks of their eyes. Yeah, die there. In the farmer's field, I could always hear them coming, grazing slowly through the tall grass. Listening to them move, I felt the presence of Thomas, his yellow hair. I prayed on hooves, the sound of them pushing through the grass. There was something about horse eyes – the depth, the darkness, and the sideways placement on the head. The black holes spoke of secrets. A strange and interesting secret – so much hidden behind such a small, dark space.

I knew all about secrets. *If I were thinner, I wouldn't want to die.* In this field, sometimes I had a break from the thoughts. And sometimes I didn't. Sometimes, I wished the horses would crush me thin, and I could turn into smoke, entering the land of ghosts, finding Thomas there. Maybe he'd be grinning. A wicked grin, smoking one of Dr. Dad's cigarettes. Maybe I could shut my eyes and wish myself into Thomas' smoky breath.

Deep down, hidden under my blue dress, I had a feeling. Maybe if I wore my blue dress every single day, I'd never have to worry about fitting into anything else again. Yeah. Barefoot, blue dress. But at some point, Margene would have to wash it, and then what would I do? I would rather stop breathing than have to try and fit into another dress.

The clouds were on wind time. I knew when it was time to go inside by the sound of the horses grazing out there; they bent their necks down when it was time to go in. When it rained, they let the drops roll down their coats. I stood still with them, my breath even, feeling the drops on my own skin. I liked swallowing rain, but I couldn't get the dress dirty, so I headed down.

Loud and high-pitched, Margene's voice sprung up and out of the sliding back door, rising out of it: "Mary Lochmore, come inside here! Supper, Mary! I don't want to have to call you again. Come eat. Mary!"

She called and called for me to come inside, the sound fading away close to the place where the tall grass of the farmer's field turned into the cropped, mowed grass of our yard. Those days, she was always calling. Even if I were near, she was calling, always looking for me, always.

As I headed down the hill, I wished for the wind to carry me away as fast as sound, turning me into the purest cloud. So white, almost blue. I'd look like I was suffocating. Blue. Blue and blue dresses. I was thin. No, fat. I was blue. I couldn't breathe.

I looked back. The bay horse looked at me from far away. Then he and his slick, black-coated friend went trotting off to the barn where they belonged. The horses were on wind time too. It was measured by the way the clouds slipped into faces and voices that only I could see and hear. And I imagined they loved me. And I imagined Margene and Dr. Dad loved me, but I was never sure. And I imagined Thomas still loved me, even though he wasn't breathing. And I imagined that the whole world was made of horse eyes, glued together into one giant, awesome black circle.

While I moved forward, the grass bent for me, parting in great v-shapes. I began down the small hill, where the grass weakened. I moved past our swing set and Margene's tomato garden, making footprints in the rows. When I hit our back deck, freshly stained, I smelled Dr. Dad's coffee can full of cigarette butts. I liked the smell. If Thomas were there, I'd show him how I could balance on the deck railings, blowing spit bubbles.

The closer I came to the door, the more carefully I stepped. The house had become cleaner, more pure. Inside, everything was white – the floors, the walls, the furniture. White, so quiet. Shh.

I slid the glass door open, floating inside. There, I studied the way Margene's thin hand gripped a rag, gliding over glass until all of the windows were streak-free. That meant she was nervous. She looked up at me, shaking her head in a thin-lipped frown. She didn't talk much when she cooked or cleaned. She always wanted help, but Dr. Dad never helped her. I was afraid to make a mess. If I made a mess, I was afraid to clean it up wrong.

Mostly, I tiptoed.

Dr. Dad didn't talk much anymore. But he always dressed sharp. He smelled sweet and spicy and smoky. If I got close enough, I loved to breathe him in. He had shaved his mustache, and the skin under his nose was weirdly white, except the place where the dark scar fell, forking into his lip. He drank weekday, bar gin, and weekend, driveway beer. If he didn't have a staff meeting, Dr. Dad came home from Chiron Hospital, grabbed a drink of Beefeater Gin from his bar, and disappeared to the back porch to smoke a few Vantage menthols. Lone Lochmore party.

Margene finished making pork chops and two side dishes, both homemade. She wore a clean, white apron. Studying her, I knew Dr. Dad must be in a bad mood. If Dr. Dad was in a bad mood, she made pork chops. Pork chops were his favorite.

At the dinner table, when Dr. Dad raised his brows, glancing right, he wanted salt. When he looked left, that meant he was tired. After we sat down to pray, he fell asleep in his pork chops. Then he woke to move to his lazy boy chair in the den, where he passed out in front of the TV.

Margene took off his shoes, shaking him. "Jack," she whispered. "Jack."

Lights flashed on Dr. Dad's face while the shows changed scenes. Even drunk, Dr. Dad looked sharp. Drooling, but well-groomed.

Margene gave up, covering him with a white blanket.

Dr. Dad was out. Out like a light.

Margene started cleaning again. She cleaned the den. She cleaned the den again.

Alone in my room, I was restless, searching for motion. If I stretched up to look out my window, I could see the farmer's field; I could see the shapes of his horses there, two shadows steadily grazing. Sometimes, they trotted, tunneling through the tall grass. Nightly, I stared out at them. Or perhaps they were peeking in. Whatever the case, they moved, and when they moved, I whispered, *I will have one, Thomas.*

If I tried hard enough, I could almost hear their hooves tearing up the ground. I could almost see their bodies parting oceans of tall fields. I imagined them kicking up and out of their frozen frame behind my window, breaking loose to tear through the glass. Somewhere near the panes, I swore I could hear them breathing. Windows and walls started speaking to me.

Many mornings, I woke restless and cranky, recalling each move the farmer's horses had made in the field the night before. I imagined them coming to me in a slow walk, sending me a message through their eyes. I heard, *Shorty, bring me in.* It slid through my brain like mind butter.

Then I looked in the full-length mirror hanging from my door, checking my skin for cloud people dust that could've leaked out on me. Then I worried. Even on gray days, Margene said that a kid like me could get burned. She was always worried about skin and moles and clothes fitting. Everything caused cancer. And she worried about scrubbing and folding and making dinner. And where was Thomas? And when would Dr. Dad be home? And the ironing. And cleaning. Margene's silence was her own song as she scrubbed, imagining there was dust. Margene gave me looks, looks that said she was nervous. Nervous about gin and lazy boys and black boots. Nervous about one day losing to the dirt.

Five.

I had nothing better to do. Even though it was dark, The Bible Beater kids were out playing in the cul-de-sac. Ever since Thomas was gone, I ran wild and Margene was always yelling at me. We all started playing "Kill the Man," a tackle football game that made no sense. When I caught the ball, I ran my butt off before the biggest boy with zits squashed me. I was the only girl around, but I was a tough cookie.

I had the ball tight in my crooked arm until one mean kid ran up behind me, grabbed the back edge of my Velcro tennis shoe with his hand, and jerked my leg hard, slamming me headfirst into the grass. Facedown, flattened by the force of the fall, I heard laughing. But I still had the ball. I wouldn't let go. I gripped it, resting there, waiting for quiet. Finally, silence came, and I stood up, brushing myself off. Without a tear, a yelp, or the slightest cry, I threw the ball away.

The boys stood still, surprised, showing me respect because I didn't let go, even after being flattened. Skinny and awkward, I got tackled the most, but I knew how to fall.

Margene had already been screaming at me to come inside when the worst thing ever happened. I missed one easy catch. I kicked at the grass, disturbed.

A tall kid yelled at me, "Nice miss, Fatso!"

"Shut up!" I yelled back. But then I thought about his words. I thought about how his dark eyes shot out a mean light. I thought about Captain Blackeye. I felt the fury, the thunder inside. I studied the tall kid's face. I thought about my pirate sword. I hated his fat face. Then the bad thoughts came. *Find your sword, Shorty. Blow the man down!*

I went to find Margene. I didn't want to be a tattletale, but I couldn't stand listening to the bad pirates in my head anymore. I knew Captain Blackeye wanted me to join him. I wouldn't let him take me. I wasn't made of sticks and stones. I was all skin.

Margene listened, studying me while I cried. "You and your sad hazel eyes. My Mary," she said, running a hand through my ratty hair.

I told her about the tall kid, how I was Fatso.

Margene nodded. Margene wanted to fix things. Then she picked up the phone. She made a Doctor's appointment.

A few weeks later, Margene and I sat in a small, white room, facing one of Dr. Dad's friends, a plastic surgeon.

I felt a little better. I wasn't going to be Fatso anymore.

Margene explained my fat problem to the Doctor.

I sat there quietly, listening in, running a hand over my stomach.

The Doctor shook his head at Margene. In one hand, he twirled a pencil, moving it from bony finger to bony finger. "Margene, your daughter is actually too thin for her age, according to the charts. Surgery would be utterly impossible. Not to mention illegal. Absolutely ridiculous. Mary is fine just the way she is." He touched the top of my head, smiling.

I leaned closer to him. He smelled sweet, like pipe smoke. I didn't smile back, but I breathed him in. And I knew he was kidding. I knew he could see my fat there, my lead belly.

Margene responded, "Just do something as a favor for Jack." Her lips quivered. Her right pointer finger twitched. "Or, if you don't do us this favor, I could let all of Chiron Hospital know about what happened with you and that young patient. I'm sure you wouldn't like that at all," she said, pulling her yellow hair back tighter in a rubber band. Then she crossed her arms under her big chest, waiting.

The Doctor turned red, gripping his pencil, breaking it in two. For a second, he wasn't breathing; his cheeks puffed out like a balloon. Like his air was tied off at the neck. Then he breathed out and said, "I'd rather have my secrets revealed than hurt this child. Now leave here now, and I don't want to see you back here again. Does Jack know about this?"

Margene shook her head "no."

Margene tried again. She tried pulling strings.

I listened quietly, waiting, holding my stomach, feeling bigger and bigger. The surgery had a fancy name. Margene called it "getting Mary's stomach pinned back." I imagined the surgery. I imagined the Red-faced Doctor sucking fat from my stomach, turning me into a flat surface, a flat floor made of human flesh. I imagined staples in my skin. Sick from visions of bloody fat and guts moving through a sucking tube, I threw up all over the room.

Margene panicked, searching the room for towels. I knew she was worried about cleaning things up.

"The Nurse will take care of it. Take this child home now," the Red-faced Doctor said.

Margene grabbed my arm, and we left.

The whole next day, I couldn't stop vomiting, thinking about stapled skin. I started having horrible stomachaches that came from nowhere. Somehow, Margene got me a prescription for painkillers, but they weren't helping. My entire middle ached, throbbing. *Maybe I've been shot. Captain Blackeye took me out in my sleep. But Thomas isn't here, so I can't be dead, can I?*

Since the Doctor wouldn't do the surgery, I had to figure something out. So I wrapped an Ace bandage around my middle as tight as I could, every day holding my stomach in, covering my chest and belly, imagining that I was a pirate injured from a wicked swordfight. *I am your First Mate, Shorty, the biggest, baddest pirate in all of Scallycat.*

The whole next week, the strange stomachaches were unbearable. I wrapped the Ace bandage tighter and tighter around my middle. My chest and sides ached, but I ignored it. *I am the biggest, baddest pirate. No one can touch me.* Margene gave me more pills. Swallowing painkillers and more swallowing, I made my Ace bandage tighter. And tighter. I couldn't breathe right, but I had to wrap myself, to pull my body in. Smaller. Tighter. Flatter. More. I only ate apples.

A few weeks later, I removed the bandage. I smiled, hoping I was smaller. I asked Margene how my fat looked.

Margene's skin looked tusk-white. She said, "Uh...it's hard to tell."

When she thought I couldn't hear, she told Dr. Dad to not to let me get a hold of that Ace bandage anymore under any circumstances.

I felt better, and the aches were fading, but when I studied my belly in the mirror, all I saw was my same old stomach covered with bloody sores, the skin chafed raw from the tight wrappings. Under the rashes and dried blood, there was blue and black. I studied the blue. The ocean under my skin. The bruises. My stomach was flat, but the right side still stuck out a little bit, I thought. I was sure I messed it up. The right side.

Margene said we'd get the blood off with paper towels later.

Dr. Dad handed me some antibiotics.

I ran my fingers over the bruised, cut-up skin. After the blood was gone, my belly looked better, except for the scars. But that right side stuck out a little. I could tell. And I couldn't stop thinking about the fat right side. The side I messed up on.

To celebrate my new look, I put on some tight jeans, then headed outside to find the Bible Beater boys. Surely, they would like me now that I wasn't Fatso.

When they saw me, they all turned red, staring at the ground. Everybody was turning red around me lately. I figured it was the new style.

"See my new body?" I asked them. I put my hands on my smaller hips.

They nodded. Their faces turned darker, crimson. Then neon. Then they ignored me and threw the football around.

I ran back inside, heading to my room. Disgusted, I stripped down, hiding under the covers, feeling my flat stomach. I realized the starvings and wrappings made no difference. *I messed up on the right side.* I stared down at my crooked right wrist. It sure ached.

When my belly was still healing, Dr. Dad got transferred to the University of Welch Hospital in the Midwest. We moved in the middle of the night. We told no one –not the Bible Beaters down the block, not the mountains, not the horses or fields, not the willow tree. Not even God. But I was sure Captain Blackeye knew. I was sure someone sent him the message in a bottle.

Six.

The City of Welch

Our new house was roomy and red brick, set in the end of a cul-de-sac in Highland Township, a wealthy suburb of Welch. All around, fresh houses were springing up out of their graves on Welch ground. Mud was everywhere. All was similar – the streets, the kids, the construction sites, but there was no willow tree, no farmer's field, and to the neighbors, I was the Lochmore's only child.

Living in Welch made me feel fatter. When I told Margene, she scrubbed the floors of our new home. Shiny, slick, slippery white floors. Then she swept, mopped, bent down on her hands and knees and checked the corners of the room for crumbs, for garbage, for all of the lost things. She searched each crack. Something was always missing. Something was never found.

It became normal to wake up, walk groggy to the shower, feel a lump in my throat and dread the day ahead. I had anxiety for breakfast with fat free milk. Day and night, the racing thoughts were there: *If I could lose weight, I'd be fast enough to kill Captain Blackeye.* Quietly, I listened to the rumbling voices, the thunder inside.

I told Margene about the fat thoughts, crying in her bed nightly.

Margene wanted to help. She made it her mission to make it go away. She told me not to worry, that we were going to do something about the fat.

I stopped crying, but I was scared. I thought back to the stomach wrappings.

Later that week, Margene and I barreled down Sidesaddle Avenue in her SUV. She pulled into a place called Diet Planet.

They weighed me in at 105. I knew I was Fatso, but I didn't realize I was a sea monster. I felt hot, ashamed. They handed Margene and me a food plan, and we stayed there for an hour-long meeting, where some excited woman shared her story about her 50-pound weight loss.

I was the only 11-year-old in the room, but the ladies welcomed me. I looked at the charts, deciding on a goal weight – 92 pounds.

From weekly visits and lectures, I learned to read labels, weigh, measure, and count calories. I learned how to starve myself. I discovered low-cal sweeteners and gum. Tea filled me up. Hot bouillon. I was a star dieter. I was a master.

Every week, Margene took me to Diet Planet. On the drive there, I shifted in my seat, nervously waiting for the moment when they weighed me in. I counted calories in my head, adjusting and readjusting numbers. Numbers wouldn't leave me alone. I saw them life size, in full color. Suddenly, my brain was numbered, overcrowded. My brain was being upturned. By numbers. By pirates. By fat pirates with bodies made of numbers. Someone was inside me, attacking, searching for booty.

If I lost weight, everything was all right. But then, after the Diet Planet meeting, as soon as we left the building, the battle was on again. I had to make it through another whole week, worried about what the scale would read the next time. There was no end to the talk, the fat pirates in my head.

Soon, I weighed 94 pounds. Dr. Dad said I looked fragile and sick, showing off a drunken, sad smile. But my goal was 92, not 94. Or was it 88? *My* goal was 88. I carried that number in my mind. *88. 88. 88.* I couldn't stop losing.

Margene and Dr. Dad put me in a Catholic school, St. Genevieve's. My uniform barely hung on to my tiny frame. My skin was loose on my stressed bones. I had so many numbers to keep track of, so many bad pirates to please. Friends' parents made remarks about my dangling uniform. They whispered "sick," "too thin," "sad girl." Margene whispered back, "My Mary has always been just skin and bones, ha ha."

I started running. It was a lot of work – counting calories, exercising, trying to study and hold it all together. If I slipped and had too many calories one day, I'd beat myself up. *Big, fat pirate.* The next day, I starved harder. It wore on me, but it also helped me hang on to life; it helped me forget that I wanted to join Thomas in heaven.

One morning, when I was getting in the shower, singing, "Yo, ho, ho, and a bottle of rum," Margene walked in on me. She saw me naked.

Through her frosty orange lips, she gasped, "Oh my God! Mary!"

I was shivering. "What?" I muttered.

"Your ribs are showing! It's scary. No more Diet Planet. It's over."

Over. Over. I thought, *What do you mean, over? 88. I'm working hard. 88, 88, 88. I'm not at my goal yet, am I Thomas? 88. 88. 88. Or am I there? I haven't weighed myself in a while. I'm scared of the big, fat pirates coming to get me. I have to be small so I can swing from the sails, the ropes, travel from ship to ship like a ghost.*

I made up new diets, munching on sugar free mints and gum. My stomach hurt constantly, and sometimes, the stabbing pains were so bad, I studied the scars, the place where I had wrapped myself, where the bandage had rubbed, and Margene usually let me stay home from St. Genevieve's on the bad days.

At the dinner table, I made my own sandwich.

Margene yelled at me to come to the table and eat the meal she prepared.

I refused. I ate my lite wheat bread with one slice of fat free turkey.

Dr. Dad shook his head, sipping his beer.

And I swore that somewhere close by, Thomas' owl eyes were watching, looking down on me, waiting for me to fade into a ghost. I ate my sandwich, picking off crust.

Margene's food wasn't safe. Margene wanted me to eat her food *and* be skinny, and I had no idea how to eat normal people food. I knew I wasn't normal. I was Thomas' First Mate, Shorty, and I wished I still had my eye patch. I only wanted to see half of me.

Dr. Dad ate Margene's food.

Margene ate her food and picked at Dr. Dad's plate when he passed out again.

I wanted to *stop the thoughts* or starve myself until I could no longer hear the thunder inside. If I were light enough, maybe I wouldn't need to breathe anymore. Like Thomas.

Seven.

Thomas would've hated the St. Genevieve uniforms. He would've said, "These suck." When Margene took me downtown to be measured for a new one, I was terrified. They were itchy, and they left red marks on my stomach like I just got wrapped up in a rubber band. I thought about what Thomas would look like in the stupid dress pants and tie, and that if he were there, he'd probably wrap his tie around his head like a karate master. That thought made me laugh some.

Nuns were in charge, and I figured Thomas would've loved to run up behind one of those old ladies and pull down her black and white hood, revealing a mess of gray hair that stuck out like a bird's nest. That made me laugh a little more.

All the time, I got sent to the principal's office for rolling my eyes and not eating and looking at heavy metal music magazines during lunch. I loved the way rock stars wore devil makeup, sticking out their long, painted black tongues. I wanted their skinny legs. I wanted to wear the creepy-cool leather pants and costumes.

Constantly, Margene and Dr. Dad were called in to school for meetings with the St. Genevieve principal, and it got to be so often that it really became old, but usually, by the time they left the office, they all forgot about me being bad. I mean, I had straight A's, and Dr. Dad paid some extra cash to St. Genevieve's, so I came out without a scratch. Really, it was easy.

I was just glad the uniforms covered the awful scars that stretched across my stomach. The scars had faded into long, dark, wormlike creatures that were forever imprinted on my belly. Every night, Margene and I rubbed Vitamin E oil there, wishing them away. But I couldn't stop staring at the nasty scars. I rubbed more oil there, praying and wishing, but I could still see the wormy shape, thinking, *God, devil, whoever, make it go away. Something bad.*

After school each night, I worked out on an ancient, loud exercise bike in the den. Twenty minutes, then thirty. And if he was actually home, Dr. Dad yelled at me for making too much noise while he was trying to watch crime shows on the TV and pass out. So I switched to running around the neighborhood in the light, in the dark, whatever. Even when strange cars followed me, I didn't go home. Instead, I ran faster. If Captain Blackeye was going to kill me, he'd have to be really quick. Even though my clothes were loose, I ran. Dirty-nailed and fast, I was a wild tomboy. When Margene wasn't looking, I shopped in the boys' section. I thought about what Thomas would pick.

When Dr. Dad came home from Welch Hospital, he smelled sweet and spicy and sometimes nasty. Some Saturdays, Dr. Dad took me with him to the quickie mart, where he bought a 44oz. Mountain Dew, later dumping it out, refilling his cup with vodka. I wasn't an idiot, and I knew what he was doing, but it felt like our secret vacation.

He drank and drove. Together, we rode around in his smooth, new white Cadillac. Rides with Dr. Dad were always too quiet. I kept wishing Thomas was there to bust up the scene.

Tongue-burning hot chocolate for me. I tried so hard not to spill. Spilling was a disaster. So what if Dr. Dad was drinking vodka again? We didn't talk about it. So what. Dr. Dad drank. And when he drank, his face scar twitched, zipping across his cheek, a juicy, dark, thin skin mark. I was glad some things, like scars, were always there.

Sometimes he smoked, and it never bothered me. I wanted to smoke too. Sometimes, he'd move his lips into an "O," popping out smoky rings, one after another. I liked the smell of his smoky car, and his smoky, suede Saturday jacket. And I liked the way he drove, slow and steady, sometimes in between the lines and sometimes not. If he moved at all, I could hear his clothes brush together. He never turned on the radio. Driver and passenger, like snakes, we silently weaved through the Welch streets.

Closer to home, I reminded myself to be a good pirate.

Dr. Dad pulled over again. He always forgot a newspaper. At our second stop, random men in suits greeted Dr. Dad. He was like a Welch rock star. When he shook hands, his body jerked around, and he looked normal for once.

Back in the car, I ran my hands along the door lock. Inside, the car was dark reddish, and it smelled like dusty roads.

When Dr. Dad answered his cell, he whispered about brains. He was a brain guy. Research Doctor, Margene said. I never understood what he was saying, and I didn't want to know, really. I was afraid he'd figure out what was going inside my brain, and that he might want to cut my head open and fix things like Margene was always doing.

I pressed my hand against the window, feeling the cold glass. I thought that if I wished hard enough, the glass would bend, and a hole would open, making a tiny escape. I pressed my face against the glass, wondering what would happen if the windows shattered. I pictured myself falling out, hitting the sidewalk, making a bony mess on the busy street. I wondered if Dr. Dad would save me, save my glass body.

The car silence was so thick, it was nearly solid. The air seemed to be made of heavy clouds, ready to spill. Taking a dead man's curve, the car easily turned, bending and blending with the road. It was cold in there. No, hot. I didn't reach to change the heat.

At dinner, I watched the way Dr. Dad's thick, pink hands grabbed his fork, his knife, slicing and stabbing steak. Every second, I watched his hands. There was no telling where those hands might go or how slow or how fast they might move. No telling.

Later, when Dr. Dad drank at his bar, I watched his hands grip the glass. When he went outside to smoke on the deck, I watched him through the window. I watched him light up. Inhale, exhale. I made my mouth move into an "O," like him.

Bored, I watched Dr. Dad pass out in the den. First, his eyelids closed, soon reopening in a flash of lashes. Then his lids moved gently, like a hummingbird's wings. His thick hands dropped their fold, falling over the arms of the chair. He breathed heavily, coughing, and then he was out. No waking him then, for sure. Dr. Dad moved and breathed like a quiet wolf. He rarely cracked, but when he did, he truly growled. He might slap Margene. He might grab her, shake her. No worries, there was no blood, no bruise. Only red marks here and there, then silence. A million nights of pink hands, red cheeks, smeared orange lipstick, empty glasses, and silence. Everywhere, blurry colors.

Then something changed. One day, out of nowhere, Dr. Dad sat me down at the dining room table, a scene that always made me feel like I was trapped on a deserted island.

He cleared his throat. "Mary, I know you see me drinking," he said.

I shrugged, listening, staring up at his scar, watching it move while he spoke.

He coughed. "I need to tell you some things. I've done a lot of harmful things. I've been hiding bottles everywhere. At the hospital, at home, in my car. I have a disease. It's alcoholism. Your Grandpa had it too. I'm telling you because I've been sober for three days now, and if I start acting different, that's why."

"Okay," I said. "But I never really noticed that much. I mean, Thomas and me both knew. We just knew you weren't around, and when you were, I was scared sometimes." I was scared he might go away – into his study, out to Welch Hospital, and on and on. I wanted him there, drunk or not drunk, smoking or not. I didn't care.

He gave me a stiff hug, patting my head. One tear hung out under his left hazel eye, wetting the top of his scar. "I'm so sorry, little Mary. I just haven't been here. It's been bad, everything with Thomas. I know it's been bad. Margene and I are doing the best we can to manage. I know you are too."

I smiled, acting happy, but I was worried. Dr. Dad was acting strange, talking and everything. I wasn't so sure about all of the talking.

Then I was glad that he left to go smoke out on the deck. Through the window, I watched him smoke, just like old times.

One night at the dinner table, Margene and I were alone again.

"Eat, Mary," she said quietly. She had almost given up on me.

Just the two of us. That'd been happening a lot, and I

was sick of it. Sick and tired. "Where's Dr. Dad?" I asked her, putting my hands on my hips.

One piece of fake blonde hair drifted down from her pony tail, across her eye, cutting it in two. The smile slid off of her face. Her boobs bounced when she jumped up from her chair, hurried to the stove, picked up a monster-sized spoon, and started stirring something. Then she turned around, slowly. "Beats me," she said. She stirred and stirred.

I ran up to my room. I didn't want to eat anyhow.

Dr. Dad stopped parting his hair on the side. Instead, he ran his fingers through the waves, letting the hairs go freestyle. He bought shiny, bright-colored shirts and joined the gym. His cheeks filled out. Every morning, he swallowed vitamins. He slept through the nights. He started talking more. And he started yelling at Margene.

Then he avoided Margene. She followed him around the house, always reaching for him. She followed him into his study, saw that he was reading, and left. She followed him into the den, cleaning around him.

After a while, they barely even brushed arms.

I watched Margene clean and hurry, clean and panic. She lost track of what she'd cleaned, and she cleaned it all again, becoming Dr. Dad's shadow while he moved from room to room, one hiding place to another.

No one mentioned Thomas anymore. It was as if I'd never even had a brother, as if Margene's vacuum had even cleaned up the memories of Captain Tomcat.

Something was coming. I knew something was coming.

Part Two. The Wanted Pirate Jeffrey

Pause. Play.

One.

Four-legged creatures. Far away from the Southern Scallycat farmer's field, lost in the Welch Midwest, I still felt close to the horse's shape and smell. Me, half-wild. Even in my room, I swore I could hear hooves splashing through oceans. And I swore, when I put an ear up to my walls and listened close, I could hear horses snorting and whinnying.

In sixth grade, I begged Margene and Dr. Dad for riding lessons. Finally, they agreed. First, we had to buy a riding helmet. So Margene and I ventured just outside of Welch to the town of Mitgard, searching for family-owned Griffin Farm, where there was a small tack store.

That first curvy drive down the two-lane road, we passed a shack of a restaurant called Mommy's. Across the street was The Black Spot, a deli/thrift shop/food mart, a small town general store. The neighbor's yard was littered with protest signs and Jesus quotes pinned up on huge pieces of plywood. I thought that the Scallycat Bible Beaters would've liked it there.

The Black Spot was a good place to get thick turkey sandwiches; the meat was stacked so high, we could barely get our mouths around them. I forgot to worry about calories. Then I *noticed* that I wasn't worried about calories. Then I thought, *Maybe this store is magic.* Then I wiped off the mayonnaise in case I was wrong.

When Margene and I were done stuffing our faces, we drove on. Less than a mile down the road, we came to a monstrous sign that read, "GRIFFIN FARM, BOARDING, LESSONS, SALES, TACK STORE," in red and black.

Pulling through the front gate, we made our way down the potholed drive in Margene's SUV, bouncing through the gravel. White clouds rose up from the wheels. Margene swerved, trying to miss the holes, but we jarred all the way down the long drive. Beside us were enormous fields. Griffin Farm had acres and acres of land – front fields, side fields, back fields and a number of small paddocks. Everywhere I looked, black fences rose up out of the ground, marking off separate turnouts areas.

Horses were turned out in the right front field, and all around them, there were massive jumps made of telephone poles and railroad ties. Quietly, I settled in my seat, staring out the window with my mouth slightly open until I noticed I was drooling.

Margene concentrated on swerving. Her right pointer finger twitched while she drove. She looked side to side, getting frustrated with the driveway, but I thought that her face looked different. Maybe the drive and the horses were calming her too. Just a little. And a little calm was a lot for Margene.

When we came to the parking lot, I looked right. In front of the lounge, some barn workers were sitting at a picnic table. Some were eating. Some were smoking. Their clothes were filthy. Hair full of sawdust, they looked serious and tired. Then one older woman limped over, hobbling as if she had a wooden leg. A cigarette hung from her lip. In a hard tone, she barked orders at the others, telling someone to call the blacksmith. The schoolhorse, Teddy, had lost a shoe.

On the far right, there sat the front ring made of dirt and sand – a huge oval with half-painted jumps lying around. I was afraid that if I blinked, Griffin Farm would disappear. I was careful. Following Margene, I walked lightly, trying hard to appear serious. If Thomas were there, I knew he'd make fun of my stiff steps.

Inside the lounge, a loud, deep voice boomed, "Hello there, welcome to Griffin Farm! I am Sandra Lee Griffin, one of the owners here. Big Mike is the other. He's my husband, but he's at a horse show." She held out a long, strong hand. "And I hear they're winning!"

Margene shook her hand. "Thank you. We need some lessons and a helmet for my girl Mary here," Margene said.

"Where you from? I recognize that accent…" Sandra Lee asked.

"Down South, Scallycat, the mountains," Margene answered.

"Oh, some good horse shopping around there," Sandra Lee said. "Come on, I'll show you around the farm."

I looked out the windows, spying on one boy who was riding in the ring. He was small and short legged, like me.

Sandra Lee tapped my shoulder hard.

I looked up at her. Way up.

She pointed out the window with a long finger, a knotted, dry twig. "That's little Jeffrey out there. He's watching things around here while the other two of my boys are at the show. Come on now, we don't have all day. Horses to feed and ride, hay to unload. No time to dilly dally around here," she said.

Margene brushed some dust off of her dark, clean jeans. Slowly, she followed Sandra Lee, giving me a look that meant, "Be good."

Sandra Lee moved forward. When she moved, her long legs jutted out from her body like two poles, swallowing ground. She was thin and naturally pretty, with brown, wide-set eyes; her skin was clear and light, and when she smiled, she moved side to side, her grayish-brown hair swinging at her shoulders. She towered over Margene and me, and her voice was strong, but sometimes, there was a soft curl at the ends of her words.

All about the lounge, there were ancient, worn chairs with orange vinyl cushions, and the furniture looked bruised and beaten. On the scratched, wooden table, a large horse head ashtray rested; it was dirty, overflowing with butts. And there was dust. Everywhere, dust. I loved the dust, the grimy lounge. I breathed in dust. I'd never felt so dirty. I'd never felt so alive.

Ahead of me, Margene stepped carefully, avoiding the piles of dirt someone had forgotten to sweep up. Margene was probably thinking about a shower right then and there.

Horse show ribbons and cobwebs covered the walls. The ceiling drooped, and in parts, it looked like it might cave in. One side of the lounge was made of glass, a sheet of windows for viewing the large indoor ring; it reminded me of a stadium, and the footing looked chocolate brown and cotton-soft.

I wanted to put my bed in the lounge, live there. I quietly followed Sandra Lee and her muddy boots. She made tracks across the checkered floor.

Margene talked with Sandra Lee about the riding program, the trainers, and the schedule.

Next to Sandra Lee, I felt small.

Sandra Lee led us through the swinging door of the lounge, through the tack room that smelled of must and leather, home for rows and rows of saddles, and into the "Main Barn," as she called it. In front of us, the barn aisle stretched out long and wide. The Main Barn held forty to fifty horses, all shifting in their stalls. I smelled manure, hay, and the "horse smell" – a mix of hair, sawdust, leather, skin, and animal. *I'm breathing it, Tomcat.*

As we walked down the aisle, some horses poked their heads out to greet us, some searched our hands for treats, some sifted through hay, and some stood in their stall corners, ignoring us. I looked in, listened to them, and watched them move. All the while, Margene and Sandra Lee muttered about kids and lessons. All I wanted to do was crawl inside one of the stalls and rest my head against a warm, furry neck. I wanted to bury myself in the hay. I wanted to dive inside the walls, the wooden planks.

Then I heard the sound of hooves click on the aisle. There was sweaty Jeffrey, done with his ride, wearing black chaps with fringe. Pulling at the neck of his t-shirt, stretching it, he wiped his face. Then he stared at me curiously, taking off his helmet, which had left behind a sweaty ring on his head of brown hair. He ran a hand through his flattened hair, and it stuck straight up. He left it this way.

I smiled. He looked goofy.

He didn't smile back. He waved hello, and his mouth was serious. His eyes were set wide, like Sandra Lee's. He was slow to blink. Then his horse shifted sideways. "Whoa, ho, ho," Jeffrey said in a deep voice. And the horse stopped dead. He patted the neck. "Good boy," he said. Then he looked at me again and squinted.

Sandra Lee said to Margene, "Jeffrey can hardly see without his glasses on. Don't mind him if he seems rude." Then she marched us on to see the backfield, the side ring on the hill, and the "New Barn," where the expensive horses lived. Through the barns we drifted, then back to the tack store and lounge, where Margene bought me a black velvet helmet and a package of ten lessons.

"Well, we'll be heading out. I need to get supper on," Margene said to Sandra Lee.

Sandra Lee nodded. "Put some meat on this girl's bones if she's going to be a Griffin rider. Around here, my boys are like garbage disposals. Put anything in front of them, and they'll eat it right up. They're at that age where everything goes right through them. Ha, ha."

Margene nodded. "Mary eats like a bird. Always has."

The barn phone rang loud, making me jump. Like a hunting cat, Sandra Lee leapt down the aisle to answer it, yelling back at us, "See you in the lessons!" Out of breath, she reached for the phone, yelling into it, "Hello there! Griffin Farm!" She lit a cigarette.

I stared into some stalls until Margene poked me and said, "Don't get too messy now."

I ran my hand along some dusty stall doors.

Margene had to drag me out to the parking lot. As I climbed in the SUV, I glanced back at the picnic table in front of the lounge. Jeffery was sitting there, drinking a Pepsi, ankles crossed. When light hit his boots, the heels started shining. He still had his spurs on.

I smiled at him again.

He waved goodbye, squinting. His mouth was serious. Then he shoved his hand inside a bag of Cheetos, ate a handful, and licked his fingers one by one. He held up his orange thumb at me.

I held up my dusty thumb at him, hopping in the SUV, shutting the door softly.

Margene's engine was already running. "Look at you, you're filthy," she said.

"Yup." I smirked. I wore that helmet on my head the whole way home.

Two.

Fat, brown Velvet was a gentle bay mare. She was as wide as she was tall. When Velvet turned her head to look at me, she looked like a brontosaurus. Shakily, I climbed up on the mounting block to get on, and before long, after Sandra Lee adjusted my stirrups, I was riding. Well, Sandra Lee was leading me around the ring. She had a hold on me, hooking a long rope, a longe line, onto Velvet's bit. I kicked and kicked at Velvet's sides, but no matter how hard I tried, Velvet refused to trot. Maybe a slow first lesson, but I was hooked.

My second lesson, Sandra Lee put me on Ft. Scott, a chestnut, and he gave me the trot that Velvet wouldn't give. While riding, I forgot about Dr. Dad disappearing all of the time. I forgot about Margene who cleaned and cooked and asked me if I wanted food.

Each week, I looked forward to the after-school afternoons when I knew I needed to grab my helmet and boots. I'd rip off my St. Genevieve uniform, throw on my purple jeans and an old t-shirt, and then it was time to go to the barn, my barn, Griffin Farm, red and black, the barn's colors, my colors, the colors of blood and pirate flags.

Quickly, I moved up from beginners to intermediate to advanced lessons. Then I started jumping, and Dr. Dad decided it was time for a pony. First, we leased a large pony, Genie, and I learned about horse care – brushes, hoof picks, bridles, saddles, saddle pads, and the list went on. The expense was never-ending. We weren't as well off as most of the lesson kids, but I was right in there with them.

Then the horse shows began – first, the local shows. The small, local shows were quick – one day, all day; we hauled our horses there, collected ribbons, and went home.

There were good days and bad days for the Griffin boys and me, but I was hooked on jumping, showing, and the rush. On good days, I brought home the ribbons and felt a natural high. On bad days, I hid in my room, only coming out for riding lessons or school. Winning was everything. I was a Griffin Farm rider, a winner. I had to be.

I went to the barn every day. I rode Genie, and I begged Sandra Lee's husband Big Mike to let me ride more. Quietly, he looked at the horse list. He usually found something for me to ride. I rode anything. Good ones, bad ones, scary ones, I rode.

Before the horse shows, I was a train-wreck-mess of nerves. I had near-insomnia the week before, practicing courses in my head. And I was terrified that my show clothes wouldn't fit. So I rode more. I rode three or four horses a day. I rode without stirrups. I rode with a crop stuck between my elbows to keep my back straight. I rode bareback. I practiced. I won ribbons. When I won, Buddy Griffin, the oldest, gave me a high five. Jeffrey, the middle one, nodded and slapped me on the back. And Michael, the baby, was usually sitting somewhere getting sticky, eating ice cream.

Soon I spent most days at the barns with my hair tucked up under my helmet neatly, like Sandra Lee taught me. My legs were poured into jeans and some hand-me-down chaps. At horse shows, I wore breeches, tall, custom, leather boots, and wool show jackets, even in the dog days of summer.

Jeffrey and I knew the feel of reins. Blisters became a part of our skin. We compared calluses. We knew what it was like to pile in a hotel room, back late from a show day, only to wake up at five a.m. for more practice, carrying our saddles in one hand, and our dry-cleaned show jackets in the other. We knew what it was like to catch a catnap, curled up on top of tack trunks.

In the hotels, we took turns at quick showers, barely staying awake through fast-food dinners. We knew what it was like to be away for a long, horse show weekend, to miss a day or two or three of school.

Dr. Dad drove me to the barn on some Sundays when he wasn't at Welch Hospital. He was always on time, but on the way there, he rushed anyway. Dressed in his tan sport coat, he focused on driving while I reached to feel the soft brown patches shielding the elbows of his jacket. On the way, a coffee cup knocked the edges of its holder, but even as we arrived and braved the Griffin's pot-holed drive, Dr. Dad's drink never spilled.

At the barn, we went our separate ways – me, down the long barn aisle to greet Genie, and Dr. Dad, into the fly-infested lounge, where he watched and waited for me, glancing over some other father's shoulder to catch part of the University of Welch football game on a portable TV.

When the riding lesson was done, we always took the long way home – Dr. Dad steered the Cadillac through curves, slowly crossing the first set of train tracks. He always looked both ways. There were few houses on our sides – mostly old trees, old hills on his side, and the Little River on mine. And every week, I pointed at the yard with the miniature horses; there were three out front, grazing next to the homemade sign that read, "Keep Out." We could count on those scenes.

We had no long talks of Dr. Dad's patients, school or my too-tight jeans. It was only Dr. Dad, staring out at the green side, and me, staring out at the river's blue, and in those colors, those blurry moments of car-side picture shows, it no longer mattered if Big Mike had looked down at the ground again, shaking his head at me, angry when I'd messed up on a jump, stomping the heel of his paddock boot into the sand. It didn't even matter if Big Mike had praised me in a booming voice. It didn't matter that I was covered in sawdust and sweat, that the smell of horse seeped out of my pores. All that mattered were Dr. Dad's hands – one on the gearshift, one on the wheel, and the way his grip grew tighter when we crossed the tracks for the last time. Here, I felt the cool, leather seats, so much smoother than reins, and I began to imitate his grip, his feel of stillness, his quiet ride, and Dr. Dad, my silent driver, looked green, looked blue, then green again, leaving those colors behind.

For a moment, he halted, released the wheel, then used both hands to turn, creep out, and silently slip to join the stampede on the gray highway, making it look so easy, leaning back for a straight stretch, steering me closer and closer to home.

Silently, we drove. I tried to gauge his expressions, making sure my shoes didn't have mud on them. If they were dirty, I put a towel down. No footprints, not a trace. And here and there, I felt some peace sitting with him in the white Cadillac. But there was still a sea of fear inside me. I wanted to be near him in his space, watching him, but Dr. Dad was the master of cool, calm, closed-up, and sometimes collected. Impossible to read. I worried about getting hushed.

Three.

I always liked it when Sandra Lee was driving, because she sped like a maniac; she could care less about cops. She was driving because she was smoking. That was the usual order from Big Mike, who thought that the driver window sucked out smoke better than the passenger one.

Jeffrey never called her "Mom." Like Margene, she liked her name, and that was that. Big Mike, in the passenger seat, was their Dad, but none of the boys ever called him that either. To the boys, they were Sandra Lee and Big Mike. That was the way it always was, and that was the way it stayed, much like everything else at Griffin Farm. Chores, watering time, feeding time, riding time – everything was as predictable as the signs of a dying pony – stopped eating, stopped making manure, ended up belly-up, then rolling in the stall. That meant the intestines were about to twist. And that meant she was a goner, and even if they'd called the vet by that stage, we all knew when a pony was near-dead, whether or not she was still breathing. At that point, there was nothing left to do except stand at the door of the stall, wait, and watch her give in. It was too late for prayers.

Jeffrey and I were in the backseat middle. As luck went, we were always sitting there, and we never complained, accepting the bumpy placement in the Thunderbird.

Buddy was squished next to me on the right. Two whole years older, he was fourteen. He stared out the window. Buddy wore a plaid suit that day. Unless he was riding, he always wore mismatched plaid suits, just to wear a suit. No other reason, other than that he liked strange styles. And for some reason, Buddy always got away with his strangeness.

We were out on Griffin family errands, the "house kind". When we ran farm errands, we took the Red Dodge truck. On house errands, food and clothes and such, we took the Thunderbird, and Buddy wore strange suits. More than once, Buddy told Jeffrey and me that he was going to be a rock star, and if he kept wearing weird suits, maybe he wouldn't have to be a farm worker like Big Mike. Jeffrey and I believed Buddy. Absolutely.

Jeffrey shifted, whispering to me, "I hope we get home soon. I have stalls to clean. And we all know Big Mike won't get to them."

I nodded, patting him on the leg, which made him jump. Jeffrey and I knew that Big Mike wasn't really a farm *worker.* He paid bills and told the barn help what to do. Jeffrey and I knew a lot of things that little people shouldn't know, complements of Buddy. We'd learned all of the best cuss words from Buddy.

Sandra Lee made sure the boys were busy, "outta trouble and clean," she always said. And it was true. Jeffrey couldn't get into much trouble since he was always picking hay out of his hair and smelling like horseshit all the time. In my head, I mulled over the sound of *horseshit,* and a smile spread over my face. I felt it freeze there.

Jeffrey punched my arm and went, "What?"

"Nothing," I said, smirking.

Skinny Buddy bounced in his seat, catching my thought. "Fuck," he whispered to me, testing Sandra Lee. Buddy loved attention. The summer before, he used the horse clippers to shave his hair in a circular pattern, so that the top of his head looked like a bullseye. Big Mike knocked him around some, but Buddy told me it was worth it, that the girls at school liked his bullseye.

"Watch your mouth, Buddy, or I'll fill it with manure," Sandra Lee yelled back while she drove, glancing up in the rear view mirror, then looking back at the road, speeding. Side to side, frantically, she scanned the side of the road, probably watching for animals. And then she sped on.

"Sorry, Sandy Lee," Buddy said, smiling sweetly, batting his long white lashes, running a hand through his thick, white-blonde hair.

The boys looked nothing alike. Jeffrey's hair was dark brown. Michael's, a sweet dirty blonde. Buddy swore to me that they'd all been adopted until Sandra Lee pulled out the birth certificates one day and said, "See, now? You all came from my stomach, so stop messing around. But you all looked like little adults when you popped outta me, that's for sure. Damn, three C-sections is one too many for any woman."

They *didn't* look alike, but they rode horses alike. Before they even learned to walk, all three knew how to steer a pony. For the Griffins, riding was more familiar than eating, sleeping, or crawling. And while riding horses, whether taking lessons, goofing off, or having races in the front field, the body form of the three boys was exactly the same. I'd spend hours watching them ride. The only way to tell them apart was the different heights of their black helmets. Their knees bent at the same angle in the saddle. Their top halves were thin and muscled. Even their hands gripped and pulled the reins the same way. When they trotted, their compact chests often rose and fell together, posting to the same rhythm.

Next to Jeffrey, Michael groaned. "I'm sick, Sandra Lee." Only ten, always a sicky, Michael was a smaller version of Big Mike. Both of them had hair that lightened in the summer sun. Michael had a wide smile and green eyes that were often teary. His eyes were see-through, newborn creepy, and they stayed that way past the baby stage. He would tan a deep brown in an hour. People were always saying that Michael was beyond cute. More like a live doll. People said that right in front of Jeffrey, which made him groan. Sometimes I groaned too, just because.

Jeffrey looked like Sandra Lee, with brown hair and fair skin that burned and peeled and freckled more at horse shows. Jeffrey was forever fighting his shedding skin.

Buddy looked like no one, not even a neighbor, in the face. To me, sometimes Buddy didn't even look like a human being. His nose was narrow, defined. His cheeks were hollow. His hair, that strange whitish blonde. His eyes, blue and squinty. He was as slinky as a barn snake, slithering around the barn aisles, driving the tractor like a madman, and everyone wanted to know Buddy, but no one really knew him. Buddy was always complaining that his eyes hurt. He didn't tan. He always stayed about the same color – pale white. Unlike Jeffrey's, his skin was flawless, especially his slender fingers. After a weeklong horse show, Buddy might turn beige. Then burnings and peelings. Then back to white. And at horse shows, Buddy always won, regardless. He beat the other kids over and over, but he never stressed about winning or practicing the way Jeffrey did. He could look at a course once and remember the order of jumps, no problem, while Jeffrey had to study the courses over and over again. A natural, Buddy would enter the show ring, jump jumps, and win every time. While he rode, he was so relaxed. Sometimes he hummed his latest favorite rock tune. While Jeffrey was silent, concentrating, Buddy was singing and riding and winning.

But at the shows, something did drive Buddy insane. The loud speakers. The sound, the announcer's voice, bothered his ears constantly. And he had sensitive sight and touch as well. Buddy could find a lost shoe in a field faster than anyone. He had the softest feel on his reins. Guiding a horse's mouth, Buddy barely had to move. Buddy was a walking sensory machine. All the girls loved him, including me. It was easy to love a ghost, but I knew Buddy was untouchable. He'd never get pinned down. Never, I knew.

Following Buddy's lead, Jeffrey said, "Ass."

"Dick," Buddy said.

"Pussy," I said, joining in.

Jeffrey blushed.

Before Sandra Lee could yell at us, Buddy yelled, "Here comes the circus! Here it comes!"

Buddy wasn't talking about a real circus. Jeffrey and I always hoped Margene or Sandra Lee would take us there, because we wanted to see unicorns and tight ropes, but Sandra Lee thought the real circus was abusive to the animals, so we never went. Still, every now and then, I dreamed about riding an elephant. And Jeffrey did too. We both wanted to beat Buddy to it. Beat Buddy at something for once.

Michael whined, "I might puke, seriously, you all."

Jeffrey inched closer to me. Michael rarely bluffed.

Sandra Lee stepped on the brakes, squealed over to the side of the road, and said to Michael, "There, throw up, get it over with." She was all Griffin business when she said it, as if she were ordering more hay for the barn.

Big Mike said, "Easy on the car, Sandra. You're killing the brakes. This Thunderbird's not for road racin,'" he said. He belly-laughed, *heh, heh, heh.* Then to Michael, he said, "Get over it, you're a Griffin boy. We don't get sick." He didn't laugh, looking at Michael.

Michael threw up anyway. When Big Mike wasn't looking, Michael cried a little.

Then we went on down the road, heading back to Griffin Farm.

As we approached the black gates, Buddy bounced in his seat so high, his head hit the ceiling. He took my hand and said, "Hang on, Mary, we're goin for a circus ride!"

Jeffrey hung on to my other hand.

Sandra Lee hopped out of the car to open the gates. She took her cigarette with her. It hung from her hand like an extra, stick finger.

Big Mike sat quietly. He never helped. That was the rule with the Griffins. The driver opened the gate.

Sandra Lee looked back at Big Mike, waved her cigarette, and said, "You're sitting there like you think these iron things are gonna open on their own."

Big Mike smiled and nodded. "You're the driver. It's your job. Besides, I like to watch you do it. Reminds me of the first time I watched you. Remember? Remember what happened after that?" He winked.

Sandra Lee turned red and said, "You might have to remind me when we get back to the house."

"Great, that means I'll have to do all the work if they have their alone time," Jeffrey said, scowling.

"Alone time?" I asked.

"Sex, Mare," Jeffrey said, smiling for once.

Buddy laughed and said, "Fucking."

I blushed and said nothing. Buddy had won again.

When we hit the driveway, the ride began. Pothole after pothole threw us out of our seats.

Buddy shouted at Jeffrey, "Here's the ride, boy, hang on! It's a wild one this time, a real mustang! Hang on!" Buddy's blonde hair shot up from his head like an old Q-tip.

Jeffrey hung on to me.

We all held hands, bouncing around in the back seat. Even carsick Michael. We knew the timing of each hole, and for each one, Sandra Lee sped up for a better jolt.

Sandra Lee witch-cackled.

Big Mike yelled, "Slow down, woman, you'll ruin the tires!" He shook his head. "Damnit, I told the help to fill these holes with gravel." Big Mike said that daily.

Sandra Lee smiled and said, "Hang on! We're almost home! Hang on!" Getting closer to home, Sandra Lee was always dramatic. She let go of the wheel for a second and said, "No hands!"

Big Mike grabbed the wheel just in time to steer the Thunderbird away from crashing into the black fence. "Watch it, Sandra. We just fixed the fence from the last time you hit it."

Sandra Lee looked at him, went, "Humph" and sped up, hitting a big pothole.

Big Mike was knocked to the right, hitting his head on the passenger window. Slumping down, he hung on to the edge of his seat.

When Big Mike relaxed, Sandra Lee slowed down. She looked at him and said, "Sit down, Big Mike, we're not done yet."

"Lord," he said, rolling his eyes.

The driveway was long, twisty, and even though I knew chores were coming, down the drive, I felt like a human cannonball. *Fire in the hole, Tomcat.*

Jeffrey flew up and out of his seat, giggling and bouncing.

Sandra Lee was going even faster than usual.

Buddy whooped, "Mad ride, Sandra Lee. Hit the gas!" Buddy was right. It was a mad ride. We *were* at the circus.

Beside me, the black, freshly painted fences of Griffin Farm magically sprung up from the grass. In the fields, the horses lifted their heads, then went back to eating. The grass was lush, thick, and wild. All of the troughs were filled to the brim with fresh water.

When Jeffrey flew from his seat the last time, he waved at the boys' first red pony, appropriately named, Red. Michael's idea. Jeffrey told me he thought it was a stupid name, but Michael had been cursed by a wicked toothache that day, so Jeffrey let the name slide.

By the time I could see the house – red brick with white pillars, huge black letters spelling GRIFFIN over the door – Jeffrey had settled back in his seat, letting go of my hand.

Buddy held on and announced, "Home!" Whenever he said that, Buddy had this pop-eyed stare, as if we'd arrived on Mars. When he smiled, it was all teeth.

In the circular drive, Sandra Lee slammed on the brakes.

We all scrambled out of the car, and as usual, Michael lagged behind, catching his shirt in the Thunderbird door, then tugging it out, tearing it.

Big Mike carried Sandra Lee inside the farmhouse, and they disappeared.

Jeffrey and I stared at each other, laughing.

Sex. Fucking. Buddy had taught us all about penises and what they did. They *fucked.*

Buddy grabbed Michael and Jeffrey, each by one hand, yelled back at me to "Come on," and we headed to the barns. When Buddy walked, he bounced with an erratic hop, jerking his left arm around for no reason other than to look like a cartoon. And to pull poor Michael off of the ground every now and again.

Jeffrey scurried to keep up with Buddy's stride. At every moment, it seemed that Buddy was still on a drive with Sandra Lee. While he walked, he sang, jerking in a quick limp, for no reason other than to limp. Buddy's head was surely *in* Mars. Flat ground or not, he hopped around like a lizard on hot ground. Sometimes, he would walk a thin line, as if he were balancing on a tight rope, carefully, slowly, one foot at a time, both hands spread out for balance. He never just *walked*. It was as if he was always hoping for strangeness, a mishap, a mistake, something lost, something found, anything to change the course of the day, even if the change was terrible.

I began to think that Buddy *was* from another planet, that even though Buddy walked and talked on Griffin land, his mind was trapped in a place where dreams were real, where horses spoke, where driveways held elephants, trapeze swingers, and circus games. Buddy lived for speed and jolts and rock and roll and holes.

Four.

Jeffrey and I had just finished riding, and I'd fallen off, but I didn't care. My crooked wrist hurt, but that was about it. Outside of the barn lounge, we sat at the picnic table, eating Moon Pies, which was the best we could get out of the barn workers. Margene forgot to pack my lunch again, and Sandra Lee had a full plate of lessons, so we were stuck with junk food. Actually, Jeffrey and I were used to it. I nibbled mine, worried about calories.

The weather was growing cold, steel, crisp. Jeffrey and I were both bundled in our thick, short jackets. His was green. Mine was blue. We both had hathead. We both wore tight leather chaps. Mine were gray hand-me-downs from Buddy. Jeffrey had on the black ones that day; he had seven pairs of chaps, seven different colors, all worn out.

Jeffrey picked up a few cigarette butts out of the horse head ashtray and said, "Come on, Mare, let's go smoke 'em."

"All right," I said. Jeffrey could talk me into anything, just by glancing at me with his googly green-blue-gray eyes. Googly, because Sandra Lee had just bought him some new black-framed, thick glasses. Actually, they suited his oval face.

While we ran behind the barn, I had to yank my bra straight. I didn't have a chest like Margene's mountains, but I still didn't need to be showing mine to the world.

I was slower than Jeffrey. My paddock boots were too big. Earlier that year, Sandra Lee had found me the boots in Jeffrey's pile. The Griffin boys had more horse gear than regular clothes. And Buddy had the most, because he was the Griffin Farm star.

Buddy might've been the oldest, but by then I knew he was crazy. Jeffrey was normal I guess. Too normal, so serious. And Michael, well, he was cute, and he and most others knew it, but man, he was whiny. And we all knew that.

While we smoked, Jeffrey kept his eyes peeled for Big Mike, Sandra Lee, and the barn crew. I ran my hands along my purple jeans because I had dust all over me. My fingernails were black from brushing horses and picking out hooves. Margene had told me a thousand times that those jeans were "bulky-looking," but by then I was starting to ignore her. Jeffrey liked them, and that was enough for me.

"Hey, your fly's down, Mary," Jeffrey said, blowing out a smoke ring.

I looked down, feeling at my chaps, lifting up my black and silver leather belt, checking it out. My pants were fine. I looked back up, saying, "You suck."

"Ha, made you look," Jeffrey said, pushing his glasses up on his nose.

Jeffrey was always fiddling with those new glasses. He lost the last pair when we were riding in the front field, messing around, having races, when Slick, the three-year-old black horse, bucked Jeffrey off. After about five hundred hours of looking, Jeffrey and I gave up on the old glasses and went back to the barn.

When we finished smoking, Jeffrey stamped out both the butts hard with the toe of his black paddock boot. Jeffrey had the fancy, new zip kind. Mine were just cheap and laced.

As always, Jeffrey looked at me seriously. He said, "Lord, I still have to pick out some stalls and feed. I don't even know where Buddy is. He disappeared again. Probably out in the field playing air guitar. And Michael, we all know he's useless."

"I'll help you," I said, wondering if I did look fat in my purple jeans. Whenever Margene saw those pants, her mouth drooped all funny like she was about to drool down her shirt. I looked at Jeffrey's skinny legs, studying the way his jeans hung on his hips.

Jeffrey grabbed my arm for a second, then let go, looking me in the eye. "I can tell you're worrying again, Mare. Your jeans look fine. I like them. All of us like them. Us Griffins anyway, and that's all that matters. Come on, those horses are gonna be kicking at the walls if we don't feed them soon. You know I always have to do everything around here."

I smiled. "You do." Truth was, I was afraid to wear a different pair of jeans. I was afraid of sizes. Margene kept trying to get me to change, but every few days, I'd just throw the same ones in the washer, slipping them back on, making sure they still fit. On the days when they felt loose, I was relieved. On the days when they felt snug, I was crabby to Jeffrey, and I didn't ride as well.

Jeffrey joked that I had my own uniform, which made me think about the stinking nuns at St. Genevieve's until Jeffrey led me into the barn, hauling bales of hay onto the cart.

All around us, the horses shifted in their stalls, whinnying and knocking against the walls. I breathed in dust, wood shavings, and the smell of manure. It felt like home. I thought of the farmer's field back in Scallycat. The fresh, greenish hay matched Jeffrey's eyes that day, and the sawdust was the color of Thomas' hair. I was glad it was getting colder. We didn't have to swat so many flies.

Jeffrey filled a coffee can full of grain, measured it, and dumped it in a feed bucket. One stall at a time, he carefully poured the grain.

I spaced out, following him.

"Would you help me, before I tip the cart and pop you one?" Jeffrey said, staring back at me with hay in his hair. Jeffrey had this look in his eyes. It was the same look he had when he put his hand on my forehead, holding me back when I tried to punch him. His eyes bugged out, and his face held a frown that looked like a smile might bust out any second, making his cheeks explode. But the smiles rarely came out. That was Jeffrey.

"All right, here, geez." I grabbed a few flakes of hay and threw them in a pony's stall, wrapping the bailing twine around Jeffrey's head. "Caught ya," I said.

Wearing the twine like a necklace, Jeffrey chased me down the barn aisle, yelling, "I'm gonna catch you, now, sucker. You better run!"

Both of us stopped when we heard Big Mike's booming voice yell, "No running in the barn!" We stopped cold. Big Mike had the spooky, mysterious, whispery way of a horse trainer. When he spoke, we listened.

The riding held us together, but Big Mike watched over us all. Everything about Big Mike was lean and loose. His eyes were a soft, see-through green. He had lines around those eyes, and his skin was weather-roughened from years of teaching outside. He lived and breathed horses. Once, I caught him tasting the sweet feed. I never saw a horse act up in front of Big Mike. And I knew how to deal with quiet types like Dr. Dad. When Big Mike was there, that was enough.

Big Mike wasn't like the other trainers who wore fancy belts and expensive chaps. He wore old, stained, loose and long jeans that hung on his frame; they were as thin as tissue paper. His cowboy hat and sweaters were riddled with holes.

Then Big Mike's boots click-clicked on the aisle, and he disappeared into the indoor riding ring as fast as he came.

It took us forever to feed, because Jeffrey made the hay cart tip, and we knew we had to clean up all the hay and grain from the aisle before Big Mike came back, or he'd make us do morning stall duty, which was a bear.

Then Jeffrey made up some story about how he was going to win Champion at the next show. I agreed with him, even though I knew that Buddy would beat him. Jeffrey really didn't have a chance. Buddy was crazy, but he was the best rider at Griffin Farm. He was the best in all of Mitgard. No one else even came close. Big Mike, Sandra Lee, and the whole horse world were always talking about Buddy. And Jeffrey hated it. I mean, he loved Buddy. We all did. But Jeffrey hated the talk.

We hurried into the lounge. The heat was cranked in there. Big Mike was quietly sweeping. A barn cat scurried across the floor. She looked sick.

"We did everything. It's done. We're done," Jeffrey said to Big Mike. "And that cat looks like it might kick the bucket."

Big Mike nodded and kept on sweeping.

Jeffrey shook his head, shrugging. "It's never good enough," he whispered to me when Big Mike was down the hall in the office. "And damn, he hates cats."

I patted Jeffrey on the back. "It's good enough," I said. "It is."

Jeffrey laughed nervously, sitting down at the round lounge table.

I sat down with him, waiting for Margene to pick me up. She was always late. Usually, Big Mike kept the barn open just because I was still there. Sometimes, Sandra Lee saved us all the trouble and gave me a ride home.

Jeffrey breathed slowly, folding his hands like he was praying.

I did it too, even though I didn't get religion. Neither did Captain Tomcat, and that's why we were the most powerful pirates in all of Scallycat.

Sitting in the dusty lounge, Jeffrey and I had this game. We stared at each other, mouthing words, trying to figure out what we were saying to each other without actually speaking. I thought about how the horses were probably rolling in the mud outside while we were in there fooling around.

Jeffrey mouthed, "Mary's jeans are so cool."

I mouthed, "Jeffrey's glasses are so cool."

Jeffrey mouthed, "Mary needs a black horse."

I mouthed, "Jeffrey, train Slick for me."

Jeffrey mouthed, "Mary, do it yourself, lazy bones."

I smiled.

Jeffrey mouthed, "I'm worried about Buddy."

I mouthed, "Oh, he's just Buddy."

Jeffrey mouthed, "No. It's something bad. I'm worried."

I spoke. "What do you mean? What's bad? You

know something?"

"I just have this feeling," Jeffrey said. "Like horse sense, you know. Something awful, I'm telling you, you know what I mean?"

"Yeah, I do know," I said.

And then Jeffrey mouthed something else I couldn't quite read.

"What was that one?" I asked him.

He blushed. "Did ya see that mare Sandra Lee brought back from Scallycat?"

"Nope, where?"

"Out in the back field tonight, I think. Hm. She's around. What a pretty thing. Hey, Mary, lets hold our breath."

"I don't want to."

"Come on," he said, breathing in, shutting his mouth tight. He started to turn red. His cheeks filled up.

"Stop it," I said, grabbing his arm, shaking him.

But still he wouldn't breathe.

"Breathe, damnit," I said, shaking him again. "Jeffrey, stop. I mean it, stop. Breathe."

Jeffrey released his breath. Swoosh. He chuckled. "Chill, Mare," he said.

I folded my arms quietly, rolling my eyes. "Don't do that to me. Ever again," I said. "Ever."

Jeffrey nodded. "Okay, okay, I hear you. Don't have a freakin' heart attack."

He never got mad at me. But I got mad at him. He always rode the troubled horses, the real tough ones, the crazies and the young ones and the downright pissy rearers and buckers. So he fell off a lot. And when he fell off, he always tried to scare me by lying there on the ground too long, holding his breath, acting like he was dead. I'd run over to check on him, and every time, he'd jump up, saying, "Whoa, that was a wild ride!" Then I'd try and punch him but I never could. Jeffrey was too quick. Holding his breath and running away from me were the two things that Jeffrey had perfected. Even while wearing tight chaps, he could run. But he always came back.

Margene was really late.

Loudly, Jeffrey said, "Get ready for the next show, Mary. Get ready to watch a real rider. Me." He pointed at his chest, grinning.

From the office, Big Mike shouted, "I heard you, that's right, you're a Griffin rider and Griffins always win!"

Jeffrey's mouth turned all serious. He fixed his glasses again. Then he took them off, wiping them clean, sliding them on, sliding them off. On.

By the time Margene pulled in the driveway, the ring lights were out, and only the lounge was still lit.

"See you tomorrow," Jeffrey said. "Maybe you'll grow an inch by then."

I stood up and smiled. "Maybe you will," I said. "If you're lucky."

Before I left, Jeffrey whispered, "Really, about Buddy, I'm worried, Mare. Something awful, I'm telling you."

I shrugged. "Use your deadlights, matey," I mouthed back.

"Huh?" Jeffrey said.

"Just keep your eyes open. Time will tell," I said.

"I guess so," he said, feeling at his chin with his hand. Then he reached forward, touching my crooked wrist. "How'd you get hurt, Mare?"

"Shipwreck," I said, turning to leave.

"Seriously, tell me," he called out. "Someday, you'll tell me."

I heard him, but he thought I didn't. I was pretty much gone.

In the car, Margene was listening to some new age tunes that made me edgy. Her fake blonde hair was slicked back in a tight bun. Before I sat down, she spread a towel across the seat. Her frosty orange lipstick cracked when she said, "Don't get the car dirty, Mary. Take your boots off."

So I did. And I thought about Jeffrey's clean glasses. And I thought about Jeffrey's classy, zip up paddock boots, and how I'd like to have a pair of my own, how I'd like to be able to go home with him and leave my boots on.

The next day, Saturday, Big Mike, Sandra Lee, Buddy and Michael were away at a local show, a one-dayer. So Jeffrey and I were home watching things as usual. We couldn't drive yet, and we still thought beer was gross, so after we each rode five horses and made sure the afternoon turnouts were done, we combed the fields for treasure.

Jeffrey always let me pick up everything so he could spend time making up stories about the junk. Mostly, we found old horseshoes. Jeffrey said that the stones I found were fossils or Indian arrowheads. One time, I found a comb with a few missing teeth. He said it would turn my hair black if I used it. I told him he was nuts. But that night, just to prove his story right, I dyed my hair black. When Margene saw my new look, she dropped a metal spoon on the kitchen floor, and it bang, banged across the tiles.

I smiled and smiled. That moment, I decided that I'd keep it black forever.

Dr. Dad didn't even notice.

That day, Jeffrey and I found a rain boot in the field. It was dark green.

"Don't touch it," I said, backing away. My hands started shaking. Then my arms. My legs. My whole body rattled. Everywhere, bugs.

"Someone might be looking for it," Jeffrey said, tugging on the boot, picking it up.

Suddenly, I pictured Captain Blackeye's face. Sticks and stones and black eyes and black hair and pale skin and broken bones. Blood. Thomas' yellow hair. I threw up.

"Geez, you sick?" Jeffrey asked.

"I guess so," I said, wiping my mouth on my shirt. I spat. My eyes felt wet. "Sorry, didn't mean to do that."

"It's all right, hey, what is it, Mare? You can tell me, you know you can," he said, holding that green boot. Jeffrey's eyes, even through his glasses, were suddenly neon.

"I used to have a yellow-haired brother," I said. And I told him about Captain Tomcat. About the pirate hunt. I told him about Captain Blackeye's boot. I told him about Scallycat, the mountains there, and how Margene and Dr. Dad were shaky. I told him about Thomas' yellow hair, the police line, the crime scene tape. I told him that we never found Captain Blackeye, the killer, that everyone knew the Lochmores stopped looking. Everyone knew. Well, they thought they knew. Really, I had never stopped looking. Secretly, I would never stop.

Jeffrey ran his fingers along the fringe on his chaps. Quietly, he put the green boot down, burying it in the grass. He patted me on the back. "Listen, we'll just leave this green boot right here in the field for someone else to find. Now, come with me. We've still got to fill up the water troughs."

I nodded, following his skinny behind. Together, we went in the Main Barn. I liked the smell. And so did he. I knew this by the way we both breathed it in at the same time, making the same sound, then slowly breathing out, sharing the wind.

That night, Margene forgot to pick me up at the barn again. Dr. Dad called to check on me, but by then, the rest of the Griffins were home from the horse show, and we were all too starving to wait for my ride home. Big Mike had skinned our supper. Fresh fish. Sandra Lee fried it just right, so it didn't taste "too fishy."

Jeffrey, Buddy, Michael, and I sat in our seats at the table, waiting for Sandra Lee's homemade meal.

Michael whined, "I'm starving!"

Jeffrey sat quietly.

Buddy studied his face in the plate's reflection. He stuck his tongue out at himself, then laughed, saying, "Good to be back playing here," to his imaginary concert crowd, I guess.

I watched Sandra Lee. Her face was the texture of an old shoe. I knew I'd better eat around her. Sandra Lee usually sent me home with biscuits or bread, saying, "We need to fatten you up." She made everything homemade, even hamburger buns. She talked to her cookies too. Probably because Big Mike was always watering the ring or having serious chats with the female vet.

In the barns, Big Mike frowned a lot, constantly yelling at Sandra Lee, "Stop fiddling around. You never stop moving." Big Mike did the same thing, though. When I tried to show him the blisters on my hands that appeared from gripping reins, Big Mike just kept on telling stories to the farrier while making a list of horses that needed new shoes.

We all ate, except for Buddy. He talked to the crowd he saw inside the plate.

Big Mike stared at him, shook his head, and went on eating.

Wide-eyed, Sandra Lee studied Big Mike.

Big Mike shrugged.

And Buddy went right on talking to his imaginary rock and roll fans.

Everything was just as it always was, except Jeffrey kept touching the toe of his boot to mine, which was becoming annoying.

Later, waiting for Margene, Jeffrey and I sat on the porch swing, staring out at the horses' dark shapes, watching the way the shadows shifted across the fields that night. Wildly, Jeffrey pumped his legs, and for a moment, I wondered if he'd pump them right off. We waited until the swing was at its highest point in the air, sat on the edge, then jumped over the side of the porch into the grass.

There, in the cool grass, I touched Jeffrey's straight brown hair.

He looked at me with his serious face. His glasses were crooked.

I scrunched his hair between my fingers. Not long before, I had cut his hair, which was a bad idea. I knew it wasn't too straight because he was trying to roll up horse leg wraps at the same time. Sandra Lee said she'd shave my head with the horse clippers if I tried it again. When she said that, Jeffrey smiled on the inside. I could tell.

I pulled my hand from his hair.

We climbed back onto the porch, sitting back on the swing for another ride. Off in the distance, the horses moved, no more than slowly grazing black shapes.

"Margene's always late," I said. "Where is she?"

"I dunno, Mare," Jeffrey said, rising.

We sat back on the swing until the clouds disappeared, and the thin moon peeked into the sky with its white eyelid.

"I'm scared," I said.

"Of what?" Jeffrey asked.

"I'm scared I'll lose the horses and my purple jeans."

"I'm scared too," he said.

"Of what?" I asked.

"I'm scared I'll lose to Buddy again at the shows."

I moved closer to him. "I'm scared Dr. Dad will leave."

He moved closer to me. "I'm scared Big Mike will go to a horse show one day and not come back."

"I'm scared of yellow hair," I said.

"I'm scared of getting kicked in the head by that new green horse," he said.

"I'm scared of you," I said.

"Why?" he asked me.

All I could think about was the way he looked after a bad fall, when he held his breath, the moment before he rose, letting me know that he was all right. All right. Suddenly, it was hard to breathe. "I'm just scared of you, that's all."

"You shouldn't be. I'm always around. I'm harmless," Jeffrey said. "I'm scared of Buddy, of something awful."

"Did you say something to Big Mike? Maybe you should tell him."

"He's too busy, Mare. He doesn't look up unless a fancy, winning horse trots by."

"But maybe you should try and talk to him. About Buddy."

"I think he already knows."

"Yeah, he has the horse sense too."

"Mary?"

"Yeah?"

"I'm scared of you more than I'm scared of something awful."

I smiled, but I'm sure he couldn't see it. Maybe the teeth.

The porch swing squeaked. The chain on one side broke, sliding Jeffrey into my lap. Our noses bumped, and he kissed me. Jeffrey's kiss was wet, soft and sloppy. I felt like he was using the same air as me for a second. My chest. It hurt. I tasted him. I was hungry.

He pulled back and said, "You're a good kisser."

"I've had lots of practice," I stated.

"Sure," he said, kissing me again.

Then Margene barreled down the driveway. Her headlights blinded us.

"See ya in the morning," Jeffrey whispered. He tilted his head down, chin against his chest, hopping off the swing.

Margene honked her horn three times, and the whole Griffin farmhouse came alive with light.

He turned to look at me. Half of Jeffrey's face was lit.

I put my hand on the light cheek, thinking about how I'd like to get marooned in that moment. Turning on my boot heels, I left the porch, heading to the SUV, making sure to take off my boots before I got in.

That night, I slid out of my purple jeans, rolled them up in a ball, and threw them out in the garage garbage cans. Then I buried my head under the covers, which was something I didn't usually do, because it was so hard to breathe like that. For some reason, I didn't want to breathe so badly any more, unless I was breathing with Jeffrey.

Five.

Man, sometimes Margene went with me to the horse shows, and when she did, she packed food and more food. It took her forever – preparation, plastic containers, labels on things, and the SUV was jam-packed perfectly as well. There were weeks of anxiety and furious rustling for Margene, and her busy ways leaked out on me as well. I counted bridles, breeches, and show shirts, making sure everything was in order, labeling plastic bags for shampoos, brushes, and toothbrushes, all vacuum-sealed. Margene was terrified of leaks.

When we arrived at the show grounds, Sandra Lee wanted to know what we ate on the entire trip. In detail. Then back at the hotel, Sandra Lee and Big Mike made us eat out, buying meals that were fancier than anything Margene ever made. There were always seconds and thirds. Sandra Lee made us test everything.

Margene fell into Sandra Lee's food schedule as well. Nightly, I pulled at my tight show breeches, wondering if they would fit me the next day. The Griffin boys talked about horses. All I could think about was my full stomach.

Jeffrey and I spent a lot of time working and not getting paid for it, but it was fun managing the show stalls, just the two of us, while the others were out riding or longeing horses. It felt like we were escaping the adults, on our own kid adventure. Of course we rode too, but not as much as Michael and Buddy.

After the kiss, hanging out with Jeffrey was a lot like being with Dr. Dad. We didn't talk much. Really, I was afraid to bother him. Still, it was nice to be near him, and by the look of Jeffrey's watery eyes behind his thick glasses, I think he liked it too.

On those trips, we were focused on the show – winning, and work – not each other. I watched what he did, and I tried to move like him. When Jeffrey fell off of a horse in the show ring, he would paint a crazy maniacal smile on his face, and everything, my whole world, felt out of control. He went along with the falls, letting it happen. I fought to stay on.

But other than almost killing each other with brooms and hoses, we got along at the horse shows. There, Jeffrey and I had a truce. It wasn't a spoken peace treaty; rather, there were too many distractions – that kept our kid heads busy enough for us to be in the moment, forgetting about porch swing nights.

Michael was happy sitting on the ground, the butt of his breeches turning brown.

Buddy was too busy winning to notice us, and Big Mike and Sandra Lee moved so fast, their bodies seemed to be made of one strange skin blur.

But the horse shows began to haunt me. When we bedded the stalls down for the night, I wanted to set the horses free.

Jeffrey was always checking the door latches, making sure the horses were shut in tight for the night.

I heard one restless horse paw at the stall, scraping at the walls, trying to escape. Watching them, listening to them, I too felt like I was trapped in an unfamiliar nest. I lost a lot of sleep over those scraping hooves. Several times, when Jeffrey wasn't looking, I opened the latches, setting them all loose on the show grounds. We always found them, but several times, Big Mike let Jeffrey have it, blaming him for the loose horses. Jeffrey knew it was me, but he never said anything. He took

Big Mike's words inside, sticking out his bottom lip. He stood still. He didn't crack. He was dead serious.

Around Big Mike, Jeffrey and I were on our best behavior. Even Dr. Dad acted like a puppy around Big Mike. When Big Mike shook his hand, Dr. Dad often stuttered. Big Mike was a smart, quiet man with a strong memory, like Buddy, but his looks were like Michael's. In public, he was calm, cool, and often mysterious. All around the horse shows, people knew his teaching voice. His words were few, sure, and to the point, and every student listened to him as if he were the President.

Back home from the horse show, Margene weighed herself, announcing if she'd gained from eating hotel meals. Dr. Dad kidded her. And then Margene weighed me. She kidded me. A joke. Each time I stepped on the scale, I trembled.

Six.

Even before Jeffrey mentioned his worry, I knew there was something strange about Buddy. All in the town of Mitgard knew that something was strange about Buddy. And just when I thought I had him figured out, Buddy would do something like carve the letters "BG" on his arm with a razor blade, making his own personal tattoo. People whispered around the farm, but pale Buddy was a Griffin winner, and that bought him respect. At the horse shows, he was unstoppable, and all of Mitgard knew about that too. Cutter or not, Buddy was a winner. And winners could cut or shave their heads or smoke weed or drink or jerk-walk, and there was nothing anybody did about it. Buddy was a strange, Mitgard legend, a white-haired misfit hero, a chalk-pale Superman. Yes.

One day, the boys and I were walking down to The Black Spot store to search for junk food. Sandra Lee and Big Mike were busy out fixing the tractor or sending a stallion's sperm across the country. So we walked.

Carefully, we headed down the narrow side of Mitgard Highway. The cars flew past so close to me that I could feel the wind speed.

I stepped on the heels of Jeffrey's boots, making him crack up for once.

Michael was dragging behind, looking cute, like he should be on a Christmas card.

I nudged Jeffrey with my nose. I was a foal. He was my mother. That was the game.

"Stop it," Jeffrey said, shoving his hands in his jeans. "Or I'm gonna fall in the road and get flattened."

"Oh, you'd bounce back up," I said, laughing and tossing my black ponytail, a long, straight, black whip of a tail. A snake. I jogged to keep up with Buddy's pipecleaner legs. And so did Jeffrey.

As usual, Buddy was in front, our leader. He was jerk-walking like he did, grinning something evil, like he had a plan in that head of his. He always had some plan. A plan to mess up the barn later with a stink bomb. A plan to spray graffiti all over the new town fast food joint. Or a plan to steal some food from Mommy's Restaurant. That day, like any other, I was sure he had a plan.

Buddy had always been popular, but by the time he was fourteen, every girl in Mitgard ran after him. They were always hanging around the farm, calling out his name while he rode. After he dismounted, he'd pull off his helmet, and Buddy's pale blonde hair hung in his face, or it jutted straight up out of his scalp. His hair was never combed, and it was full of crazy cowlicks. Then he'd swagger over to his fans, smile at each and every giggling face, and hug a few lucky girls. Sometimes they squealed, loving his wild white hair.

Buddy turned around to aim a rock at Jeffrey, then stopped to ruffle Jeffrey's hair, saying, "Easy, middle bro, easy now. I was just kidding around. I wouldn't throw it at ya."

Jeffrey laughed, relaxing.

I laughed too, but I half believed Buddy might throw that rock.

In the back, Michael mumbled, "My stomach hurts."

"Geez, you're a baby," I said, marching along.

"Be nice now, Mary. You're not our real sister, but you're close enough, so be nice," Buddy said, pulling my ponytail.

I blushed, hugging Buddy's thin arm.

Smiling, Buddy patted my head like I was his dog.

Together we tore through The Black Spot, grabbing Doritos and Mountain Dews, then headed back to the farm, again braving the side of busy Mitgard Highway.

It seemed like a long hike back. In the cold, sometimes the walk was murder.

Buddy pulled up the collar on his coat, shivering.

"You're crazy wearing that," Jeffrey said. "It's a thin coat, ass."

Buddy stopped and said, "Cuss words are cool, but don't ever call people names to their face. You know, you might hurt somebody. And then you might die. And then you might never be able to say you're sorry. You never know what might happen."

Jeffrey stared at Buddy, one hand on his Doritos, one hand at his chin. "You trying to prove something?"

Buddy said, "Yeah, to the whole fucking universe." He laughed and kicked some gravel with his boot, jerk-walking forward. "Now come on, dickweed, it's cold. Ha, ha. Hey, I love you."

Jeffrey shrugged, looking back at me. "You see what I mean?" he whispered. "Weird."

I pulled the rubber band out of my hair, letting it fall down thick and messy.

Jeffrey was straight-faced and serious all of a sudden. Too serious.

Buddy *was* weird all right, but it was cold out, and I was too tired to join in.

Michael trailed along, moaning, holding his middle, staring at the ground. His green eyes shone, matching the shade of his winter coat.

"Buddy, we better hurry. We have all those horses to get clipped for this weekend," Jeffrey said, hooking his small hands on his narrow hips.

"It'll get done," Buddy said, smiling. Buddy never cared about horse shows. He'd rather chew on some grass, smoke some grass, sing, or study cracks in the road. That's what he was doing – studying cracks in the middle of Mitgard Highway, while a semi-truck barreled toward him.

Calmly, Buddy looked up, stared at the truck, then dove for the side of the road just as he was about to get mulled down. Then he stood up, smiling and humming. Buddy was tempting the God or devil or whoever it was you met when you walked the plank. Then he crossed the street right in front of a minivan.

Jeffrey shook his head, looking at me sideways.

Across the highway, Buddy ran a hand through his white hair and yelled at us, "Come on, now, it's all damn clear, you wussies." With his light blue eyes and thick, cotton hair, he looked like an alien – a wispy, white, smiling creature dressed in a suit of dust. Troubled dust. I knew he did booze and pot. I knew he'd had sex with some of the barn girls, and they were all still in love with his bleached face and shocking, red smile. It was the strangeness that drew everyone inside his pale, daring world.

Even Sandra Lee got sucked in. She never punished him for sneaking out, for getting liquored up before dinner, for taking some girl up in the hayloft, or for riding bareback at midnight after he got stoned. She never punished him because right in the middle of the barn lounge, Buddy would wrap his skinny arms around her, kiss her cheek, and she'd forget about it. Poof.

Sometimes Big Mike grounded him and gave him more chores, but when a horse show was coming up, Buddy could drink and screw whoever as long as he won. Again and again, during the lessons, Big Mike said, "You're my Griffin winner, Buddy. Don't you ever forget that." Then he'd ruffle Buddy's hair. Buddy would look at him with the small eyes he had when he was buzzing and throw Big Mike a crazy grin. Buddy was untouchable.

All about safety, Jeffrey waited for a long, clear shot before he crossed.

Slowly and carefully following, Michael and I crossed the road together, holding hands.

In silence, we walked on. The boys and I turned quiet when we came closer to the farm; the presence of the horses calmed us down. And usually things stayed quiet – by the time we reached the Griffin gates, Michael stopped complaining about the weather and his aches and pains.

But as we walked down the driveway, Buddy's alien ways grew into something otherworldly all together.

Michael threw up his Doritos on the gravel.

I reached for Jeffrey's hand. His hand was thick, dry, cold.

Jeffrey pressed his thumb into my palm.

Buddy crossed the driveway once. Then twice. Then again. He scratched his head, yelled at the horses, yelled at the air, yelled at someone out there. "I'm gonna be the greatest rock singer Mitgard's ever heard, you hear me! Yeah, you hear me. I hear you too. I'll be a big star on stage. I hear you. I hear you too. Damnit, shut up, I hear you." Then he shook his head, hitting it with his fists, saying to Jeffrey, "Come on, pardner, let's go home," like nothing had happened.

Buddy lit a cigarette. Took a puff. Threw it out. Lit another one. One after another, on the way down the Griffin gravel drive, he chain-smoked and smiled, and when he smiled, I felt like I was melting into the tall grass.

Jeffrey and Michael eased closer to the Griffin fence, hiding from Buddy when he twitchy-walked in the front.

I shrank to the sidelines too. "You're right. He sure looks strange," I whispered to Jeffrey, pulling my hand from his. "Stranger than usual."

Jeffrey nodded, holding a finger to his lips. "Shh," he said.

"Hey Buddy, you know Dr. Dad's gonna get me a new pony!" I was trying to bring him back, bring him back to us.

"You're too good for a pony!" Buddy yelled back. "We'll find a big, black gelding for you! A woman's horse. Maybe Slick."

I smiled. A woman's horse. Buddy thought I was a woman.

"No. She needs something older, more trained," Jeffrey stated.

"Naw, she needs Slick," Buddy answered, smoking and twitching and going to his planet, wherever that was. "And I need to get me a band. I've got bigger plans than this farm could ever handle, you hear that, little bro?"

Michael wiped his mouth.

Buddy bowed down for no reason. "Thank you, thank you," he said to the air. "It's good to be here. I'll be back next time on tour."

Jeffrey's eyes widened.

I raised an eyebrow.

When we made it to the farmhouse, Sandra Lee didn't know what to do with Buddy. By then, he was talking about how he was going to get a record deal. At dinner, he told Sandra Lee and Big Mike that they better watch out, that he was going to be the next Alternative Rock sensation. He knew because the highway spoke, telling him he was the "one." But Buddy didn't play any instruments. Even when Buddy begged, Big Mike never let him pick up a guitar. Big Mike thought music was for sissies, and Buddy couldn't have any distractions from his riding practice. So Buddy sang while he rode. Buddy could sing and whistle louder than the rest of the boys, but he didn't know any real songs other than the songs of horses whinnying.

That night, figuring Buddy was just stoned again, Sandra Lee gave him more horses to ride and more chores to make him forget what the highway was telling him. It didn't work. Buddy came back to the farmhouse talking to Jeffrey and me about how the horse names were code for him to follow, that the codes would lead him to his record deal. Someday. Somehow. From Someone. Out there.

So Sandra Lee and Big Mike gave him more chores until Buddy was doing all of the boys' farm work and helping the barn crew. He remembered every single chore, not missing one turnout, one call to the vet, one lost shoe. Buddy remembered things, things like language, colors, what kind of paddock boots a person had worn two years before. He remembered lyrics and words, sayings he'd heard long ago. He remembered the exact shade of a girls' shirt, one he had seen once at a horse show. He remembered the angle at which her tears fell when he told the girl there was someone else. A lot of someone else's. He remembered road signs, billboards, and street maps. All of the words were telling him something. Buddy was deep in his head, and he kept getting deeper.

When he got deeper, he would twitch-walk more, like a white-haired man made of lightning.

And every time I looked at him, I could see the lightning. Every time I heard him sing, I could feel the thunder inside. Inside him, inside me. It was our storm, our world.

Before sleeping, when Buddy should've been about to drop from all of the farm work, Jeffrey said that Buddy came into his room to tell him about the way he remembered things. He told Jeffrey about women, about how they were God with skin on.

One time, I heard Buddy talking to Jeffrey in the tack room. He said, "Watch out for the boarder girls. They disappear on you. If I were you, I'd hang on to Mary like she was your own arm, bro. She's a good one. And besides, she likes your glasses, man. Go get her. Get her." Then he left to smoke a bowl behind the house.

Sometimes Jeffrey and I smoked weed with Buddy, but this night, Buddy was freaking me out a little. Even though I was scared for Buddy, I was intrigued. I wanted to *be* Buddy just for a few hours, to see what that alien world was like, just to see what it was like to be the best rider in town without practicing much, to see what it was like to frighten people and draw them in at the same time, just by looking at them. Even the bullies. For a moment, I thought that I might be one of the people inside Buddy, as if I could manage to crawl in there. I loved Buddy and his strangeness.

I told Jeffrey this. And he agreed. "I sure as hell love him, he said. "I'm lucky. I have my own ghost brother. And we better stick by him. I mean, he's going to be a rock star someday I guess, isn't he, Mare?"

"Sure is, Jeffrey," I said, staring at my boots. I could hear some guitars, the beat of drums, the monstrous noise. I could hear the thunder inside.

The next day, Buddy stayed in bed, so Jeffrey and I had to do extra chores. More watering and carrying buckets, which was a pain, but we were used to it. Every now and then, Buddy had his days when he wouldn't leave the farmhouse for anything. When he was up, he was up. When he was down, he was back-flat to his bed, staring at the ceiling, barely humming.

After Jeffrey and I rode three ponies apiece, we went inside to check on Buddy again. We made sure we took our boots off. Sandra Lee sure didn't want us tracking in any mud, whether or not Buddy was dying.

As we walked up the stairs, Jeffrey said, "I hate it when he does this." He slipped on a step, and I pressed on his back, holding him up.

Michael wandered in, bug-eyed and half-naked.

Sandra Lee called the vet.

Big Mike felt Buddy's forehead and said, "Feels fine. Don't be lazy, now. You're a Griffin." Then Big Mike headed out to bush-hog the backfield.

Buddy still wouldn't move. No one could find anything physically wrong with him. He just refused to move. He said that he needed to rest the thoughts in his head, that they were moving around, spinning around like tractor wheels. The music producers were calling, he said. Calling and calling, and he had to stay put so they could find him. He was waiting for his big break.

Watching him, pulling on his arms and legs, trying to get him to rise up out of his bed, Sandra Lee forgot supper.

After cleaning all of the stalls, doing our homework together, and clipping some horses, getting them ready for the next show, Jeffrey and I knew we'd have to make our own dinner. In the kitchen, Sandra Lee announced, "You're on your own."

Margene called, asking where the hell I was, but I ignored her, handing Sandra Lee the phone. She covered for me. "Mary's helpin' us out, Margene. Don't you worry about that girl. She's got a good head on her shoulders," she said. "Thin though."

They talked for too long. And when I saw the frown on Sandra Lee's face, I knew that Margene had broken down and told her that Dr. Dad was drinking again. Which he was. My house had grown so quiet that even bare feet seemed to pound on the floor. The smell was back – the sweet smell of liquor seeping through Dr. Dad's pores. Sweet, like wicked sweat candy dripping all over the spotless floors.

Since Sandra Lee was taking care of Buddy, Big Mike was lost in the field or talking horse deals on the phone, and Michael was hiding, Jeffrey and I made spaghetti from a jar. It wasn't too hard, but by the time we were done, we were covered with sauce.

"Nasty, like blood," I said, looking down at my dirty shirt.

Jeffrey slurped a noodle. "Big Mike's gonna kill me. I forgot to turn the ring lights off."

"He'll get over it," I said, flicking some sauce at him.

"Shit," Jeffrey said, grinning a little, then frowning again.

"He might wash your mouth out with saddle soap though."

"Fuck," Jeffrey said. "That's what your parents do when they're in bed together. They fuck."

"Shut up," I said. "My parents don't sleep together. Dr. Dad sleeps in the chair downstairs."

Jeffrey shut up.

We ate spaghetti. Big Mike never came home, and Sandra Lee stayed up in Buddy's room.

Michael reappeared.

Jeffrey handed Michael a plate full of spaghetti, patting him on the butt.

Michael smiled. His green eyes sparkled. Then he sneaked away to watch TV in the den.

"Since we're all alone here cooking, it's like I'm your wife," I said to Jeffrey.

"Sort of," Jeffrey said, scooping mounds of spaghetti into his small mouth.

We were quiet until I did the dishes, making sure to scrape them all shiny clean, the way Margene had taught me. Then Jeffrey and I went upstairs to check on Buddy.

Sandra Lee and Buddy were smoking in his room. Buddy was sitting up, but he looked paler than before, and Sandra Lee looked thinner and paler too. If he was locked in his room, so was she. If he was smoking, so was she. If he was sick, so was she.

Still, the horses were fed, Big Mike went out checking the fences in the dark, and the stalls were spotless. Everything at Griffin Farm was business as usual. The show must go on.

The next day, Big Mike had the barn crew layer the fences with fresh black paint. On the outside, Griffin Farm looked like a winning, top notch barn, which it was. The

Griffins were always in the ribbons. Big Mike made sure of it, even if he had to drug a spooky horse every now and again.

While Jeffrey and I were refilling buckets, checking for ice, Big Mike said, "Buddy better be back to normal for the indoor shows. Enough of this band and rock star nonsense."

Jeffrey took a hammer to an icy bucket.

Then, days later, Buddy suddenly popped out of bed and tore around the barns, riding, cleaning, and shoveling, practicing his jumps, creating tiny white tornados in the aisles and tack room. Then he was back down again, strapped to his bed, talking about horse names and record labels, wearing a three-piece suit. When he was down, the rich boarder girls called and called. The vet prescribed Buddy some sedatives, which turned Buddy into a sleep machine.

Hanging on Big Mike's few words, following his moves, we traveled to bigger shows. Saddle sores grew on our calves, our seats, and the insides of our knees. Backs ached. Shoulders knotted up. At St. Genevieve's, I often fell asleep at my desk.

Soon, Dr. Dad bought me Slick, the black thoroughbred gelding. Slick was nearly 16 hands, a four-year-old with huge, dark eyes, and he had freakishly long eyelashes. Boyishly cute and talented, but young. I felt deeply connected to Slick – his jumping ability, but mostly, it was his eyes. I knew he could hear my thoughts, sensing things. When I put my arms around Slick's neck and felt him breathe, I found peace in the rhythm of it. From black mane to black tail, he was mine.

I rode and showed Slick on the circuit with the Griffins, ignoring my sore, crooked wrist. I was too busy working, training, grooming, teaching lessons, and showing. With Slick,

I moved up the levels. Slick carried me through many difficult courses.

The week before a show, I practiced obsessively. I rode any horse Big Mike gave me, even if I didn't like the horse. After a long horse show weekend, if I rode well, I felt high for a short time. Then the adrenaline rush of winning would fade, and I'd be back down again. I felt a sinking letdown. My racing brain was still there.

My hands turned thick and rough, blistered from reins, often decorated with Band-aids. My back ached daily, and sometimes, I had to walk or ride hunched over like Jeffrey and Buddy; our backs were all screwed up. We could count on it – the dull pain was always there.

At the hotels, Big Mike was supposed to watch us, but he rarely did. We stayed up late, stole beer, ate pizza, piled in each other's rooms, then woke up at five a.m. to braid our horses and ride. Wearing our show clothes, we tried to stay clean. We all lost sleep. We knew how to wait all day to show, to train and train, all for three minutes in the show ring, when we were judged against each other and the other barns.

Home from the shows, we all hung out in the barn lounge, surrounded by Big Mike's show ribbons and dust. Even after we dusted, there was dust. We sat on the orange cushions, and truly, our seats made dents in those chairs. Buddy and Jeffrey battled each other at cards, their hands moving to play so fast, the numbers blurred.

In the barn lounge, at the round table, we fixed our "hat-heads," we zipped up our chaps, we fixed broken bootlaces, we cleaned tack, we poked at each other. And sometimes we were just there, silently sitting, buying time before Big Mike would stride by, slipping on his deerskin gloves. Truly, the gloves had more holes than skin. But when the gloves were on, that meant it was time to get our horses ready to ride.

I was tired. Damn tired. But the motion, the rhythm of the life, however jumpy, allowed me to crawl into the horse world I remembered – the one where Thomas led me through the Scallycat fields. But the rich boarder girls usually made eyes at Buddy, rode, and went home. They talked about boyfriends, sports, and school. They whispered about me, "that weird girl with black hair." Like Buddy, I knew I was different. There was something lurking inside of me that was as dark as Slick's deep eyes. I knew Captain Blackeye was still out there, within Buddy, within me, made of sticks and stones and boots that moved to kill.

Seven.

I was on my way to a horse show down South. Margene wasn't coming, and Dr. Dad was lost somewhere, acting like he was fixing people's brains at the hospital, but really searching for his next drink. Margene tried to hide the bottles, but I wasn't stupid. By then, nobody said anything about anything, and that worked out just fine. Ever since Thomas was gone, that just seemed easier.

Big Mike and Buddy were in the Dodge truck, pulling nine horses. Sandra Lee, Jeffrey, Michael, and I followed behind in the Thunderbird. In the car, we were quiet. Well, Sandra Lee sang along to some old blues on the radio. When we pulled into The Horse Park, we found our stalls, and the madness of arriving at a show began.

Three grooms unloaded the horses. With sweeping, long strides, Sandra Lee hurried over to the show office and back, checking the class schedule for the next morning. Jeffrey and Michael bedded the stalls down with shavings. Buddy, Big Mike, and I unloaded the saddles, brushes, show curtains, planters, bridles, and all of the other equipment. Setting up at a horse show was like building a house in one day. Everything had to go up fast and look perfect. We finished the job in one hour, and then it was time to ride.

Michael rode three ponies.

Buddy rode six horses.

Jeffrey rode Michael's ponies again, and then he schooled another problem horse, making sure they were all in tip-top show condition.

I rode Slick after Buddy had ridden him. He got the horse ready for me every time.

Then we gave the horses a little medication, hay, grain, wrapped their legs, and headed to the hotel.

Everyone was beat, but not too beat for dinner.

The brothers stayed in one room. Jeffrey and Michael were always in one bed. Buddy was in the other.

I stayed down the hall with Mandy, Liz, and Liz' mom. Mandy and Liz were some boarders. They were all right, but kind of spoiled, and they didn't really like me, because they were jealous that I was like one of the Griffins. But it just made sense for us to stay together.

As soon as I was done getting ready for dinner, I went on over to bug Jeffrey in his room.

I knocked twice, softly.

Michael answered, opening the door. He smiled a toothy smile. "Hi Mare," he said.

I ruffled Michael's hair, then sat on the bed with Jeffrey. He was still covered with horse grime.

Jeffrey and Michael fought over the shower until Buddy said, "He's littler, let him go." So Jeffrey backed off.

Then Buddy stripped down, laughing at Jeffrey. "You snooze, you lose, you two!" he yelled, sneaking into the shower in a naked blur.

I turned my head, blushing.

By the time Jeffrey got his shower, it was bitter cold. He yelled this from the bathroom: "Buddy, you suck!"

Buddy and I laughed hard.

There was another knock. Big Mike and Sandra Lee poked their heads in. It was time to eat.

We went to the hotel restaurant, which was full of horse people – people I knew, and people I didn't want to know. Some were the competition. Some were friends, but all of us were there to win.

Jeffrey ate ribs that dripped all over his clothes.

Michael had a cheeseburger.

I had a kid's meal. I wanted to look good in my breeches the next day.

Liz and Mandy mostly talked.

Except for Buddy, we were all acting nervous. Buddy ate a steak, slowly slicing it, talking to it. He whispered, "Sorry they had to kill you, little buddy." When he looked at me, he smiled and stabbed a big piece, shoving it in his mouth. Then he shrugged. "I eat it, but I hate myself for it," he said. “When I’m a rocker, I’ll be a vegetarian I swear.”

Jeffrey chewed on his manly ribs and looked at me with wide eyes. “Oh, crap, there he goes again,” he said.

When we returned to our rooms, I ditched Liz and Mandy because I heard that Buddy had scored a twelve pack of beer. I ran down the hall to hang out with the boys.

Buddy handed Jeffrey a cold one.

Jeffrey sucked it down.

Buddy handed Michael a cold one.

Michael, even at 10, took large sips.

Buddy handed me a beer, and I kept up.

Buddy finished off the rest, and I knew I had to go back to my room. It was near ten p.m., and we had to be up at five a.m. to braid the horses. When I reminded them, everyone groaned.

Five a.m. wake-up call. I slid on my breeches and boots, grabbed my saddle, and rushed to meet Sandra Lee outside. Big Mike and Jeffrey were already at the show grounds longeing horses, wearing them out so they'd be calm.

Buddy started acting strange again. His show shirt was on inside out. His tie was cockeyed and loose, and he had that look in his eye. I knew, watching this look, that Buddy was going to win, but also that Buddy was losing his mind.

At the showgrounds, Liz and Mandy were already cleaning tack. Buddy rode their ponies first, later passing them on to them so that they could practice.

Big Mike barked orders at the girls while they practiced, getting ready for their first class.

Michael sat around, slowly eating a danish.

Jeffrey and I rode ponies and horses, and the rides all ran together. After a while, I hung on and jumped, and the animals were just there beneath me. It was way too early to think of anything new. One, two, three, jump, while Big Mike barked, "Heels down, sit up straight! You look hunched over like an old lady, Mary!"

When we were done practicing, the horses were braided, and the announcer was testing the speakers, Buddy put his hands over his ears. "Goddamnit, turn that shit down!" he yelled.

Sandra Lee felt his forehead. "You okay, Buddy? You know this is a big show for us."

"I know, but Jesus, tell them to turn that shit down," Buddy said.

"I'll see what I can do," Sandra Lee said, smoking her cigarette.

It happened at every show.

When Buddy, Jeffrey, and I were cleaning tack in the tack room, Buddy started talking to the reins. "There, now, I'll get you all clean, so that I can be a Griffin Winner. That's right. I'm a Griffin, and I win. Hey, I love you, reins."

Jeffrey pinched his arm. "Buddy, who are you talking to?" he asked.

"My bridle, little brother. It's good luck. Try it."

So Jeffrey started whispering to his saddle, just for kicks.

And so did I.

That day, Buddy was Grand Champion again. Whenever he rode, he hummed a song he'd recently heard on the radio. I could hear him singing as he rode past the in-gate. He won without even paying attention.

Jeffrey did all right. He won two classes, but in the third, his horse stopped in front of a jump, and he almost fell off. He didn't cry, but Big Mike gave him a look that made me want to shoot one of the Jack Russells that was running around loose. It wasn't Jeffrey's fault. It never was. He always rode the hardest horses, and Big Mike didn't want him to look weak, so Jeffrey couldn't wear his glasses when he showed. And Jeffrey tried contact lenses, but it didn't work with the sand rings, the stall cleaning, the shavings, and the dust. After many tries and infections, he just gave up. Sure, he made mistakes. Jeffrey couldn't see.

Michael was Reserve Champion in his Pony classes.

I won a few seconds and thirds. Good enough.

Buddy's winnings covered up our losses, but by the end of the show, while Buddy and I were packing up trunks, I watched him move. He looked skinny and wild, jerk-walking, limping because his back hurt.

On the way home, Jeffrey and I rode in the back seat of the truck. Buddy and Big Mike were up front.

Buddy was stoned. I could tell because his eyes looked squinty.

Big Mike didn't seem to notice. Driving carefully out of the horse park, he said, "We need to stay in tip top shape for the next show. We need to keep your points going, Buddy."

"I don't want to go. I'm so damn sick of it all," Buddy said quietly.

"Aw, come on now," Big Mike said. "You're my Griffin winner." He glanced at Buddy, punching him in the arm.

I wanted to say something, anything, to help Buddy before he lost it. I swallowed.

"I want to be in a band. Not a rider. I *never* wanted to be a rider. You're the one that wants me to win," Buddy said. He had a wild, strange smile on his face.

"Boy, you're the best rider in this state. You want to throw it all away?" Big Mike gripped the steering wheel, slowly guiding the truck and trailer onto the highway.

"Yup," Buddy said, scratching his head. "I sure do, and I'll write songs about it all." He whispered, *You ass.*

Big Mike said, "You give up now, and how about I tell Sandra Lee about all the weed you've been smoking, and how you stole all the booze from my liquor cabinet. How about that? You want me to kill your mother like that?"

"What do you care? I know you're cheating. And I know who you're banging too," Buddy said, knocking his hand on the window. "Hello? I hear you, I'll be out of my dressing room and out on stage soon," he said to the window.

Jeffrey looked at me, turning red.

I raised my brows.

Both of us shrank into the back seats, listening close.

With that, Big Mike took a thick fist and popped Buddy in the cheek. "Don't be saying things like that, you hear me? You're a Griffin rider, and there's no damn record deal coming!"

"Yeah, I'm a Griffin rider," Buddy said, rubbing his face, barely backing off from the blow. Then he scratched his head and said, "Quiet" to himself. Then he hit his own head with a hand, softly. He scratched his head again, looked at me and said, "Make them be quiet, Mare. I know you get it. You're weird like me. I can hear too much. Everything's so loud. Make them be quiet."

I leaned forward and whispered in his ear, "I'll help you be a rock star, Buddy."

"Mary, stay out of this," Big Mike said. His green eyes softened, and he put a large arm around Buddy's shoulder. "Jesus, son, I'm sorry I hit you. I've never done that. There's just so much pressure." His face reddened.

Sickly, Buddy smiled and said, "Yeah, pressure. I'm your Griffin winner. And there's another Griffin winner too, isn't there, Dad? There's another one in your bed when Sandra Lee's out teaching lessons."

Jeffrey sniffled.

I offered my shirt sleeve to Jeffrey, and he shook his head "no."

Big Mike stepped on the gas.

Silence. For two hours. Silence, until the black fences of Griffin Farm sprung up from the ground. We were home, driving down the potholed drive, just another circus ride.

When we arrived at the farmhouse, unloading our ribbons, hanging them on the walls, Buddy hummed, dropping his saddle on the kitchen floor. He winked back at me. "Pretty lady," he said.

I unloaded the leftover food into the cabinets.

Buddy loosened his tie and took off his riding show coat. He ran a hand through his whitish hair. "Mary, come here," Buddy said, pulling me into the bathroom.

I looked back at Jeffrey, and he mouthed, "Go."

"What is it?" I said to Buddy. I shivered a little.

"When you look at me, my head gets quieter. When you talk to me, things aren't so loud and scary. And the music helps too. When I'm singing, they can't get me, those people, those voices. I know you hear them too. The music and the noise. I know you get it, don't you, Mary?"

"I dunno, Buddy."

"All I'm saying is that it's our little secret, k?"

"Okay, Buddy, whatever you say, but I don't understand."

"It's okay, you're too small to understand. When you're older, you'll be cleaning up some messy stall, and then you'll get it all. Sooner or later, shit'll hit the fan between me and Big Mike. And then Jeffrey's gonna be the Griffin Winner. You keep him, because he'll stick around. Jeffrey is strong. He can take the hard horses, and he'd do anything to help you. We have to hang on to whoever helps us. We have to, you hear me?"

"Okay, Buddy, I hear you," I said, pulling at my breeches. I had to pee.

"I'll be gone someday. I'll be a big star, and I'll get to hear the crowds howling at me, instead of those sounds in my head. It's so fucking loud, Mary."

"Okay, Buddy."

Buddy put his hands on my shoulders, looking straight at me with his alien blue eyes. "Just so you know, I love you like a sister, and in my book, you and Jeffrey are the real winners," Buddy said.

"Thanks," I said, smiling wide.

"I always get the easy horses. That's why I win. You can handle anything, and later, when times get harder, you'll be strong enough to take life. You might not get this now, but someday you'll remember me saying this stuff, and you'll realize I'm right. I'll disappear from people's minds, and you and Jeffrey will ride on."

I shrugged and squirmed. I really had to pee.

And so did Jeffrey. He was banging on the door, yelling, "Christ, guys, get out of there!"

"All right then. Go help unload the trailer, kid. And remember what I said...you two are the real winners. But you better piss first...you look like you might wet yourself," Buddy said, grinning.

I unzipped my breeches. "Get out first," I said, pushing him in the belly.

"Yes ma'am." And Buddy jerk-walked out of the bathroom, scratching his head, muttering to himself. Then he looked back at me and said, "Hey, I love you, I love you all," right before he shut the door.

Just before Margene picked me up, Jeffrey and I saw Buddy walking alone out in the side field. He hopped on a gray horse bareback. Then Buddy looked around, making sure the coast was clear, and he started singing. Softly at first. And then he let loose, really howling.

Jeffrey knew. I knew. The way he howled. It was our secret.

Eight.

At the next horse show, I tied Jeffrey for Champion in the Children's Division. It had been a sweet show. The Griffins were in the ribbons again, and everyone's skin was cracking from the cold.

Back in Mitgard, while I helped Sandra Lee and Big Mike unload the trailer, Jeffrey tucked the horses in. The horses walked slowly, heads hanging low, worn out from the show, returning to their familiar home stalls, settling in for the night.

Jeffrey had a winter wind burn. He was shredded.

Buddy had stayed home. He had enough points, and he was way ahead of his age group in every division. And he was supposed to stay home, to "make sure the barn crew gets the work done," Big Mike had said. Truly, Jeffrey and I had agreed that Buddy wasn't well again. We knew the barn crew workers each did the jobs of three men. So there was no reason for Buddy to stay home other than that he was sick again. The big, sick, Griffin Farm secret. Any day, he'd be on the cover of every Rock magazine in the world. Secretly, Buddy said, the truck axle was telling him this message. He was gonna be a big, big star. Maybe on another planet, but he was gonna be big.

It wasn't raining, but it seemed like it should be because the sky held on to its steel, gray, cold fullness. And the Griffin land had been hard and starving for weeks. When I looked out into the fields, even the horses looked parched, freezing, thinner. Every being was stuck in a brittle, cold drought.

Filthy, Michael and Jeffrey raced to the red brick farmhouse.

I stayed behind, watching their small, tight butts move. They were both still wearing their tall riding boots. Jeffrey's were tight and too short. He'd shot up an inch lately. His brown hair was plastered to the back of his head.

I was ancy, shifting in my boots. Jeffrey and I still had to pick out the stalls before bed. I hoped Buddy was awake because Buddy was fast with a pitchfork, and he was so much stronger and taller. He could carry two hay bales at once, and Jeffrey and I could only handle one apiece.

Crawling through Sandra Lee's legs, Michael sneaked into the house before Jeffrey.

When Jeffrey tried to swagger past Sandra Lee, she moved to block him, yelling, "Outside, Jeffrey. It's your turn to do the night check. Have Mary help you." She pointed a long, knobby finger, shaking her cigarette at me.

"But I'm hungry," Jeffrey whined.

"Me too," I whined.

"When the stalls are picked out," she said, smiling. She handed Jeffrey and me two cartons of chocolate milk, which we gulped down. Then she winked and handed Jeffrey a pack of Bazooka gum as bribery.

"All right," Jeffrey said. He turned to me, grabbing my hand. "Let's go, Mare. Let's get it done." He rolled his eyes.

Sandra Lee said, "That's my boy. My winner. My Griffin Farm Champion."

Jeffrey popped a piece of gum in his mouth, handing me a piece.

We chewed and chewed, heading to the barn together.

Griffin Farm Champion. Jeffrey had beaten all the kids. For once, he'd be in the Mitgard paper instead of Michael or Buddy. I chewed my Bazooka, popping a bubble. I smacked it. "You're the best rider ever," I said to him.

Jeffrey said, "Thanks, but let's be real here. Buddy wasn't there."

"I know," I said. "So what."

Jeffrey put on his serious face again. "But you tied me, remember? You're not so bad yourself."

"Luck," I said.

"No, you're good," he stated.

"I might cry," I said.

"No you won't. You never cry. Not even when you get bucked off."

"I know. But I'm so happy I might start crying today."

The sky grew darker. I didn't mind storms. Neither did Jeffrey. Sleet or scorch or hail or snow, we worked outside. And even if we were cold or wet or scared, we never showed it to Big Mike.

Jeffrey looked up and sighed. "Snow's comin' Mare."

"Yup," I answered. I sighed too. That meant we had to bring the horses in.

We started gathering horses from the fields. We both brought in two horses at once, which was dangerous, but it was faster that way.

Then, in the distance, I heard Sandra Lee calling for Buddy. Over and over. I shivered, looking at Jeffrey.

He scrunched his eyebrows, hanging on to two lead ropes. His glasses were so crooked; he had to tilt his head to see.

I hoped the horses didn't decide to bolt. Big Mike always said, "Remember that lady out in Highland who got her arm ripped off that way? You'd better listen to me...bring them in one at a time." But we never listened. Saving time, sometimes, we grabbed three or four horses at once.

Sometimes five. A lot of things at the farm were dangerous, but faster.

Again, from the farmhouse, Sandra Lee called for Buddy. "Dinner, Buddy, dinner!"

Jeffrey shrugged.

My stomach rumbled. I trembled, feeling the thunder inside. I looked up. The sky was wrong.

We brought the horses in, checking for lost shoes. We didn't look at the hooves. We could tell whether or not one was missing by the sound of hooves beating on the aisle. The rhythm of it.

I handled feeding the grain alone while Jeffrey smoked. When it was time to do the hay, I took a drag and stamped out his cigarette.

Jeffrey smiled for once.

I smiled back. At twelve, Jeffrey and I were strong, but it still took a while to do the hay. I helped him steer and wheel the cart to the hay barn, glancing back up at the black sky. I wasn't scared, but some of the horses were. They whinnied and shifted, speaking to each other.

"It's all right," Jeffrey called out to the horses, his voice echoing down the barn aisle.

"Yeah, it is, there now," I added. I listened, hearing my voice carry. *Now, now, now,* the barn aisle said.

The old hay cart was hard to maneuver. It creaked and went sideways instead of straight. With hay on it, it was ten times harder, and by the time we were done, we were always covered with hay and every piece of my body itched.

If Big Mike were there, he would've been done by then.

I hung on, helping Jeffrey steer. Several times, we almost knocked each other over, but we both laughed and held on. I was so glad Jeffrey was laughing for once. I loved the sound of his throaty, deep, rare laugh.

Jeffrey slid the giant, rusty hay barn door open. He turned on the lights.

I heard a few mice scatter. I saw their swift shapes dart across the floor. *Swish, swish.*

Jeffrey looked up, slowly. Slowly. Gasping.

I looked up too. And then I saw the shoes. The polished dress shoes. I looked all the way up. I saw the white hair sticking straight up. I saw the pale face. Milky, snow skin made of plastic. The expression – blue eyes wide with fear, mouth stuck open in a sideways grin. The tie, striped, wrapped around his neck under the thick rope. I saw the suit jacket, bright blue, minus the shirt. The chest was bare with a bloody lightning bolt carved into it. And a bloody star was there. I squinted. His chest, in bloody letters, read, "See, I'm a star." He had no pants on – just his white, blood-stained underwear – and his legs hung down like bluish, stiff sticks, toes pointed. The body was still. No twitching. Buddy was hanging. Hanging from the rafters. The rope, the noose, was digging and digging, tied around his neck tight. Digging and digging.

I moved forward. I thought that if I could reach him, reach up, I could pull the rope loose, magically saving him.

Jeffrey coughed, holding me back.

I breathed in. I didn't let the breath out. I thought about Captain Tomcat never coming home. I thought about Captain Blackeye, how he was still on the loose, maybe hiding in the hay barn, how all the Lochmores had stopped looking. I thought about bugs in my mouth and yellow tape and barking dogs. I thought about flashing lights, Dr. Dad drinking again,

Margene on the porch, rocking, waiting for Tomcat to come home.

I shook. From the side, I tightly grabbed Jeffrey around his middle, taking his air away for a second.

Jeffrey put a hand over my eyes, blinding me. He, too, was shaking.

I let him blind me. I swallowed my Bazooka.

"Buddy!" he yelled. "Shit, Buddy, Shit!" he yelled again. "Fuck, Buddy, Fuck!" he yelled, as if Buddy might yell a cuss word back.

Jeffrey left me there, turning off the barn lights to make it all go away.

In the dark, I grabbed for him.

Jeffrey turned the lights back on.

Still there. Still hanging. Buddy's white face, blue legs, the bloody lightning, the bloody star, the bloody words.

I couldn't move.

Jeffrey didn't move.

I looked at him.

He looked back.

Then we both looked up. At Buddy. Hanging.

Jeffrey grabbed my hand. We started running. We left the cart, Buddy's body, and the blue behind, scurrying to the house like rats.

I tripped.

Jeffrey tripped.

We kept running.

I hung on to his shirt, letting him lead me. I itched all over. I scratched at my cheeks until they bled. Bugs in my mouth. Yellow tape. Bugs.

In front of the Griffin farmhouse door, Jeffrey threw up his chocolate milk.

I wiped Jeffrey's mouth with my shirt.

Big Mike and Sandra Lee came to the door, still yelling for Buddy. Frantically, by then. Yelling that it was time for dinner.

Jeffrey wiped his mouth again.

Big Mike said, "Boy, you ruined your show pants. Those things cost me two hundred dollars."

Jeffrey's eyes bugged out. Gray-green.

Then Michael was there, staring at Jeffrey, drooling. "You look funny," he said.

We were all staring at Champion Jeffrey who had thrown up on his breeches.

"The hay barn," he said to Big Mike, looking him hard in the eye. "The hay barn. He's there. I found him. Buddy...he's down…like a horse…with the colic...he couldn't take it...hanging there...fuck...I found him."

Sandra Lee, Big Mike, and Michael stared at him. They were mute. It was as if they were all standing outside a sick horse's stall when the intestines had already twisted, when the horse had stopped rolling. Gave in to it, gave up. There was nothing they could do. They stared at Jeffrey in silent shock, knowing it was too late for the vet, too late to pray, and too late to believe in something other than what Jeffrey said next: "Mom, he's with the bats. Hanging from the rafters."

Margene pulled in before The Blue-black Men came. Her SUV tires spit up gravel.

Before I got in the car, I looked at Jeffrey, who was staring down at his soiled breeches, scratching at the stains there. He looked up at me. Through his glasses, I stared at his eyes, looking for something, anything. Nothing. His mouth was trapped in a serious line. And no tears were coming down. Nothing. He didn't move. He looked at me. Frozen, he looked at me. "Snow's comin', Mare!" he called out. "Jesus, fuck."

I looked at him. All the way into the car, I looked at him. All the way down the drive, through the window, I looked at him. And with his mouth open, still in shock, he looked back.

Margene asked, "How was the show?"

"I am a Griffin winner," I said, resting my head against the window, the cold glass. It was much too late to cry.

Nine.

Two years later

Jeffrey and I had just turned fourteen. Buddy had been gone for two years. Big Mike had been gone for two years. An affair. With *her*. Jeffrey and Michael weren't sure about much else, other than that the "her" was someone bad, a bad nag, a mean-spirited horse. We were all still taking lessons from Sandra Lee. By then, she was stick-thin and sickly looking, and she didn't talk about horses anymore. She taught lessons, left the barn, smoked, and went thrift store shopping every day. When she got back, she always said, "Jeffrey, you should've seen the specials!" Then she disappeared, hiding in her room until it was time for another lesson.

The day was a scorcher. Together in the front ring, Jeffrey and I were in a lesson.

I took off my helmet to scratch my sweaty head.

Jeffrey said, "Man, your hair's a mess. You might think twice about taking that hat off."

"I know," I barked at him. I kicked Slick, edging closer to Jeffrey so I could hit him in the arm. Slick grunted. So did Jeffrey.

"Ow, damn," he said, scowling.

I made girl punches hurt sometimes. "Give up?" I asked him.

When Jeffrey punched me back, it caught me in the breast.

I leaned sideways, nearly falling off Slick, who spooked. "Shit, stop, that hurt," I said, turning red, hanging on to my reins. "Whoa," I said to Slick. And he listened. He always did. Jeffrey had trained him well.

The day when Jeffrey found my breast was the same day he stopped play-punching me at all.

Jeffrey turned away from me.

From the center of the ring, Sandra Lee yelled, "Jeffrey Griffin, it's your turn on the course! We don't have all day! I still have to hit the mall before it closes!"

Jeffrey glared at me, then kicked his horse, heading to jump some jumps.

I tucked my long black hair back under my helmet, staring out at the front field, which always set me to dreaming. It took a while to hide my hair and make it look neat, the way Sandra Lee liked it. By then, my hair was waist-long, all dried out from dyeing it.

I watched Jeffrey ride, envious. Since Buddy died, all Jeffrey did was practice, and it was really paying off. The boy was good, really good. All in the town of Mitgard were beginning to notice. I could hold my own, but Jeffrey was better, and I knew it. And he knew it. And it seemed like he no longer cared.

And it wasn't like I could rely on my looks to get his attention. My eyes and lips weren't big enough, and my hair was always a mess of split ends, but deep inside, I still thought that Jeffrey's eyes were like horse eyes. Often, when I looked past his glasses, I could tell if he was hungry, tired, or feeling sick. I could tell by the shade of his gray-green-blue eyes. Jeffrey's eyes said more than his words ever could. He could match my stare, he could hold it, and he didn't look away. But I knew that suddenly, to Jeffrey, I was no sister.

After the lesson, we stood far apart, cleaning tack, avoiding eye contact. I looked at the ground or my feet. I felt my fingers along the braided reins, trying not to look up. And when I was distracted, I usually pictured Buddy's bloody chest. I saw lightning bolts, stars. Every time I caught Jeffrey's blue-green-gray eye, I thought about Buddy's bloody chest. And I thought about how we had both lost a brother. Blonde-haired kids had a habit of disappearing around me, one at a time, suddenly and awfully. The shock. Like the quick shock I felt when I accidentally leaned an arm against the Griffin's electric fence.

Big Mike had left Jeffrey to clean up the Griffin mess. That ate at me. The world ate at me. The world ate at Jeffrey. I could see it in his curious eyes. But I met his strange, quiet stares with my own long looks when he let me.

After I cleaned my tack, I found Jeffrey hiding out in the back barn. He was brushing the gray draft horse, East End.

He looked up at me and said, "What?"

I took the brush from him, throwing it. East End jumped in his stall, nearly squashing Jeffrey.

"Be careful, you wanna kill me?" Jeffrey yelled.

"Stop being a dick," I said.

"I'm not. I'm just trying to get the work done," he said.

"Hey, let's go for a run in the fields," I said. "We've done enough work for this year."

He pulled his glasses off, cleaned them on his shirt, then slid them back on. "You got that right," he said softly.

"So what do you say?"

"Okay, I guess," Jeffrey answered, clearing his throat. "You might piss me off sometimes, but you still have this way of shaking me up, making me forget what I'm supposed to be doing."

I sneezed. The sawdust was thick in the air. "I guess that's good."

Ever so slightly, Jeffrey smiled. It was the first time I remembered him smiling in two years.

I smiled back. “Come on, trouble, let’s go, before you change your mind and start sweeping or shoveling shit or something.”

Jeffrey nodded, following me out of the barn into the back field. Leaving the horses behind, we ran through the tall grass. Crickets danced. Suddenly, we were lost inside the insect world, the world of green, our world. The Griffin grass came alive, alive enough to almost bring back Buddy's voice, his three-piece suit, and his white blonde hair. I could almost hear Thomas calling, “Shorty, there’s a treasure up yonder! Blimey! Sail ho!” I could almost see the Scallycat Mountains spring up around us, leaving us lost in a gorgeous, green valley, leaving us lost in our world. Ours. Forever.

It almost brought it all back alive. Almost.

We stopped to catch our breath. I bent over, gasping.

Jeffrey ran a hand through his brown hair, making it stand straight up. “Fuck. It’s all fucked up,” he said. “Fuck.” Jeffrey scratched his head.

I put an arm around him loosely, just standing there, saying nothing at first, feeling him out. Like the horses, like Dr. Dad, with Jeffrey I had to use my senses, guessing how to react. Yeah, it was our whole world. Ours. Not whole at all. Fuck. I was still out of breath. Jeffrey and I had been smoking a lot that summer. I struggled to speak. "Jeff...you…look strange," I said.

"I'm all right," he said, shoving his hands in his jeans pockets.

A piece of my black hair fell into my eyes, half-blinding me. I left it there. "You're thinking about Buddy," I said. "You have that look. Your face is all frozen. Like a statue. Hey, brother I’m thinking about Buddy too. And Thomas. It’s okay to think about them. It’s not our fault."

Jeffrey stared at the grass. "Yeah, I keep seeing his chest. The blood, the lightning, the star."

"Me too. All the time. When I'm riding or cleaning tack, I see his teeth or his smile. Then I see his scary, bloody, cut up chest. I have to keep riding or brushing some pony to get it out of my head," I said. I squeezed my arm around him tighter. Sweat leaked down my forehead.

Sweat spilled over Jeffrey's nose.

Neither of us wiped it away. I needed to feel it dripping there to remind me that I was alive.

Jeffrey shifted.

My arm fell, limp and uselessly attached to my body. My hand jutted out sideways from my bent wrist. I could feel the slight, jagged turn of the long ago broken bone, and it ached.

Jeffrey looked me in the eye. "I knew Buddy better than anyone knew him. He would've never gone and killed himself without leaving me a letter or cuss word behind as a weird joke. I know he would have. Like those suits he always wore. Or like when he was doing drugs. He always told me everything. I just don't get it. I don't get why he said nothing. I still can't believe it. And that chest. He was trying to tell us something and nobody was listening. All we did was tell him to ride and ride and win. Nobody was listening, Mare."

I sat down in the grass, looking up at him. "I'm listening," I said.

"I need to bush hog," Jeffrey said, sitting down next to me. "This grass is out of control."

"I like the grass wild," I said. "I don't get it either. I want that picture in my head to go away. I do, so bad."

"I need to clean up the mess around here," he said.

"It's creepy, all of it. I'm scared."

"Me too, me too." His voice deepened, sounding older.

I rose up.

Jeffrey said. "Sandra Lee's gone crazy. All she does is shop. The farm's gonna go under. Big Mike's gone, and those other boarders at the barn are only concerned with winning, so they'll all split soon and find another barn. Really, I got nobody but you, Mare."

I grabbed his hand, then let go.

"I'll race ya back to the barn," Jeffrey said.

And so we did. We ran through the grass, making insects dance.

As usual, I went in the Main Barn to get some horses ready to ride. But the whole time I was riding, I swore I heard someone whisper. Someone close. Someone right under my nose. Between my eyes. *Make the chest stop bleeding.*

I tacked up Rojo, a chestnut quarter horse, and J.J., a chestnut thoroughbred, leading them both down the aisle to meet Jeffrey. "You pick," I said.

"I'll take J.J. He's spooky sometimes," he said.

"All right then," I said, handing him the reins. Jeffrey was always trying to protect me, even though I'd ridden J.J. many times before.

In the ring, when Jeffrey rode J.J. up next to me, when I saw his look, I knew that he too was haunted by the body, by Buddy hanging there. But when I looked at Jeffrey's eyes, I also thought of something else. Like Buddy used to say, "When you find a good horse, never let them go, ever." Jeffrey was a good horse. But I was beginning to feel like a wild one – untrainable and reckless.

I decided to try whatever it took to make those visions go away for Jeffrey and me, whatever it took to help Jeffrey's eyes relax into human ones, rather than stay in the large, blackish, horse state of remembering, remembering that day in the hay barn, the shared vision of a dead brother. I had to make it disappear. For me. And for Jeffrey. Whatever it took.

Ten.

At the barn, little Michael Griffin was becoming popular and wild. At twelve, he had wavy, longish brown hair, and the greenest of eyes. He wasn't a tough rider like Jeffrey, but on a horse, he looked natural, and his form was beautiful. It was as if Michael was born to hang on to a mane. Michael's shapely legs carried him, and even when he fell off, it was graceful. He was spindly, beautiful, and as fast and elusive as a foal.

Whenever I spent the night at the Griffins, Michael stayed up talking to girls on the phone late into the night while Jeffrey was making dinner or cleaning up. Jeffrey never asked for help. After Jeffrey was done mopping, we ran around the backyard, acting like horses, pawing at the grass, snorting, and whinnying even though we knew we were too old to act like beasts. Usually, my chest hurt when I was with him.

But by the end of the summer, our world was shaken again.

Jeffrey broke the news like this: "I need to talk to you in the back barn when you get a chance," he said.

I looked at my watch.

"I told Michael to sweep the aisles. No worries," Jeffrey said.

I knew it was serious. The "back barn" conversations were always serious. And that day, Jeffrey's clothes were way too clean.

Slowly, we walked down the long Main Barn aisle, heading out back. There, Jeffrey turned over some empty buckets, making us makeshift seats in the spotless aisle.

He sat down.

I sat down.

He held his head in his hands.

"What is it?" I asked him.

He looked up slowly. "Sandra Lee can't hold it up anymore. We're selling it. We're selling it all."

"Tell me you're kidding."

"I'm not kidding. And nobody else knows, so don't tell the other boarders yet…well, what's left of the boarders anyhow."

I nodded. My mouth felt loose. My teeth chattered.

"Are you moving out of the farmhouse too?"

"Yeah, but we won't go too far. There's no money, Mare."

I swallowed hard.

"You need to find a place to board Slick as soon as you can," he said.

I hugged him. "When?"

"Sometime after the next show, all hell's breaking loose. Not sure about the details yet. I'll let you know. You know what else?"

"What?" I asked him, ready for the worst.

"Whenever you leave the barn for the night, my eye starts twitching. Sometimes it twitches until I see you again."

"Really?"

"Really." Then Jeffrey kissed me. He started at my forehead, moving down, hitting my cheeks, my lips. He kissed my neck. He licked my neck. Suddenly, I was his salt block.

I took off my shirt, breathing in the horse smell, breathing in Jeffrey, breathing in the horse smell. It was hard to tell the difference.

Jeffrey kicked the buckets down the aisle, and then he looked at me wide-eyed.

Moving to the hard, cold ground, I stretched flat on my back, waiting for him.

He traced a finger along the faint scars on my stomach, feeling the texture. He didn't ask any questions. Instead, he kissed the scars. He licked them.

And when Jeffrey was inside of me, he stared me in the eye. He didn't look away. He could match my stare. He could.

It hurt, and I liked that it hurt.

A tear slid down one side of Jeffrey's face, landing on my lip.

Eleven.

It was my last show with the Griffins. We'd all been to the Horse Park, and Slick and I were truly stars. Not only did I ride well, but I also won several classes and ended up Grand Champion in the Junior Hunter Division. Sandra Lee, Dr. Dad, Margene, Jeffrey, Michael, the Griffin boarders – everyone was there to watch, and they hooted and hollered after I finished my courses; they were clapping like maniacs. Even Slick looked proud, holding his head high in his stall, reaching his nose out to my hands, searching for treats.

All around the show grounds, people patted me on the back, congratulating me. I was so surprised at winning Champion that I kept squeezing the long ribbon to make sure it was real. I felt so full. Any moment, I thought my chest might burst from the strange, new hour of joy.

On the way home from the Horse Park, I struggled to keep my eyes open as Sandra Lee barreled up the highway, smoking and swerving. We'd all been awake for five days almost literally, and the adrenaline of the week was fading. I decided I wasn't going to school the next day. I deserved a break.

Margene picked me up at the barn, and as we drove down the long driveway, she was strangely quiet. Usually she drilled me for details, wanting to know how I planned on doing better at the next show. But this day, with her right pointer finger twitching, she concentrated on driving. Then she looked in the rear view mirror, coating on some frosty orange lipstick. The car swerved, nearly hitting a deer.

We entered our spotless house. Clean, so clean, it was more sterile than a hospital. No dings, no dirt anywhere.

Everything – the cabinets, the appliances, the furniture – was sparkling new.

Carrying my saddle in one arm, I took my boots off at the door and scrambled inside, dropping things as I went, huffing and puffing.

I looked across the white kitchen, scanning the room.

Dr. Dad sat quietly at the table, staring at his hands. Then he whispered, "Come over here. We need to talk to you." His lightning scar made a weird cheek river.

I was shaking, afraid they'd found out about the beer I drank at the horse show. Slowly putting my saddle down, I slid my way across the beige wood floor, wearing boot-blackened socks, and I made it over to the family room easily. The whole house was large, open, and spacious – a slick, white slide. When I walked through the halls, there was rarely anything in the way.

After I sat down, Dr. Dad spat out more words than I'd ever heard him say at once. Sleepily, I listened, missing most of it. But I'll never forget the last words he spoke: "Margene and I are separating. We didn't want to tell you before the horse show because we knew how important it was for you."

I laughed out loud. I thought they were kidding around. Then I looked at Margene. Her skin was gray-green. Her eyes, swollen and bloodshot. She looked small and weak.

I sat down next to Dr. Dad, who looked lost. There I was, back from the show of my life, and suddenly, Dr. Dad was leaving Margene. I'd be damned if I was gonna stand there and listen to them cry and moan about how their marriage was trashed.

I stole Dr. Dad's cigarettes and ran outside. Lighting up, staring at the stars, I wondered if Buddy had found a home inside one of the planets. Buddy and Thomas, my universal light switches.

Two days later, Dr. Dad left our Highland home, finding an apartment in Mt. Kormet. Really, Dr. Dad disappeared, and then there were only two of us. Oddly enough, Margene's makeup disappeared as well.

Soon after, one shadowy day, I was relaxing at the barn, cooling Slick out, letting him graze. Calmly, I studied the arch of his dark brown neck, running my hand over his half-wet coat. I listened to him shift. Every few minutes, he nudged me to another spot, where the grass was taller, thicker. And sometimes, he nudged me just to touch me.

I heard the lounge phone ring. One of the boarder girls yelled out my name. The barn crew took care of Slick so I could answer it.

Margene was on the other end, cry-talking that I needed to come home. She needed me. I hung up the phone, running back outside. I grabbed at Slick. More than once, I hugged his neck.

Someone put Slick in his stall. The barn manager with the gimp leg gave me a ride home.

I found Margene in Dr. Dad's walk-in closet with one of Dr. Dad's plaid shirts wrapped around her shaky frame. And on her legs, his hospital scrubs. Even the feet. She looked up at me weakly, reaching toward me.

I stared at her, confused. I didn't move from the doorway.

"Come here, I need you," she said, reaching for me with both hands, which were covered with rubber gloves.

I stood unmoving, still wearing my sweat-stained riding jeans and T-shirt, my dirty socks stained from my paddock boots. I watched her cry, wearing Dr. Dad's plaid shirt. I wanted to shake her, to make her get up, but I didn't move. I didn't want to feel the loss like her. Thomas and Buddy were enough. Dry eyed, not blinking, I stared at Margene.

Her crying wasn't loud. It was a deep, guttural cry, the sound of a baby animal, a sound that haunted me. Soon, she stopped reaching for me, wrapping Dr. Dad's shirt tighter around her shaking body. She stopped crying and curled up in a ball, twitching.

I watched her. Dr. Dad was gone. Margene was gone, lost inside the walk-in closet. I knew Slick would be gone soon. Griffin Farm was disappearing. Thomas was gone. Buddy was gone. Inside me, a storm of terror spun. My whole world rose up, slapping at me, beating me. I didn't move. I was alone. I wanted out. And I understood completely how Buddy must've felt. Buddy's way or some other way out. Over and out. Out and up. Or out and down. Wherever. Anywhere but earth.

That night, when I crawled under my yellow sheets, I heard a knock on my door.

Margene cracked the door open. "We're going to sell Slick," she whispered.

"I know," I said.

"We can't afford riding lessons anymore," she said. "Not with us paying for two places to live, with your Dad gone and all."

"Aye."

Margene shut the door.

I thought about lightning bolts and Captain Tomcat's yellow hair. We were the most powerful pirates in all of

Scallycat. I thought there must be a new field somewhere, a new field with new treasure. Or a new field with another lost, black boot.

Someone had a grip on me. Captain Blackeye was poking fingers inside of me, creating holes, digging into me; I was a spider web, about to be washed away in one swipe. The bedroom grew bigger, stark yellow and blue, then white and ghostly, as pale as Buddy's skin. Shaken, I scratched at my crooked wrist. I scratched and scratched. There, blood. I wanted to crawl under the bed like a tomcat.

Part Three. The Dreaded Captain Blackeye.

Stop. Fast Forward. One year later. Play.

One.

When I turned fifteen, Slick was gone. Jeffrey had sold him to a little girl on a Southern farm. Griffin Farm had been leveled, the horses had all been sold, and the rings and barns were no more. It had happened fast. The Mitgard land was a hotbed for business heads – what was once the farm was now a corporate communications headquarters. No more than a large, flat building with small windows rested on the green fields. Black asphalt divided the place where the front field used to be, the place where Jeffrey and I used to race, tearing up the land.

I thought about the angle of Jeffrey's knee when he sat in the saddle. I thought about his thick, small hands, his black-rimmed glasses, his small nose, his crooked teeth.

Margene thought it might be good for me to see the land, so every now and then, she took me to Mitgard. Or maybe she just needed an excuse to get out of the house. I begged her to go a different way, but Margene wanted to fix things. She wanted to fix depressed, black-haired me, the girl who slammed doors and told Margene to shut up.

Margene kept in touch with Sandra Lee for a while. They talked in whispers, and I'd listen in at Margene's bedroom door. They talked about Big Mike and Dr. Dad, and how men never did anything but leave. On this, I agreed. But after a while, the phone calls stopped, and we all fell into our separate lives, lives absent of hooves and muddy rings and horse show ribbons.

Every day, I thought about calling Jeffrey. I thought about hunting him down in his new house in the suburbs of Mt. Kormet, but every time I thought about it, I saw Thomas' yellow hair. I saw Buddy's pale face. I saw him hanging there. His bloody chest. Lightning. I felt the thunder inside.

The horses tugged at me, but I couldn't bring myself to hear Jeffrey's voice, to see his serious mouth, to gaze at his curious, ever-changing eyes.

I was in my thinnest stage. To make up for selling my horse, Margene bought me a bright blue, Polo bathing suit, right on time for Liz and Mandy's boy-girl pool party. They thought it might be fun to have the barn crowd get together, even though the farm was gone. Margene made me go.

Proud of my skinny self, I swam and played with the rest of the kids. When we dried off and got dressed, we decided to play Spin the Bottle in the basement. I hoped no one thought I looked fat in my blue suit.

When I was kissing some skinny, blonde-haired kid in the bathroom, he stopped and said, "You're the girl who hung out with Jeffrey all the time. I used to take lessons there. Not much, because we didn't have money, but I remember seeing you."

Surprised, I said, "Yeah."

"I know Jeffrey pretty well. He moved down the street from me. Sandra Lee bought them a small, older house. So sad, them letting go of all that land," he said.

"I thought he might come today," I said.

The blonde kid looked down at the ground.

Liz banged on the bathroom door. "What are you guys doing in there?"

"Shut up, Liz," my kisser said.

"How is Jeffrey?" I asked the kid.

He looked up at me with round, chlorine-reddened blue eyes. "You want to know the truth?"

"Yeah," I said. "The truth."

"He got into some pot and shit at that new school he's at. He's been in rehab once already. Sandra Lee made him go. But he can't stay sober."

I nodded. I gulped. "Well, thanks for the kiss," I said.

"Sure, I'm Gus," he said, shaking my hand.

"Thanks for the kiss, Gus."

"I'm sure I'll see you again. I'm sure of it," Gus said, smiling.

Fully, I agreed, smiling back.

When Margene picked me up, my suit was still half-wet, so she put a towel down on my seat, protecting the leather.

"How was the party?" she asked me. While she drove, she twitched her finger, tapping the wheel.

"Stop doing that," I said, grabbing her finger. "Stop it!" I yelled.

Margene jumped, and the SUV swerved to the other side of the road. Just in time, Margene steered us straight. She yelled back at me, "Mary, don't ever do that again! If you don't shape up, you'll have to go live with your father."

"Fine," I said.

It was quiet in the car. I thought about what Gus had said. I thought about Jeffrey, and what he might look like in pajamas, shaking in rehab. When I got home, I ran up to my room, writing in my journal: "JEFFREY. I MISS YOUR FACE. BUT GUS KISSED ME. I'M SORRY." I read each word out loud, hanging on the sounds. I believed that if I concentrated hard enough, my visions might come true. I wrote about insects, tall grass, Jeffrey's cheeks that flushed when he had a wicked windburn. I wrote about Buddy's sensitive ears, and Michael's shining green eyes. I wished Thomas was there so I could show him the words, so he would say, "It's good, Shorty," so he could ride with me, ride the high seas.

Alone, I fixed my hair and eyes, talking to the mirror. There was nothing but the glass and me. *Fat, ugly, sick-o.* I could not *stop the thoughts.* When the horses were there, when Jeffrey was there, I had a break from the thoughts. But now they were back. *If only I were thin, Jeffrey would love me. Maybe if I rode again, rode better.* All I could think about were Jeffrey's triple-colored eyes, and how I wanted him back with me, riding beside me, feeling the rhythm. I wanted it all back. I wanted everyone back whole.

And then one day, Jeffrey sent me a letter from rehab:

Hey, Mare
Call me. I'll be home soon. Write me if you have a bad week and feel like exploding. I'll do my best to call too, once I get clean. Our house in Mt. Kormet sucks. I hate it. I miss the fields, don't you? I miss the mares. Sandra Lee is addicted to shopping, and I think Michael is gay, but I guess we all knew that. I'm not. Of course you and I already knew that. He's not as pretty as you though. Don't tell him I told you that. Well, I gotta go. Smoke break time.
Seeya,
Jeffrey

A few months later, I got another one:

Christ, Mare
I'm fucked up. I'm in another hellhole. I'm shaking and sick. Withdrawal and shit. But even though I'm a sick horse, anyone that you date has to go through me first. You know I'm like you're brother. I'm begging. Mail me a picture. Nothing here is as pretty as you.

Miss ya,
Jeff

I never replied. The letters got shorter and stranger, until our whole relationship faded away into an awkward wall. Jeffrey's words turned tough and curt:

Mare:
Why won't you write me back? After everything. The farm. Buddy. The field. The back barn. Never mind. Forget it,
Jeffrey

I was afraid to mess up his sobriety, and I didn't want him to know about my darkness. I didn't want Jeffrey to know that I was forcing food down, that I wasn't sleeping much, and that when I did sleep, I dreamed of pirate swords and throats, my throat, slashed to red ribbons. So I didn't write.

On my sixteenth birthday, I stole quarters from Margene's top dresser drawer, buying smokes from a machine down the road. My bleach-blond high school friend Katie was newly driving. We were on our way to a party. Word was that there was a lot of weed and booze there. On the way, we stopped to pick up Katie's older friend, my Spin-the-Bottle kisser, Gus. He walked out of his front door playing guitar, then hopped in the car with us. I hadn't seen him since the party when we'd kissed. He looked spindly and mischievous, more long-legged than any boy I'd seen.

Soon, I was rip-roaring drunk on Peach Schnapps, and somehow Gus and I ended up in a dark basement together. I wasn't scared until he started giving me a backrub.

Gus and I kissed a little. Well, Gus kissed me.

I was stiff, like the dead.

We moved upstairs to a small bedroom. There was a futon, but we sat on the floor, facing each other.

I couldn't look him in the eye. I was afraid to mess something up, like I was always messing up Margene's floors. I touched my hair, making sure it looked all right. I thought my jeans looked too tight. I wondered if Gus thought I was fat, ugly, gross.

I slipped my shirt over my head.

And so did he. Gus pressed his chest against mine. He shivered.

I shivered.

Then we lay down, sandwiched together, chest to chest, like that.

Gus fell asleep, smiling.

Drunk and dazed, I stared at the ceiling, wide awake. Waiting.

In the morning, bug-eyed Gus wore sunglasses.

I felt nauseous. I wondered if he thought I looked fat in the light. Quickly, I slipped on my shirt.

Gus strummed his guitar, singing to me.

When he sang, I felt a strange calm, as if his voice wiped away the others, the crowd in my mind.

Then he paused, taking off his sunglasses, staring at me through his round, blue eyes. He smiled and shrugged. “I'm sure I'll see you around,” he said. “I'm sure of it. Life is weird that way.”

“And will you remember me when you're famous?” I asked him.

“Remember you? I won't have to, Mary. You'll be in the tour bus with me,” he said. Then he started singing about crossing the ocean.

I hummed along until Katie yanked on my shirt, and we scrambled to the car, reeking of booze and cigarettes.

Back home, I showered before Margene had the chance to smell me. And then I went outside, staring at the dark, cloudy sky. I wished for lightning, and it came.

The next night, driving a red Olds, chain-smoking cigarettes, I sped down the street to meet Katie at a college party near the University of Welch. We sat in the grass in a fraternity house backyard, where I met a freshman. I didn't know anything about him, other than that he was so drunk he could barely walk, and he needed a ride home. I offered.

Escaping Katie, I helped the guy to my car, driving him to my house. Margene wasn't home. I wasn't sure where she was, but the whole house was spotless.

I got in bed with the freshman, and we played house. We had sex, and then it was over.

In the morning, I drove the freshman home. I never saw him again.

Guilt crept in. Then a crushing anxiety about diseases, pregnancy, sin and sex and feeling nasty. Girls at school had relationships. There I was, smoking, wondering what the freshman's name was. *Still smokin' Tomcat.*

Two.

Soon after, Margene got sick. Margene took a head-trip.

I called Dr. Dad, filling him in. When he came over, he had a yellow leather suitcase. He said, "Honey, I'll be staying here again." Dr. Dad seemed sober, but he looked worn.

"Okay," I said. And that was that. Dr. Dad was back home.

That night, Margene set an extra place at the dinner table, a place for Tomcat.

"Stop it, Margene. We need to let go," Dr. Dad said. "Thomas is not coming home. Not ever."

Margene sniffled. Then she cried out loud.

Dr. Dad took a hold of her wrist tight enough to make her shake.

She struggled, trying to rid herself of his grip, yelling, "I can set any goddamn place I want to! I made your perfect homemade food! It's my kitchen! If you don't like it, leave again!"

Then more wrist grabbing, the throwing of silverware.

Glass breaking.

Dr. Dad touching Margene's hair.

Margene slapping his cheek.

Me slapping both of them. "It was me! I was the one! I found the boot! I pulled on it! I woke him up! I woke up the bad pirate!" I yelled. Then I calmed down and stated, "Yeah, I woke up the killer."

Then silence. A dead silence.

"None of it matters. None of it's going to bring Thomas back," Dr. Dad said.

Margene reset the table for three.

Dr. Dad sat down, watching. Then he rose, helping her. His large hand brushed across her pink-nailed one. He held her hand, gripping it. He pulled her close, hugging her. He kissed her cheek hard.

Margene took the kiss.

I sat down. I saw Thomas' ghost. I was sure that their touch had been enough to make his face reappear. Suddenly and painfully and peacefully and sweetly. I imagined that he would reach to hold my hand and call me his First Mate, Shorty. And we would all laugh together in the white kitchen.

If I could just escape Dr. Dad's Scallycat accent, the high pitch of his pain, a pain that even he, a surgeon, couldn't heal, and if I could just escape his white coat, if I could just escape Margene's clean kitchen, maybe then I'd feel whole. I had to get out. Either that, or I might become another knife in Margene's sharpened set.

After the kitchen incident, the scene at home was getting weirdly old – for weeks, Margene had been in bed, buried under thick, white covers. She was never down that long. For the first time, dirty dishes sat in the sink. Crumbs on the floor. Dust on the blinds.

Dr. Dad told me she had a sinus infection, but the recovery was taking way too long. Those weeks, I tiptoed into Margene's room, afraid to wake her. I was terrified of seeing that look on her face – downtrodden, anxious, pale, and fragile. And she was shrinking. Her whole body seemed to be melting into her king-sized bed. Sheets perfectly ironed and tucked in, no lines. Then she blew her nose again, quietly crying into one of Dr. Dad's old handkerchiefs. Mostly sniffles and hidden cries. Bedridden and anxious. I could tell that she was holding back, and it spooked me.

Sometimes I sneaked up to the side of the bed, quietly saying "hi," or saying nothing at all. Sometimes, she reached for me, looking for a hug. Not knowing how to talk to her, after a while, I went out and got drunk with Katie instead.

Dr. Dad went to work and tried to hold us together. He bought us fast food or TV dinners, but Margene wouldn't eat. Dr. Dad was less talkative than ever, trying to work and work out and go to sober meetings and take care of Margene and me. We went through the motions and kept our schedule. Go to work, go to school, ask no questions, expect no explanations. When Dr. Dad came home, he brought pizza. Margene didn't touch it. I threw mine in the garbage. Everyone was looking thin. One wiry house in Highland.

Margene was there, upstairs, blowing her nose, but a thickness hung in the house, an oppressive, ill feeling that wouldn't go away. Every now and then, Dr. Dad and I peeked in on Margene and her handkerchief. After a while, the sight of her hiding in a white-sheeted cocoon, moving only to use the bathroom, filled me with a churning fear. I thought her sickness might be catching so I stayed away.

Then came anger. I started thinking, *Get up, damnit.* Like Dr. Dad, my lips were trapped in a thin line. Captain Tomcat, the most powerful pirate in all of Scallycat, would've known what to do. That thought made me feel a little lighter, just for a moment. I mentioned it to Dr. Dad. He winced.

Sometimes, Dr. Dad would crawl into the bed with Margene, and even though her head was infected, when I saw him there, things seemed all right, as if Thomas were looming above us in the room, as if we were whole again, as if the Lochmores were once again four instead of three.

Finally, one day, without warning, Dr. Dad announced, "Margene is sick."

Margene got up. From her antique dresser, she pulled out bedclothes, carefully folding them, making piles on her bed, packing. Then, as Margene floated down the hall in her see-through nightgown, Dr. Dad followed behind her, carrying a huge, blue suitcase.

I didn't know where she went until Dr. Dad took me to Welch Hospital to visit her. And even then, I thought it was about her sinuses. I had to figure it out by reading Doctors' lips and straining to hear Dr. Dad's whispers to his doctor friends. Finally, I came to, talking to Thomas in my head. Ghost Thomas and I agreed. We were at a psych ward. Margene went nuts.

When she walked down the hall to greet me, she looked strangely spacey, ghostlike, wearing a loose gown. She appeared so tired, I wondered if she might fall asleep standing up. She was crying up something awful – the kind of cry that held a tangible, throbbing despair. She was thin, and I wanted to shake her, to snap her out of it. I felt like there was a wall between her and the rest of the living. An imaginary police line, some CAUTION tape. And if we crossed it, she might break into pieces. Dr. Dad and I were with the living, and Margene was on the side of the dying. There was a life and death game going on, and Margene might not win.

It stank in there like urine and disinfectant. New to psych meds, Margene acted groggy. She walked funny. She tried to smile, but it came out looking more like a wet, sad smirk, a down-turned half moon. When she held me, she hung on so tight it hurt. I wanted to push her away, brush her off, be gone with sick Margene. All I had were the people in my head – Buddy, Thomas, Jeffrey. Sometimes Gus. It was getting crowded in there.

Dr. Dad was busy going to meetings and working. Margene was in the psych ward. Anger festered inside me, turning inward. My head was full of pressure, as if I lived and walked inside the deep sea. *I should be the one locked up. All hands on deck. I am the baddest pirate in all of Scallycat. I should be the one, you landlubbers.*

The Doctors explained Margene's condition to Dr. Dad. I overheard that she was overwhelmed and depressed, and they were trying different medications on her – antidepressants and anti-psychotics. She wasn't responding very well, but they were going to keep trying. She seemed so tired.

Dr. Dad zoned out, staring out windows, staring at ceilings and floors.

Margene cried more, but the rest of the time, she was creepy-glowy, on the edge.

She came home a week later. Dressed in beige, her gold seashell belt hung loose at her waist. She was bony, but she started coming out of the bedroom, making homemade meals and cleaning again, but I couldn't shake the image of Margene blowing her nose under the white sheets, how she didn't move to clean it up. And how I didn't help her clean it up, because I was afraid of a dirty Margene.

Dr. Dad was afraid too. I overheard him talking to her shrinks. I heard them say that it might run in the family.

After a few weeks, Margene started eating again. She rose, dressed, put on her frosty lipstick, and fixed pork chops, because those were Dr. Dad's favorite. She stopped taking the medicine. She cleaned. Everything was eerily normal. The bad, secret breakdown was gone. She scrubbed. She scoured and polished and waxed and scraped and mopped and folded and used her fingernails to scrape it all clean.

I pushed it out of my mind.

Dr. Dad stayed. That was enough.

We never talked about it again. We never talked about it at all.

After Margene's breakdown, I sat alone in the kitchen, eating a bagel with one slice of fat free cheese. Drinking my diet soda, my head started racing, as if someone had a grip on my skull, rattling and shaking it. My heart beat, my head beat. My whole body beat at me. There was a throbbing thunder inside me. The world blurred, shifted, intensified. Everything pulsed around me; all shapes appeared distorted. I was trapped on a beach, buried in sand. People appeared, random strangers, ghosts that walked around me, moving around me rapid-fire. Faces melted. Girls were laughing, eating, dripping, made of wax. I choked on my breath. I shook my head. I thought someone had a hand over my mouth. I wiped my lips to make sure there was nothing there. I was being smothered, crushed by the atmosphere. I gasped. Someone was coming. Captain Blackeye. Any moment, someone would put hands around my neck and choke me just enough to watch me struggle, letting me live. Any moment, my hair, the kitchen might catch on fire. My scalp tingled, itched. I scratched my head, feeling around my hair for hidden ants. Any moment, ants might burrow into my brain. Bugs, everywhere, bugs. And where was Thomas? And where was Buddy? And where was Jeffrey? And why weren't they there to help me get rid of the bugs in my head?

Slowly, blurry-eyed and half-conscious, I floated through the house, trying not to brush against ghost shoulders. I moved, inched my way down one wall, then the next, terrified. Around me, the ghosts turned into evil cartoon characters. Uniformed, robotic monsters. Then I ran. Out of breath, I ran. I sprinted to Margene's room.

She was making the white bed.

Quietly, I said, "Help me."

Margene was unfolding the sheets. I heard the sheets snap open. I heard her tuck them in. All around me, ghosts were floating and floating. Each small sound fired at me – the sound of the starched sheets snapping, the sound of Captain Blackeye walking down the hall one footstep at a time. I was in a war zone of sheets and bugs and boots.

Margene smoothed the comforter down. "Settle...down...Mary," she said.

But I could hear the pauses in her voice, the uncertainty. She breathed heavily, backing away from the white bed, carefully choosing words. "What's going on? Whatever it is, we'll take care of it," she said.

Then I remembered *her* hospital trip. I knew that she knew the terror.

"Everything is so loud, and I'm seeing things, things like ghosts in here," I said. My bottom lip trembled.

Margene moved forward, putting a hand on my shoulder. "How long has this been going on?" she asked.

"Since before Thomas was gone," I said. "For as long as I can remember." My eyes spilled. I shook. Head to toe, I shook. "There are people. In there. In my head, Mom."

Margene nodded, calling Dr. Dad. "Mary's having a nervous breakdown," she stated into the phone. Then she listened, mumbling answers. Quietly, she pressed the phone into her cheek.

Margene hung up. She dialed again, making me an appointment with the school counselor.

I ran my crooked hand along my scarred stomach.

On my first appointment, stuck in the counselor's office, I was quiet and withdrawn, afraid to speak. The counselor had to draw words out of me one at a time, first grade style. After a while, Margene ended up talking to the psychologist more often than I did.

I showed up, but I didn't tell her that Thomas, Buddy, and Jeffrey were all still in my head. I didn't tell her about the lightning in my mind. The black boots, the bugs, the caution tape. Instead, I drank.

Three.

Margene was sleeping and Dr. Dad was at the hospital, so I sneaked out, picking up Katie at her parent's house. In the car, through her thick lips, Katie rattled on about her boyfriends.

I didn't tell her about the men in my head.

While I was driving, Katie handed me a long-necked Bud Light. The bottle was ice cold in my crotch. Water dripped slowly down the sides, slightly raining on my jeans, making spots. I felt the bottle sweat. I gripped it, turning it up, drinking it down in a few labored gulps. I felt an intense pull in my chest. My head cleared. I felt taller, thinner. I felt a deep, strange, warm comfort. I wanted more.

I turned up the radio. Heavy metal. I sang along.

"Calm down, Mary," Katie said. "And watch where we're going. We don't need to be getting pulled over."

I drove faster.

Katie rolled her eyes, lighting a cigarette.

"I like the rush," I said.

"How are your parents doing?" she asked me.

"Dr. Dad's going to meetings again. And therapy. And he's looking skinny and pale. Margene wanders around afraid, lost, and confused. As usual. How about yours?" I asked her.

"Dad's always working. Mom sits at home in the mansion and smokes," she said, picking up another beer.

"It's sloppy, but Dr. Dad seems to be growing stronger. Margene might lose herself, or she might crawl out of it. I'm not sure."

"I hear you, I know what you mean," Katie said, sucking on her cigarette with those fat, red lips. "Have you heard from that guy you liked…the one from the barn…what was his name?" Katie asked.

"Jeffrey," I said.

"Yeah, heard from him?"

"Well, in my head I have," I said, laughing.

Katie laughed back.

Then I started to see the signs in things again. Billboard sayings sent me messages, messages from God. I looked over at Katie. She was quietly staring out the window, drinking her beer. I figured she hadn't heard God's voice, so I kept my mouth shut, drank and drove. It was as if I were a child again, resting in the grass with Thomas, staring up at the cloud people, but instead of imagining them talking to me, I could actually hear them. I thought maybe Thomas was better off in heaven.

Then I heard a strange, deep, guttural tone. I was sure it was Captain Blackeye. His voice was the loudest. Thick and throaty. He laughed and said, *Ahoy, matey.*

"Did you hear that?" I asked Katie.

"Hear what?" she said, running a hand through her greasy bleached hair.

"Never mind," I said.

"You're acting funny. You need to get laid," she said.

"You got that right," I said. *Still smokin', Tomcat. Still smokin', Cap'n.*

With one hand, I held the steering wheel. With the other, I reached out at the face floating in front of the windshield. Every time I reached out to touch the vision of Thomas, my fingers spread, and he slipped through the spaces between them, leaving me with an open, reaching, useless crooked hand.

By the time I was seventeen, hills and horses haunted me. I thought about knives, all the sharp things. When I drove down the road, at each curve, I thought about going straight. I dreamed about getting fatal diseases, drank and smoked pot, my mind riddled with Griffin flashbacks. I thought about the last time I stood in Slick's stall at the farm, leaning against his warm body, his thick, soft coat, while he nudged me with his nose, saying goodbye. I thought about the day I played tag with Slick in the field for the last time, when he followed me up and down the fence lines and how when I left, from behind the paddock fence, he followed Margene's car down the drive, hurriedly trotting, lifting his nose, searching the air for the last of my scent. And then he was gone.

Alone in my room, I had Scallycat flashbacks too. The Scallycat Mountains seemed to rise around me, and I could hear Thomas calling my name. *Hey, Shorty, I spy a treasure! It's a biggun!* I thought about the days spent in the dusty lounge of Griffin Farm – the black fences, the farmhouse, the boys, and the back field. I missed staring at Sandra Lee, studying the cigarette hanging from her lip, nervous about the long ash. I even missed Michael's whining. I spent a lot of time in my room, thinking about mountains, wild seas, and sharp things.

Katie and I hit the world of drunken parties. At first, once a week. Then three. I woke up on random couches, in random beds. I slept with whomever I ended up with, wherever I ended up. I discovered free booze and nameless sex. I had a talent for drunk driving and strange luck when it came to avoiding cops. Several times, I almost passed out while driving, waking up just before I went off the side of the road. Once, I made it all the way back home only to fall face-first on the hard ground, knocked out cold. Still another time, I came to out of a blackout going 100 mph on some highway with no headlights on, heading to Scallycat. Piss was everywhere. I woke up at the Super 8 Motel, at random country houses. I woke up with a band. Then another band. Miraculously, I never got a DUI. I never even had one small wreck. I never got a ticket.

Katie liked heavy metal and tattoos and hard liquor. We were a good, tough match. We slept with frat boys and band guys, crawling into random beds, passing out.

Every now and then, I'd wake up in a random bed and think, *What would Jeffrey think of me now?*

I started writing illegible entries in my journal. All caps. Suicide letters. I drove past the land where Griffin Farm used to be, studying the grass, and the land seemed smaller. There was no place to search for treasure anymore, but I knew I was still Shorty. I knew it. I had to believe it. I had to believe in something. I needed my eye patch. I needed a straight right arm.

Four.

One winter night, Katie and I hit a frat party. Gus was in a band by then, and we'd heard that they were playing that night.

At the show, countless drunken blondes danced in the front row, waving bodies in Gus' face.

Gus gazed my way, smiling and singing.

I danced a little, smiling back.

He looked at me. Well, I thought he looked at me. It was hard to tell with the flashing lights.

While he sang, he twisted his lean body around on stage. Gus looked older. Sweaty and mysterious, he moved carefully, like a sexy snake.

When the show was over, after he packed up his equipment, he waved Katie and me over. "You guys can come hang out at my place if you want. It's kind of a 'lonely man' apartment, but you're welcome there."

We hopped in his blue tour van, sitting together in the passenger seat. Katie was halfway on my lap, bouncing and giggling and singing there. It was snowing something wicked, and Gus drove carefully.

We didn't talk much on the snowy ride; we all spaced out, watching the road.

Then Katie whispered, "He's a celebrity around here now, Mary."

I smiled. "I guess," I whispered back.

Gus' apartment was clean and reddish – red walls, red couches – with black, hard, contemporary furniture surrounding the fluffy couch. I scanned the room for booze. Nothing but burgundy colors and clean all-wood floors.

Gus said, “Make yourselves at home. I’m gonna change. I’m all sweaty.” He flashed a toothy smile. “It was hot in there, eh?”

“Yeah,” Katie and I said at the same time.

We sat on the couch, licking our lips. Cotton mouth.

Then Katie whispered in my ear, "He wants you to follow him, you dumbass." She nudged me.

“Maybe he wants you,” I said.

“No, come on, wake up, he wants you,” she said.

Katie and I lay on the couch together until, laughing and half-drunk, she kicked me out.

I moved down the hall into Gus’ room, sitting down on his bed, on the side by the heater. There, I stared at the wall with my head propped on my hands. The heat was on high. Soon, I could feel my feet again. I breathed deeply, lying down next to him, pretending sleep.

Gus sat up, creeping over to the heater, twice feeling the air, so close to my leg that he was almost, almost touching me. Back turned to me, he sat on the edge of the bed, warming himself.

It was five a.m. at least.

Then he returned to his side of the bed, resting next to me. I heard his body rustle the sheets, twisting and turning, restless. He inched his way over to me, moving on top of me. Gently, he breathed all over me, from my forehead to my toes. He kissed my shoulder, my neck, my cheeks. He didn’t kiss me on the lips. He simply breathed on me, touching my face, inch by inch.

Then we slept curled up together, feeling the welcome heat of the room. Gus interlaced his fingers with mine, gripping both of my hands. Like spiders, his fingertips moved across my crooked wrist. Then one hand drifted down, pushing up my shirt, feeling my scarred belly. We each held a hand up, pressing our palms together. His long fingers swallowed my stubby digits.

All night long, he wrapped his long arms around me, holding me tight against his chest, pulling me close, narrow hips to narrow hips. He was soft, warm, and sweet. A breathy gentleman.

In the morning, Gus jumped out of bed, hurrying to the shower. Then he poked his head around the bathroom door and said, "Hey, you look pretty there. You look just right, just sayin'."

I smiled, turning over in the twisted sheets. Then I rose groggily, finding Katie in the den. We each held a hand up, feeling our hot foreheads, and the familiar ache of a hangover. We didn't have any other clothes to wear, so while Gus dressed in his room, we quickly washed our faces in the kitchen, swishing water around in our mouths, more than ready to get on out of there.

Katie walked outside.

I waited at the door.

Slick-haired Gus came out of his room.

Gus and I shared a few awkward smiles.

He drove us back to my car, which was still parked at the frat house. A thick-bodied kid was passed out on the front lawn.

Gus hugged me. He waved at Katie.

"See you around, mate," I said.

Gus nodded. He winked. "I'm sure of it."

On the way back home, I thought about the Singerman. That night, I made sure that I went to bed feeling a little hungry. While my stomach growled, I gripped a stuffed horse hard enough to choke the living.

Hanging out at bars, I'd often hear girls whispering about Singerman Gus and me. Sometimes, brave ones would ask me if it were true that he took me home.

When they asked me, I answered with this: "Arrrgh."

Much of the time – the concerts I saw, the places I crashed – was a mystery. I passed out at random houses, in cars. I woke up with bruises. It was a dangerous ride, so I drank more.

At eighteen, Katie and I decided to blow off college. We both scored jobs at The Greater Welch Thrift Store so we could find some good, cheap rocker clothes. We moved into an apartment in Mt. Powder, the artsy side of town. We got pierced. We got tattooed.

I was looking forward to a party house. Bring it on, Singermen. I could take out any Captain Blackeye.

I listened to Gus' music for a while. He never called, so I trashed his music. Then I pulled it out of the trash, missing the sound of his voice, the way it calmed my head, my head that held the storm. But I was afraid that within Gus' crowds, I blended in, just another small, black-haired, hazel-eyed horse in a wicked, wild herd.

While drinking and driving, sometimes I saw horses fenced in, calling to me from the road sides. The horses lifted their heads, staring back at me, as if sending me messages through their deep eyes. In a place lost inside me, I could still hear the sounds of horses breathing – the thick in and out through the nose. I thought the horses were saying, *What happened to you?* Or maybe it was Jeffrey speaking. Or Thomas. Or Buddy. The voices were running together. Even Gus worked his way inside me, singing inside my skull.

I began taking long drives. Fast, reckless drives. I drove to Scallycat and back. I drank on the way. I aimed for holes and bumps when everyone else swerved. Taking speed, I could stay awake and drink and drive longer than anyone I knew. Gripping wheels, I lived on long hours. And while I drove, I repeatedly saw them – random horses spying on me from their grass positions. I saw one gelding squint, and I felt his rage. I saw one mare's wide eye, and I felt the depths of her loneliness. When I stopped to touch one, the large nose pushed against my chest. Then the eyelids drew back. *Feed me. Feed me.* But my hands were empty. I had nothing to give.

In my apartment one night, the power went out. Katie had disappeared for a few days, which was nothing new. On the dirty floor, in the dark, sitting cross-legged, I drank warm beer, scrawling block letters in my journal. Outside, some kids were sled riding. I was sure they were maniacs.

The next day, I realized my journal was missing.

I tracked down Katie at Welch Thrift Store, calling her. "Have you seen my journal?" I asked frantically.

She paused. "No, don't even know what it looks like," she said.

"Well if you see it, don't open it," I said.

"Okay."

We hung up.

Later, Margene called, drilling me with worried questions. Katie had found my journal, read my writings, and called Margene, letting her know that I was alcoholic and suicidal.

"Is it true, Mary?" Margene asked me.

"That bitch!" I yelled. "The words were mine. That world is mine."

"She's trying to save your life," Margene said.

"I don't need someone saving my life," I said.

"Your Dad and I are concerned," Margene said.

"I don't need Dr. Dad saving my life either."

Margene was quiet. For once, she had no idea how to fix things.

I hung up.

When I saw Katie that night, I rolled my eyes at her, shaky and sore. She handed me a bottle of wine. I shrugged, drinking it down, and we never mentioned the journal again.

The next night, I woke up near the Horse Park. Groggy, trying to patch together the details, when I got home, I realized that Margene had called the cops, reporting me missing. I told her to stay out of my business.

Katie's Dad had connections at Welch Music Center, so we often scored VIP passes to concerts. Parking up front with the limos, we slipped into the private Club, getting served every time. Most nights were gone to me, except for the flashing lights.

At one concert at the end of the summer, I saw Jeffrey. I grabbed Katie's arm, hanging on to her, watching Jeffrey across the rows. To my left, about ten rows back, he was dancing, but he wasn't holding a drink. He wasn't smiling, but he was moving, rocking back and forth to the rhythm, the way he used to when he rode.

Jeffrey looked my way, stretching his neck. He started working his way down the rows, heading toward me, snaking through the wild crowd.

I hid behind Katie. I didn't want Jeffrey to see my mean spirit away from the barn, away from the crisp fields.

"I have to piss," I said to Katie.

Katie tossed her bleached hair and smiled a drunken smile. She said, "Damn, this is a good song," through her big, cracking lips. Then she followed me out of the rows, and somewhere in the crowd, I lost Jeffrey. But even as we left the show that night, I could almost feel his stare burning through the back of me.

Back home, I sat on the floor of my apartment, listening to Gus' voice wail, his songs trailing out of my stereo like an angelic alien. I took in the haunting sound of his voice, shutting my eyes, smoking. Dr. Dad had quit by then. On the day he quit, a curious hole appeared in the middle of the wall in Margene's spotless white kitchen. Whether he punched it or she punched it, I wasn't sure.

I cleaned the apartment. Again and again, I cleaned it, but the picture frames still looked yellow. The stain. All yellow. I left it.

Christmas was coming, and I knew Thomas was in all of our thoughts again. Smoothly and slowly, he'd seep inside our minds, and then the old pain took a knife turn, butter-spreading across our world, coating our hearts with a thick season of yellow sorrow. So it was easier not to call or visit Margene and Dr. Dad. Sometimes, silence counted for something. Instead, I sent mental notes. *Thinkin' of you. I'm all right.* But I still felt a deep, lasting hunger that bit at me, tearing up my middle, churning and pouring upward, resting in my throat. I was hungry for words, but my speech tasted bland. I wanted to live within Gus' songs. I was hungry for the mystery, the mystery between two music notes, the mystery between two bodies, two souls joining, and for an instant, becoming one. I was hungry for long, thin arms that wrapped me inside a skin wave of peace, arms that swiped away my cravings, touch that left me feeling clear and sleepily full. I was hungry. I was a whore. I was fake. I was glad Thomas wasn't around to see his First Mate slipping into liquid. My eye twitched. The right one. I cracked the knuckles on my wrecked hand. Crack, crack.

Five.

I was at The Crow's Nest, a dive bar in Mt. Powder. The shots came by the glassful. It was seedy and small, but the tunes were surprisingly good. The place was kickin' and packed. The Crow's Nest held the kind of musicians who played with desperation and depth, because the tunes were a part of their lifestyle as much as eating.

In the music zone, I drank pints, making eyes at everyone. Things were loose and urgent, loose and mean. All around, love was quick and wild. Good music, hidden talent, and utter, hilarious crap. Fights, make-ups, breakups, and low-lit rooms. It was late. Nowhere else was open. There, a wet, musical dream.

I saw Gus here.

The crowd spilled out into the street.

Next to me, Gus smelled earthy, thick, rich, slightly sweet. His scent alone made my body twitch.

Later that night, I sat on the sidewalk outside the bar. The streets were so quiet that I could hear the sound of car tires spitting up ground. It was so late, barely any stragglers were out. Then I saw a slim shadow.

Gus sauntered up, sitting down on the ground next to me. "Hey, there, you look like a little dreamy bird."

I smiled. The night was clear. Not hot or cold. Somewhere in between.

"Do you need a place to stay? You look lost, Mary," he said.

"I do, yeah," I said.

We held hands until the street cleaner came. I followed Gus' rusty blue van through the Mt. Powder streets as he led me back to his apartment, and the warm, reddish rooms. This time, we entered through the back door.

Gus smiled a lot as we climbed the steep stairs, stepping lightly, trying not to disturb the quiet night.

Behind him, I studied the way Gus' yellow hair hung loosely, wanting to feel each strand of it, to grab it, to hang on.

Opening the door to his room, he looked back at me, smiling. "Welcome. Enter," he said. Suddenly, he had a rougher, older look, like a train hopper, mixed with a brutally handsome, pale face. Eyes, the bluest of blue, like Thomas.

He had changed his room. It was softly lit by blue Christmas lights strewn across the ceiling. Made of sticks, a giant ball hung from the middle of the ceiling; it was Gus' personal makeshift planet. And truly, the whole room made me feel safe, yet warmly lost. A soft-lit outer space.

Gus turned on the stereo. Guitars called out like children. Tiny, distant screams.

Surely, I was shooting somewhere. I saw stars.

He kissed me up and down and up. Then he stopped.

Our breath was even. Close. My body shook and ached.

I woke in the middle of the night next to him. And when I woke, I felt a radiant side cramp. And to wake and ache and still want to be near him – that was new. It was a shared, sweeping night. A good skin trade.

When he woke, Gus traced his guitar-playing fingers all over me again. All the while, he smiled.

I wanted to stay in that starlit room. I wanted to stay wrapped in his smooth, white arms. Again, I shook and hurt, feeling the release.

But under the warm sheets, I knew it was time for another exit. I stood up, I threw up, and headed to sleep the rest of the night on his couch.

Gus brought me a towel. He wiped my mouth. "You need help," he said, pausing for a moment to touch my cheek. "I want to be with you, but you're dating the booze instead. I've always wanted to be with you, but you need help."

"You're dating your band," I said, coughing.

"It's not the same," he said. "It's work. They're like family. My life is big enough for you too, but not like this."

"I should go now," I said, sitting up.

"Stay the night," he said, grabbing my hand, stroking it with his long, slender, musical fingers.

"It's not the right time," I stated. I felt my eyes fill up a little. I was sure the rest of me was vanishing.

"Mary, it'll be the right time when you decide it is," Gus said, pushing a hand through my knotted black hair.

"I know you're right about the drinking. I have a hole inside of me the size of a small planet, and no one can fill that sucker up. No one but me I guess. So I'll meet you again after I can find some life size Band-Aid or something." I looked down, shrugging. "I don't know what to tell you. I've always felt fucked up."

Gus ran his fingers along my crooked wrist. "Hell, honey, we're all fucked up really, and it seems like we're all here to help each other not be so fucked up or at least distract each other for a little while. Girl, I hate to admit it, but you make my heart hurt." Then he wrapped his long, thin arms around me, hugging me tight.

"I love it when you do that," I said, feeling his bony chest press so close.

Six.

I knew I needed help, but I couldn't stop and for a long while, I decided that I may live and die as a gutter drunk. I woke up from blackouts driving somewhere, anywhere, covered in vomit, piss, or booze. Searching for Captain Blackeye, I used men to buy me drinks. I charged up credit cards. I sold plasma. I pawned jewelry. I never missed work. Every now and then, I thought about Dr. Dad and how he was still sober. Katie and I laughed about it. I decided that I was going to die drinking. So be it. Katie and I were the two peas thing.

I worked at Welch Thrift, drank with Katie, and hid the bottles when Dr. Dad came over. When I visited Margene's white kitchen, I tried not to breathe out on her. She knew that alcohol smell. Sometimes I stole booze. Later, I gathered bottles, driving down the street to several different garbage cans, scattering the trash so that even the garbage man wouldn't know. Even sober Dr. Dad had no idea. Or maybe he didn't want to see his little black-haired Mary drunk and pierced and so wrecked.

Several times, I showed up at Gus' apartment in the middle of the night, drunk and dirty. He welcomed me in, taking care of me, washing my clothes, and then we ventured out on long, late night, twisty drives. I slept on his couch, on his floor, but I never slept with him and never stayed through the night. It was never solid, but I thought of him as a gentle, sleeping bear. We were like air together – sexual and scented, but never quite concrete.

But one night, after he wrestled a gin bottle from me, pouring it out in the sink, I stumbled outside, cussing at him, cussing at his apartment, cussing at the rain. I left. Again. I didn't look back.

Seven.

It was a night full of fog and cold mist, fit for apparitions. Hauntings. Outside, an ambulance started the siren song. Ominous and loud, it echoed, as if announcing a death. But the eerie sound calmed me. By then, I'd become familiar with the droning city sounds of my Mt. Powder home. I knew I was far away from the horse smells, and the crisp, sweet-green air of Griffin Farm, and each day, I knew I was slipping deeper into the dark alley noise.

Writing in my journal, I sat in the kitchen, remembering the willow tree in the backyard of our Scallycat home. I wrote of Thomas buried in wispy branches, where everything had seemed ancient and magical. Dreaming of trees, I felt comfort in the feel of my black hair brushing across my cheeks. Some of it hung loose, and some of it was braided in thin plaits. I knew Gus liked it that way. I'd become a hippie type for him. I dressed in tattered jeans and thin shirts. Short nails, no makeup. My jacket was green corduroy. I wore scented oils. Most hours, my feet were bare.

My throat was dry and scratchy from smoking and repeated bouts of drinking-induced tonsillitis. My fingers hurt. Stretching my fingers, wishing life into them, I thought about Jeffrey's long stares through his thick, black-rimmed glasses.

Then I heard the sounds of Katie rising, banging around her room, waking from a strange, late nap. I heard the rustle and the "Shit, I'm still loaded," when she fell, dazed and hungover. Her white figure crept into the kitchen. Like a ghost, she floated, stepping lightly. Then she turned my way, staring at me with huge, tired eyes. She studied me, puzzled and alert, like a wild animal, one hand on the fridge, one hand feeling her middle. Only a thin t-shirt covered her tiny shape.

The cream, wrinkled, papery shirt looked like a second skin. She stood still, like she might break. Like a sleepy child. Then she stuffed a bagel in her mouth. She bit down, then spit it out.

"What are you doing?" I asked her, laughing.

"I thought I was hungry," she said. “But I think I’m too sick.” Small bruises, facial half-moons, rested under her deep brown eyes.

I stared at her in the soft light.

“What are you doing?” she asked.

“Brooding, ” I said.

"Same," she said, sitting next to me. The neck of her shirt fell over one shoulder. She left it hanging there, touching my arm. Then she tiptoed away.

That night, when I crawled under my covers, I barely slept, restless and kicking the sheets. I heard the screaming of sirens. I cracked the window, feeling the wind's breath.

The next day at work, I kept my routine – fold, sort, hang up clothes, keep or throw out donations, smoke break, ring up Sandra Lee twice – but I felt shifty behind the register when Katie gave me change.

That night, back home, Katie moved slowly. A yellow bun bobbed on top of her head.

I joined her in the kitchen for a smoke.

She smiled. "Hey Mary, you want to go for a walk for a change?" she asked me.

"Yeah," I said. “Before it gets dark. You know these streets get rough.”

“I know,” she said.

We picked up our coats, heading outside.

With one hand, she let her bleached hair down. "Look at the moon," she said, gazing up.

It was a thin slice.

Then we headed past the stores, down the side streets, and into Mt. Powder Park. It started drizzling. Her bleached hair was stuck to the sides of her face like paint.

We climbed crooked trees and rested on the stone wall by the overlook, gazing out at the city of Welch below us. Our feet dangled there.

"This place freaks me out at times," I said. “Reminds me of things.”

"Not me. I find it peaceful," she said. "We don’t do this enough,” she said, hands around her knees. Her thick lips spread red and wide.

I shut my eyes, drinking in the pale, fresh light.

Then she jumped up.

I tried to catch her, but she was already gone, heading down the muddy hill in a wild, full run.

She waited for me by the car. It was late, but we decided to go out anyway, heading home to dress warmer.

Katie searched through my closet for something clean, deciding on an old pair of jeans and a flannel. She wrapped a black scarf around her long neck.

Quickly, I changed clothes in front of her.

Katie wandered around my room, studying my family pictures, focusing on one of Thomas and me when we were little. "You look so serious for a little girl, staring up at your brother," she said.

"I always wanted to be him," I said.

"Why?" she asked.

"Thomas lived to play. He was content with just that," I said.

Katie raised a brow. "People forget how to play."

I thought about the moon. The thin slice.

Katie chuckled. "You're always so serious," she said. "Let's get outta here."

We headed to The Crow's Nest. I looked around. No Gus.

Back at the apartment, Katie and I stumbled around the kitchen. She fell, landing on me, knocking me over. "Hey you," she said. She said it softly, in a singsong, medium tone. We passed out on the tile floor.

Time was moving slowly. Sickly hilarious and dreamy. Somewhere in the middle of the night, I felt her hot breath hit the back of my neck. Then I turned, slowly facing her, breathing in her scent – pot, booze, and patchouli. I wanted to stop the insanity, but Captain Blackeye was still on the loose. And so I turned over, sleeping on.

The next night, we headed to Welch Music Center to see Gus' band. I was used to seeing him play small clubs, frat parties, and fields. But within about a year's time, Gus was a megastar. At the show, I watched men fall for Katie. Everywhere she turned, some guy wanted to put her up on his shoulders. And it was easy. She was so light. It seemed that suddenly, everyone was looking at her. Everyone but Gus. It always seemed like Gus was looking at me, watching me, making sure I was still standing.

I didn't wait for him after the show. I had sea legs.

After the concert, Katie and I crashed at a crack house on Vine Street. Passed out people were strewn about the room, sleeping wherever their bodies fell. Katie and I ended up on a dirty mattress next to each other. It was late into the night. Three or four. I stared at the ceiling.

She looked at me and said, "What is it?"

I whispered, "Move over."

She laughed, "I would but you steal covers." Then she rolled over, coughing hard.

I coughed. "There are no covers."

On the floor, someone groaned.

Inside, I heard a voice say, *Captain Blackeye's ship is near.* The tone was baritone.

Eight.

One day, Katie packed and left, moving in with Gus' bass player.

Hiding alone in my apartment, I drank and chain-smoked. Hollow, I felt as if she took my insides with her on the move.

I woke half-drunk and hazy in some backyard on the outskirts of Welch. I had no idea what his last name was. Some naked hippie was next to me. I woke up on random floors, futons. I woke up on the ground, the street, in the gutter. I was on an endless circus ride, hanging on, spinning and spinning. I nearly stopped talking. I felt like no one heard me anyhow. Lurking in my gut, I felt an endless nausea. Way beyond Katie, something was missing. Everything was missing. I consumed countless drinks, smoked weed in random bands' vans and tried my hardest at passing out. Nights of insomnia haunted me. Days, I walked around tired and bewildered. My tolerance was too high.

Katie sent cards with paintings on the front. Cards with hearts drawn in red marker. No writing, no words but, "Iloveyou. Hey you, Iloveyou." The words ran together, dripping red across the page. She always said it like that. *Iloveyou Mary*. Hurried, strung out.

Sometimes, I stayed up for days when I got on a roll. I blamed it on Katie, but my head rushed with words, and my body was tense and tight, full of anxiety. Surely, I had bugs crawling on my skin, bugs in my hair, bugs. Lightning in my toes, my fingertips, between my eyes, lightning. I got another tattoo. The pain felt good. In the pain hour, I was distracted from the withdrawal, the shakes.

Nine.

Bored one night, I drove to The Crow's Nest. I sat alone, watching the blues band, which wasn't bad. I gulped a beer down, eyeing the drummer, and then I saw Jeffrey.

Standing in front of me, he looked thinner, older. Smoking, appearing deathly serious, he hugged me. "Good to see ya, Mare," he said.

Slurring, I backed away from him and said, "You suck at staying away."

He laughed, surprised. "I do?" he asked. Calmly, he stated, "Maybe so, but you know I couldn't ever give you what you needed. I mean, I tried over and over. I did."

"How the hell could you know what I need or needed?" I asked him.

"I know we both went through a lot of shit at the farm, and there's no going back there."

"I don't want to go back. I just want to find out the truth," I said, nearly falling off of my bar stool.

"I don't know the truth. You don't know the truth. About Thomas or Buddy. We'll never know all of the truth about anything. We'll just never know why." He stared out from behind his glasses, waiting. His lips looked full and wet.

"I don't know what to say," I said.

"Me either."

And all of it came rushing back – the fields, the horses, Big Mike and Sandra Lee, the short, black-haired, dusty girl I used to be. It all came back. "Jesus, Jeffrey, I don't even know what's real anymore," I said.

Then the band got louder.

Jeffrey yelled in my ear, "I'm real. I am so real. My eye still twitches when I think of you. Every fucking time. Come over. I have a place in Mt. Kormet, my own place. Come home with me, we can talk. We can catch up, make it new."

I went back to my beer. "I don't…want…new," I slurred in his ear. I didn't want him to know me again. To know me like that.

Jeffrey hugged me. Then he turned his back, walking away. He was still bowlegged.

"You don't know me! You don't know me now!" I yelled at him, slurring, falling off my bar stool.

He turned around once, shook his head, and left.

Somehow I made it back to my apartment in one piece, passing out on the couch. The next morning, I wondered if I was dreaming, if it had happened. I wondered if I was made of more than a filthy shadow.

An otherworldly feeling started at my chest, moving through every part of me – every vein, every inch of skin. It felt wrong, frightening. It hurt. It was hard to blink. My skin felt taught, like I'd had a facelift. Someone was trying to tell me something, and I couldn't figure out who it was, what the message was. I heard Jeffrey's voice inside me. There he was, in my head, loving me, hating me, torturing me. *Hey Mare, hey Mare, the hay, Mare.*

I wasted my money on booze. Then I sold some of Margene's jewelry. Tired and hungover became the norm. I'd had enough of drinking. I still drank. I prayed for sleep. I worked out. I had to stay thin. Then I heard Gus' voice inside of me, singing, *Please God, make Captain Blackeye go away.*

Nightmares. I woke thinking that mad people were in my room. Surely, there were dead people in there. Mean ghosts coming back for revenge. Daily, I had panic attacks. Nightly, I had night sweats. Captain Blackeye began to visit, living in the closet, hiding between my old riding breeches.

And then there were more visitors. I plastered my walls with pictures of singers. Whole walls of Singermen. I started to think that they could hear me too, that some day we would all meet, that the songs were written directly to me. And they were all in various cities, waiting for me. And Gus was the leader. I wanted Gus to sing out a reason for me to stay in his starlit room.

I tried to tell Margene. She wanted to fix things. She wanted to erase my tattoos. So she suggested laser removal places. I ignored her. To me, everything was just another scar.

I was shaky. I could not stop drinking. And just like Dr. Dad used to, when I passed out, no one could wake me. When I woke, I whispered, "Dear God, help me."

I drove to Mt. Powder Park. Nearby, a couple hugged, saying a teary goodbye. Staggering to the stone wall overlook, I sweated. I wanted to curl up there forever, lost in the wild grass, the overlook, the field, any field of green. I knew the land, the feel of it, the trees and stones and lovely grass. I thought about hills and horses, shaking there. *What has happened to me, Tomcat?* I heard thunder. The thunder inside. *Fire in the hole, Captain.*

Ten.

One Sunday, feeling hung-over, I sat with Dr. Dad in his Highland home kitchen, when I overheard Margene talking on the phone to Sandra Lee on the phone. So I drilled Margene later, finding out that Michael Griffin had moved to Violet, a small town on the East coast. Sandra Lee was worried sick about him, Margene said. Sandra Lee thought he was dealing. My ears perked up while Margene was busy ironing Dr. Dad's shirts; I stole her phone, digging through it, finding Michael's number. Katie said she would cover for me at work. I packed my car, visited Dr. Dad at Welch Hospital, and gave him a quick "goodbye." When he hugged me that day, he held on.

When I reached the outskirts of Violet, I called Michael. In a slow, sing-song voice, he said hello, giving me back road directions to his place.

I hadn't seen Michael in so long, I barely recognized him. Little Michael Griffin was no longer little. An extremely tall, wiry fellow with watery, squinty green eyes greeted me at the door. His hair was highlighted with blonde streaks, and I was struck by how much he looked like Buddy.

Michael wore nothing but baggy overalls. His skin was reddish tan. He didn't talk much, but when he did, everything he said was as sweet and smooth as a lyric.

Michael hugged me, beaming. "Maaarrrryyy!" he shouted.

"Good to see you, handsome. This is a nice place," I said, feeling his body tremble.

Michael nodded. "I'm housesitting."

"For who?" I asked him.

He ignored me and said, "You look like you need some rest. Come here."

He pointed to a makeshift bed on a tie-dyed futon in the side room.

I lay down.

Michael sat next to me, touching my shoulder. "God, you're gorgeous," he said.

I rolled my eyes. "Oh please. You need glasses like Jeffrey. How'd you end up here? Sandra Lee is worried to all hell."

"I know," he said. "I just couldn't stay in stupid Welch. People weren't shutting up about me looking like Buddy, and it was driving me insane."

"How's Jeffrey? I ran into him a while ago. It was kind of…well…a mess."

"He's all right I guess. Good as he could be. Sober I think. And acting like he's in charge of everything all the time, just like always."

I laughed. "Yeah, that's old Jeffrey for ya."

"You need to start eating, Mare," Michael said. "I mean, you're hot, but so thin."

I looked down, shrugging. "Whose place is this?" I asked him.

"Well, my boyfriend's. Met him at a horse show back in the day, and things kinda stuck. It's not the best, but it's better than being alone." His manner was mild and calm. He lit up a joint. "He still rides some, but I never do. Can't even go to the shows to watch. Just too much for me, you know?"

I nodded, taking a hit.

Grinning, Michael adjusted his overalls.

The house was strange. Very strange. Although Michael dressed like he was poor, the house was enormous and expensively decorated. Room after room, it was all plush. Seemed like his boyfriend was a wealthy, new wave hippie. Or a dealer.

While I rested, Michael made me an organic, vegan dinner. We ate in the spacious, silvery kitchen. There were too many rooms to count.

Michael glanced around. "He treats me well. He does. Well, when he's home. I have a lot of alone time, that's for sure."

"I know what you mean," I said.

"You seeing someone now, beautiful?" he asked, and the old spark came back in Michael's green eyes.

"It's complicated. Never any answers," I said.

"I hear you," Michael said, kissing my cheek.

Later, alone, buried in tie-dyed covers, I tossed and turned. I was a long way from Welch. I thought about Jeffrey. I was a long way from him too.

The next day, Michael gave me the waterfall tour of town. He had turned into the gentlest creature. And while we were driving, he began to unload. Watery-eyed, he looked at me and said, "It's awful, people looking at me like I'm a ghost. It must be even worse for you and Jeffrey. You were the ones that found Buddy there…in the hay barn."

"Every day, I see him. Every single day," I said. "Michael, you should come home."

"Probably," he said. "I think my boyfriend's getting laid every weekend at the horse shows. Really, I know it, but I don't do anything. I just sit here and smoke up and wait for him like a sad little boy." Michael rolled his eyes. "Men, I tell you."

"Come back with me. It'd be good for you to see Sandra Lee. It'd be good for her to have her baby home."

And we smoked another joint.

Michael agreed. "What the hell," he said.

Taking our time, we shopped for organic cheeses, breads, and fruit to take on the trip. When we started out, Michael drank pure juices, ate organic, and smoked weed. By the time we hit halfway, Michael started smoking cigarettes and eating cheeseburgers again.

With Michael, I felt warm, loose, chilled out. He had that way about him, making me feel like I was in the right place in the car with him. It was so hot in the car; it felt like my body might melt right into the seats. Just like the old summer days at horse shows, both of us were stinking and dripping, and we didn't care.

After a while, Michael was bare-chested, with the top of his overalls pulled down, the buckles hanging at his knees.

We switched. While he drove, I rested my head down in between the seats, and he stroked my black hair with his soft, manicured hands. Moment by moment, as we sped on, there was constant touch. All hugs and head strokes.

I breathed in his natural cologne.

At night, when he placed a hand on my head, I could almost see Griffin Farm spring up out of the road, rising and rebuilding right there in front of us. When the sun died down, and the sky was filled with pale flames, we listened to random stations, and the hum of street and tires. The stars broke out; they were magnificent, and Michael's gentle driving was hypnotic.

On the drive, we were half-naked, happy, and alive, and I hadn't had a drink in while. I felt as dry as brittle, August Scallycat field. We clung to the road wildly, drastically, welcoming the heat, so glad that we were two. We were stripped down, surviving. We were Griffin winners, moving and riding.

When we reached the outskirts of Welch, the night was thick with black air. We drove straight to Sandra Lee's place in Mt. Kormet.

I knew I was looking worn, but when I saw her, I realized she looked worse. Weathered and tired, the map lines in her face had webbed out into new territory.

"My Mary! My Michael! My baby Griffin!" she yelled, smoking, sucking it in, blowing it out.

She welcomed us inside. The place was cramped and everywhere, there was junk. Saddles, bridles, knick knacks, junk. Sandra Lee glanced around. "Pardon the mess," she said.

"She won't throw anything away," Michael whispered to me.

Sandra Lee made us sandwiches. Our plates barely fit on the kitchen table, which was full of magazines and antique figurines.

Sandra Lee picked up a ceramic doll and said, "This one's worth a pretty cent."

In my ear, Michael whispered, "She's obsessed."

"I heard that," Sandra Lee said. "Ha, ha. Most people think this stuff is trash, but I know better. I have an eye for the treasure."

"You do," I said.

Michael nibbled, nudging me hard. "Don't encourage her," he said. "My stomach kind of hurts."

"My baby, always the sicky," Sandra Lee said. "All grown up, but still the sicky."

I laughed. "True," I said.

As we went upstairs to sleep, Sandra Lee shouted after him, "You look like old Buddy more every day."

Michael winced, hurrying up the steps. "See what I mean?" he said to me. "I hear it every goddamn day."

"Yeah."

We slept in the guest room together, cuddling in a queen bed.

"Does Jeffrey ever come over?" I asked him beneath the sheets.

"He takes care of her, buys her groceries. Jeffrey always takes care of everything. You know how he is. Sandra Lee can't really function anymore, other than to go spend money she doesn't have. Big Mike cut her off long ago."

"How is Big Mike?"

"All right I guess. Heard he got married. Jeffrey and I haven't talked to him since he left. He has a tack store, and sometimes he judges at the horse shows, but he doesn't ride or teach anymore. Can't stand it."

"I miss it," I said.

"It's in the blood," Michael said, nodding.

We woke wrapped up together. We got dressed in front of each other, the way we used to change clothes in stalls or in the tack room at the barn, without even thinking about it. It didn't seem strange then, and it still didn't seem strange. It was Michael, my green-eyed brother, and it was good to hear his sing-song voice.

I sneaked out of the cluttered house before Sandra Lee woke up, heading back to my Mt. Powder apartment, calling Margene and Dr. Dad to let them know I was still alive.

But I felt restless. I needed a drink. Sleepy-eyed and dirty, I took a long shower, feeling the water cut through my dust-darkened skin. I scrubbed myself with soap. Then I did it again, uncovering layers of filth. I thought about horses, the moving beauty of riding, and the way that Jeffrey and I once rode like two twin birds, lost and gliding.

I gulped, swallowing water, wishing for sawdust, hungry for hay, grain, and wine.

Michael called the next morning. He said, "Mary, you know, instead of staying here, we could get a bottle of wine and drive forever."

I thought about it, smiling. I thought about it long and hard. After our journey home, there we were, wanting to leave again.

Michael waited on the other end, whistling.

I didn't answer.

"My head hurts," he finally said.

"Yeah, mine too," I said back. And I knew he knew that I wasn't going anywhere, that this was now our world, wherever it took us, even if that meant facing the ghosts.

Man, I was thirsty.

Eleven.

The weather was dry. Welch's seven hills were bright, solid, planted against the sky like cardboard cutouts. When I stopped at a gas station, I was quick in, quick out, hearing voices, ready to roll. As I drove up and down the hills, the scene rocked with hazy heat.

I parked along the side of the Welch Thrift building, spotting Sandra Lee's car there. To the roof, it was packed full of beads, rocks, twigs, and random junk.

Katie was working. She was a cool cucumber, gripping my hand, spitting out, "Hello Mary."

I waved at Sandra Lee, who already had a full cart. She was engrossed in studying the knick knacks behind the glass case. Finally, she creepily smiled and waved back, digging in her pockets, searching for her cigarettes, making sure they were still there.

While I was ringing her up, I had a vision of Jeffrey. His hair was thinner, and his thick hands were reaching for me. Bloody Buddy and bloody Thomas watched us. We were in the mountains. Bloody Buddy and bloody Thomas watched us. Then we headed further up the mountain. Stars and the like. Jeffrey was a jumpy, catlike creature. His expression changed into a blinkless stare. I shook him, yelling his name. He wouldn't blink or move. I held him there, outside in the awesome dark, the quiet night. Naked Buddy slipped through the forest. Naked Thomas slipped through the trees. Naked, hanging, bloody Tomcats and Buddys everywhere. I held Jeffrey. His bones jutted out, testing his skin. He was rotting. And still I held on.

When I came to, Sandra Lee handed me her money. I banged the register closed, moving out from behind the counter, walking slow and smooth, like a cheetah.

Sandra Lee stated, "Michael's gone again. No word." Her eyelids fluttered.

But I felt my horse sense kick in. I knew that he was still alive.

A few days later, when I got off of work, I called Sandra Lee to check on Michael. She invited me over. "I'm warning you though," she said. "Jeffrey's here trying to sort through all of my clutter, but come on over anyway." She used her old horse trainer voice. Not going was not an option.

It was evening. I drove up and down the hilly streets into Mt. Kormet. All around, cars were neatly parallel parked.

Sandra Lee let me in, handing me an imported beer. "Jeffrey's upstairs," she said. "He's trying to sort through my clothes and throw stuff out, but I won't let him, heh," she said.

I had the shakes. I tried to hold myself still, calm, quiet. I tried not to hear the people in my head, the visitors, the bad pirates.

Sandra Lee and I chain-smoked in the cluttered kitchen.

When Jeffrey came in, he looked dead serious. "Hi," he said.

"Hi," I said back.

"How are you, Mare?" he asked me. He didn't move for a while. Not at all. Then he squinted.

"You're not wearing your glasses," I said.

He reached in his pocket, pulling them out, sliding them on. "There, that's better," he said. "Now I can see you."

We ate spaghetti from a jar. Sandra Lee did all of the talking.

Later, Jeffrey and I sat on the front steps, smoking, watching the neighbors drive in and out, watching garage doors rise and fall.

I swore that I heard the click of a horse shoe hitting the street. I swore that I heard a whinny.

"Good to see you," he said. "But I can smell the booze, girl."

I looked down. "I gotta go," I said. I was restless.

Jeffrey nodded. "I understand. Do what you gotta do." He reached forward, hugging me. "Hell, I know what it's like. I've been there. I've been right where you are."

I swallowed. Then I left.

I barely scraped by, hanging out with street people, sleeping on floors, scrounging for drinks or drugs, crashing in random beds. Dirty and loose, I looked like a walking stick, and I was every bit as much of a wreck on the inside. Margene couldn't fix me. I stayed away from Dr. Dad and Jeffrey as much as possible. I was afraid, since they were in recovery, that they would see me drink and know my secret. Find me out.

Since I didn't have to go into Welch Thrift until noon, I usually made it. Sometimes I didn't, but for some reason, no one said anything. One day at work, when my boss sent me to the back to tag some shirts, I never returned to the register. Instead, I curled up on a bed of shoes, passing out.

I started partying at dive bars that were close so I didn't have far to drive home. I woke up in a preppy kid's bed. I woke up with a traveler. I woke up alone. It was always a surprise. I woke up shocked, checking to see if there was blood anywhere. Time after time, I ran out of men's houses with no shoes, no shirt, no bra, searching for my filthy car. Sometimes, just for fun, I'd curl up in fetal position, convinced that Captain Blackeye was coming to kill me. I thought I was suffocating. I was in a man's car. A woman's car. On the ground. At a concert. In the mud. He was coming to kill me. I woke up in woods, apartments, on floors. I starved myself. I gorged myself. I deserved to get a disease. Then I started wishing for one. Repeatedly, I was stricken with fevers. My throat was worn thin. It was maintenance, or I shook.

Sometimes cops appeared at my apartment parties, and I had to scramble to hide my stash of goods. Consumed by fear, I had to be high or drunk just to proceed through daylight. Random people started showing up at my apartment. Purple hair, piercings, tattoos of every kind. Even the walls had holes. Loneliness hung thick in the air, and by then, my only possessions were a few clothes, my car, and my shoes – too-small black high tops riddled with scratches and tears. Any other belongings I'd once had, I'd pawned, sold, or traded away. Filthy and unsafe, it became the norm to feel sick. Nearby, there was always someone strange, someone shifting on the floor, someone screaming.

Sometimes I traveled to see Gus' shows, later sleeping in my car. The music, the crowd kept me feeling half-alive. Sometimes I braided my whole head so that it wouldn't turn to knots. Showering if I were lucky, my clothes were thin and torn. My feet were blistered and swollen. I was a long way away from the well-off, horse riding, St. Genevieve Catholic schoolgirl I used to be, and I knew it.

Part Four. First Mate, Gus.

Stop. Play. Pause. Play.

One.

In the middle of the dog days, Welch was unnaturally hot and seemed even hotter when the air conditioning busted in my Olds. All around, the ground was yellow and dry. Dr. Dad was constantly pulling out the sprinklers and reminding Margene to move them. She always did. Then she moved them again and again.

Those two were finally getting along. Margene volunteered at a hospital out in Mitgard, just a few miles from where Griffin Farm used to be. She had stomachaches and trouble sleeping, but she seemed to be working through it. After going to therapy with Dr. Dad, Margene had a new slew of friends, and she smiled more, coating and coating her lips with her famous frosty orange shade. Dr. Dad was still quiet and serious, but he was steadily sober, and his hair was turning silver. Distinguished waves. Dr. Dad was still doing what he always wanted to do – saving lives and studying brains. He called me. She called me. I answered half of the time. All around me, it seemed like everyone else was growing up and getting better.

Stuck at Welch Thrift most days, trying to avoid Sandra Lee, I was searching for some kind of escape from the booze, escape from the people inside.

Closing up one night, Katie and I sweated and locked the money in the safe, deciding on a rock show to hit. Gus' band was playing at Welch Rock Festival, and Katie's Dad scrounged up some tickets for us.

When I picked her up, Katie looked slender and fine; she was quiet around me, and at times, seemingly cautious. But when we started drinking at the bar, Katie became more talkative. And the more she grew at ease, the more I felt a secret jealousy. Katie had that bleach blond hair and those thick lips, and no matter what band was playing, when Katie was in the front row, people looked at her. Not me and my black hair and boyish ways. Always Katie.

She laughed like a bird – high-pitched, loud, and hard. Her laugh bugged me to the core, but she stuck around, and that was enough.

We snaked our way through the crowd. It was packed, so packed that we held hands while we weaved. The stage lights beamed out on the crowd, blinding us.

Then Singerman Gus appeared from back stage. He was so lean, his arms and legs were mere poles covered with skin. His hair was yellow, then darker when he moved into a shadow. Then yellow again.

I hid behind a tall hipster, watching Gus until I heard the loud, high pitch of Katie's laughter.

"I swear the drummer's looking at me," she said. "Weird."

"Probably," I said back, watching wide-eyed.

I heard the sound of Gus' voice through the speakers. His medium tone, clear and solid, drifted into the room, calling out to me like a lone, hungry, cold, forgotten horse left behind in the field. Then he tripped, and his voice cracked.

The sound of Katie's squeal.

Gus laughed, singing on.

"Gus is looking at you!" Katie shouted.

"Nah, it just seems that way. He can't see me with that spotlight," I said. Curious, I walked forward. The air grew warmer. The light, brighter. I squinted. I lit a cigarette, holding it with my bad arm. I held my smoke near my side, hiding it.

Katie waved a guitar pick in my face and said, "I caught it. You want it?"

I nodded, and she slipped it into my hand. It was orange and used, with the emblem rubbed off. I shoved the pick in my pocket with one hand, tossing my smoke down, stepping on it, then stepping on it again, making sure it was out for good. I was still afraid of barn fires.

I moved to the front row, looking up.

Next to me, Katie looked bored. She might as well have been filing her nails. "I'm leaving," she announced.

"You mean now?" I asked.

"Yeah. Now. I'm gonna try and score with that guitar player from the opening band," she said. "Don't have much luck with bass players, ha, but I keep trying."

"Okay, be careful."

"I will. No worries," she said. She grabbed her purse and left, like that.

She'd find a way home. I shrugged, glancing back at Gus.

For a moment, watching Gus rage at the mic, watching him lean forward and back, his tall body rising and falling like the sun creeping up or down in a rear-view mirror, I felt free again. Then I shrank down and drank. Reaching my arm above the crowd, I felt the heat of bodies and breath. I leaned against the stage. Almost there, Gus, almost there. Stumbling, I grabbed at my dress, pulling the neck of it down, showing some collarbone.

As Gus sang, it threw my mind back to the open, untouched land I used to know. The crowd became a wild field surrounded by rolling hills. The air turned fresh and clean. The green, the yellow struck me. The herd was dancing, smacking hooves on the bar floor, running from lightning.

After the show, I scrambled out back, sneaking back near the tour buses. I was early. Dirty, drunken fans were all around. A forest made of filth, grimy shoes, scuffed boots, we stood in a line, waiting for Gus, shifting and smiling, as if waiting for some quick pony ride.

It was nearly 3 a.m., but it was still hot. Next to me, a round-faced hippie sold jewelry. She showed me her flat, glass case. "Only ten dollars apiece," she said.

I stared at the copper bracelets and silver rings in front of me. I pointed at two bracelets, ready to buy them, when I heard a loud voice boom behind me.

"I need a ring!" the voice said.

I turned around, facing the loud man's chest that was covered in a skin-tight, sweaty, blue t-shirt. I looked up to see Gus' blue eyes. The hair was yellow, yes, but the roots were darker, a soft shade of light brown. His eyes were wide-set like mine. His lips were smallish, like mine. His cheeks, high. Like mine.

"I think you should get that ring," I said, pointing at a thick, copper ring with a Thunderbird carved into it.

"That's strange," he said. He reached under his t-shirt and pulled out his necklace, a silver and turquoise Thunderbird. Then he raised his pole arms and said, "When Thunderbird came down to the earth, lightning filled the sky!" His voice was loud, but still somehow soothing.

"When *what* came down to earth?" I asked him, studying the sunken cheeks, the small lips that curved like mine. The familiar face, and his similar features comforted me. Gus had this way of helping me tune out Captain Blackeye, if only for the night.

He said, "The Thunderbird! Wind and cloud spirit. Some believe it carries a lake on its back. That's where the rain comes from. It's the guardian of the sky." He stood near me, playing with the ring on his right hand, grinning wide. "Good to see you, love."

When the Thunderbird came down, lightning filled the sky! The words played over and over in my mind. My brain's CD was skipping.

He ran a hand through his yellow hair. Pieces stuck up. Pieces stuck down, flattened. His windswept hair was the color of the dusty Griffin lounge.

I felt a headache coming on. Wiping sweat from my forehead, I felt an aching vacancy there. Surely someone had shoveled a tunnel behind my eyes. Hell, I was dizzy. One lone lightning bug flashed neon. Then a strange summer rain trickled down like a soft kiss. Mosquitoes came out to kill. I looked around, but there was nowhere to hide.

Near the end of the crowd line, Gus was signing autographs.

I was last.

When he reached me, he stared, biting his lip.

"You sounded good," I said to him.

"Thanks for coming," he said, hugging me furiously.

"I've been coming." I looked down. I looked up. I looked him in the right eye. "You don't always see me."

"That's what you think, Mary Lochmore," he said. "But you're wrong. I see you. You don't fool me. And when you're not there, you bet I notice. I can feel it in my gut. Sorry I sound so cheesy," he said, grinning. Then he reached forward, hugging me with his long arms again, pulling me close.

I felt his damp chest, his damp belly. I felt his slick arm skin on my slick arm skin, sliding there. Skin on skin, it was smooth, slippery. He smelled like rain.

Backing away from me, he said, "Listen, Mary, I always see you down there. I see you watching, and you don't watch like the others. I know you're hearing it, I mean really hearing it. I know you always have."

"I'm hearing it," I said. "You better believe it. I hear fucking everything."

He hugged me again, then leaned back, looking at me. Gus winked. "Stop worrying so much. I can see it in your face. I do it too. That's the trouble with us sensitive types. Girl, you need a vacation."

"Damn straight I do," I said, smiling.

"Hell, we both do. I'm tired as hell. This road life is wearing on me."

Suddenly, the sky shifted, and the clouds hovered above us. Then a hard rain fell, cooling things down, letting loose.

The rest of the fans ran for cover.

I stood still, opening my mouth, feeling the drops hit my tongue.

And so did Gus.

Water slid down his face. His hair turned flat and slick. He said, "Listen, I have to go do the meet and greet thing. Part of the deal, or my manager will kill me. But I'll see you soon. I'm sure of it. I know we have a weird history, but every time I see you I know we're not done. And every time I talk to you, I sound like I'm fourteen, ha. Damn, sorry."

I nodded. "I love it."

We stood in the downpour. We each held up our palms, cupping some rain into our hands.

I grinned.

Gus grinned.

Through wet lips, we both smiled. The sky shuddered, flashing yellowish white. *When Thunderbird came down, lightning filled the sky!*

That weekend, I headed to a club two hours North of Welch to see Gus. I was right on time. As I looked around the crowd, colors and words became directions, as if everything was hooked into a secret vibration. I wasn't sure, but maybe it was God. Maybe I had ESP. Everywhere, signs, whispers in my head. I couldn't shake the whispers. *Thunderbirds.*

After the show, I went back to the hotel with Gus. We lay on the bed together, resting our heads at opposite ends.

"Everything's always bad timing with us. I mean, I've got this tour going on, and I'm going to be gone 'til god knows when. It'd get old for any girl. I mean, it does. I keep trying it, but girls usually get sick of it. People think I must be all wild and getting laid every night, but really I'm just sitting in my hotel room by myself, eating Cheetos and watching the Science Channel, ha," he said, running a bare foot along my shoulder. Then he moved, sliding along the bed, switching directions. Facing me, he said, "One day it'll be just right. Ah, fuck, let's hope so, Jesus, haha."

And when we kissed, we kissed the same way. It was smooth, urgent, and I felt a certain rhythm. Lip to lip, we kept the beat.

Then he pulled back. "Bad, bad timing, Mary."

"Always," I said.

"You know I'm with someone? I mean, kind of. Only a matter of time before she gets tired of my travel and noise too. But you know I'm with someone, right?"

"I sense things," I said. "Horse sense."

He nodded, moving back around, his head at my feet, and we slept this way, at opposite ends.

The next morning, Gus kissed me goodbye and said, "Remember the Thunderbird. Lightning filled the sky."

"Lightning," I said. "I'll see ya next time around." And I left Gus, but it was only the beginning of my time spent with the monstrous, winged, legendary Thunderbird creatures.

On the way home, I looked for signs, for directions, but everything seemed to be a dead end. My secret. Dr. Dad wouldn't get the Thunderbirds at all. Like when I was little, when Thomas and I saw cloud people. No one got that either. It wasn't even worth it to try and explain.

Then I saw a Thunderbird car. I followed it for a while. Maybe the Thunderbird God was telling me where to go next. I had to follow the cars. I took many detours, listening to the universe, the cars, and the signs. I was on an adventure, yes, and the Thunderbirds would lead me back. Back to Scallycat or back to Griffin Farm. Back with Buddy or Jeffrey or Thomas. Back with Margene and Dr. Dad. Back to searching for Captain Blackeye. I wasn't giving up.

I could feel and turn the wheel. But inside, I heard this: *Follow the blue car. Still smokin' Tomcat. Dirty car. Dirty bird. See you soon, Gus. I'm sure of it. I hear you, Thunderbird. Dr. Dad moving out and moving in and cutting up heads. Dirty bird. Turn, no, straight. Stop. Rewind. Play. That license plate means stop here. Soon, love. I need to go to South, win a horse show. That's a Southern plate. I hear you. There's another one. Thunderbird. Turn left. Hurry. He's losing me.*

I drove on, following Thunderbirds, listening to the tangled web of words in my head. A puzzle, another language, a wicked calling. My brain tunnel was cavernous and sticky. More signs crept in, giving me God's directions. I focused on Thunderbird cars, billboards, license plates. Someone was trying to tell me something. Buddy or Thomas, from beyond the grave. There was something I didn't know, some secret. Some *thing* was trying to tell me something, some creature, only I couldn't figure out who or what it was. License plates became a one-way, direct phone line to God. I wondered if God had call waiting. I had to figure out what *they* were trying to tell me, whoever *they* were. Sometimes the voice was Jeffrey, Sandra Lee, Margene, Dr. Dad, or Katie. The messenger list grew longer.

Then it got worse. I began focusing on the order of words in my head, the specific letters. *Maybe I should pay attention to lowercase words. Pay attention to "bird" and not "Thunder." No, uppercase. No, nouns.* The codes came at me with a curious force, as if I were a secret detective trying to figure out where Captain Blackeye was living. Maybe he would live inside me forever.

When Margene and Dr. Dad had me over for dinner that night, I picked at my food. While they asked me about Welch Thrift, I desperately tried to decode their words, their letters, their messages. Repeatedly, I shook my head.

"Mary, you need some rest. You've got circles," Margene said.

I nodded quietly. Captain Blackeye was somewhere out there, hunting for me. He had missed me when he killed Thomas, and I knew that he was still after me. I knew it. I knew I was possessed by a pirate. I had to listen to the voices, the codes. Someone was trying to tell me where that bad pirate was. Someone was taking me on a ride through the high seas. *You're a dirty bird. Ha, ha, ha.*

Two.

Even when she was smashed, Katie dressed well, but she often caused messy scenes that involved bruises, cuts, broken lamps, and wrecked furniture. On and off, she lived with Gus' bassist, but when it got messy, she came over, and we held wild parties at my apartment. Most of the people who came were Mt. Powder locals. Most we didn't even know. There was never enough booze around to quench our heavy thirsts.

We'd oversleep, tear over to Welch Thrift to work, then start drinking until we passed out each night. We couldn't function without it, and we knew it, and we didn't care.

I avoided Dr. Dad and Margene, convincing them that I was busy working. Nights, I started writing fiction in block letters. I could whip out thirty solid pages of fiction in one night, no problem. All in scratchy caps. Mornings, I woke with strange men, strange women, strange wounds, my floor carpeted with bottles. The days went like this: crawl to work, write, drink, puke, pass out, maybe piss the bed. Sometimes I ate.

And I couldn't stop my aching mind from spinning words and thoughts at me. I made suicide plans. *Wrists, maybe. Gun? Pills?* All day long, visions of deathly plans floated inside me. I thought about Buddy. I thought about the hay barn and the rope. I thought about good pirate knots.

Katie and I were knocking down drinks somewhere deep in the hills about an hour from Welch, and she had talked me into going to one of Gus' shows because by then Katie had a reputation, and I usually just did what she said. She was always stealing cases and breaking things – chairs, bottles, basically wreaking havoc. Like Dr. Dad, I was a quiet drunk. Mostly, I remained alone and depressed, following Gus around. I figured I'd die drinking, and even Margene couldn't fix me.

That night, Gus played a mean guitar. His voice was strong. He was slick and fast when he moved across the venue floor in his usual twisted dance.

I wanted to be smooth and wild, that one tough girl beating the rest at getting his attention. But I was a one-woman chugging contest who puked in the bathroom when no one was looking. Maybe I wasn't a star like Gus, but I *was* a star at cover-ups, the queen of liquid lunch. I could chug and cheat and pass out cold, then drive my car. No one caught me. I was a monstrous, winged bird.

"When are you going to get up and dance?" Katie asked. "I'm bored."

"After the first three songs we'll go up there," I slurred.

Then we sipped more and said nothing. Those days, it was a lot of nothing – nothing to eat, nothing to say, nothing to do but drink.

Katie lifted her beer, downing it. "You want another?" she asked me.

"Yeah," I said. I'd planned on three. Just three. I already felt sick, but I needed another one. I was nervous.

Katie returned, handing me another full bottle. She said, "I think I need help, Mary. I think I have a problem, you know, with the drinking. I need some help." She sipped and sipped.

Wide-eyed, I stared at her. Then I heard Gus singing. I crawled up through the crowd, near enough so that he could see half of me. In the music zone, I lifted my chin, staring up at tall, wide-eyed Gus. Then I looked at the lights, and I couldn't see anything at all. I couldn't tell if I was standing or floating. I breathed in, breathed out. I felt like my body was slipping out from under me, sliding into space, leaving me invisible. I danced to remind myself that I was still alive.

When the song ended, I hurried back to my half-finished beer.

Katie looked me in the eye again and said, "I need some help. I can't stop drinking."

After Gus sang his guts out, something happened inside me. Suddenly, staring at Katie, it all came back – the faces of men I'd used, the hangovers, nights pissing in my bed or car, days stealing from gas stations, dark times when I pulled blades on my own skin, dirty tattoos and pregnancy tests, the cold, wet streets, and all of the loss – losing Thomas, Buddy, Griffin Farm, even Jeffrey, losing my Lochmore character, my body, my mind – these moments flashed in my brain. I envisioned Dr. Dad's scarred face nearly splitting in two when he said he was leaving Margene, Margene's face when she cried on Dr. Dad's closet floor, and her relief the day he came back. I saw my own bloated, red face, my body shuddering, me crying in my horse's stall, dreaming of cutting my wrists. I looked down at the crooked, wrecked wrist. I shook my arm, trying to fix it, to make it whole, but my hand still jutted out sideways. Mary, the broken circus freak.

I thought about the times I jerked Jeffrey around. I thought of Slick and Gus and Thunderbirds. I thought of Captain Blackeye, the lost boot, Thomas' yellow hair turning red, then dark brown, covered with blood. I thought of The Blue Men searching for Captain Blackeye and how they gave up. We all gave up. It all came back, and so did all of the liquid – anything that would make me melt into nothing,

nothing, nothing, always talking about how I was going to do something, something, something. Nothing.

I stood up. I was driving.

Katie rose, following me. She said to my back, "Gus sounded great. And he was looking at you again."

"Maybe," I muttered. "But that's just Gus. Up there, he's in his zone. He likes to shine on stage and look. Nothing really comes of it."

"Not yet," Katie said. "I just think you two have something."

"We have something all right, but I sure as hell can't figure it out."

"Maybe you're trying too hard," she said.

"Definitely," I said, gripping the wheel. Driving, I concentrated on the road. The double, the triple yellow lines. Carefully, slowly, I weaved my way back to Mt. Powder.

Katie and I sat on the couch, drinking more. It was hard to keep track of anything anymore. Nights blurred together, drink after drink, kiss after kiss, endless hours of hard-ons, hands, lips smacking, rough, misleading sex, and all of the using – using people for money, liquor, a place to stay, any place.

"It'll be all right…won't it Mary?" Katie asked softly, sipping. Usually she wanted to pass out. But that night, Katie was strangely sensitive. Her fingers brushed over my shoulder, slowly crawling. Like bugs, like worms.

"I don't know anything," I said. "Except I'm beat. And I'm sick." I heard the sounds creep in – my people, my visitors, my mind fans, my Thunderbirds. I saw yellow. All over the room, all over my skin, Katie's skin. Yellow.

We hugged, crying just to cry.

I thought about the countless men I'd been with – the faceless, bodiless, nameless men. I'd trained myself to see the parts I wanted to see, to feel the parts I wanted to feel, to hear nothing but sighs and groans and the sounds of kisses, the slobber and the breathy, drunken grunts. Mornings, I'd trained myself to run until my feet were raw.

I broke free of Katie's hold and said, "I need help too. With the drinking. I can't stop either. I'll go with you to get help."

"Really?" she asked.

"Yes," I said. Deep down inside of me, one voice howled to break free. It screamed there. It was a voice I'd stuffed for years, a voice that'd been hidden since the childhood moment when I stood behind the police line, waiting for Captain Tomcat to come home. I felt the onslaught of years of stifled screaming. I felt the lightning, the thunder inside. I gave up. Finally, I gave up.

"I can't stop," Katie said.

"Me either," I said.

"Let's drink on it and think about it tomorrow," she said.

"No," I stated.

"Why not, we've already started. C'mon, just one more drink with me," Katie pleaded.

"No. I want more than this," I said. Over and over, I heard it: *I want more.*

Katie looked at me blankly, her eyes bloodshot and dull.

She rose from the couch, fell down on the carpet, and picked herself up, laughing. She drunk-waved at me, stumbling, smacking her face against the front door, soon opening it.

My head buzzed, full of bees.

Katie turned and smiled weakly. "I'm leaving," she said, slipping out the door.

I stared at the wall. Suddenly, living wasn't about winning horse show ribbons, scoring kisses or even making it to work. It wasn't about being a big star like Gus. It wasn't about trying to find love, lost inside my lone field. It wasn't about treasure. It was about Dr. Dad being clean, this speck of hope. It was about believing in *I want more.*

I felt warmth in the place between my eyes. I saw a strange yellow light. It was soft, glowing there. *Hurry, Shorty, I'm here.*

Three.

Sober. Day One.

Withdrawal. Panic. The shaking. The cold sweats. I was busy – busy repeatedly checking door locks, convinced that someone was coming to kill me. I had wild tantrums, howled, raged, and felt the shock of a newly sober mind, one waking from a long, dark, sleep tunnel. My thoughts were too slow. Then too quick. Every inch of my skin and bones was aching for alcohol. The cravings were constant and maddening. I scratched one leg, then the other. I hugged myself, rocking. I scratched my scalp, my arms, my lips. I scratched. Bugs. Maybe I could scratch them away, scratch myself clean. I curled up on the floor mattress, praying under the twisted sheet. There was nowhere to go, nothing to do. Except for the couch covered with cigarette burns, I had sold everything else to buy liquid lunches.

Still wearing my clothes from the night before, I made my way out of my room, leaning on walls, searching for the phone. I shivered. Cold. No, hot. I gripped the phone, shivering. No, sweating.

I called Dr. Dad. "It's gotten bad," I whispered into the phone.

"What's gotten bad, honey?" he asked. That day, he didn't pick my brain much.

"The drinking," I said.

"Get to a meeting," Dr. Dad said. His voice quivered. Then he was quiet.

I hung up. I stared at the phone, stared at the wall. I couldn't think of anyone else to call, so I sipped soda, smoked, worried, drank tea, drank more tea.

Me, the couch. My body sank into the couch, then it twitched. I was freezing solid. No, I was on fire. My hair was on fire. My body was on fire. I stared at the wall and tried to forget that I was on fire.

I rose, staring at the dirty mirror. My skin. Bloated, red. My eyes. Black circles, black makeup running, streaking across my face like war paint. My face was a bruised apple. An inch of brown roots peeked out from my black hair. I heard a siren wail outside. My ears hurt. I made shadow pictures on the wall. I watched the shapes move and thought, *I'm not gonna drink today. I'm not gonna drink today. Maybe if I don't drink for the next five minutes. Yeah. Then I can have a drink. Five more minutes. Scratch that. Five seconds. Then I can have a drink. Five more seconds. One, two, three, four, five. Okay, now five more. No drinking for five more seconds.* I talked back to the cravings. I wondered how the hell Jeffrey made it through the first day.

In the evening, I went to my first meeting. I drove out to Mitgard, thinking that maybe Jeffrey went to meetings there. But inside the small room, a handful of strange old men sat in a circle, drinking coffee. Some coughed or chewed tobacco. Someone sneezed and someone said, "Bless you." No Jeffrey. No one my age at all. My head hurt. My hair hurt. I pulled it, yanking some out. The pain felt good.

I picked up a white chip from the silver-haired cowboy who was handing out coins. The white chip symbolized "surrender," the sober people told me. So I held on to it. I wanted to live or maybe I didn't. Maybe I just needed something to hold, something to grip. I looked down at my crooked wrist, feeling the edges of that chip. I felt the cool plastic. I felt.

People shook my hand and said, "Glad you're here." The big-nosed jerk next to me smelled like firewood. He gave me a blue book. Then I had two things to hold on to – a chip and a book. I listened, staring at blurry, sober faces. One man's cowboy hat reminded me of the horses, hills, and fields that were my homes before the drinking began, before liquid Mary. It was his hat that made me, for the first time that day, not think about a drink. I clung to that vision of the man in the hat. The man, the hat, hope.

When I returned home, Katie had busted into my apartment. She was working on a bottle of wine.

I told her I went to a meeting.

She laughed.

I told her I was serious. I watched her glass, studying the level of wine. I smelled it. I could almost taste it. *Maybe one taste. Just one. So close. So fucking close.* Then I scurried off to my room, sitting cross-legged on the carpet. I knelt down, praying for help, praying to the Sky God, the Thunderbird, for help, resting my forehead against the tobacco-stained, yellow wall.

I crawled out the window, slipping onto the building roof, looking out over Mt. Powder, then looking further, looking all the way out over the city of Welch. I sat there, staring up at the stars, feeling the cool wind, hearing the soft hum of street noise. I wondered if someone could die from crying. I thought I might jump off of the roof. I felt a colder wind. I felt aches and shudders and a fear beyond fear. I felt.

Four.

Sober. Day Two.

I wasn't dead yet. When I woke, I scratched and scratched myself to make sure. I hadn't had a drink for a whole day, and I wanted to celebrate with a beer. I deserved a celebration. *One beer. And maybe booze it up at The Crow's Nest. That wouldn't count.*

I knelt down, praying out loud: "Great Spirit, fuck you. I'm sick and tired of hearing this shit in my head, but please, I don't want to drink today." Then I got dressed.

Katie was in the kitchen, hungover. Her hair, moppy and ratty-blonde. She gave me a dread-look.

"You don't live here anymore. Why are you here?" I asked her.

"I have nowhere to go," she said.

I left her in the kitchen. I had no idea how I was going to make it through the next day without a drink. I put one foot down. Then the other.

We headed to work in separate cars.

That night, I went to a meeting downtown, where some guy my age looked at me and said, "You're in the right place."

"I'm feeling a lot, but at least I'm feeling," I said. I felt weak from crying. I grabbed a meal, a cookie.

Smiling people handed me phone numbers. I wondered where they were all going after the meeting, but I was too tired to find out.

When I got home, I found a soda. There was still a whole twelve pack of beer in the fridge. That wasn't nearly enough. I grabbed some tea and my soda, heading to my room to write. I felt in my pocket for my white chip. Still there. Still sober. *Damn, I hate Margene for being so clean. I hate Dr. Dad for giving up, for not finding Captain Blackeye. I hate Jeffrey for not calling me. I hate Gus for not hunting me down. I hate Thomas for losing his life. I hate Buddy for hanging. I hate horses, my body.*

I sipped my tea, drank it, and pissed. Made more tea, drank it, pissed again.

God, I hate tea. God, I hate God.

Five.
Sober. Days Three & Four.
from my journal:

GOD, IF YOU'RE THERE, I DON'T WANT TO DRINK. I FEEL CRAZY, AND I THINK I MIGHT DIE FROM CRYING. I DON'T KNOW HOW I WILL KEEP UP MY JOB. SO TIRED. GOD, I HOPE NOBODY PULLS KNIVES ON ME TODAY, INCLUDING MYSELF. I HAVE TO KEEP CHECKING THE DOOR. SOMEONE'S COMING TO KILL ME. CAPTAIN BLACKEYE IS COMING. TO SET ME ON FIRE. TO MAKE ME WALK THE PLANK. STICKS AND STONES AND MUDDY BOOTS. IF I CRAWL UNDER THE COVERS AND PULL THEM TIGHT ENOUGH AROUND ME, HE CAN'T GET ME, CAN HE? I AM SHAKING, AND I DON'T WANT HIM TO KILL ME. OR WORSE, LEAVE ME ALIVE, LEAVE ME LIKE THIS. HE'S OUT THERE AND COMING TO GET ME. I DON'T KNOW HOW PEOPLE SLEEP WITHOUT BOOZE. I DON'T KNOW HOW TO KEEP HIM FROM KILLING ME WITHOUT SOME BEER. HE DOESN'T KILL ME WHEN I DRINK BECAUSE I PASS OUT FIRST. DEAR GOD, I DON'T KNOW HOW I'M GONNA SORT THROUGH THE CLOTHES AT WELCH THRIFT, AND THAT MAKES ME MORE SCARED THAN CAPTAIN BLACKEYE COMING UP THESE STAIRS TO KILL ME.

MARY

I met a cute guy on day four. He looked like a heroin addict – tall, skinny, open-mouthed, left eye squinting, walking on air. A sick version of Gus. I was in a smoking meeting, and the junkie was the only one not smoking. I wasn't paying attention at all. I was shaking too much. And I thought about whiskey. That's what I needed – a little kick. Meetings weren't bad. I could smoke and drink coffee, and while I was there, I usually didn't want to kill myself.

I went home. I didn't think about people killing me, but I did think about hands. All those hands that'd touched me at night, all those strangers. A pile of useless, cut off hands. Gore. *Maybe I could cut myself. Maybe another piercing, a tattoo. Anything.*

God, I wanted a shot.

I went to another meeting, and the junkie wasn't there. And neither was Jeffrey. I started to wonder if maybe he'd relapsed. Maybe he wasn't going to meetings. Dry. Or he'd moved. Or he'd gotten married.

Six.

Sober. Days Five & Six.

I woke up drooling, wondering what it'd be like to put a needle in my arm. At the meeting that night, the cute addict wasn't there. I didn't want to eat too much, so I needed more coffee. I stared at the wall, thinking of Jeffrey, our first kiss on Sandra Lee's porch swing.

from my journal:

DEAR GOD, I DON'T KNOW WHAT I'LL TELL MARGENE AND DR. DAD IF I RELAPSE. I MISS SLICK. FUCK DR. DAD FOR SELLING MY HORSE. I'M NOT GONNA EAT ANYTHING BUT PRETZELS. I HAVEN'T HAD HOT FLASHES OR SHAKES ALL DAY. I DIDN'T FEEL LIKE PUKING DURING THE MEETING. BUT I DID THINK ABOUT STICKING A NEEDLE IN MY ARM. GOD, SPIRIT OF THE UNIVERSE, BUDDHA, HIGHER POWER, BIG FAT MAN IN THE SKY, OLD HORSE, WHOEVER YOU ARE, I DON'T WANT TO KILL MYSELF. EVEN THOUGH THE APARTMENT SMELLS FROM ME SMOKING TOO MUCH IN HERE, I WANT YOU TO KNOW THAT TONIGHT, I MADE SHADOW PICTURES AGAIN. THEY WERE PRETTY. ONE LOOKED LIKE A HORSESHOE FOR SURE. BUT I GUESS YOU ALREADY KNOW THAT.

MARY

Seven.

Sober. Day Seven.

Daily, sometimes twice a day if I wasn't working, I went to meetings, but I couldn't figure out why everyone was happy and smiling when I was exhausted from trying not to kill myself, fighting wicked thoughts one minute at a time.

That night, I decided to test myself. I went to see Gus play. I chain-smoked cigarettes, and I was lightheaded and hungry, watching in an anxious daze. His bass player drank three beers. *Only three. What a waste.*

Gus smiled at me as usual when he played, and he hugged me after the show, but I was a mere shell-girl. When he hugged me, it hurt.

"You look different," he said. "Something in your eyes."

He hugged me again. It hurt again. It hurt because Gus walked away, and it felt as if he took my chest with him. There I was, standing in the crowd, my head floating in the shadows, my arms reaching, my right hand weirdly shaking, jutting out sideways.

Back home, alone, I stripped and crawled out the window onto the roof again. It was so cold, my skin turned prickly, goose bumps rising up, reaching for heat. Maybe Jeffrey would love me now that I was clean. I hadn't had a beer in a week. I couldn't remember the last time I'd gone a whole week without a cold one. Then I noticed I was naked and numb. Instead of jumping, I went inside.

When I crawled under the covers, I realized it'd been two days since I thought someone was coming to kill me. Two whole days. Was that progress? Jesus, it was sad.

I slept that night. Day seven, I slept. Shuteye.

When I woke, I said hello to something greater. And I didn't think about whiskey until at least noon. The apartment was so still, so quiet. I tiptoed, feeling small. When I flipped the switch, I believed there would be light. And there was. The whole room filled up with a curious light. Shafts of ghostly, yellow light. In the smoky room, I thought I saw pieces of hay and yellow hair intertwined.

Eight.

Soon, paranoid thoughts crept in. Criminals were after me. At night, I swore I saw ghosts wandering about the house. Any day, I'd be murdered, quartered, my body strewn about the house in a bloody mess.

At that time, Katie called me, looking for a place to crash. "Just for a little while," she said, "I'm broke."

I offered up the couch, and she agreed.

Bitter and depressed, she was nursing a wicked breakup. Both of us were a sight – not eating, not showering, depressed, and weird. But at least someone was there, someone solid among my ghosts. Dr. Dad warned me about staying away from people using, but I needed Katie, and Katie needed me.

All day, all night, Katie smoked pot from a bowl she made out of an apple, which was easy to hide from the cops. If she got caught, she said she'd just eat the thing. Made sense to me. So Katie smoked up and somehow, I stayed sober. Several nights, we stretched out on the floor together, my black hair weaving into her bleach blonde locks. Katie and I stayed up all night, most nights. We stayed in. She cooked. I chewed and thought about lost horse shoes.

But Katie came out of her depression, and her mood turned kind and giving. I started to study her dark eyes, and the pictures inside them, a tunnel of dark pictures that leaked out shards of light. Late at night, we told each other long, pointless stories about homelessness, suffering and cravings, our heavens and hells. But while she spoke, I fought against my personal visitors, the voices and the sounds within me.

I dropped weight rapidly. Soon, I had to shop in the kids section at Welch Thrift. Margene constantly invited me over for dinner. Dr. Dad called more. Katie made me organic dinners, encouraging me to eat. But I hid in my room. I had to hide. Captain Blackeye was coming for me.

One day, I told Katie she needed to leave. I couldn't handle seeing her smoke pot and drink in front of me. When I told her, Katie nodded, accepting it, shutting her eyes tight, then opening them again, letting me back in, sucking me into her dark eye magnets.

"I'll always be your friend, Mary," she said. "Always. I don't care if you're drinking or not. I'll be there. You are my soul friend. Iloveyou." And then she moved out.

My body was turning into a thin letter.

I worked hard to avoid Sandra Lee at Welch Thrift. It wasn't easy. She was there shopping every day. And if there was a sale, she madly dashed around, hunting for bargains, only leaving the store for rare moments to smoke cigarettes. I knew she'd bug me about my weight, so when she arrived, I had Katie hold down the cash registers while I smoked and hid out back as much as I could, tagging the inventory.

By asking around, I found out which meetings Jeffrey went to, and I avoided those. And I knew he drove a Dodge truck, so whenever I saw one parked in a church lot, wherever the meeting was, I'd drive away. There was a lot of running round, keeping distance. I sat on the floor. I wrote on the floor. I slept on the floor.

At a year sober, when the physical withdrawal should've been long gone, I passed out at the Welch Thrift, hitting my head on an antique bicycle. I thought my skin might shed, blow away. I thought it was my fault.

With huge, lined, baggy eyes, I tried so hard to appear better. When I looked around at other newcomers in the meetings, I saw them getting healthier each day, and I couldn't understand, with all of my hard work, my consistent sobriety and prayer, why I was only feeling worse.

I saw a nutritionist. I tried vegetarian diets, vegan diets, whatever I would eat and keep down. I followed directions. I went to countless support groups, weighed and measured my food, creating specific menus for myself every morning. Every week, the nutritionist weighed me in, monitoring my losses, which is what kept happening. Losses. I couldn't stop losing. Period. And I stopped having periods.

It was a full time job keeping track of my food plan, going to meetings for alcoholism, planning menus, following directions, reading self-help books, writing and reading my writing to sponsors and friends. I tried and tried. I worked on my health and recovery all day, every day. I'd never tried so hard in my life, and it was despairing, because it seemed like the harder I tried, the worse my mind was spinning.

I shook my head. It became harder to make decisions, to wake up and proceed through a normal day. *Please God, please let me not drink. All I want is peace of mind. I'm begging.* Confused, doing all of the right things, there was still no peace. Death was a better option than my internal, insane commotion. Beat my head against a wall. Maybe that would work. My hell. An angry mob lived inside my head and heart. I felt possessed. No human could help me. God wasn't helping me. Why was I sober? Why was I alive? Fighting dizziness, I was full of fear, nibbling on measured food, petrified and disappearing.

I started to see more signs in things. Connections came at me through literature. I had trouble stopping the connections. One word would lead me to one memory, then to a movie, a horse, and so on, until I couldn't stop the thoughts. *Please, God, make it stop.*

I spent most days trying to eat, reading spiritual books, writing, painting, and listening to Gus' music. I painted and framed enormous pieces of artwork. The sounds and voices would not shut up, and the more I tried to breathe in, breathe out and slow my thoughts down, the more I tried to grasp at internal quiet, the worse the commotion rattled. A noisy torture.

Nine.

My favorite meeting was out in Mitgard on Friday nights. On the way, I passed by the land where Griffin Farm used to be. Each week, around twenty of us were crammed into a dingy, smoky, packed room. To get a nicotine buzz, all I had to do was breathe in. The clothes that I wore on those nights would never lose the smell. I fit in.

One day, Michael Griffin randomly appeared at one of these meetings. Seems he had returned home to get sober. He looked tan, ripped with muscle. Every week, I saw him there. And every time, he'd pick my entire body up, hug me, and twirl me around high off the floor. Sometimes, his strong squeezes hurt, but even in my most disturbed moments of ill thinking, Michael hugged me. His hair was back to natural, light brown, and it reached past his shoulders by then. Constantly shaking his head to move the wispy hairs out of his shiny green eyes, Michael wore nothing but overalls, t-shirts and work boots, and he looked as handsome as ever. Sober, he loved to eat, whenever and wherever, but he never told me to eat. He took me as I was – thin and ill – and never asked questions.

Michael was newly sober like me, and he started wearing a thick, infectious smile. I longed to share in his smiles, to feel the happiness there, but I only felt a gaping fear.

One day in the late fall, when I was in the thick of a depression, one growing inside me like a monstrous, black yawn, and my body was rejecting food every which way, Michael called me up to bug me.

"What are you doing?" he asked.

"Nothing. Sleeping. I'm a mess." I said. I wasn't sleeping.

"I'm coming over," he said in his smoothest voice. "Don't go anywhere."

"No, I don't want you to."

"I don't care. I'm coming over anyhow. We're going riding."

"No," I stated.

"I told you we're going," he said.

"I can't," I whined.

"Yes you can," he said, quiet and throaty, but still firm.

"I'm too weak."

"No you're not. We're going. I'm coming over. Don't move." He didn't wait for me to answer. He hung up.

Within ten minutes, I heard his truck rumble into my parking lot.

Michael picked me up, carried me out of my apartment, and put me in his passenger seat. "You are so light," he said, smiling. "Tiny."

Resting my head against his truck window, I pressed my cheek to the cold glass.

He punched my arm softly, making a dent in my thick, corduroy coat.

He drove me out to Eastern Welch, where they had some trail horses for rent.

When we pulled in, Michael shrugged. "It's Western riding, and it's not what we're used to, since we were big Griffin show jumper riders and everything, but it's better than nothing," he said.

"Better than nothing," I said, half-smiling. "I haven't ridden in years."

"Like ridin' a bicycle," he said. "Come on."

I sat there.

Michael came around to the passenger side and pulled me out of the truck, holding me in his arms, then setting me on the ground. He yelled at the man in charge, "Hey, give her a good one! This one's a rider."

The man in the hat said, "Hm."

I rode a Chestnut horse named Scout. Scout had a kind eye. For me, he stepped lightly. He walked slowly. He was used to being last in line, so we were.

In front of me, Michael trotted on his black draft horse, Dolly. Then he stopped, making sure I could keep up with him.

Scout trotted, closing the gap.

It was just the man in the hat, Michael and me. Riding beneath the trees, for a moment, I forgot how small I was.

Michael led the way, helping me navigate the trees and rocks, a path I could've never managed on my own. I was used to riding in smooth rings made of sand, and here, there was nothing but uneven ground. And I thought, in that moment, maybe Scout was the only being that could sense how I felt. I nearly grinned, holding the reins.

Michael turned around in his saddle, staring at me. "Mary, I love you like a sister."

I nodded, feeling Scout slip, then steady underneath me. I knew Michael was trying to save my life.

Not long after, Michael relapsed. Then he returned to the Mitgard Friday night meeting looking thinner and worn. For a while, it seemed that he was back on track. I put a picture of him on my fridge. The picture was taken the day we went riding, the day he carried me from scene to scene, leading me and looking back, making sure I was still there.

Nights, while I used a plate-sized scale to weigh my dinner, Michael let me stay at his ghetto apartment, giving me a key. I always showed up unannounced, often sleeping on the couch next to his massive, flea-infested Rottweilers. The dogs, the bugs, and me. When movies made me feel suicidal, Michael turned them off, and he told me stories instead.

I prayed, just for kicks. I tried hard, but my thoughts increased to speedy, anxious confusion. Crowds shouted inside my mind, and I couldn't decipher which voice to follow. I couldn't stop writing, painting, analyzing music. I couldn't stop moving. I was sure I had a heart condition. There had to be some explanation for the awful, sick feeling. My heart hurt, beating rapidly. And when it wasn't threatening to beat out of my chest, my heart ached, always letting me know that it was there. It ached. God, it ached. My ferocious organ.

On the way to Welch Thrift, I thought about running off the road.

I spent hundreds of dollars on art supplies and frames. I broke into Michael's apartment when he was out of town. I took a shower and painted a mural on the wall. A girl, yellow hair, a red sun. Then I left.

Michael left the mural there, left the red sun. But he started to sense things. He could see into me. He could see the torture going on in there. He had seen it with Buddy.

I clung to his side and together, we tried aromatherapy, light therapy, therapeutic dance, raw foods, vitamins, herbs, veganism, vegetarianism, cranial sacral therapy, massage and reflexology, among other things. If only I could find the right herb or essential oil. Maybe a scented candle, all organic clothes and detergents. I read labels carefully, trying to make my body pure.

Then Michael relapsed again. This time, he disappeared.

Overcome mentally and fading physically, I wondered why, doing all the right things – staying sober and eating organic – I felt considerably worse. I kept treating the symptoms – my weight, the anxiety, restlessness, alcoholism, depression, exhaustion, insomnia, and on and on. I found no remedy.

One day at work, I asked Katie if she knew of scented oils that would help combat racing thoughts.

Sadly, she looked at me, running slender fingers through my hair. "Mary, you have some wicked roots. You want me to come over and help you dye your hair later?"

"Sure," I said. "I'm taking a smoke break, okay?"

Katie nodded. "Take all the time you want," she said.

I picked up the phone, whispering into it. I told Dr. Dad I wanted to kill myself.

I heard him breathe heavy, yelling, "Margene! Get the hell in here. It's Mary. She needs you."

I hung up.

Codes and signs wouldn't leave me alone. Walking through the streets of downtown Welch, license plates started sending me messages. Bumper stickers gave me directions. I read into them, conjuring up meanings, acting out on whatever I uncovered. Custom license plates were the worst, toying with my head. Everything around gave me directions on where to go, what to think. I saw a picture in a coffee house. A painting of a little girl swinging. I thought, *I can go higher. I miss swinging with Thomas, the fields and him, the remains, the ruins. Jeffrey ruined me. Jeffrey was on drugs, Gus isn't but maybe he should be, what's the word, Thunderbird, what's the word. Us, her, me, you, him, her, it, I can go higher.* Then, I'd see another license plate, and another chain of thoughts would begin. Each moment was crazed, loud, voice-busy, a broken answering machine eating the tape.

At first, I thought that God sent me the messages. Then things grew much darker. I couldn't take a drink without thinking the arch of pouring water meant something. I made connections as far back as St. Genevieve's, on a one-way, hellish word train. Deep inside, twisted between other voices, a little girl screamed, *Help me. God, help me.* This small voice spiraled inside of me, then bellowed at me, until I finally gave up, silenced by despair. I could barely speak. I couldn't stop thinking long enough to express anything.

I tried to appear sane. Faking it was exhausting, but I couldn't sleep. Then I lost the tired feeling altogether. My panic attacks became more severe. The world vibrated and pulsed around me. One day, some sign led me to the local mall. Inside the mall, I stood at the top of the escalator, woozy. My heart started beating erratically, light hurt my eyes, and senses intensified, particularly my hearing. The universe pulsed around me – big, loud and out of control. A distorted circus. A mad cartoon. People were melting. The whole mall was melting. I thought that if I stepped on the escalator, I might slip inside of it. I stood at the top, waiting for the panic to subside, but the bright lights hit me like lightning. Quickly, I backed away, running out of the mall into the parking lot. The day was gray. Cars were everywhere, like spiders. I shook my head. Spiders.

I thought I was a bad, bad girl. Guilt-ridden, isolating, I thought that I wasn't working hard enough spiritually. I thought about Gus, his Thunderbirds. I wanted to catch up. So I dove into Native American spirituality, buying and reading any book I could find. I saw visions of Thunderbirds on streets, t-shirts, plates, movies, books, billboards and inside store televisions. Then I focused on Thunderbird cars again. On my days off from Welch Thrift, I drove all night, waking up in Scallycat, then driving back. I followed the cars, assuming the vehicles were leading me to a cure.

One day, I followed a T-bird to Sandra Lee's house. Wearing all black, I made sure she wasn't home. I made sure Jeffrey's truck wasn't in the driveway. Then I wandered around the yard, taking pictures of thin trees. I thought that God led me to those trees, that it was my journey to be there with those trees, however skinny they were.

Katie assumed that I was merely turning into an eccentric artist who loved road trips.

Dr. Dad told me I was quiet lately.

Margene called relentlessly, trying to lure me over for dinner.

I was quiet because I had to be. I didn't tell anyone that God talked to me directly through the cars. At first, God was soft, quiet, indirect and easy on me. Then God had a muffled voice. Then the voices stopped sounding like God. They turned clear-cut, loud, and mean.

Near the end, I drove to Sandra Lee's again. Something led me there. Maybe a car or a billboard, but I assumed this house was the location where I would soon start an enormous spiritual institution. I drove up the driveway and took pictures, ignoring that I was trespassing again, envisioning my future inside her home. I thought it was my calling. I dreamed up plans and visions of the institution I would soon create. I was to be a great, revered leader. And Sandra Lee, well, she'd just have to move out.

In notebooks, I madly scribbled plans for huge projects and visionary institutions. Mary, The Great Spiritual Leader, drew diagrams, sharing them with anyone around. I talked of my plans at work. I mentioned it to Dr. Dad, and he seemed entertained. But I didn't tell Margene. I thought I might "jinx it."

I drew up childlike architectural plans on poster-sized drawing paper, naming every employee and their positions. The building, the plans, to me, were more real than the real world itself. Everywhere, my visions. I thought about Buddy, how he dreamed of being a rock star.

Dr. Dad thought it was cute.

I explained my plans to Katie at work, spreading the word. As far as I knew, she didn't pass it on.

Sometimes during the day, I'd visit Sandra Lee's house twice, three times. I was always in the car, taking roadtrips, heading to work or Sandra Lee's, dreaming up spiritual plans. And I was the great spiritual leader, Captain Tomcat's First Mate, Shorty.

I called in sick, made up excuses, had Katie cover for me.

Billboards became messages from God. Road signs, newspaper headlines and finally, all letters turned evil, sending me messages. Vowels laughed. I hit my head with fists, subtly jerk-walking down the street. I tried hard to hold myself together, but it was hard to walk. It was hard to talk. It was hard to blink. Every movement became a concentrated effort. I was scared stiff and felt stiff, talking randomly, jumping from subject to subject with little pause for breath. I had to remind myself to brush my teeth and hair. Forget shaving. Letters swarmed inside my head like flies. It was all some sick joke. God was a joke. I hated God. God hated me. I hated me. I had to stop breathing.

At Welch Thrift one day, Sandra Lee was shopping. She pulled me aside. "Mary, I need to talk to you," she said.

"Sure what's up?" I raised a right brow.

"I know you've been coming over when I'm not home. I just haven't said anything, dear. I think it might be a good idea if you see someone. You know, a professional or something." She put an arm on my shoulder. Gently.

I cried a little.

Towering over me, Sandra Lee hugged me.

Katie handled the registers like a master.

"We've all had it rough," Sandra Lee said. "I mean look at me. Let's face it, I can't stop shopping, and Big Mike is shacked up with God knows who. Jeffrey's the only one that seems to be holding on, and even he's shaky, taking care of me and all. So don't think you're the only one, kiddo."

Her hug was loose. I felt her huge hands press into my back. I smelled her familiar scent – stale tobacco and something sweet, like the sweet feed we used to give the horses. She let me go, pulling back.

"I'm gonna start my own barn one day, a different kind of barn, and I will be the leader," I told her.

"I'm sure you will, honey. I'm sure you will," she said. Then she left to go smoke.

The rest of the day, I tagged kids' clothes, searching for shirts to fit me.

Part Five. All Hands on Deck

Press Pause.

One.

Just like in my riding days, I did whatever Sandra Lee told me to do, but my first Doctor prescribed anti-depressants alone, which made me exceedingly worse. Alone in my Mt. Powder apartment, I had a severe panic attack. My heart, my chest beat forcefully. I thought that I was having a heart attack. The whole world painfully throbbed, vibrating around me. Out of breath, nearly passing out, I called 911. Soon, a huge hand covered my face with an oxygen mask. Uniformed, white-coated people placed me on a stretcher, delivering me to my first psychiatric ward, St. Joseph Hospital.

Margene and Dr. Dad had no idea how bad I was. I was alone in the hospital. No visitors. I wasn't clearheaded enough to call anyone. I was in an ugly zone.

They tried numerous anti-depressants and anti-psychotics, many doses and kinds. Like a stubborn horse, I balked at treatment, but as thoughts worsened, I choked and swallowed pills, disgusted. Nothing put a dent in my otherworldly mood. None of the medicines remotely worked. Minute by minute, I slid further into a deep pit. A painful, horrifying head tunnel. My world.

The ward was clean and quiet. Everything was shockingly white – so vivid that it hurt my eyes. The place was bare. Except for beds and sheets, there was nothing in there. White, all around. It seemed like the moon, and I wondered if I was turning into a space creature. I thought about Buddy, how he would fit in there, his white skin blending with the white walls, white floors, white sheets. He'd be invisible.

The ward was full. One girl, W., wrote me a check for five dollars. The memo read: "from God." She sang and smiled while she wrote bad checks. From Jesus and Gandhi. Amen.

A. was a longhaired, blonde guy about my age. In a hyper manic phase, he tried his hardest to bust me out of my psychotic zone. A. would not stop talking, and it was impossible for him to stay on one topic or make sense. One minute, he wanted juice, then smokes, then pot, then coffee, then candy. Then he had to change his jeans, his shirt, his face. I didn't know his last name or where he was from, but A.'s flushed smile was steady. His lips were crimson, spreading across his face like a fresh cut. He was kind and free-spirited in his manic dance. Staring at him, I knew we were both psychic.

After a week, I heard from the Thunderbirds. I had to get out to follow them, to go wherever they might lead. I convinced the Doctors I was better, acting calm, mentioning nothing about my divine surprises. At first, the Doctors told me I had schizoaffective disorder. But right before I left, they changed the diagnosis to a "psychotic disorder not otherwise specified."

Without too much trouble, they let me out.

Free. I thought about guns. When I thought about it, I felt calm.

One month later, I ended up back at St. Joseph's psych ward. I don't remember driving there. I don't remember being picked up by an ambulance either, but somehow, I was locked up. Again.

That second stay, a legally Blind Doctor diagnosed me with bipolar disorder. Another round of medications that weren't working. Again, I convinced them that I felt better, and I was released, but they signed me up for day treatment just to make sure.

A. got out the same day, and we were in day treatment together, sneaking out whenever we could to smoke cigarettes.

One day, we skipped treatment entirely, and A. took me out in the country to spend the afternoon in a Mitgard apple orchard. I thought, I know the real me must be in here somewhere. But I could not physically feel any feelings. No joy or hate or peace. Completely dulled, life entered a peculiar state. Numbness. All the while, the messages, the litany of words and voices, beat at my brain without a break. I didn't believe I would feel again. Even watching A. pick apples and spew out manic jokes, I couldn't feel humor. I would smile, forcing my lips to move, but I couldn't feel warmth. Even the panic was gone. Everything was gone. My feelings, my senses, everything had disappeared. I was still falling, slipping, losing to Captain Blackeye.

A. tried hard to make me laugh, hanging from trees by his knees, acting goofy in the apple orchards, but eventually, he gave up. We shuffled to my car, heading back to day treatment, both of us weary from one day away from St. Joseph's.

The next day in treatment, A. suggested that I smoke pot.

I told him I was sober, and amazingly, I *still was* sober.

He laughed and looked at me weird, grabbing my arm, then letting go.

"I'm serious," I said.

"I know," he said, giving me a hug.

I never saw him again.

Upon discharge from day treatment, I was diagnosed with "bipolar disorder with psychotic features."

This time, the Blind Doctor called Margene and Dr. Dad. They had no idea how bad I was until they saw me, so thin and petrified that my eyes sank into my skull. They didn't *ask* me if I wanted to move home for a while. Instead, they made me.

They packed for me; I was too weak to lift and move clothes. I felt small, fragile, and useless. I had trouble getting up, much less try to carry boxes.

Driving me to their Highland home, in the car, we didn't speak. I stared out the window. When we arrived, I hit the couch, staring at the ceiling. All I thought about, in between the relentless thoughts, was how I might manage to break free from Margene and kill myself. I made detailed, gruesome plans.

By then, I'd swung completely into a comatose-type depression, and I was still having psychotic symptoms – messages, grandiose thinking, racing thoughts and referential thinking. Signs, signs, signs. There was no relief from my hurricane of thoughts. I hated music, writing, sex, breathing, horses, life. All I felt was sinking despair and weighted, tender muscles. I was so sore and stiff, I could barely walk.

Dr. Dad found me a new Doctor – one of his Welch Hospital buddies was a bipolar specialist. Trying medicine after medicine, I endured countless side effects, but no relief. Even when people talked directly to me, I pictured myself hanging, lifeless. I wished for a slashed throat.

I slept in bed with Margene. Dr. Dad slept in the guest room. They had me on 24-hour suicide watch. I could barely talk or walk. Reading was too difficult, frightening. Watching TV or movies was unbearable, too much information for my overcrowded brain. I envisioned my body falling from Welch bridges. Several times, I eluded Margene, stole her latest SUV and drove to the river. Pulling over once, I almost had the guts to jump.

Then Margene went on vacation with Sandra Lee. Dr. Dad had me under watch most of the time, but one day, while he was at work, I found the spare key to Margene's SUV, went in the garage, turned on the motor and breathed in carbon monoxide. Waiting, I messed with the radio. I couldn't find a good song. Groggy, I was pissed. My suicide was taking too long.

The next thing I remember: another oxygen mask. My body was strapped down on a stretcher in the emergency room. Then some specters, some white-coated men, transported me to the psych unit, where I gripped my familiar hospital duffel bag and a stuffed horse. My admission diagnosis was "bipolar disorder, depressed. Depression & suicidal ideation, anxious, isolation, past history of alcohol dependency."

I was there for a little over a week. Out for two days, then back in.

Talking the Doctors into giving me a pass, Margene and Dr. Dad busted me out one evening, taking me out to dinner at some Mt. Powder artsy restaurant. I sat and sulked at the restaurant table, sinking in my seat, spaced out like a robot, unable to speak.

Margene ordered food for me.

I couldn't sit still. Instead, I wandered through the restaurant. I never made it back to the table.

Dr. Dad had to hunt me down. He found me in the men's bathroom, curled up on the floor. He handed me a cigarette, and I took it, lighting up, staring at the tiles.

"You will get better, Mary. You have to believe it," he said, sitting on the floor with me. He put an arm around my shoulder.

I stared up at his silvery hair. I studied his lightning scar, his forked lip. "I don't believe in anything anymore," I said. I tried to cry, but I couldn't. "It's gotten bad. It's gotten bad, Dad."

Even though he'd quit for years, Dr. Dad lit one up, smoking with me. Together, we smoked in the men's room, breathing in and breathing out.

"I won't let you give up," he said, looking me in the eye. His eyes looked so blue that night, as blue and round as a cartoon owl.

"You have Thomas' eyes," I said.

He winced, nodding. "Tomcat would be pulling for you too," he said.

I agreed.

Dr. Dad pulled me off of the floor, whispering, "Come on, let's go before Margene breaks down the door and wrestles us both." He held my crooked arm while we walked back to the table. Slowly. He held my arm all through the rest of the dinner. Even when I didn't eat, he held on. Even when I didn't respond to the waiter, he held on. And when dinner was over, Dr. Dad led me to the car. He held on.

In the car, Margene was driving. The blues hour was on.

I listened to the music, trying to ignore the messages the lyrics were sending me, trying to just feel it.

Margene started humming.

Dr. Dad started humming.

I felt a gurgle in my throat. It was something.

Dr. Dad reached back, touching my right arm, the one with the hospital bracelet wrapped around my bent wrist. "I wish I could take it away from you. Your Mom and I, we won't stop until you're better."

I let him stroke my wrecked wrist.

In slow motion, Dr. Dad led me from the car back inside the hospital, back to the unit, back to my bleached room. He hugged me.

Margene hugged me, wrapping an arm around my scarred stomach.

I chewed at the skin around my fingernails.

The next day, Sandra Lee visited. She hung out near the side of my bed, shifting in her shoes, leaning from one thin, long leg to another. Her dark grayish hair swung at her cheeks.

Buried under the sheets, freezing and fragile, I asked her, "I feel like I am made of glass. Am I see-through?

"No, you're as solid as they come. You're a Griffin rider. You're a winner," she said, stroking my ratty black hair. Moving closer, she asked, "Do you want me to tell Jeffrey you're here?"

I told myself to blink. My lips wouldn't form words. My arms couldn't reach to give her a hug. I mouthed, "No," moving my head back and forth, letting it fall to the right side.

Sandra Lee stood still and strong, leaning against the bed, combing my hair with her fingers, making my horse tail smooth. "Hey, listen, being on the right side of the dirt makes it a good day," she said.

Two.

Flat on my back, on the stretcher, I was trapped. Gently, the bed moved, rolling forward. The Tall Male Nurse pushed me from behind. He was quiet at first. I was glad he stepped softly. My ears were on fire with sound – even the slightest whispers turned into harsh noise.

The Nurse paused for a moment, fiddling with something. He rustled. The bed stopped cold.

I stretched my neck, glancing out the hospital room window. Early morning, it was barely light out, from what I could see. I looked only for a moment, but I caught a quick vision of the outside sky, a sky that was fading from black to gray. The window frame was a thin rectangle filled in by thick, dull, shatterproof glass. Then my neck felt weak, snapping back, cracking like kindling. My head fell, weighted down and loosely attached. I thought, *Maybe I could try it again? Hold my head up. Maybe I could see outside, be outside? One, two, lift it. My head.* Then, from somewhere deep in my mind, I heard this voice: *You're never getting out, Mary. Never.* The tone was deep, guttural. Captain Blackeye. Then I heard this: *Hang on, dancer. Thanks for coming to the show.* The tone was medium, a male tenor. Like Gus.

As the Tall Male Nurse pushed me out of my room, I moved my eyes right, left, then up, staring at the ceiling. My eyeballs worked. Easily, I could control them. I rolled them, my eyes. But I had trouble with the lids, particularly the shuttings. Open too long, my eyes hurt, dried out. The sting. I managed a squint. *Better.* I squinted at the stark, white ceiling. Blinding, ghostly, blurry, painful white. I told my lids to shut, and they did.

Tucked in tight, strapped down by two layers of thin sheets, I heard the Tall Male Nurse say he didn't want me to fall. *Or escape,* I thought. My body sank into the cushion, and I imagined the dent my slight weight would leave behind. I wondered, if I tried hard enough, could I sink through the bed, turn invisible and slip away, blending into the ground?

I opened my eyes again, peering at the place my chest would be, if it weren't for the sheets. My body was hidden, unmoving under the tight cloth that covered me from my toes to my chin. There, at my neck, the crisp, starched sheets hugged my throat like a pale necklace, a fat, hemmed choker. My arms and legs were heavy, cemented to the bed, refusing to move. Even the slightest wriggle or twitch was difficult, complex. It wasn't worth it to try. Besides, there was no reason for motion, nowhere to go.

But my damn nose itched. *Okay, now move the right hand. Pick it up. Scratch the nose.* Twice, I told myself this. No response came from arms or fingers. While I struggled to move, my skin felt tense, stretching and pulling around my being. Severe, taut, rigid. Any moment, I thought my bones might protest their lock-down home inside me, threatening to tear through my useless, thin skin mask, bloodily breaking free, rupturing the surface of me, killing all cells and edges. I thought my bones might escape me to rest inside another body, a true, functioning body that was running on the right mind time, operating quickly, giving out grips, sips, swaggers, and a thousand different grins. I thought about how people took grimaces, raised brows, and nose blows for granted. I wished for one grin. Nothing.

Each organ protested my frame. My stomach ached, empty and sore. My lungs felt fragile, moving with effort, no more than kid balloons, leaking air. More than breathing, I shivered.

Beneath me, the stretcher wheels rolled, squeaked, and moaned. One wheel thumped like a broken grocery cart. The simplest sounds – the busted wheel, the occasional rattle of the metal bed frame – echoed in my head, bellowing into my eardrums, joining the rest of the sounds in my head – from dull, garbled, baritone words to the high-pitched screaming. It was hard to tell the difference between the outside racket and my people inside, the crowd in my mind.

I was on my way down. On my way to another white room, where I'd get my first treatment. ECT, Electro convulsive therapy, the real name for shock treatments. No one was fooling me.

The day before, the Tall Male Nurse had shown me the video about ECTs. While he pressed "Play," he acted friendly, smiley, then sat on the bed with me like old times. Muscle-cut and dark, he was. A looker. At the end of the video, he peered down at me, saying, "You all right? You all right...in there?"

I nodded. I didn't know what else to do. I was twenty years old, and he was giving me a lesson in the course called ECT 101. Then I knew what to say. I moved my lips. I asked him, "If I have...treatments...will I still…have to take… medications…later?"

The Nurse looked down, twitching his huge, white shoes.

I knew that despite all of his smiling and pats on my back, even he wasn't sure if the treatments would work. I thought maybe I was one of "those," a hopeless cause, a chronically mentally ill patient, one who would never come back to the living. It wasn't spoken, but he knew and I knew that these treatments were a last resort.

The Tall Male Nurse pushed me further down the hall. Earlier, I'd caught a glimpse of his hands, his large forearms, his flawless, butter-shiny, brown skin. While he wheeled me through back hospital corridors, I tried rolling my eyes back in my head to see him again, but all I could see were the lights above me, the lights that burned into my sensitive eyes. I saw spots.

The Nurse cheerily said, "Well, hey down there, it looks like you're waking up a bit."

I tried to talk back. I pursed my lips. I chewed. I raised my right eyebrow. I tried to raise the left. I clenched my teeth. I moved the bottom lip and breathed in, but words weren't working. I made myself blink twice, which meant, "I'm here."

He started humming. His humming pained my ears, pissing me off, but I was a good girl. Mute. While he wheeled me through the endless halls, I watched the lights flash above me, counting each one. *One, two, three. Where was I? One, two...please, God, let my arms and legs work. Let me sit up. Let me fall off of this stretcher. Let me slide into the tile, turning into a square, a patch of flat skin, flat body, flat flesh. Let something fall. Crush me and this bed. Let me turn into a tile line, blending into the floor. No one but the spiders would see me then, would they, God? Please take my life. Please let this be over. I am a barn spider.*

I was so depressed that even my speech was a slurred effort. I had to consciously order my arms and legs to work. *Okay, move finger. I want to die. It hurts. Move thumb. Help me. It hurts.* In my head, I talked back to the relentless thoughts. *Shut up. You are not real. I deserve real. I deserve real love.* Then I heard this voice: *Mary, we got you. You're not getting out, ever. Die.* It repeated over and over, like an evil tape recorder with no "Stop" button. Captain Blackeye had a telephone line connected to my ear. I understood why people held a handgun to the head, pulling the trigger. Anything was better than my open-eyed, comatose depression. I lived and moved to the rhythm of heartbreaking, guilt-ridden, sometimes graphically violent mantras in my mind: *Shorty, we know where you are. Watch for us. Arrr. Captain Blackeye and his men are coming for you. You're never getting out of here. You, fat, dirty...you should hang yourself before we do. Ha, ha, ha.*

Wheeled around corner after corner, I watched the lights again. I counted, *One, two, wait, slow down.* Then I lost track and gave up, listening to the voices, none of which came from friends. *What's the word, Thunderbird?*

We entered the elevator. Inside the electric box, the Tall Male Nurse was still humming, and in the closed space, the sound pummeled at my harshly sharp ears. Again, I told my hands to move, to pull out from under the covers, to reach up and cup my ears, shutting out the droning sound. But my palms pressed against the bed, flat and useless. I thought about moving my fingers. I managed a pointer finger twitch. Then I gave up, letting the sound intensify, vibrating inside me. Between the lights and the intense sound, even my senses became the enemy, and there was no escape.

I muttered, "I've felt like this…for years…when is it going to get better?"

The Tall Male Nurse touched my shoulder, reassuring me. He said, "Many people have ECTs. It's a common treatment."

I envisioned my body trapped inside a can of black paint. Captain Blackeye was holding me down. I was drowning, near death, choking on tar-thick fumes, my body charred, burning alive, refusing to die.

The elevator moved. I wanted to sit up, to study the numbers and floors, but I couldn't. I wanted to piss, but I couldn't. I wanted to breathe slower, but I was panting. Stuck open, my eyes were desert dry. I forced my lids shut, concentrating on blinking. I wanted to say, *I want out of here so I can kill myself,* but I was silent.

The Nurse sniffled and stopped humming.

I counted lights again. Wicked, never-ending, those lights. I was freezing. I was so awake. I felt every hair on my arms and legs. I felt the hairs under my armpits, scratching there. Dr. Dad had thrown out my razor. Every hair moved under the sheets. I was half-dead and hairy, but still conscious.

The halls smelled like bleach. The smell entered my nose and stayed there. I tasted the metallic, bitter air, an awful detergent. Each of my senses was magnified, as if I were trapped in a movie theater, stuck in the moment before the previews ended, before the senses adapted to the rush of blaring visions and music. Everywhere, noise.

Blinking became too difficult. I shut my eyes. When I shut them, I heard this: *Mary, we got you. Marooned here, you are, matey. Ha, ha, ha.* It was a familiar voice, among the many, a guttural, angry one. A mean, sick horse. I opened my eyes again, hoping the words would go away, but they didn't. Instead, someone cackled at me the whole rest of the way to the pre-ECT area, a place that was full of patients, blinding white, and dead quiet.

I squeezed my eyes. I tried for one tear. Nothing.

The Tall Male Nurse wheeled my stretcher into its parking place. "I'm leaving you now," he said, "but they'll take good care of you here. I know they will." Then, in a black and white blur, he left.

Here, the Anesthesiologist mumbled some words to me. He smelled sweet, like Sandra Lee's cookies. His hair and eyes were black. His skin was as milky and pale as whipping cream. When he smiled, his lips spread across his face, sensuous and thick, wormy.

"You have all of your jewelry out?" he asked me.

I nodded, "yes." He was one of the "normal people," responsive and quick, able to lick lips and smile. I had two labels for people in the hospital – one, "the living." Two, "the suffering." Or, "us."

Then a Faceless Nurse came in, hooking me up to the IV. I was used to needles by then, and I didn't flinch. Rather, I welcomed the pain. The Faceless Nurse placed suctions all over my chest, sticking the tiny circles to my skin. My chest was made of saucers. Tubes were everywhere, monitoring my vitals. I wanted to ask the nurse if the treatments would hurt. I wanted to ask her if she thought it would work. I was afraid I'd end up as a wandering derelict, waving my arms, causing scenes on a busy street. Or I'd end up living in the woods, smelling like feces and grime, later resting somewhere, anywhere, the gutter.

The Doctor came by to visit. He was soap opera handsome. I remember thinking, *I wish I could write so I could write about him. Maybe someday I'll be able to read again. Talk. Ride horses. Maybe. God, if you take me right now, I'll make you a deal. I'll come back as someone better. I'll save Thomas. I'll save Buddy. I'll do it right. Dear God, please.*

The Handsome Doctor explained the procedure, but I didn't hear him. Instead, I stared up at the lights. I was a horse. I was a pirate girl, Thomas' First Mate, Shorty. No one could touch me. I was not in the hospital. I was not about to get ECTs. Instead I was a Thunderbird, a monstrous winged creature, a legend flying somewhere, out in some vast, newly gray sky.

I screamed for Thomas.

Then they put me out and gave me the juice.

Three.

After my first ECT treatment, after they removed the vital-monitoring suctions on my chest, my skin was covered with red rings; it appeared that I had a severe case of ringworm. I closed my blue gown, covering it up.

The Tall Male Nurse took me back up to floor ten. He pushed me quicker than before. It seemed that I was flying through the halls, on an eerie stretcher ride back up, up, up. I counted the ceiling lights while we flew. My first treatment was over, and I didn't feel any different. Just spacey.

"You might lose some memory," he said softly.

But I remembered every voice, both inside and outside of my head. *Mary, we got you. We got you.* They were all still there.

There I was, back in my quiet room. At last, my quiet room, alone again in bed. Every forty minutes, someone came in to call me by my name, to make sure I was responding, to make sure I was alive. Several times, Nurses urged me to go to groups, but I stayed in bed, staring at my crooked wrist. It was hard to know where my hands left off, turning into fingers.

The Handsome Doctor came in. He asked, "Are you having any suicidal thoughts?"

I looked at him. He was one of the living. I remembered what another Doctor had told me: "You must wade through this storm." I wondered when the storm would cease. *What' s the word, Thunderbird?*

Again, the Handsome Doctor asked me how my thoughts were. Then he spoke a few paragraphs about med changes. He repeated, "Are you having suicidal thoughts today?"

I felt something wet under my eye. A tear. I said, "No." And I knew, by the way he ran his hand through his silver-brown wavy hair, that he didn't believe me. I wasn't going anywhere.

He took some notes. Then, in a flash of white, the Handsome Doctor left.

I stared at my curious fingers, moving one at a time. Why did it have to be so cold? Or maybe it wasn't cold at all. Maybe someone turned off my body heat. Or maybe I was too thin to feel the slightest warmth. *Go ahead. Burn me.*

I tried to sleep. Sleep didn't work. There were too many messages to decipher, too many words in my brain. But I reminded myself I was lucky. The others were worse. Damn, they were bad off. Damn, it was cold, colder still at each end of the hall. Again, I piled thin, white sheets on my thin, white skin, making it into some kind of borrowed cocoon. *And still I shiver. All I do is shiver. More than eating, I shiver. More than sleeping, I shiver. I shiver more than breathing.*

Over and over, I opened the same magazine. I tried to read the same page. I thought, *Now, I will try to read the same page.* Then I thought, *I read to try the same page. I read the same to try the page.* It was no use. *I try another page. Another I page try.* I couldn't concentrate long enough to put a sentence or thought together. And the pages I did read, they came into my brain out of order, disguised as confusing anagrams and puzzles. The people inside me were messing with my reading again. It was despairing and maddening. I couldn't read better than a first grader. I shut the magazine. I opened it again. The sentence read: "What is the best body for your age?" I read it once. Then I saw, *hat is the OD for you, g.* Then words sent me messages in code. *H is the best for you. His body four. He overdosed.* Then I racked my brain, trying to figure out who overdosed. Maybe Michael Griffin.

Reading was impossible.

E. passed by my door while I was trying to read. I looked up at him, because he was cute with large features – large brows, large eyes, large lips. E. was about my age, but he had an old man's gut. All day long, he paced the floors. He had deep dark, brown eyes. Rabbit holes. *If it weren't so cold out in the halls, and if my heavy legs would work, I'd walk with him.* Mostly, his walk slipped into a staggering shuffle. Really, it was no more than a creep. *Maybe I could keep up. Maybe I could reach the floor with my feet.* Then I heard, *Crazy Mary, we got you. Anyday, you're walkin' the plank. Surrender.*

The Tall Male Nurse looked in on me, doing rounds, making sure I wasn't bleeding. He told me it was time to take my medicine.

I choked it down.

When he left, I pulled my aching body out of the covers. Put one foot down. Then the other. Shuffling like E., I made it to The Recreation Room. One foot at a time. It was right across the hall. Ten steps. It took me ten minutes. Scattered about the Rec Room, there was a guitar with no strings, board games with missing pieces, twenty movies I'd seen so many times, I knew the words. I knew the gestures. I heard the messages, the secret messages coming from each twitch or blink.

S., the lawyer, played chess with E. There were no queens, so I wasn't sure who was going to win that way. S. seemed so calm, like me. Eerie, the kind of calm that made me wonder what horrible mess was on the inside. I liked skinny S., and he liked me. He knew Dr. Dad. That somehow made us buddies. I understood his quiet diet.

I told him I'd felt calm when I tried to kill myself, and he agreed. There I was on a quiet trip. I'd go wherever it would lead. It felt so right. It felt like an end to the shakes, the racing thoughts, the voices, the night sweats, the fear, God, fear. No more.

I'd wanted to end it. So did S. He had the bandages on his arms to prove it. My suicide attempt failed and so did his, and I could tell he felt utterly disappointed, like me. I watched them play chess, and I started talking back to my bad thoughts. *Stop it, you are not real. I deserve real. I deserve real love.*

Then Margene showed up, and we played Uno. Around us, people were screaming and yelling. One patient thought he was God. Another thought she was called to ride her bicycle across the world, and she didn't even own a bike. Another thought the spirits told him he'd be the next President. I prayed that the ECTs would shock me back warm, back with the living. I prayed to be able to read and write again. I prayed to see horses, cats, to feel hard kisses, to feel a hand running over my stomach scars in the morning, to feel a good, long stretch. To feel my heart again. Or pain. Anything beating.

Margene and I couldn't find the threes. She thought she had a full deck, but they were missing, those tricky threes. No one could find the threes. I felt weird, missing threes. God, I missed them. I missed missing. We never found them, the threes.

There I was, back in my quiet room. At last, back alone in bed. The threes were bugging me. I figured there was a planet with missing socks, guitar strings, threes, and razors. I was still missing those threes. And then I realized that I was missing something. Threes. Those damn glorious threes. My God, I was feeling something.

Four.

Neatly ordered, the Arts and Crafts Room was a tight fit for the sick ones. Us. That summer, the ward was crowded, and all around me, the others were playing with paper. We were a bunch of depressed, manic, and psychotic patients crammed into a walk-in-closet-sized space, making preschoolish projects. Mostly with magazines and glue. Nothing sharp. Often, we used our fingers to tear pages apart. Every now and then, some lucky ones were allowed to use safety scissors, the kind with serrated edges – plastic, dull teeth, hard to maneuver.

The Yellow-haired Arts and Crafts Nurse appeared to me as a blurry-edged being, a shadow, a TV with bad reception. Mostly, I saw the back of her head. Her face was another face among the faces. But her high-pitched voice was startlingly clear, a voice that flew out of her mouth, hitting the ceiling, bouncing off of the room's white walls, and landing in my ears, rattling my head, purring inside of me, then hissing, as if I had a snake trapped in there, upstairs, behind my eyes.

I struggled to cut and paste amidst the Nurse's echoing voice, and the low murmur of voices around me – the nonsensical chattering, the mumblings, and the occasional groan or yelp. But overall, like me, the others concentrated quietly on the task at hand – a collage on construction paper. We were supposed to make two that day. One collage for the present and one for the future; that is, we had to show the staff where we wanted to be, and how we wanted to feel once we made it to the outside.

I knew that "Arts and Crafts" was a fancy name for the staff's opportunity to watch me. Each day in the ward, moment by moment, Nurses and Doctors measured my moods, checking for progress, noting my motor skills, weighing my ups and downs, making notes on my chart. It seemed that every time I looked up, someone was watching, taking notes.

I tried to fake it, but I kept dropping the preschool scissors until I finally gave up, using my hands, tearing my magazine to pieces. When the Yellow-haired Nurse glanced over, I made myself sit still and smile.

Day two of Arts and Crafts, we worked with leather. We were supposed to make belts, belts that we weren't allowed to take with us until we left, due to the possible risk of hangings and chokings. We were supposed to stamp patterns into the leather. I talked back to the sounds in my head: *Shut up, I'm busy.* Then I thought, *Maybe I can make a belt. I'll try.* All I had to do was stamp and press, stamp and press. But I searched through the bins of blank belts, pulling them out one at a time. Hundreds of belts. I pulled each one out, holding it up to the light, checking the length, trying some on. But there wasn't a belt small enough for me. I searched and searched through the tangled stack, but no luck. So I settled on the smallest one I could find. I stamped crooked flowers and random letters into a belt I would never wear. I breathed in, breathed out. The room smelled like leather, like horses.

I had to ask the Yellow Nurse if she had any smaller belts. I held mine up and said, "Do...you...have more? Doesn't fit."

The Yellow Nurse glanced at me, smiled all teeth, and shook her head "no." Then she looked down, making notes.

I hated the flowered, nonsense-lettered belt, but I put it on, thinking that maybe I could sneak out of there wearing it. I pictured my lifeless body hanging from some height, my neck wrapped in leather flowers, my mouth open and ugly, my body jerking, then still.

The Yellow Nurse took notes. Her face looked flat, like a pancake with features.

I didn't want to cause a scene about those belts. Those fucking belts.

The Yellow Nurse told me to hand over the belt.

I did, reluctantly.

The next day, we made decoupage vases. I worked hard, pasting magazine faces to the vase, cementing them there with a clear, sticky cover, turning the curved surface into a vase full of frozen people, faces trapped under the sticky, gummy glue. The trapped paper people stared back at me. The faces were frozen in time, frozen in gestures, like me. The faces called out to me, speaking to me. *You're stuck too. You're in here, with us.* I talked back to them. I tried to fight Captain Blackeye, the evil. Then I was surprised that I felt like fighting. *Leave me alone. You are not real.* But the vase faces stared at me. And even though it was my creation, it seemed that everything I touched – everything inanimate – was alive, speaking, laughing. Mutiny.

When my vase was nearly done, it was time to fill out an evaluation form. The Yellow Nurse wanted us to recognize our progress. I thought that any minute, someone might turn on cartoons and hand me some cookies and juice. Force me to take a nap. Despite the Nurses' efforts, I was barely functioning at toddler stage.

I filled out the evaluation, judging my skills at making the decoupage vase:

Occupational Therapy
Work/Task Skills Group

St. Joseph Hospital, Department of Psychiatry

Self-Evaluation

Name: MARY LOCHMORE

1. What are your goals for the Work/Task Skills Group?

TO MAKE A VASE, A DECOUPAGE VASE.

2. How would you rate your performance on this activity?

Very poor Very Good

1 2 3 4 5

THE NUMBERS LOOK THE SAME, WHAT DOES IT MATTER. I AM SHARK BAIT.

3. If you would do the activity again, what would you do differently and why?

I WOULD USE DIFFERENT PAPER AND SMALLER PIECES. MY HAND HURTS. SWORD FIGHT.

4. What were your thoughts while working on this activity?

WHEN IS THIS OVER. MUTINY.

5. List distortions in your thoughts, if any.

NO ANSWER.

6. What rational responses can you substitute?

WHEN CAN I BEGIN A NEW PROJECT, SOMETHING MORE CHALLENGING. SOMETHING WITH THREES. WE COULDN'T FIND THE THREES. WHO CAN PLAY UNO WITHOUT THE THREES.

7. How does this activity apply to everyday life?

LIFE IS A SERIES OF PIECES THAT NEED TO BE GLUED TOGETHER CAREFULLY. THERE'S AN ANSWER IN THE PATTERN. I THINK. FUCK.

8. What will be your goal for yourself while working on an activity?

MY GOAL WILL BE TO BE PATIENT WITH MYSELF, ONE PIECE AT A TIME. MY GOAL WILL BE TO BE MYSELF, PATIENT, A TIME AT ONE PIECE.
MY PIECE WILL BE TO GOAL MYSELF, BE PATIENT AT A TIME.
MY ONE PIECE WILL BE THE GOAL. ONE WILL, ONE TIME PIECE, ONE.
ME TATOO IT MYSELF ON PIC ATE. I ATE TOO MUCH. I AM ILL TOMCAT.

Thank You.

Five.

The smoke was thick, nearly solid. The box, the room, was gray-yellow, stained by nicotine. I aimed for the small hole on the side of the wall – our community lighter. Confiscated by the staff, real lighters were considered weapons. Not for lighting. For burning.

"Inside the smoking room, someone is talking to me," I sang. I sang instead of talking. It seemed easier. I could hear Gus in my head. He was helping me sing.

Around me, other shadows and ghosts hummed along. We were smoke people, made of thin vapor. We were in the vapor zone.

When I sat down on the bench, I made out one face. S. was in there. He looked up and said, "Thank you...for singing."

We smoked quickly, puffing in and out before the Nurses came back. I felt sick, breathing in the second hand and first hand, but I smoked on anyway. Everywhere, people complained about rotten, splitting headaches.

Some girl in the corner was crying a little. Smoking and crying, dropping ashes on her hospital gown. Her wrists were bandaged like S. She was a skeleton girl. All I could see clearly were her tiny feet, her slipper socks. Makeshift psych ward slippers, the soles half-black from floor grime.

S. said, "You better stop singing and start smoking before they come get us."

"Okay," I said. In my head, I heard, *What's the word, Thunderbird, what's the word? You're never getting out of here.* I sang, "Thunderbird in the smoking room."

The skeleton girl in the corner stopped crying abruptly. She asked, "You hear them too?"

Six.

I had a hold of my stuffed horse by the leg. I sat in the bed, hanging on to the animal, too weak to grip its whole body. I called out to the Nurse, begging her for more sheets. I thought about going to the Rec Room to watch T.V., but I was still afraid of the T.V., and all of the sounds and messages inside that wicked box. So I stayed in bed.

The Nurse told me the good news. Since I moved up a few levels, I was allowed to go with the group up to the roof. Packed in, we rode the elevator up. We were quiet patients, awaiting our turn at fresh air. When we reached the top floor, the elevator doors opened, and we followed the Nurse single file, marching through the corridors one by one, ever so gently, ever so slowly, reaching the outside. There, the light hit my eyes, forcing me to concentrate on blinking.

A rooftop playground spread out before us. Some patients remained still, squinting at the light, unmoving. Others threw a flat basketball around. I stood in the open air, staring at the barbed wire fence lining the entire square, rooftop area. I thought that fence was there to test us. Like I could be the one patient brave enough to get down and dirty and bloody and climb the fence and jump. Over the edge. Down below. Some patients played hopscotch or catch. I thought about jumping. I wondered what my fingers would look like with barbed wire sticking out of them instead of the fingernails. Then everything I touched would be sliced open.

About fifteen minutes later, when we came down from the roof, I made my way into the T.V. room, searching for E. He was manic enough to do the talking for me. He wasn't around, but I saw the guitar. I made myself walk over one step at a time. I picked it up. But there were still no strings.

Someone could cut herself with the sharp ends of strings, yes. Why the guitar was there, I had no idea. Maybe Gus was coming.

I scanned the room. Around me, the others were drinking juice or decaf, having snack time. Some made eyes at me, but I could tell they weren't looking for a connection. They stared through me, lost in their own heads, sipping from plastic cups, eating canned fruit with sporks.

In the corner, there was a checkerboard with no pieces. And countless VHS cases with no tapes inside. It wasn't the Nurses' fault. Things disappeared on psych wards. Patients were ingenious when it came to self-mutilation. The obvious no-nos were taken away – razors, pocketknives, nail files, curling irons, hair dryers, and any over-the-counter drugs, anything that would possibly cut, burn, electrocute, or cause an overdose. Even board game pieces couldn't be trusted. A red or black checker could get lodged in a throat, an easy choke. If someone twisted off the end of a pool stick, the screw was sharp enough for a cutter to bloody-decorate an arm or leg. A ping-pong paddle could knock out teeth. Polyester pants could hold the neck, and the body's weight, without tearing, enough to make someone pass out until the material gave in. Toothbrushes and hairbrushes were weapons for bulimics. Mouthwash and cold medicine were shots for the drunks. Everything and everyone was dangerous.

I wasn't hungry, but I wanted to touch something. In the kitchen, besides a drawer full of gummy candy, there was no sugar, no caffeine, and of course, no forks or knives. Not even plastic ones. Only the plastic sporks. Every regular household object became a weapon. I grabbed a handful of gummy fruit and sat down. I unwrapped one, tasting it, chewing. Then I had another. Across the table, T., the thick, depressed kid, moved his lips to smile at me. His smile was forced, a difficult curve. But in it, I saw, not the hell inside, but the hope. Then his smile was gone, slipping away as quickly as it came. He stared at me with big eyes. I knew he was missing his smile. I knew he wanted it back. I knew it.

I wanted to hug him. Then, suddenly, my arms rose up, and for a moment, they were working, remembering how to hug. Then my arms fell back down, and I ate another gummy fruit because I needed to practice chewing. Then I realized it was sweet. I felt a slight rush. It was something. Pieces got stuck in my teeth. Red, cherry pieces. Glorious pieces.

I started humming one of Gus' songs. Slowly at first. Then singing. T. was listening, hanging on to the sound through his lost stare, staring at me from the side, like a horse.

Seven.

Words were coming back to me. I was able to speak again, but I had lost track of days. The Tall Male Nurse told me it was Saturday.

Sandra Lee appeared at my door. She looked worn and anxious.

"What?" I asked.

"Mary, I'm sorry. I know you told me not to, but I told him. Jeffrey. He's here, in the hall. If you want me to tell him to leave, I will," Sandra Lee announced.

"Let him in," I said quietly.

Sandra Lee disappeared.

When I looked up again, Jeffrey was standing in the doorway, holding a single yellow flower. "Hi," he said, staring at his gym shoes.

"Hi," I said back.

"Can I come in?" he asked, peeking above the yellow flower.

"Sure," I said.

Jeffrey moved forward. He reached up to straighten his thick glasses, handing me the flower.

"Can you just set it on the dresser?" I asked.

"Sure," he whispered. Then he moved closer to me, looking me up and down. "Sandra Lee's been giving me updates," he said. "I've been so worried, Mare."

"Join the club," I said, turning over in bed, nearly covering my head with the sheets.

"Look at me," he said. "My eye's doing it again. That twitching thing. It's like a Mary alarm or something."

I turned back over, staring at his glasses, then staring beyond the glass, into his gray-green-blue eyes. I was nervous, worried the colors might suck me in. And I knew he could be moody, and sometimes his serious looks came across as downright mean. I could never quite get close enough to him, even when he sat on my hospital bed.

"Have you heard from Michael?" I asked.

Jeffrey looked down at the white floor, running a hand through his messy brown hair. "I guess he's alive," he said, putting a hand on my shoulder. "He overdosed about a week ago, but they brought him back."

I nodded.

"Did Sandra Lee tell you already?" he asked.

"No, I just knew something happened. I always seem to know when a Griffin is lost or found," I said.

Jeffrey squeezed my arm. He looked smart, tough, strangely small, handsome, and untouchable. His lips wavered with a full, deep red shake, wet and almost womanly. His skin was pale, making his eyes stand out on his face like pool balls surrounded by black frames.

He smiled and cried at the same time. "I'm just praying that Michael hangs on. If he goes back out again, I don't think he'll make it."

"Are you still sober?" I asked him.

Jeffrey answered, "Yes, years now. And I heard you are too. That's great, Mare. I wish Michael would get it. Every day, I wish. But every time I talk to him on the phone, he's in a different city, buzzing on whatever. Sometimes, I can tell by his voice whether he's on cocaine or heroin. Sometimes not. I feel like it's my fault. After we sold the farm, all we did was get messed up, hung out, and survived. And I taught him how to get fucked up. It was me." Jeffrey's eyes barreled into me. A curious mustang.

He continued, "Anyway, he went back to the East coast and found his boyfriend with someone else. He just lost it then, really lost it. Came back to stay with Sandra Lee, but ended up downtown on the streets again and overdosed. We don't even know who found him this time, but one of these days, no one's gonna be there to save him."

"Using isn't pretty. You and I know that. And you know it's not your fault, Jeffrey. You know it's his choice," I said, pulling the sheets up to my neck.

"I know, Mare. But I feel like if Buddy were here, he'd know what to do," he said, looking up. "But it's just me holding it all together."

I paused, listening quietly. Then I responded, "You know you've been doing all you can. Just you being there, being here, it's enough."

Jeffrey's expression was hard and rough. He had one hand on his chin and another on the bed, on me. He smiled weakly.

"We are a disturbed duo, brother," I said.

"Always have been, but you know what?"

"What?"

Jeffrey touched my cheek. "I think Buddy had what you have. The bipolar thing. I think he needed a doctor, the meds, a shrink. We just never saw it. We were too worried about winning and the farm to see it. We were too lost in our lives. God, I wish I could rewind time. I wish in a weird way…that he was in the bed next to you."

"You don't wish he was here. This place is a lonely planet. It wasn't your fault, Jeffrey. It wasn't my fault or Sandra Lee's or Big Mike's or even Michael's fault. Buddy was sick, yeah, and he wanted to go. And he did. Horrible, the way he did. But for whatever reason, he wanted out. He was tired of winning, brother."

Jeffrey took off his glasses, wiping his eyes. His head hung down low, his chin resting on his chest. "I just wish we would've seen it, that's all. Just wish we would've found him some help before it was too late."

"I know, and I wish I could've saved Thomas somehow, but there's nothing any of us can do. I'm just trying to get better, and I don't know if I ever will."

"You're the bravest woman I know," Jeffrey said, sliding his glasses back on.

"Thanks," I said. "Thanks for coming."

"And you're too good for me. Always have been," he said, lying down in bed with me.

"I think it might be the other way around," I said.

"Let's face it, we're both as insecure and neurotic as all hell."

"You got that right," I mouthed.

Jeffrey nodded.

And for the first time that week, I slept.

The whole next week, Jeffrey visited. Some days, Margene and Sandra Lee dropped by, and we all played cards in the Rec Room. I had trouble following the numbers, but Jeffrey helped me through it. Some days, Jeffrey came alone, and those days, we usually slept, packed in my tight twin bed like two cigarettes in a full pack.

Jeffrey helped me into the community kitchen. He often fed me when I refused to eat. And when I was too stubborn to swallow a meal, he brought me candy from the gift shop, saying, "Now I know you'll scarf this down." And I usually did.

Jeffrey's tough intensity and sad eyes drew me in again. A pupil magnet. I clung to him while we walked the hospital halls. He had a strange ability to intimidate the other patients wherever he swaggered, all bowlegged and serious. Even though he was a thin, small-bodied man, when he moved past the rooms, no one ever shouted at him. No one asked him for money. From his brown hair to his dirty gym shoes, Jeffrey's vibe screamed, "Let me be." Slight, but it was there. Even amidst the chaos and the psychotic screams, Jeffrey made me feel safe.

Some days, it was dead quiet. Other days, people were howling. The days blended together as I waited for my next ECT treatment, barely responding when anyone talked to me. I could only respond to Jeffrey's touch, and even that response was slight. My home was a hospital bed. My mind was sloppy and extreme. My voices were rough and loud; they yelled, they cussed, and I banged on my head with my fists, wanting to kill them, wanting to kill Captain Blackeye.

Each morning, in the dark, I walked back and forth, pacing through my small room. Then I'd pace the halls. Walking the halls, I watched my back, daydreaming about Scallycat in between the racing thoughts. I remembered when light was barely peeking through the sky, revealing the mountains. On a cloudy day, the mountains were barely visible, no more than waves, a blurry, magnificent sea. But on a clear morning, the ridges poked at the sky, cutting into it, the divine edges searing the blue-gray atmosphere, reaching for the rare sun. I remembered when Thomas and I looked out to the Scallycat Mountains, wishing on them, wishing for all things great and small, wishing to one day tame the wild horses and live forever in the glow of the sun, resting in a field somewhere together, gripping manes.

When I wasn't with Jeffrey, I hung out with S., the lawyer, and E., the hallwalker. And sometimes I just stayed alone, wasting time. So much time. I watched the clock, day after day. I watched the minutes. I watched the second hand. Time was maddening. I was desperate for a quiet place to crash, desperate for one night away from the patients and the noise. Countless mornings, feeling sick from medication side effects, I threw up and panicked, wondering how long it would take me to get up and clean it up. When I reached over, I felt the cool metal frame that held my hard, thin hospital bed.

In the afternoons, I sat in the Rec room, writing in my journal in block letters, writing the same sentences over and over, trying to make words work, always looking over my shoulder.

Jeffrey would show up and interrupt me every time, yelling, "Hey, what're you doing? Stop writing! Come in here, they got candy hidden in the drawer for you, Mare."

I wanted sugar. I wanted some sort of high, any high, anything to change the way I felt, and Jeffrey knew that. He needed it too. As we downed sugar, I wanted to walk down the street, holding his beat up fingers. I wanted to touch his arms, arms that were pale and rough. I wanted to touch his quick, thick hands. How I wanted to feel one of his callused fingers on my cheekbone.

Jeffrey beat me at Scrabble. He let me win at Rummy. The guts and grime of our lives, our losses, held us side-by-side as we played board games in the white rooms.

One day, I was sitting up near my small, barred window. My only light came from the fluorescent panels in my room. I thought about piercing my nose with a safety pin I'd stolen out of Sandra Lee's latest Welch Thrift dress, but I knew it would leave blood on the sheets. I thought about the mess, how Margene would have to clean it up.

Jeffrey found me there. He stared at me, scowling. He said, "Hey, what do you think you're doing with that safety pin?"

"Nothing," I said, staring down at my pajama pants, and my worn, barely blue thrift store kid's half-shirt.

He shrugged. "Come on, let's go get something to eat."

So we did.

In the kitchen, Jeffrey said, "Margene says they're letting you out today. You better get rid of any sharp things."

I raised both brows. "Really?"

He nodded, slurping some Jell-o. "Eat, Mare," he said.

I stabbed a tater tot with my spork.

"You have more color," Jeffrey said.

"I guess," I said. "I'm still having trouble reading. And the T.V. still drives me mad. Too loud."

"Buddy always used to say that too," he said.

I nodded, agreeing. I had my dessert. Vanilla pudding. Like soupy cardboard.

Back in my room, Jeffrey helped me pack my few belongings. He folded my underwear carefully.

Before he left, he said, "You call if you need anything."

"Yes," I said. I thanked him, and Margene and Dr. Dad trickled in, driving me to their Highland home. I had the sickest feeling about the move. At the hospital, Jeffrey and I were bonded in the land of white rooms, our white world. Those days, short visits were all either of us could handle. I thought of the night at the hospital when I saw two patients get in a fist fight. The hippie kid got his face smashed in, his eyes poked into a bloody mess. The Doctors weren't sure if the kid would ever see again. I thought that without Jeffrey, I too might end up blind.

Eight.

Outpatient, I had fifteen ECT treatments, on a Monday-Wednesday-Friday schedule. I forced myself into a cocoon state, blocking it out. I felt dread, dread that I wouldn't get better, and dread that I'd have to endure more treatments. My life felt eerie, spacey, and I developed a hard shell.

After each treatment, Margene, Dr. Dad, or Sandra Lee sat by my side in the recovery room. Other times, no one was there. Just me, my tubes, suctions, and my depressed head. I felt the same at first. No better. Then for the rest of the day, I was monitored. I prayed to feel tired, but I still couldn't sleep.

I felt no pain before, after or during the ECTs. But the hospital ceiling lights, the vision of them passing over me like an evil strobe, was cemented inside a crevice of my brain. A haunting, posttraumatic memory.

I felt as if someone had placed a filter on my brain. The real me was lost deep inside my heart and head, abandoned in a tangled field of estranged synapses. I felt fragile. I became the pirate girl, riding on a Thunderbird, wading through a wicked storm. I forced myself to live in the land of pirates and vapor, to block it out. I floated somewhere above the mountains of Scallycat, in a high sea made of sky. Because I had to. Because brushing teeth was a difficult chore.

I told myself that it was a story. Yes, a story I had written to Thomas in block letters, and any day, I could delete the text, turning it into something new, my real life, the real me.

DEAR GOD:
I AM POSSESSED.
LOVE, MARY

Over and over, I was wheeled in, stripped down, got zapped, then went home. It was a bizarre way to spend a morning. After each treatment, I sat on Margene's couch, bored and unsettled, unable to concentrate. For nearly another entire year, I was stuck in the comatose depression. All I did was sit and smoke on Margene's couch, constantly restless, but unable to find an outlet for my silent fury.

Finally, after the ECTs, extensive therapy, and more medications, my brain began to function more. Barely. I was slightly better. That is, I had suicidal thoughts only half of the day. So gradual, it was hard to tell improvement at all.

I stuck close to Margene and Dr. Dad. They were familiar with my vacant look, my slow responses, and my death wishes, but they were learning about the bipolar illness right along with me. Since I was forced to sleep in bed with Margene, we grew closer. I learned that she was more than Margene who tried to fix me. She was patient. Margene never gave up on me. Never.

And there were times when Sandra Lee came over to see Margene and me, and the three of us hung out in the basement together. Together, we stared at the wall at the Highland home. The white, clean wall.

When Margene couldn't watch me, Dr. Dad took me to work with him. He gave me my room to hang out in, handing me coloring books. And while I was there, I'm sure he got nothing done. Nights, he drove me to meetings, sharing recovery with me. When I sat outside on the back porch to smoke, he watched me from the window, making sure I stayed alive.

Nine.

One night, Margene let me leave the house for dinner with Jeffrey. He picked me up, and we hit a fancy fish joint.

By then, he'd found a full time job selling cars. Not glamorous, but he was paying his bills, and he had new shoes. Several times, he said, "Order something, Mare. You need to eat. I'll get it for ya," but I acted like I wasn't hungry.

After his meal, we drove downtown together. I knew Gus' band was playing acoustic on the square, but I didn't tell Jeffrey.

Downtown at the show, next to me, Jeffrey stepped lighter. His mood was loose and cool. Jeffrey was my street twin. "Hey, this guy sounds good," he said.

I nodded. "He rode at the farm way back when."

Jeffrey raised a brow. "Really?"

"Yeah, we need to get close."

When Jeffrey walked ahead of me, short-striding through the crowd, people moved for him, opening up space.

Somewhere in the middle of the night, I weaved through the crowd, snaking my way to the front row, staring up at Gus, losing Jeffrey. I was trapped in Gus' zone, the zone of medium tones, yellow hair, and blue eyes. When Gus sang, he rolled his eyes around. Then he looked at me, grinning. Just like old times, I grinned back, giving him the peace sign.

Later, I found Jeffrey sitting alone on top of an enormous speaker, nodding his head to the beat. He looked like a watchdog sitting up there, grooving out.

I climbed up on the speaker, sliding in next to him. My left leg touched his right, brushing against him, then settling in place.

He punched my arm and said, "Where have you been? I've been worried sick."

"Wandering around," I said. Moving closer, I put my arm around him.

Jeffrey jerked my arm from his shoulder and said, "Don't, Mary."

"Don't what?"

"Don't disappear like that then act like it's all cool," he said, sliding his glasses off, wiping his eyes.

I said, "You disappear all the time too. Your face is impossible to read. I never know when I can even touch you. You're just so far away all the time, and I'm really sick of it, sick of trying to figure you out."

"Christ, Mare. I saw the way you looked at that singer. I might not see very well, but I'm not blind. I can see you're into him. You just got out of the nut ward, in case you've forgotten. So stop touching me. Would you just let me enjoy the show?" he asked, knitting his brown brows, zoning out, staring at the stage.

"Yeah, I'll let you be, let you watch the show," I said, hopping down from the speaker, turning my back to him, walking away.

Jeffrey followed after me, yelling, "Are you leaving? I drove, in case you forgot."

I walked on. I didn't look back. What I didn't realize was that I had Jeffrey's wallet and keys in my bag. I took the bus to my old Mt. Powder apartment.

The next day, I woke up startled and confused. I looked around. Safe. I was in my floor-bed in Mt. Powder, relieved that the scene was familiar. My head throbbed. My thoughts were thick, racing, and depressed. I picked up the phone, listening to message after message from Margene and

Dr. Dad wondering where the hell I was. I hung up the phone, lying down on my floor-bed, relieved to be alone. Until I heard the yelling. I looked up.

Jeffrey stood above me, hands on his bony hips. He yelled, "You know why I'm here! You have my goddamn wallet!"

"It's on the desk," I said quietly. I shook slightly. Jeffrey's blue-gray-green eyes turned black, shooting through me.

He stared. Blood rushed to his cheeks. Then Jeffrey whipped his small body around, turning his back to me.

I followed him across the apartment.

He was searching through his wallet.

"What the hell? You think I stole something from you?" I yelled at his back, trembling.

"Nervous habit, I always check," he said, facing me. He slid his wallet in his pocket. Hands on hips, he stared at me blankly.

"I can't believe you," I said.

Jeffrey moved forward, bumping my shoulder hard. Then he backed away, leaving my room, hurrying down the hall.

I followed after him, all the way out the front door of the building.

There, he stopped. He didn't look up. "I don't want to talk about this. Not now." His voice turned shaky and quiet. Then he did look up. He stared. His bottom lip twitched. Quickly, he said, "I can't talk about this right now. I can't." Then he walked away in a blur, the heels of his shoes brushing together. Swish, swish.

I watched him disappear. Then the loss was stored somewhere inside, churning and burning. The shock.

I called Margene. "I'm at my old apartment. Mom, I'm okay," I said.

A few weeks later, Dr. Dad dropped me off at a twelve-step meeting in Mitgard. I saw Jeffrey sitting across from me. He stared at his hands for an entire hour, doodling in a notebook. Afterward, he drove out of the lot without saying anything, rolling down the street playing punk rock, burning past people in his truck. A bullet. He wasn't wearing his glasses.

Ten.

I got rehired at Welch Thrift and moved back into my Mt. Powder apartment against Margene's wishes. Sick or not, I was still as headstrong as a mistreated horse. Margene was perpetually in a panic, wondering if I'd try to kill myself again. And so she cleaned. Her Highland home reeked of bleach.

Recovery was so slow; it was barely recognizable. At work, while sorting through donated clothes, I thought about slicing my veins with the box cutter in the break room. *It'd be easy.* That was the process. In my head, ghost pirates swabbed the deck. Hauntings.

I worried that I wouldn't wake up for work. I worried about my speech, wondering if the words came out smooth, fluid. I had a hard time speaking to Katie, and I overheard other coworkers say that I was the "spacey, strange girl on acid." I stared back at them with seal-like eyes. I walked on a thin, slippery, glass plank.

It took at least a year before I could walk and talk normally again. I practiced forming words at work, slowly making my way through syllables: "Hello... can... I... help... you?" My sentences held long, slow pauses and sometimes, I'd gaze at people too long, making them look down and scoot away from me as if I had an infectious disease. But I couldn't help the long stares. My brain was still in slow motion, and it took me longer than most to respond, smile, look away, wave an arm. I had to remind my eyelids, fingers, mouth, legs, and arms to work, to move, to shut, to wriggle, to stride.

As I completed simple chores, I was suddenly severely shy, meek, and bizarre. Katie knew why, but she never brought it up. I was trapped inside a bottomless secret. My thoughts went like this: *Okay, now, count the clothes. Good. Hit buttons on the register. Good. Now give change. Say, Thank you. Now what? Someone is looking at me. They all know. I know they know. God help me. I want to cut myself.*

When Katie and the new workers were hanging out, I'd walk into the conversation, and they'd turn silent and scatter. Once, Katie said, "You're looking a little better. You're not moving so slow."

"Uh, thanks," I said, staring at her until she looked away. I wasn't thinking deep thoughts. It took me a while to blink.

Everything – getting up, washing, making my bed, seemed like an enormous task. Showing up at work was the main focus of the day. And as soon as I got home, I tried to sleep. My apartment was dark many more hours than it was light. Then I'd go to a meeting and go to bed. Work, meeting, bed. For a long time, the schedule didn't vary.

I took medications and gained weight, religiously visiting the Doctor. Barely, I stayed with the living. I feared that if I did too much, or if I were overly affected by the outside world, I might end up back in the hospital. So I stayed in my cocoon apartment.

My life equaled little more than showing up. I didn't talk to anyone unless I had to. I barely covered the basics. First grade student on meds.

I had wicked night sweats. Nearly every night, I woke drenched, paranoid, and confused, annoyed that I had to wash the sheets again. It was sloppy, but I showed up at Welch Thrift and appointments, fighting other medication side effects – weight gain/loss, water retention, sun sensitivity, shaking, frequent urination, skin rashes, nausea, dizziness, incessant thirst, dry mouth, increased/decreased sexuality, constipation, stomach aches, headaches, backaches, restlessness, insomnia, fatigue, and more.

Finding the right medication was grueling. Most meds didn't take effect for three weeks. So I experienced no relief mentally, plus added physical problems from side effects. One anti-psychotic med caused a severe, traumatic reaction. One mood stabilizer made the world appear cartoonish. I had allergic reactions, intense paranoia, and other experiences that made starting a new medicine a terrifying mystery. It took two years before I was stable on three meds that remotely worked. Even then, from summer to fall, dosage changes. If I became more physical, meds were altered, and on and on.

Doctors made decisions based on feedback, but the powerlessness and uncertainty made it a scary guessing game. I felt like a lab rat. I was Dr. Dad's own personal brain patient, and even he couldn't find a cure.

I experienced panic attacks while I was ringing up customers. Between movement problems and misconnections, each afternoon, I was exhausted and ready to crawl home to my dark room.

On the long drive home from Welch Thrift each night, I stared at the CD player in my car, telling myself to put Gus' music on. I thought it'd be nice to hear his voice, but it seemed like too much work to drive, open the CD case, and slide it in. I'd get confused, distracted, and couldn't follow through with my plan. Then I drove home in silence, teary, unable to do it. After months of this drive-home struggle, finally, one day, I moved my hand while driving. Then the next day, I got out the CD case. The day after that, I pulled Gus' CD from the case and put it in. The process took months.

After that, I had another problem. I had to drive and take the CD out. Change it. I couldn't. I listened to Gus' CD repeatedly for months.

Through work, I became better at communicating with my voice. Beginning with childlike scribbling, I relearned how to write, block letter by block letter. I didn't read for a long while. Over time, words came back to me, but I lived with posttraumatic stress – flashbacks of hospital lights, patients, and scenes, and the constant worry that the illness would come back and seize me, destroying the life I'd worked so hard to recreate. Fear hung thick, a humid reminder, but after I experienced some level of mental soundness, I thought the illness had vanished.

I fought side effects and residual symptoms, but I began to feel like a normal person. Like a sober, living, breathing regular person. I could laugh and cry again. At 22, I was so grateful it hurt.

On Sunday nights, Margene and Dr. Dad had Sandra Lee and me over for dinner. Margene cooked. And she didn't hang out on the porch waiting for Tomcat to come home. Instead, she stayed at the table, drinking coffee, telling Sandra Lee and me that we could smoke in the house.

One Sunday, in Margene's spotless kitchen, I stared hard at Sandra Lee.

She was silent.

I looked at Margene. She pressed her frosty lips together in a thin line. She had that look. She needed to clean something.

I sucked in air. When I let it out, my shoulders shook.

Margene put her arms around me. She said, "You're pulling through. You are a rock. I can feel Thomas with us, here in the kitchen. I can feel it. Right about now, he'd be running in saying, 'Now how come you all look so serious?'"

Sandra Lee smoked and smiled.

Margene wanted to fix things, and for the first time, I wanted to let her. We shared a long, shaky hug in her spotless kitchen.

Sandra Lee spooned up the last of her supper.

Dr. Dad poked his head in the kitchen. "You all right, ladies? It's awfully quiet in here, ha ha."

Margene shooed him away, rising and turning on the radio.

Margene and Sandra Lee started singing along to old blues. Then they began to dance, jerkily stepping on the smooth, white tiles.

Sandra Lee laughed. "We're terrible, Margene."

"We are, but who cares. This song reminds me of Scallycat. I miss it down South sometimes, don't you?" Margene asked me.

I nodded, watching them dance. Then I stood, breathing in the smoky air. When Margene grabbed my wrecked wrist, helping me dance, I shook and moved and realized something – I knew that Thomas was somewhere out there, running through a field of treasure, riding a black horse, trotting down a freshly painted fence line, following me.

Eleven.

Katie called, checking in.

We met at a downtown Welch coffeehouse.

Her skin was smooth and clear. She shone, but her eyes were red. She said she was tired from long days of tagging clothes. Sipping her drink, she told me about her recent trip back to The Crow's Nest. "All the old people are still partying it up there. I haven't been there much. I realized I don't miss them."

I blinked twice.

"I broke up with that bassist, kicked him out for good. I got my own place now. It's small, but it's mine," she said. "You know, it wasn't about the fights. It was the quiet that killed us."

I nodded.

We went for a slow downtown walk, holding hands, backtracking and making circles. We drove to Mt. Powder Park, stopping at the overlook. We visited Mitgard, and I showed Katie the fields and trees, telling her stories about Griffin Farm. I showed her all of my hiding places.

This time around, being with Katie was easy, natural. We were like grade school buddies, playing together, thrilled that we were two.

Katie started coming over, dying her hair blond, helping me dye mine black. We'd watch old movies with wet heads, feeling sexy and new.

One night, like two kids, we took a bath together, and as we lay naked on my floor-bed, I stroked my hand across her stomach and swallowed. Somewhere, out there, I swore I heard a rattle. Someone was shaking a coffee can full of grain. It was time to feed, to do turnouts. I smelled leather.

Katie looked at me with watery, reddish-brown eyes. "It's good to be like this, isn't it? Just us." She smiled through her thick lips.

I smelled her earthy smell, looking up at the lashes that fanned her brown eyes. I stroked my hand across her belly. Then I felt the ribs there.

I reached to hold her hand. I held it loosely, and her palm covered mine, in a soft, sweaty grip. We fell asleep like this.

When I woke, she had already split, but I still thought about her loose walk, her newly tender, calm manner. I thought about touching her gentle hands. Just us.

That night, at a meeting, after nearly two years of avoiding him, I ran into Jeffrey, who was looking handsome, unpredictable, and elusive. Wearing a t-shirt and faded, torn jeans, he looked at me, then looked away, staring at his arm, the floor, the ceiling, the wall.

On the way home, I got off at the wrong exit by mistake.

I forgot to eat dinner. I hardly slept.

Soon, I started dropping weight. Then I got downright skinny.

Margene blamed it on stress. Dr. Dad blamed it on the meds. We all brushed it off. It'd pass.

Here and there, when I looked at graffiti or license plates, I heard messages. I told the Doctor. We worked through it. I took a week off from Welch Thrift.

The other workers whispered about me when I returned. Katie didn't say anything. She had her own wild world going on. She was pregnant. I carried her secrets, and she carried mine.

One day, on a smoke break, Katie said, "Will you go with me to the center? I don't have anybody." Her thick bottom lip quivered.

"Sure," I said. In the back lot of the Welch Thrift, we drew up the plan, figuring out how much it would cost for her to get the abortion. I said I'd chip in, that I'd borrow some cash from Dr. Dad.

"I owe you one, Mary," she said, looking up at me with watery eyes, her bleached hair framing her face into a dark-eyed saucer.

I touched her hair, tucking a piece behind her ear. "Listen, you don't owe me anything. We've been at this too long together to be keeping score here. Just know that I've got your back, sister."

Standing up, Katie cried, clutching her middle.

When Katie and I got back from the Women's Center, she looked bluish-pale. I took her home to her apartment in Mt. Kormet, tucking her in.

Katie closed her eyes, clenching her thick lips tight. Then she looked up at me and said, "I will never forget this."

"Get some rest, girl," I said. "Call me if you need anything."

"Okay," she muttered.

"I'll cover your shifts this week," I said.

"Okay," she muttered. "It's gone, isn't it, Mary?"

"Yes, it's gone," I said, heading for home.

Back home, I had a message on my land line. It was scratchy, but the high-pitched tone of Michael Griffin was unmistakable. The words were hurried, panicky. What I caught was this: "Mare…money…bus…call me if you can help." And he left his number. So I called it.

I picked up Michael downtown. When he got in the car, I touched his hand. I felt each of his silver-ringed fingers.

He felt each of my fingers. Touched each knuckle. Michael was bone-thin, white, and he was missing a front tooth.

That night, I nursed him while he went through withdrawal, shaking and puking and screaming, "God it hurts, it hurts." Straight-faced, Michael stared at me, widening his green eyes. He whispered, "Help me." He was utterly mad. He leaned forward, kissing my cheeks, my throat.

I let Michael do whatever the hell he wanted to do.

"My stomach, Mare, it hurts like razors," he said, kissing me. Then he ran to the bathroom to vomit.

All night long, I held a cold towel against his forehead.

After a few weeks, Michael was eating again. When I wasn't at work, we hung out in the apartment, listening to tunes. At Sandra Lee's, we had back porch dinners, and we acted happy, but we were all on the edge.

Michael and I slept on the floor of my apartment and sometimes, he'd even kiss my cheeks. Things were intimate, warm, loving, and many days, we laughed so hard, Michael would get sick again, the same way he used to when he was little, marching about Griffin Farm, cracking up, then throwing up on his pony saddle.

We were both broke. We'd sing along to Gus' music in the car, and we sounded good together. Michael's jeans and shirts were huge; he always wore long sleeves to hide the track marks. He was covered with tattoos by then, but his lips were unmarked, still full and beautiful. His long light brown hair was always a stringy wreck, but he was sensitive and passionate, and I loved every inch of his sensuous mess.

"If I wasn't gay, you'd be Mary Griffin," he said to me daily.

Michael didn't sing to me like Gus. And he wasn't intense like Jeffrey. Michael, the street punk, was at my side, and I wanted him there, because Michael was desperate and real. And I felt real with him.

When I sang with Michael, whether in the car or on Sandra Lee's porch, the intertwined voices created the most glorious nights. Sky-shakers. That was God.

One day after a meeting, Michael told me he relapsed again. He was shaking and sobbing, hugging me. He wouldn't let me go. But I peeled his skinny body from mine. Hand by hand, arm by arm, I pulled him off of me. When I backed up, feeling my chest slip away from his, I felt the emptiness there, as if a part of my body was still stuck to his clothes. I said, "You know you have to move out."

With wet eyes, he quietly said, "No. No. Yes. Yeah, Mary. I know."

After that, he'd show up at my apartment in the middle of the night. At first, he'd surprise me, knocking on the door, smiling wide, saying hello. He'd hug me, look around, and leave. Then he started asking for money, telling me he was sorry. Each time he showed up, he looked thinner, and I knew he was on heroin again.

One day I got a phone call from Welch Hospital. Michael had a collapsed lung. Dr. Dad and I busted past the Nurses to sit on Michael's bed.

Dr. Dad patted the top of Michael's wrecked hair, leaving us.

I sat on the bed with Michael for hours. I fed him candy.

The last time I saw Michael, he appeared at my apartment around three a.m. His bones pushed at his skin. He had swallowed a bottle of pills. Then he said, "Mary, I'm dying." He didn't die that night. He disappeared.

But six months later, Dr. Dad called me in the middle of the night. "Mary, are you sitting down?" he asked quietly.

"Yeah," I said. "It's Michael, isn't it?"

"Michael Griffin died last night. Complications from an overdose," Dr. Dad stated like the surgeon that he was.

"I guess…this time…he didn't come back?" I said, choking on saliva.

"No, he didn't come back," Dr. Dad said. "I was there. The Doctors did everything they could. Everything."

"Where was he found?"

"He was out in Mitgard. He'd been living in an abandoned warehouse. Someone was taking him food. I'm not sure how he was getting the drugs."

"There are always ways," I said.

"Yes, always." Dr. Dad said. "You and I both know that."

"Dad?"

"Yeah?"

"Who found him?"

"Jeffrey."

That night, Sandra Lee called me, leaving messages, crying and confused. I didn't answer or call her back. Instead, I sat on the couch, listening to the ring. It was so loud. While sitting on the couch, I rocked back and forth, as if I were still riding Slick. I held myself, crying and breathing in, searching for the horse smell.

Twelve.

The next morning, Sandra Lee busted down the door of my apartment, yelling, "Mary! I've been trying to reach you!"

Still in bed, I started to rise, but she jumped on the bed.

I tried to get up, but Sandra Lee's hands were as strong as Jeffrey's. She held me down.

"Why didn't you answer my calls?" she asked me.

"I'm sorry, I just…"

"I wanted to tell you that there was a note," she said, releasing her grip.

I sat up, listening.

"Michael wrote about Buddy."

"What about Buddy?" I asked.

"Michael saw Buddy messing around with the rope, talking to it, measuring his neck. Buddy told him that he'd just gotten in a band at school. Remember how Buddy always wanted to be a singer…but Big Mike wouldn't let him do it? He thought it'd take away too much time from the riding."

I nodded, listening close. "He did want to be a singer. He had that look. He would've made a good lead man. Singing was the only thing that made his head turn quiet. He told Jeffrey and me that all the time."

"Yeah, but there's something else. Michael wrote that Big Mike knew about the rope too. And he still wouldn't listen or let him quit riding."

"Are you serious?"

Sandra Lee took a deep breath. She wheezed. "Yes. Big Mike thought Buddy would snap out of it, like he always did. But it wasn't long after that that we found his body."

"I found it. Jeffrey found it. In the hay barn," I stated.

"Yes. And Michael was destroyed that he never said anything to the rest of us, that he kept it a secret. He wrote that he hated himself, hated his secrets, that he couldn't live with them anymore." Her eyes filled up. Wet, spilling over. She leaned back, wiping her lids with her strong, long fingers.

"Why are you telling me this now?"

"Because I don't want this to happen to you too. We need to stop this now, stop blaming each other and ourselves. The farm is gone, and no one can bring the horses back. No one can bring the boys back, but the show must go on."

"Does Jeffrey know? About the letter?"

She nodded. "Jeffrey read the letter first. Jeffrey always knows everything before everyone else."

"Yeah, he does." I swallowed. My eyes stung. My wrecked wrist ached. I rose up. Across the way, in the kitchen, I saw Captain Blackeye staring at me. *Ha, ha, ha, Mary, we're back.*

"Where are you going?" Sandra Lee asked.

"Nowhere." Shaking, I made coffee. There, while pouring the water, measuring spoonfuls, counting carefully, I had flashbacks of the psych ward lights looming above me as the Tall Male Nurse pushed me through the white halls. There I was on my stretcher. All around me, lights were flashing. Like photographs, like a tricky sun on a cloudy day. Lightheaded, confused and scared, I couldn't find the coffee cups. I banged around, looking in cupboard after cupboard. Still, no mugs.

Finally, Sandra Lee moved across the room, helping me hunt until we found them right where they were supposed to be, on the right upper side.

As we drank, Sandra Lee said, "Mary, no matter what Big Mike would've done with Buddy, whether he let him sing or ride, Buddy was sick, and we just never took care of him right," she said, her head hanging low, her bottom lip hanging low like an old horse. "We took care of the herd and the farm instead. I was probably ordering grain while my son was dying right under my nose."

I reached forward, hugging her. "Buddy was sick like me," I said.

"Yeah, and by taking care of you, it sort of helped me in a way. God, not that I ever hoped you'd be sick, but I'm just saying. It's strange how things come back around…kind of like the way we used to train a green horse by cantering in circles, remember? One day, after all those circles, you get on that horse, and the thing just knows how to bend and steer all of a sudden like magic. But it takes work too."

"Magic," I said, releasing her. "Circles."

I called Margene. Soon, Margene, Dr. Dad, and Sandra Lee were all sitting in my apartment, drinking coffee. When he thought I wasn't listening, Dr. Dad whispered to Margene, "Mary doesn't look good."

In that moment, Dr. Dad and Margene were so close; I thought he might reach his hand out to hold hers. Instead, he lifted up a finger, holding it to her lips, silencing her.

Margene jerked back, picking at her fingernail polish. She picked it off. She scratched and scratched at it. She looked Dr. Dad in the eye and said, "Don't ever tell me to be quiet again. I'm done with your silence. I'll say whatever the hell I want from now on."

Dr. Dad's eyes widened. His lightning scar twitched. He ran a hand through his silvery hair and said, "All right then." He reached forward, sliding a finger along her flushed cheek.

I had a dream about Gus that night. In it, I went to see him play, and after the show, he kissed me goodbye, gazing at me for a long time. Then he left in his usual hurried, long-legged, rocker stride. His steps were fast, but light. Gus moved jerkily quick, but gently, and I was convinced that his eyes held not one, but many shades of light inside the sockets.

I woke up, looking in the mirror. My black hair was dry, sticking out every which way. My lips were dry. Under my eyes, dark circles. My whole face was puffy. We'd all been crying some about Michael.

That evening, forgetting dinner, I dyed my hair black again. Fresh. This took a while. Two boxes of dye barely covered my long, tangled hair. Maybe cool, but nowhere near pretty.

I wanted to cut something. I dug around the apartment, finding the Swiss Army knife I used to carry at the barn to cut twine. Slowly, I carved a lightning bolt into my arm. *What's the word, Thunderbird?* The pain felt strange. The lightning cut wasn't deep, but it was large enough for outsiders to see, so I quickly covered it up with a cartoon Band-Aid. There, better. I shrugged, figuring the scar would fade. I wanted a bloody drawing, a release. That was all. I didn't want anyone to see. I glanced back at the mirror. My freshly dyed, slick, black hair made my skin turn into chalk. I could die by eraser.

Then I dressed in black and blue, forcing myself to go out on the town. I was on the edge, but I painted my face calm. The more distressed I felt, the more I pursed my lips, trapping my mouth in a tight hold that told no secrets. My eyes felt dry. *Whatever happens*, I told myself, *I will wait to cry.*

It was the middle of December, and the scene was gray – the look, the feel of the night was steel cold and dry-skyed all around. All ground was wet-shadowed by yesterday's rain. A damp blanket covered the Welch earth.

I looked all right, but I only looked all right. Black hair, black eyeliner, I had that tired face, and I felt the place underneath my eyes slightly swelling, begging for ice. I felt the small, black, stubborn half-moons growing there. Still, I didn't have the energy for any more makeup, a base coat.

I parked a few blocks from the bar. The streets were quiet, coal-dark, and the land was the perfect kind for muggers, full of buildings, thin alleys, broken streetlamps and little noise. I stuffed everything in my pockets – smokes, money, ID – and threw my purse in the trunk. I didn't want to be a walking target. I walked swiftly, with purpose, my street walk. I knew how to slap on a serious face. Jeffrey had taught me well. Still, I hurried to the bar. It was cold, not freezing. A thin coat was enough. While I crossed the street, heading inside, I pulled my black, ratty hair back in a slick, tight ponytail. *Better.*

This section of Welch was full of dark shapes and beady eyes. All around, men hung out in groups, wearing skullcaps, play-punching each other, giving quick handshakes, shooting the shit. I watched them shift around in the shadows. I studied their stoned, cracked out, lost faces. Some were mean. Some were quiet and shifty. And some, simply silent, watching, looking me over, checking me out, then looking away when I caught a stare and matched it with my own.

Small all around, a mugger could've tackled me with one finger, but no one touched me. I was a ghost made of steam, smoky and solo. *Try hitting vapor, madmen.* I marched down the sidewalk, and no one asked me for money. No one reached out a hand. No one even came close.

I licked my lips, which made the dryness worse.

Inside, the lights tinted the room blue. In my head, I heard this: *Lightning filled the sky!* In the crowd, with a busy tongue, licking those lips, I gazed at the stage. There was Gus. Home from tour, he was playing a small, local show just to keep busy, I assumed.

Two songs in, I felt my eyes widen, stuck open. I wasn't in front or in back, but instead, lost in between. Hidden, but when the bodies shifted, I appeared to the world, one girl among the numbers, another mate on deck. My sight blurred. I felt a strange energy in the room. Butterflies. I felt my heart push at my chest, panic attack style, beating there, reminding me that I was still alive, and the room turned calm and brilliant. For a moment, the music made me forget that I was another small listener with so many unwanted voices inside.

I was on the edge. Again.

I sneaked up to the front. Gus seemed even taller and thinner when his slender fingers grabbed the microphone. He wailed into it, standing out in front of the crowd like a laser pen in the land of pencils. Sexy. Alien. Magic Man.

He looked at me. Shyly, he looked. He sang. Softly, he sang, then louder.

I looked back, drinking it in, drinking in the fear and the noise.

His eyes were big and round, drawn comic book style on his face, set wide, way too big for his lips. Like mine.

Music notes beat up through my chest, settling in the throat. I forgot to breathe, and then I remembered, and when I remembered, I counted the breaths. Something inside that bar was haunted, full of light and mean color. People were wax. Melting in front of me. Melting.

I moved right, raising my wrecked wrist.

Gus watched me move.

I swayed to the music. I shut my eyes, and when the band was done playing, I hurried away from the bar, rushing to the car.

On the way home, here and there, when I saw a license plate, I heard voices rumble inside of me. I thought Gus was talking to me. *Hello Mary. Thanks for coming.* Then Captain Blackeye. *We're back. Do you like fish food? Thanks for playing.*

Later, back home, I prayed to whatever was out there. I sat cross-legged, hoping and humming alone, gently coming back to the same tune.

It was the middle of December. I was on the edge.

In bed, I saw Gus' face floating there. His eyes were large and looming above me. His ghost whispered at me while I drifted off.

When I woke, the buzz from the show was still there. I pictured Gus' long arms. I wondered what they'd feel like wrapped around my small frame. Then I went to work.

At work, I played Gus' music. Then I sat outside behind the store, hearing Gus' voice in my head. *Leave work, Mary. Leave.* So I left Welch Thrift. I never went back.

Home, I smoked. Gus was inside me, moving my arms and legs. I could feel him in my heart, resting there, tugging at me. I tried to move and shake the thoughts. But all day long, while I was cleaning or eating, I heard Gus. *Mary. The band's coming to see you. Mary, thanks for coming.* His voice was a soft, medium tone.

In the meantime, I started getting emails from the real Gus. The first one was simple:

dear mary:

thank you for coming to my show! it was so good to see you out there. a bass player i know knew your friend katie. she gave him your email and he gave it to me and anyway, here i am. hope this isn't creepy. you are a hard one to hunt down sometimes. i remember your cool last name too. lochmore. god this is creepy, i know. but i don't care. after all this time, so good to see your hazel eyes. hope to see you around again. don't ever let go of being dreamy. i've missed seeing you. your face. you inspire me. remember way back when…we played spin the bottle. i'm going on tour soon. stay beautiful.
rock and roll,
gus

This started an email chain between us, and the more I read his words, the more I felt connected with him:

dear mary:
i sent some cds off to the west coast. i think we still have a deal, but wish me good luck. you never know what the hell will happen in this business. its always fun to hit the fedex with the record labels' addresses on the packages because i hope someone looks over my shoulder and sees the writing and thinks i'm cool. :) so you quit your job. good for you. when i'm home, i have a stupid day job, which is cool. i can't believe they haven't fired me yet, but don't tell anyone because people think i'm sort of famous. i'm really a nerd. i like drawing stupid pictures and looking at stars. i painted a picture of you, and i thought about sending it, but i don't think it's good enough. i hope you're doing something beautiful right now. you inspire me. please come to the next show. i hope you don't think this is weird, but send me a photo of you. i love your face. gus.

Then they grew deeper:

dear mary:
it's five a.m. at least. i'm at a hotel up north. i hate this place. it's lonely as hell in this room. my band mates are drunk. i had a shot, but i don't drink really. like i said, i'm a nerd. don't tell anyone. i'm sorry it's been so long since i wrote. don't worry. i will always, always write you back. always. anyway, this town sucks, but the tour is going well. i hope you are creating something beautiful. i'm sorry it's been so long. you are always welcome at any show. just let me know and you'll be on the guest list. i hope i see you soon. i got your pictures. you are stunning. go on and be dreamy. i am too. you asked me if i liked pirates. aye.
gus

We emailed for six months, off and on. Finally, I wanted to see if it was real. So I emailed to ask him.

DEAR GUS:
EVERY TIME I SEE YOU I FEEL THE SAME WAY. EVERY TIME I SEE YOU. I JUST WONDERED IF YOU'D LIKE TO GO FOR COFFEE SOMETIME, TO SEE IF THIS IS REAL. I'VE BEEN WANTING TO ASK YOU FOR A LONG TIME. FOR YEARS NOW. OF COURSE, WE MAY BE ARCH-ENEMIES, BUT I THOUGHT I MIGHT TRY. I DON'T KNOW IF I'M COMING TO YOUR NEXT SHOW, BUT IF I DO, LOOK FOR ME. I'LL BE THE HOTTEST ONE THERE. Ha.
MARY
P.S. THANKS FOR SENDING THE NEW SONG. NO ONE HAS HEARD IT BUT ME :)

dear mary:
i would love to hang out with you. but i don't know how i would explain that to my girlfriend. i don't think you and i could ever be arch-enemies. all that said, I would Love to hang out with You…under different circumstances. i think you are fantastic. and so easy on the eyes. don't ever stop being dreamy. don't freak out…i don't even know you…but i want to jesus. i am so confused. none of this is fair to you, but sometimes i can't help it. i'm an artist. i just feel it and it comes out. damn, i shouldn't send this but i know i will anyhow. don't hate me. i need some time or something.
peace,
gus

DEAR GUS:
SEE YOU AROUND, BROTHER.
MARY

dear mary:
i don't know what i'm doing. that's not true. i do know and i'm sorry about all of this. i'm a prick. i will let you be. be well. by the way, that poetry that you sent me…it's the best thing i've ever read. stunning. like you. sorry i'm doing it again. i'm getting out while the gettin's good, mary. but something tells me our time isn't done.
Love, gus

GUS--
CYA NEXT TIME AROUND, MATE.
MARY

mary—
aye, in the future then.
gus
ps. see i told you i would always write u back

I started hearing and seeing Gus in my head. License plates, billboards, posters, words out of random street people's mouths – I thought they were all messages from Gus. In reality, I stopped emailing him and I stopped going to his shows, but in my head, he was still speaking to me.

I started hearing other voices, voices that turned dark and ominous. *You are a dirty rat Mary, a dirty barn rat. You're never getting any better. You're gonna hang from the rafters. The hay barn.* Sometimes, Gus was there, and sometimes, strangers. The good, the bad, and the ugly.

I began restudying his emails, switching letters around, decoding the words. Secret code. I thought Gus communicated to me through song lyrics. At night, I thought he was sending me psychic messages. Everywhere, whispers.

I heard his voice – a soft, male tone – echo in my head. A thought tornado. I tried to shake it, but the world pulsed around me. Then came more ideas of reference, signs, and codes. I received odd emails. Much later, I realized they were merely Spam, but at the time, I thought they were sent from Gus and his girlfriend. I'd never met her, but I suddenly believed that she hated me. Then I thought the whole band hated me. The girlfriend's family was in the FBI, and they were coming after me. Yes. I became more and more guilt-ridden, isolating and frantic, every moment looking over my shoulder, looking for the FBI.

Yard signs, lamppost signs, random buzzing and talking, all messages from the band. Night and day, the voices told me to follow the signs, that one day the universe would lead me back to them.

I thought that if I studied all letters long enough, deleting or adding letters here and there, I'd figure out what Gus and the band were trying to tell me. I'd figure out the pirate code one day for sure. I'd find the band treasure. Nouns, verbs, skip adjectives. Every third word. Anagrams. Complex letters turned into insects.

Two men at a coffee shop were music spies. They wanted to see how I would handle fame. My phone was tapped. CIA. Caller ID became code. I was sure that Gus was coming to see me. Then I thought he hated me. It was all a sick joke. I threw the cordless in the garbage. I had to find out what they were trying to tell me, whoever "they" were. The voices told me this.

Nouns turned into mind piranhas. Email code told me that Gus would be there to meet me one night, that the whole band was coming to meet me. Any moment, fame was coming to me.

I showered and sang. I did my hair and makeup, walking across the street to a coffee shop.

I didn't sit in the window seat on purpose. Email code told me that someone might shoot me if I sat there. So I waited at the bar. The band was late. An hour later, still no deal. Someone evil was tricking me.

The next morning, I woke feeling too devastated to speak. Email code told me I was too fat, ugly, and old, that the band was playing a game with me. Then the computer turned into an eye socket, a black hole. No one there except an evil joker behind the screen, cackling at me because I believed the meeting was real. My world was blurry letters, lost hope and the pain of all sound echoing, loud and piercing. All things appeared Technicolor, so bright that even while inside, I squinted.

I looked in the mirror. Beyond pale, all skin was tight, tense. My black hair, dry and ratty. Swollen eyes, full on bloodshot. My ruddy cheeks sank, dented. I was thin. No, fat. My hazel eyes were drawn comic book style, too large for my lips.

The computer might grow legs and follow me, so I drove to Mt. Powder Park to escape. Sitting in my car, I looked to my right and saw a big, blue van. And I thought the band was in there, hiding and laughing at me. All around, people were swinging legs and swallowing and skateboarding and wearing shades. It was blinding. People were laughing. At me.

Back home, I moved like a slug, smooth and slippery, hunting for sharp things. With my Swiss Army knife, I cut my wrists some, but it was too dull. Calmly, I swallowed all of my medicine at once, every pill I could find. Then I printed out a suicide note in block letters, clean and crisp, no errors, stretching out on the bed, clutching a photograph of Slick tight to my chest.

Then the pills hit. Like a detoxing drunk, I shook. One arm flailed sideways. Then the other. Legs twitched in spasms. At that moment, my cell phone rang. I crawled over to grab it. I recognized the number. Jeffrey. I didn't answer, but when the ringing stopped, I dialed 911.

Into the phone, I slurred, "Seizure, maybe. Tell them to hurry."

When the paramedics arrived, I crept around, packing well, remembering the icy hospital rooms. I lit a cigarette. Angrily, they told me to put it out or else. They were prepared to strap me down. Kneeling down, I begged to be left alone. I pleaded, shuddering, but there were too many Big People to fight.

From the ambulance, I saw crowds of wide-eyed street people gawking at me. I pulled up the hood of my sweatshirt to hide, but I couldn't stop shaking right out of it. It was so sunny it hurt.

Thirteen.

In the Welch Hospital ER, angry-looking Nurses surrounded me, holding down my arms and legs. I screamed and blacked out.

I woke up to a breathing tube, a catheter, and my raw throat was a sandy slide. When I wiped my mouth, my sleeve turned black from the charcoal they'd used to coat my insides. The stomach pumping was done. I cried because I was alive. I yelled at a Nurse to help me, to take the catheter out. He did. Then I thought the Nurse was Gus' guitar player. Aghast, I assumed the guitar player had just seen my crotch.

Alone for a full day, I repeatedly asked for a phone. The Nurses ignored me. Finally, I was allowed to call Margene. I scratchy-whispered, "I'm sick." She rushed to the ER, busting past the Nurses to see me. Dr. Dad was at St. Joseph's, digging out some brains. He came as soon as he could. Sandra Lee came. Her eyes were bloodshot too.

In the long, cold day and night in the ER, I slightly revisited the world, realizing that after going to therapy, staying sober, and taking meds religiously, there I was again, full-blown sick anyway. And *that* was terrifying. But even though I was slightly back in the real world, I kept begging Margene and Dr. Dad to tell Gus where I was so he could come visit me.

Repeatedly, Margene told me he wasn't coming.

I persisted.

She shook her head "no."

They wheeled me up to Eight West, the "no insurance ward," as we patients called it. This ward was filthy, shocking, and unbelievably heartbreaking. I felt like I was inside a horror movie, but it was harshly real, and there was no happy ending inside.

The first night, I was too petrified to speak, except I told my Margene repeatedly, "Tell Gus what room I'm in."

Gently, Margene stroked my arm and said, "Honey, he's not coming."

"Yes, but please, if he calls, tell him where I am," I said to her.

Her eyes filled up. She said, "I will."

Even inside the hospital, I couldn't tell what was real and what wasn't real. For the second time in my life, I was completely psychotic. Gone.

My roommate, V., mumbled vile profanities all day and night, angry at the voices in her head. Her toes were blackish green with grime and gangrene. Numerous times, when I came back to the room, she'd thrown up all over it. No one rushed to clean it up. But if I offered V. a glass of water, she'd snap out of it and respond to me with a quick, "Yes, I want some." Her soul was still in there, completely, as long as someone talked to her, gave her some attention. She was screaming inside. We all were.

Every few hours, the Nurses took us to a smoking room. Like fighting gerbils, we were packed in, the air thick and polluted, angry sounds vibrating the walls. I sang once and everyone quieted, listening to the echo. I imagined Michael was there, joining in on the chorus.

I couldn’t cry. Then I could. And then that's all I wanted to do. But I couldn't, unless no Nurses were looking. Afraid the man two doors down might rape me, sleep was out of the question. Like a rodent, I scurried the halls. Either that or go back to the room and V.'s cussing.

All night, patients had furious tantrums. One kid thought he was Jesus. I thought he was Gus. Another kid looked like the bass player. I kept wishing the band was trapped inside the ward with me. I thought that if they played for me, I would feel better, and I could forget that someone violent was locked in the padded room.

Mornings, we had group therapy for ten minutes. The group leader was cold to the point of abusive, and I took it, afraid they wouldn't let me out if I showed emotion. The Nurses ignored me. Treated worse than a criminal, I had to beg for a blanket and pillow. Nobody was getting better there.

During one family visit, Margene, Dr. Dad and Sandra Lee took me downstairs, where I went outside to smoke. Sitting on a bench outside the hospital, I looked up at Dr. Dad, who towered above me. I said, "Thank you so much for coming." I grabbed his soft, clean hand, my eyes spilling, studying the way that his blue eyes leaked goodness. That day, Dr. Dad breathed sensitivity and grace.

Tightly, he held my hand. His eyes were wet and round. He tried to say something, but he choked on his words. He coughed. And then he said, “Mary, you know if Thomas were here, he wouldn’t leave your side.”

Margene and Sandra Lee hovered close by, listening in, huddling around me.

“I agree,” I said. And suddenly, old pains began to rise and fall about us, settling inside our circle of skin.

Margene kissed my cheek. I could feel the mark her frosty orange lipstick made, and I left it there. When I stood, she let me lean on her. I pressed my body into her large breasts. Calmly, she held me, stroking my knotted, black hair.

Due to Dr. Dad’s persistence, after two days, Welch Hospital released me under supervision.

I recovered back at Margene and Dr. Dad's Highland home. They had started me on a new med which caused insomnia, and when I wandered outside in the middle of the night, Dr. Dad followed, making sure I didn't hurt myself. I set off the alarm more than once. Even after they took me off of that med, I had trouble sleeping. And I was plagued by the voices. By then, most of them were anything but kind.

Sometimes when I'd get up earlier than anyone else, I'd go for a walk alone, but my voices kept right up with me. I started to think that if I escaped Dr. Dad and Margene, Gus might see me on the streets, see me walking, and walk with me. How I wanted the real Gus to appear, to sing and make it all better. I thought if I saw him in person, if I heard his true voice, my own voices might go away.

I took meds, saw the doc, and hung out with family. I learned to sleep and eat again. I still wanted to die, but the voices started to settle. All that was left was an empty space in my heart, one that was reserved for the real Gus. The flesh.

I struggled with the idea of going to a show. He had a CD release party that year, but friends and family warned me to stay away. The Doctor said that the symptoms might creep up again.

There were two versions of Gus inside of me. First, there was the imaginary Gus. And then there was the real Gus, the one who played Spin the Bottle with me, the one who was tall and lean and big-eyed, the one who gazed at me while he sang on stage. And when he sang, the room turned into a calm ocean. I wanted to see the real Gus again, to know him. I didn't want to write him. I wanted to feel him, touch him, speak to him, look into his blue eyes.

Still, that year, I avoided him. And the next year. He

was on my mind and in my heart, but I stayed away. I couldn't remember exactly what I'd done while I was sick, how much I had written him. I had no idea what he thought. Maybe, to Gus, I was just another Crazy Mary.

My muscles throbbed, as if stricken with a wicked flu. Taking a shower went like this: *Okay, shampoo. Good. Open.* I talked myself through every motion. Like a child, I was forbidden from computers, shaving, driving, and being alone.

I wanted to tell the band that I was confused and couldn't help that I was confused. Part of me knew I was sick. The other part of me thought that ESP could still be real.

I forced myself to write for one minute, then five, ignoring codes and signs. Letters rose up from the page, switching around, sending me secret messages. I forced myself to read. It took months before I could finish a paragraph fluidly.

Suicidal thoughts faded, replaced by this: *You are fat, ugly, useless.* Each second, I fought my thoughts and my brain, and over time, my spirit started winning. Again.

But it was messy. I had allergic reactions to new medications. One made my mouth loose and open, my lower lip hanging there, useless. I had an ugly rash around my nose and chin. I felt like a circus freak. I had to be patient and try new medications. I had to give in.

Eventually, I returned to my Mt. Powder apartment. Unemployed, there was the endless stress of medical bills, and I was consumed by hospital flashbacks. Each day, I endured sleepwalking, anxiety, fatigue, soreness and weighted muscles, the side effects of my psychotic depression.

Frantically, I tried to uncover the missing pieces, wondering how I could make it all disappear. I wanted to find

Captain Blackeye, kill him, come clean magically, and "X" it all out.

I rebuilt myself one moment at a time. The illness didn't disappear. A year into my recovery from this mental relapse, I felt fragile again. I heard more clear-cut voices. Hundreds of combinations for letters swarmed inside of me. My life was a walking anagram. One voice repeated, *You are a dirty rat,* over and over in my head, for days. *You are a dirty rat, Mary. A dirty barn rat.* I wanted to beat my head against a wall, crack it open.

I prayed for release, for the rats to disappear from my head. When the rats went away, I saw Gus' face in windows, mirrors, random windshields. Inside cars down the road. Sometimes, I saw the whole band standing in the middle of the street, holding their instruments, laughing.

And yet, there were other lucid moments when I'd be alone in my room, when instead of the voices, I felt a love pushing through, a love telling me to ride on. Other nights, the voices were so realistic; it was impossible to not believe them. I had to call Dr. Dad, tell him what I was thinking, and let him assure me that they weren't real. Even then, I'd only believe him half-heartedly.

It took two years for the voices to fade from my mind. First, I grew more accustomed to presences, more relaxed, letting the voices and visions happen. Then I became better at deciphering which thoughts were real and which were merely coming from my injured brain. Then they came only five times a week. Then three. And so on. Eventually, there were days when I could simply get up, shower, and my mind would feel clear, relaxed, and natural. Like the early days in Scallycat.

DEAR GOD:

THANK YOU. I AM BACK. AGAIN.

LOVE,

MARY LOCHMORE

Fourteen.

I had to leave the voices behind and surface.

I knew Buddy would've understood. And I saw it in A., the blonde-headed boy who busted me out of day treatment to take me apple picking, or the psychotic girl who wrote me a bad check from God, or the Jesus boy on Eight West. I saw it in all those hidden behind locked doors on top hospital floors, brain-trapped in anguish. We knew the truth of those words. We'd been called names, dumped, abandoned, abused, fired, arrested, ignored, misdiagnosed and thrown out to rot on the streets. Because of a medical illness.

I didn't need ESP anymore, but every now and then, I sent Gus a mind thought. *I hope you are creating something beautiful. Don't ever stop being dreamy.*

To recover, I had to wave goodbye to shame. It was a process. I prayed for an end to the suffering. For me, for Buddy, for all those with brain disorders.

I was 24 years old. I understood why Buddy gave in to the circus and the noise. Reality became a gift. I began to wake up, feeling the rich, real mornings, grateful to simply sleep through the night, with or without dreams.

One day, Katie and I met for tea, and she said, "Mary, I think I'd like to travel the world. You want to come with me?"

"Nah, I'm kind of all right here," I said, sitting in a hard, green chair.

She tossed her head back, announcing, "Well, I'm gonna. Think I'll apply to be a flight attendant."

"You'd be perfect. Blonde, beautiful. You'd look pretty in those uniforms."

"I'd call you and say, 'I might be in another country right now, I can't remember.'" She smiled wide.

I chuckled. Listening to her dream, I said, "And you could hook up with all the pilots and make them all jealous."

She laughed too. "I only want one now, just one. And maybe a small yellow house, one little kid. A boy. How about you."

"I gotta go," I said, smiling. "And get outta here while the gettin's good."

I went to visit Dr. Dad. He was hanging out in the yellow-lit solarium, chilling in a red, fluffy chair, looking serene and sharp, surrounded by crimson, holding fast to a medical book. His jaw was moving, chomping gum.

I asked him for a piece, mimicking his moves, watching the way he turned pages, licking his fingers, leaning back powerlessly.

Margene walked in with the duster.

Suddenly, I thought she was the smartest, sharpest woman I knew.

"We should invite Sandra Lee over for dinner," she said to Dr. Dad.

"Uh huh," he said, staring at his book, then looking up at her, smiling through his reading glasses, chewing and chewing, his face scar moving around on his skin, making a thin-lined map.

"How was your day, Mary?" Margene asked.

"All right I guess. I didn't do much. Had some trouble with the thoughts racing in the afternoon," I said, sitting on the yellow couch.

Margene said, "I know you're sick of it all."

I nodded. "Some days, my dreams are so real, the dogs bite."

"It'll get better," she said.

"Yeah, I know." I was beginning to feel the real, solid nature of growing and living and loving and praying and getting the ax. To feel and just feel. I was beginning to move beyond my mental holes and cavities, my Captain Blackeye.

"Well, I have to get some supper on," Margene announced.

I followed her into the kitchen.

"Hey, look," she said, pointing out the window.

Outside, a gorgeous storm was ending, and the clear sky was only beginning. Margene pointed up at the clouds and said, "Reminds me of how the sky used to look at Griffin Farm. Look, honey."

And we both smiled at the gorgeous storm.

"You know, Mom, sometimes I hate this illness. Sometimes, I feel like a train wreck. But maybe my bruised brain holds a special gift. Like, somewhere inside, there's magic, a magic I can pass on, to let people like Buddy know that you can hold on," I said.

"And maybe, after all of your hearing of voices, you can hang on to one. Yours," she said. She looked me in the eye. She didn't look away. Even when that pot on the stove started boiling over, she didn't look away.

"Mine," I said.

Dr. Dad came into the kitchen. He set the table. He set it for three.

I knew I had made it out alive because I had Margene and Dr. Dad by my side. I knew that many fell through the cracks. I knew there was no real middle ground. When Captain Blackeye was around, people either recovered or died.

Back home, I looked at the pictures on my fridge – pictures of Jeffrey, Katie, little Buddy, Michael, Thomas. I had one picture of Michael. In it, he was wearing his favorite navy blue Mitgard baseball cap backwards. Every time I looked at it, I knew that if he were there, Michael would say, "Ride on, sister."

I didn't know if I was going to have another episode, but I wasn't about to sit around like a scaredy cat, waiting for Captain Blackeye's gloom and doom. Hell no. If he came around again, I'd fight that bastard pirate.

I still thought about the long, barn aisle of Griffin Farm. I thought about the races Jeffrey, Michael, Buddy and I used to have in the front field, when someone would always get bucked off, when it was usually Jeffrey, when Jeffrey would rest in the grass and act like he was hurt, pissing me off. And I thought of the day when Jeffrey and I lost our virginity together in the back barn, how it was sloppy and shaky and sweet.

At dusk, in my city apartment, I missed leaning on fences. I missed staring off into farmers' fields. I remembered listening to horses, understanding them in their silence. Griffin Farm might have closed down, but in my thoughts, we were all still riding together.

I knew I wasn't cured, but I was aware; watching for symptoms had become easier. I knew one thing for certain – my second psychotic fall led me to release the shame and bleed it out. See, with these traumatic experiences came a raging strength and fight, a fight that came from the sky and the earth, the thunder and the ground, an elemental fight to believe that I deserved true, ridiculous love, true faith, and the freedom to let my mind escape enough to dream without the fear of losing myself.

Here I was, hoping. God, I hoped. I hoped that half-sane and childlike Mary Lochmore could be trapped inside an aching mind, locked up and riddled with voices, and still come out on the other side. It had to be about today, this moment, this breath.

Eating dinner, I was crying. Not from sadness. From relief. And because I was fully in love. Not with a person, a place, a thing. I was in love with reality, and all the joy and sorrow that came with it. I was in love with the ability to feel and know that feelings were feelings, high or low, just there. I battled the dreaded Captain Blackeye, my disease. I took Captain Blackeye by the neck, and I came out alive. Twice. Facing a gorgeous storm, living inside it, living simply on earth – that, to me, became heaven. *Doin' aaright, brother. Fair winds.*

Part Six. Sea Dog Shorty.

Stop. Change Tape. Fast Forward.

Two years later.

One.

When I turned 26, there was a music festival in the city of Welch. Gus was headlining that night. I didn't tell anyone I was going. I was afraid they'd talk me out of it.

I put on some makeup. Not much. I drove downtown alone. I was shaking, terrified that seeing him again would make Captain Blackeye's voice reappear, but I drove on anyhow.

When I entered the bar, I struggled to breathe until I heard his voice – the real Gus voice – coming through the speakers. Cool and clear, his voice. As before, it soothed me, and I wanted to join him on stage, to thank him for the calm.

When he finished playing, there was a long line to meet him. I waited patiently, shaking there.

Finally, he saw me. He reached forward, saying, "Hey, I know you."

I held my hand out, blocking his hug. I was afraid of everything that night – the lights, the sound, the people, Gus' arms. But I shook Gus' steady hand with my crooked one, and my mind was quiet.

When he let go, he asked, "Heard any good music, any good voices lately?"

"Lots," I said, chuckling to myself, staring at the thin fellow. I put a hand on my heart, feeling the soft beating. I remembered his letters, his lowercase words, and the real messages in between his lines.

"How are you?" he asked.

"A little rocky, to tell you the truth," I said.

He squinted. Through his eyes, I felt concern seep out of the blue. He nodded. "Sometimes the seas can be a little rough."

I smiled and said, "Your music. Thank you."

"No thank you. Every time I see you, I start writing songs like crazy. There's something about you."

"Something about you too," I said. "Familiar."

"Yes."

And I turned away. Walking out of the packed festival, I felt lifted, lifted that even Captain Blackeye couldn't take away the love for all solid things – a curious, real love, anything but imaginary. Lasting.

Outside, Gus passed by my side, waving goodbye.

I watched the back of him. I watched him look up at the sky, studying the stars or the moon or the black.

And I relaxed. The Welch streets were quiet, still, settled, and serene.

Then Gus turned around, walking back toward me. With his long arms, he grabbed me, softly holding me there.

I felt his real, long, wiry arms hold me. Wrapped up, I felt a warm peace. The moment of arms. The quiet moment of arms.

He pulled back, gazing at me, grinning. He wasn't grinning at the crowd or the lights or the night. He was grinning at me. His gaze was long and steady.

And I grinned back. Perhaps a hug was all that was needed to create a clear, deep feeling, a feeling beyond block letters, a feeling somehow lost inside the music. Buddy was trying to tell us that. It was all about the music – the strange, unexplainable connection between the notes, the elusive, divine pattern that bled out a song. God, Buddy was trying to tell us all.

Two.

It should've been Buddy's birthday party. Sandra Lee was stirring homemade soup. Just she and I, and in her kitchen, an antique saddle took up one chair. She'd found it on one of her shopping sprees. Glancing at it, she said, "Just couldn't pass up the deal."

I laughed at her while she slurped her soup.

On the way home, I stepped on the gas and shook my head. My grip on the wheel grew hard. I glanced in the rear view mirror. *Mary Lochmore, you're a long way from the farm,* I thought. I remembered the way Jeffrey always rode the hard horses, even the ones that tried to slam him against the arena wall, smashing him like a wolf spider. Jeffrey won many wars.

Sandra Lee had always said, "Jeffrey, you have the touch with the toughens. Michael's too fragile."

Jeffrey was always so strong, and I missed his strength. Jeffrey had horses flip over on him, buck him off, kick him in the thigh, nearly kill him. At the horse shows, the other riders always joked that Jeffrey was made of rubber. When most riders would've been crushed, Jeffrey bounced up, got back in the saddle, went in the show ring, and put out his best round.

I smiled, remembering the way the three boys looked riding together, cantering through the Griffin fields, heads bobbing at three different heights.

I jumped out of the car, heading to my apartment. Someone had left the building's front door open again, the way Michael always used to forget to close the front gate at the farm. Whenever Sandra Lee found out, she'd run around the farm looking for him. She ran like a clown on crack.

Fighting medication side effects, I was tired, so tired that I was used to being tired all of the time, and I functioned in this state so well, I even had Margene convinced that I was spunky. My back hurt, my legs ached, and my eyes drooped, but I grabbed the mail, heading inside.

It was quiet, which was good. At least no stray cats were running loose. As I unlocked the apartment door, the dusk sun slid through the window, spreading a yellow sliver across the floor. It was fine.

I turned on the lights. The desk was dusty, and I tripped over my old horse boots. Kicking them aside, I remembered the pony, Red, who bucked me off once. *That pony was a real bitch.* I whispered it out loud.

"Which pony?" a voice said.

Startled, I spun around.

Smirking, Jeffrey sat on my couch.

"How'd you get in here?" I asked, scowling.

"Sandra Lee has the spare key from when you were sick," he said.

"Oh yeah," I said, throwing the mail on top of the pile.

"I decided this was stupid," he said.

"What was stupid?"

"Us not talking. I'm sick of it."

"It's been a freaking long time," I said.

"I know."

"You still sober?" I asked.

"Yeah, you?" he asked.

"Yup."

Silence.

I picked up my phone, checking messages, acting like he wasn't there. One call from Margene, reminding me that I'd told her I'd help her weed her small side garden and that I needed to call Dr. Dad and "check in."

"I know you miss the barn, Mare," Jeffrey said, moving to the kitchen. He hopped up on the counter, sitting there, his feet dangling in the air.

Standing in front of him, my jeans felt tight. I hung up the phone, shutting my eyes, breathing in. Just the mention of the barn, and I could almost smell sawdust. I sneezed. I could almost hear Big Mike sifting through feed cans, adding supplements to the grain. I could almost hear the horses pawing and snorting, gnashing their teeth at the stall walls.

"I can hear them too," Jeffrey said, catching my thought. "In my head. I can hear them when they're hungry."

I nodded.

Jeffrey folded his arms. "Listen, I'm starting my own barn. Already got it running, and I want you to work for me."

"Where?" I asked him.

"Around here, not far, just outside of Welch."

"I can't do the whole deal. I need to manage my illness, and that horse life is too much, too much stress," I said.

"Bullshit. You can take it. You'll do what you can," he said. "I just want you there. Are you going to that meeting in Mitgard tomorrow night?"

I nodded. "Yes."

"I'm going too. We can talk after. How's that sound?"

"Sounds good," I said, resting a hand on his shoulder.

Jeffrey leaned forward, hugging me with his small, strong arms. "I've missed you, Mare. It's time to just move on from here, time to keep riding. I feel better…about all of it. I've worked through a lot and now the show must go on." Pulling away, Jeffrey jumped from the counter, turned, and headed for the door. Before he left, he flashed a thin, quick smile, the best that he could do for a serious man who had strangely become an only child.

The next night, Jeffrey had a stupid, gray hat on. His trademark black-rimmed glasses were thicker, more stylish, and new. I studied his crooked teeth, remembering the time when he got kicked in the mouth, when he lost his two front ones, when Michael dug through the ring dirt to find them, saving them in a glass of milk.

His eyes were bluish, no greenish, no gray, big and round, set wide. Age couldn't change the set of the eyes, but it seemed that his nose was slightly curved at the end more than before. Age and thinness made it seem so.

During the meeting, I tried to pay attention to the war stories, stories of drugs and sex and alcohol and suicide attempts. And stories of housewives and working moms and people just there, smiling. I twirled a strand of hair around my finger, staring at Jeffrey's arm. He didn't look up. The whole hour, he didn't look up.

Outside the church, people were smoking and hanging out.

Jeffrey hugged Steve, a gray-haired man, and then waved at me.

I inched my way over. "Heya," I said. My voice felt awkward and strange. It cracked.

He hugged me sideways. "Hey yourself," he said.

I breathed in the leather smell of his jacket.

Jeffrey backed away, smiling a rare smile, showing crooked teeth. "Thanks," he said.

"Thanks for what?" I asked him.

"For meeting me."

I nodded, frozen there outside on the sidewalk, near the creepy church. We were both way too sober. I fiddled with my hair again, staring at his thick knuckles. The skin of his hands was splitting. Jeffery still had farm hands – strong and wrecked. "So where are you living now?" I asked him.

"Close to you, not far. I have a house near the University," he said, looking off, as if he was searching the fields, checking for a sick horse.

"We've been walking the same streets, and I didn't even know it," I said.

"I saw you at the grocery once," he said. Jeffrey kicked at a rock. "I didn't say 'hi.'"

I laughed. I kicked at a stone.

"So I'm married now," he whispered.

By then, the people around us had scattered. We were alone on the church path, and I was feeling shifty. Leaning weight from foot to foot, I lit another cigarette. "You're married?" I asked him, raising both brows. I looked at his hand again. He wasn't wearing a ring.

"Yeah," he said, looking down.

"Oh," I said. "Weird. I mean, good for you."

"Do you want to go for coffee?" he asked me.

"Yeah, why not," I said, shrugging.

We both wore hooded sweatshirts. On top, we both wore leather jackets. We walked. We both wore black boots, and they clicked on the sidewalk. Click, click, the same way our horse boots used to click on the barn aisle, making a simple song.

While we walked, sometimes I glanced up at him, and he could still match my stare.

I pulled my jacket sleeves down, making sure to cover my bent wrist, making sure to cover the faint lightning bolt scar there.

He touched my hand. “I’ve seen the wrist. I’ve seen your stomach. I’ve seen the scars, Mare,” he said, pressing a pointer finger against the center of his glasses, pushing them up. Then he quickly turned his head, zoning out.

He led me to his truck. Jeffrey was driving a black Dodge, similar to the one Sandra Lee and Big Mike used to drive, but his was new and spotless.

He opened the door for me, helping me up.

Jeffrey turned on the heat. “I hate this cold,” he said.

“You always were a pussy,” I said, laughing.

“Real funny,” he said, turning on some moody rock. “You always were a hardass.”

“You can’t be married,” I stated.

Jeffrey coughed. “It’s in the end stages,” he said. He coughed again.

“You have a cold?”

“No.”

I coughed.

“You sick?”

“No.”

I focused on listening to the music, staring at Jeffrey’s hands on the wheel. He gripped it loosely. I stared at his wrist. I thought about what it would be like to touch it. I thought about what it would be like to swim inside his wrist skin. I thought about his lips, and I told myself I was crazy. God knew people had called me that before. But I wasn’t crazy. I had taken Captain Blackeye by the neck. I had faced that bastard, and I was well. I was present. I was feeling. And I was suddenly so terrified to be feeling.

As he drove, I thought about the summers at Griffin Farm, the days when our sunburned faces peeled. I thought about Thomas’ skin, how it would shed too. I imagined waking with Jeffrey in the morning, living the normal life, waking to shuffle through halls, entering a chaotic kitchen full of cats and dogs, pouring the milk, and saving each others' lives over cereal.

Concentrating on the road, Jeffrey spit his words out. "I still live with her, in the same house, but it's like I have an apartment downstairs."

"Hmm," I said. "Why did you want to meet me? You said you wanted to talk about the barn. Me working for you. Whatever. Take me back to my car."

"I just wanted to see you for coffee. That's all."

"Really?"

"No." He cleared his throat. "I'll take you back to your car."

We were quiet on the way back to the creepy church.

I reached for the door handle, pulling up. It stuck, then gave.

"I'll call you tomorrow," he said from the driver's side.

And he did.

And I answered.

The next night, Jeffrey and I shared a quick, awkward dinner out, a half-date. Back at my place, in the truck, Jeffrey pulled over in the back parking lot.

I had to reach for him. As if he were a sick horse, I had to stroke his neck.

Jeffrey left the truck running.

I grabbed his hands. I pulled him in, pulled him across the seat, tugging his arms hard, feeling the reins, his arms.

When we kissed, I had a frog in my throat, but I didn't have time to clear it. The kiss stopped and started and stopped and started. Warmth crept through my chest, a warmth that spread from the top of my black hair to my callused feet. Then I felt the rush again. Surely, pieces of hay were stuck down my shirt. All over, my skin itched.

Then I backed away. "You can't be married," I stated again. As if I could wipe it away, the same way I had always wished to wipe away Captain Blackeye.

Jeffrey leaned back against the driver's side window, pressing his head against the side door. "Shit, Mary. I can't do this to you. Especially after all you've been through. I don't know what I was thinking."

"I don't know either," I said.

And then we kissed some more in the hot truck, talking tongue to tongue. Above us, the streetlamps were glowing.

I knew I should be getting inside, that I didn't need any stress. I thought about the hospitals. Margene and Dr. Dad constantly worried about me getting sick again. Lingering was the memory of shock treatments and clownish Doctors in long coats. Those memories were so close, closer than the kiss. I looked him in the eye and said, "I have to go. Now."

"I know," he whispered.

"Don't call me," I said, a lump rising in my throat.

He nodded. "I understand."

I wasn't crying.

Jeffrey wasn't crying.

I left the truck. I didn't look back. Even while I walked up the back stairs to my apartment, I wasn't crying. Instead, I felt a sinking treasure in my chest. Something was buried there, yes.

Three.

One year later

I was just getting home from the doctor when I checked my messages. One was from Jeffrey. It said, "Hey, Mare, I want you to come see the barn. Forget about all that other shit. You have to come out here. You know you need to ride."

I drove out to the outskirts of Welch. The directions were long and loose and confusing, but somehow, I found the new Griffin land. When I drove down the driveway, it was smooth. And there was no sign yet, but the fences were freshly painted black, and inside them, a few horses grazed, scattered about the grass. One by one, they lifted their heads, testing the wind, noticing my car, then settling back down to eat. *Home*, I thought. *Home.*

When I pulled in, Jeffrey had two lead ropes in his hand. "Help me bring these horses in, will you?" he asked.

"Sure," I said.

Jeffrey handed me a rope. "I'll get the bay, Sparrow. You get the black, uh, Slick. Named him after your old horse, just because."

I smiled.

Sparrow was unusually jittery. Jeffrey put a chain around his nose to keep him from pulling loose. "Usually, he only acts like this when it's cold," Jeffrey said. "His owner's in for a real treat in her lesson later if Sparrow doesn't change his mood. Guess I better ride him before she gets here. Or maybe you can."

"Maybe I can. I'm a little out of practice," I said.

"I was too. Now it's 10-12 horses a day, minimum. Even when I'm in bed at night, I still feel like I'm trotting or cantering. Sort of midnight-queasy."

"I remember what that was like," I said.

"Come on boy," Jeffrey whispered to Sparrow. With a thick-knuckled hand, he touched the horse's dark neck. Together, they walked into the barn.

Slick was jumpy as well, pawing at the ground. I put a chain over his nose, leading him in. As I walked, I didn't look at Slick. I moved forward, looking straight ahead, remembering the way that gazing ahead helped to calm the wild ones down. And it worked. Slick settled, walking calmly next to me. We headed into the barn.

When the two horses were tucked in their stalls, Jeffrey said, "Now I have to get that two-horse trailer cleaned out. It's back in the back field, stuck in some deep mud. I need it for the show I'm heading to this weekend."

"I'll help you," I said. "Well, I'll help you clean the thing out. I don't know about moving it."

Jeffrey nodded, and we headed to the field.

The trailer was buried in weeds out back. "The old thing doesn't look good to the customers. It clutters the land," he said, shrugging. "But it still works."

Near the trailer, I heard a rustle. I jumped a little. Then I saw a deer in the brush. When I got closer, I wondered how Jeffrey would ever shake the old, heavy thing loose from the ground.

Jeffrey gripped the trailer door handle.

I heard a mare whinny in the distance.

Jeffrey pulled the latch. It was stuck. When he yanked on it, it gave so much so that Jeffrey fell on his back, cushioned by the tall grass. He shook his head like a cartoon, straightening his glasses.

I lay down on the grass next to him. In my mind, I saw a mane, Thomas' mane of yellow hair. I reached out, but all I felt was air. And then I felt Jeffrey's hand, the palm, pressing against mine.

"Our fingers almost match, Mare."

"Uh huh. Almost."

I turned my head, looking at his blue-gray-green eyes. With my other hand, I picked a piece of hay out of his hair. "You know what I wish?" I asked him.

"What?"

"That it could always be like this. Me, you, in a field."

"Me too," Jeffrey mouthed. "We're twenty-seven and we're still just kids."

He was so close; I couldn't make out the nose or the teeth. Flies were everywhere. Too many flies. I knew there was something in the two-horse trailer. I knew it.

Jeffrey swatted flies out of my face. "I don't want to know what's in there. I don't want to know, girl. I'm tired of cleaning up messes." He placed his thick hands on my head. One hand on each cheek, he said, "My divorce is in the works. I'm not asking you for anything, but I just wanted you to know."

"I don't want to know what's in the trailer either," I said.

A gray mare was watching us. Her head swayed. Her lashes fanned her round black eyes.

"She's a strong one," Jeffrey said. "Forget about this trailer. Let's go in the lounge. I'm damn tired."

"Tell me what you're thinking. Straight up," I said, pulling my hair back. "You've got to talk to me at some point in this life."

"Well, here's the deal…"

"Yeah?"

"I'm married, and I love the shit outta you," he said, taking off his glasses, looking at me hard. "Always have."

"I don't want to know what's in that trailer," I said.

Four.

Leaving the new Griffin Farm, I thought about the way Michael never burned. He always had a hint of color, just a hint. Jeffrey and I always fried and peeled, fried and peeled.

Back home, I splashed water on my face, thinking about the two-horse trailer. The flies. I wondered what was inside. I turned off the faucet, listening to the water drip into the sink. I stared at myself, air-drying. Crow's feet were landing near my eyes. Then I grabbed a damp towel, clearing my face of the barn dust. *Probably just a dead animal,* I thought. *A raccoon. Yes.* But I thought of Sparrow and Slick, how they were spooking all the way to the barn. I thought about the way they jerk-walked like Buddy used to.

I swore I heard something rustle near the place where the carpet and the wall met. It sounded like mice. I pictured Jeffrey in his jeans, his lack of hips.

I called Jeffrey at the farm and heard the voice mail: "You have reached Jeffrey Griffin with Griffin Farm…" then, "Hello? Mare?"

"Yes."

"Jesus, we got a problem here," Jeffrey said.

"What…is…it?"

Jeffrey cleared his throat and said, "I went back to the back field. I went back to the two-horse trailer. There were some bridles in there. I needed them."

"Jeffrey, you have like 50 bridles in the barn. A freaking flea market collection."

"Mary, fucking listen. There was a dead one in there."

"A what?"

"A dead mare."

"Christ, which one?"

"A bay one. Found her in Scallycat."

"I'm coming over," I said. "You all right?"

"That was going to be Sandra Lee's horse when I got done training her. I haven't told her. This'll break her."

"Probably. Fuck. Make something up. Loose horses on the highway or something...don't tell her she just croaked."

"That's the thing. She didn't just croak."

"Jesus."

"I know my horses. You know I do. That mare had no signs of anything."

"Maybe she just got sick, Jeffrey. Maybe you're not as all-knowing as you think you are. Let it go, brother. Sometimes, mares just get sick. I feel a fever myself."

"Fuck your fever, come out here," Jeffrey said, hanging up.

I swore I heard mice. Here and there, through the apartment building walls, I heard a thump, a squeaky bed, a snort, a knock, like a hoof kicking against a wall, perhaps a whinny, the signs that the barn was fine, the signs of life.

When I made it to the barn, Jeffrey was already feeding the horses. I heard the sounds of various shifting and kicking. Thirty hungry horses waiting for a Griffin to finish the feed. I watched Jeffrey look in on each one; he whispered to them, loving each hoof, mane, and tail.

When he saw me, Jeffrey nodded hello.

I smiled a little, smelling the dust, leather, shavings, the musty smell of my second home. There were no voices in my head, other than the sounds of lovely beasts. I was hungry.

"You want to help me here?" he asked.

"Sure," I said.

"Sorry I was a dick earlier. I was all tore up. We need to go to the hay barn. We need some more. You want to help?"

"Okay," I said.

Together, we pushed the cart into the hay barn. When we turned on the lights, we breathed in at the same time. There was the sweet smell of fresh-cut hay, wall to wall. Greenish and heavy. Together, we hauled bales onto the cart, looking around.

"This is a beautiful barn," I said. "So clean."

"It is, Mare, it is," Jeffrey said.

"What'd you do with the bay mare?"

"Some of the Mitgard boys helped me bury her out back. She was a good one too."

"Sometimes they just get sick, Jeffrey."

"I told Sandra Lee," he said.

"What'd you tell her?"

"I told her the truth, that I don't know any answers."

"Tell me about it. What'd she say?"

"She said we'd find another mare, that we'd take another Scallycat trip to shop."

"I'd like to go," I said.

"Hell, I was planning on it."

I grinned.

Jeffrey pushed the cart, turning off the lights in the spotless hay barn, sending shadows across the freshly swept ground.

Finishing the morning feed, Jeffrey and I wandered the barn aisle, checking for loose shoes or other signs of trouble.

"It all looks good," I said, hands on my hips.

Touching my cheek with his cracked pointer finger, Jeffrey said, "I believe it does look good."

That night, after riding and teaching some lessons, there wasn't much point in going home since I'd be back at the barn again before it was even light out, before the sun or rain came down on the seven hills of Welch. And there was always something else to do – an aisle to sweep, a bridle to clean, a horse to turn in or out, a leg to wrap, a wound to fix.

I rested on an orange, vinyl couch while Jeffrey took one last walk through the fields. Then I heard him whistling.

Jeffrey quickly click-clicked across the lounge, sliding his boots off, unzipping his chaps, hanging them on a chair. He worked his way next to me on the couch, turning to face me. "I'm beat," he said.

"Me too."

"I'm working hard. I just don't know if it'll ever be enough. It all eats at me. I never wanted to be a Griffin winner. I just wanted to ride with my brothers. I just wanted Big Mike to come back home. I never cared about being the best barn. Most of the time, I just wanted to run in the fields with you. And I know I want you here. I just don't think I'll ever be normal."

I looked at his hat head, his sweaty hair. I studied his small, compact, wiry, muscular body, his dirty jeans. "I could get sick again," I said.

Jeffrey nodded. "I never rode as well as Buddy. And I never was as handsome as Michael."

"But you could handle the hard horses," I said, pulling off his glasses, setting them on the lounge table. "Can you still see me?" I mouthed at him.

"I can see you when you're up close," he mouthed back.

Five.

It was Sunday morning. Jeffrey and I decided to visit Sandra Lee at her Mount Kormet home. The kitchen was cluttered with antique furniture, dolls, vases, clothes, a life size picture of Marilyn Monroe, and loads of cat vases and other junk.

Sandra Lee smoked and made Jeffrey and me some breakfast. While she scrambled eggs, she announced, "Yesterday, I found a ceramic figurine at the Welch Thrift for 48 dollars. I can sell the shit on Ebay for twice that. And I found some odds and ends to add to my cat collection."

Jeffrey chuckled. "Sandra, you could care less about cats. You never even cared which ones were living or dying in our old Griffin barns."

"True," she said, putting out her cigarette. "But I'll rake it in on my antique cat collection."

Cutting toast, Sandra Lee took off a section of her pointer finger. "Goddamn, Mary Mother to Hell," she said. Then she taped it up.

"That needs stitches," Jeffrey said.

"Isn't the vet coming out to the barn later?"

"Yeah," Jeffrey said.

"Well, he can take a look at it."

Jeffrey shook his head at her, then looked at me, shrugging.

Sandra Lee served up our breakfast. She had made enough for three boys. She pulled her gray-brown hair back in a ponytail and said, "Jeffrey, you're my Griffin winner."

"I know, Mom," he said.

"You know Big Mike is getting another divorce," she said.

"No, I didn't know. I haven't talked to him at all."

"Well, he is," she said. "Serves him right." She pulled her cat sweatshirt around her knobby knees. She lit another cigarette. Ashes peppered the floor. Her face softened. She put a hand on Jeffrey's shoulder.

I shivered. It was freezing in there.

Sandra Lee looked down at the ground. "You know that mare that died…?"

"Yeah?" Jeffrey said.

"That mare had bad eyes anyhow. You know what Big Mike always said. One mare down, room for another one. I'm not a total cold fish, but I'd rather keep things rolling. The show must go on," she said.

Jeffrey took the cigarette from her, took a drag, and put it out. "You need anything from the store?" he asked.

"Find out what the specials are, will you Mary?" she asked.

"I will," I said.

Together, we did the dishes.

The show must go on.

That evening, after the horses were bedded down for the night, Jeffrey told me to get in the truck. He had a funny look. By then, it was dark.

"Where are we going?" I asked him.

"To see Big Mike," he stated.

"Is that a good idea?"

Jeffrey paused and said, "I don't know, but I'm going. You can come if you want. I could use someone to lean on, someone steady."

"Crap, I don't know how steady I am."

"You're the steadiest mare I know."

We drove out toward Mitgard.

Big Mike had a small house out on Mitgard Highway. While we drove, Jeffrey said that Big Mike no longer worked with the horses directly, but he still worked with horse people, and he had opened a small tack store that was attached to his home. He kept up with the horse show gossip, and he kept up with Jeffrey's winnings.

We drove past one treatment center where Michael had stayed. We drove past the shack where Jeffrey had found Michael's body. Then a quick left into Big Mike's drive.

A semi swished past us just after we turned. I felt the rumble of it, the jolt, all the way inside Jeffrey's truck. I felt my whole body shake as he turned.

Jeffrey slowly parked.

We crept up to the door. There were no lights on inside the house or the tack shop. Our paddock boots click-clicked on the sidewalk leading to the door.

I read the sign, "BIG MIKE'S TACK. OPEN. SALE ON SADDLES."

Jeffrey knocked.

I waited behind him, holding on to his shirt.

Big Mike opened the door and walked away. Then, with his back turned, he said, "Hi, son." Then he whipped around, looking at me. "Mary," he stated.

I studied the sun creases, the skin lines of an older horse man. He had Michael's green eyes, and they were red, dry, and tired looking, but Big Mike looked good on the outside. He was freshly tanned, and his gray hair was combed carefully to the side. He wore ancient, thin jeans. His button down shirt was pressed smooth.

"Well, come on, you two. Don't stand in the doorway. The air's bad for the saddles," he said.

We entered Big Mike's small house. To the right was the tack store, littered with rows and rows of saddles and bridles. We headed left, entering a bare kitchen.

"What brings you out here after all these years?" Big Mike asked, looking at the tile floor, leaning against the bar.

"I needed some bridles," Jeffrey said through his teeth.

"Yeah sure," Big Mike said, shifting around on his boots. Then he grinned. "Son, listen, it's good to see you."

They shook hands. And when they did, Jeffrey winced from the grip.

I hooked an arm around Jeffrey's waist.

For a moment, Big Mike looked like little Michael, shaking in his boots as if he needed more booze or speed. Big Mike said, "I could show you this new tack we got in. Everyone at the shows is into it. From this secret shop I found in England."

Jeffrey folded his arms. "Listen, I didn't come to talk about tack. I came here to talk about Buddy."

Big Mike nodded. "What about Buddy?"

"Before he died, before that show we all went to, did he say anything? Did he give you any clue he was going to do it?"

"Son, Buddy was sick. I should've paid more attention. You better believe that not a day goes by that I don't want to go back..."

"Yeah," Jeffrey said. "We're all stuck there."

The air was thick with the smell of leather.

Big Mike's green eyes filled up. "Buddy was our Griffin winner. But he was mental. We all knew that. Nothing any vet could've done about it."

Jeffrey said, "All he wanted was to be a singer. Not a rider. And you wouldn't let him."

Big Mike shrugged his wide shoulders. "I guess he did. When you hang around horses for as long as me, you notice things without people even telling you. Since Buddy was winning, I let him smoke pot and drink and screw whoever. Let's face it...I should've been more of a Dad than a trainer." Big Mike put a hand on his chin, feeling his whiskers.

Jeffrey pressed on. "I know he was sick. We all were, wanting so badly to win all of the time."

Big Mike shoved his hands in his jeans pockets. "You and I both know that everybody and his mother loved Buddy. Especially the boarder girls."

"The girls loved him," Jeffrey said. "And he loved music. When he was singing, it was the only time Buddy seemed halfway normal. It was like the music made him that way."

Big Mike glanced at his store and said, "You know I've got a special on the D ring bits if you're interested. You should stock up on them. And reins are two for one..."

"I saw the sign," Jeffrey said, straight-faced.

Quietly, I stood beside Jeffrey, half-hugging him. I thought Big Mike seemed weaker than he used to be, as if the horses used to give him strength, and now he was nothing but a salesman.

"We all know he was sick in the head, untreated, and I was too into the horse shows to do anything about it," Big Mike said.

Jeffrey said, "Some pieces are missing."

Big Mike sat down in a swivel chair. "Jeffrey, you don't know the half of it...what I've had to carry around all these years. And when your mother turned into a shopaholic, it was like she was going down the tubes with him. See, I had to leave her. I had to leave you all. I didn't want to ruin the rest of you like I did to Buddy."

"Ruin him? Like you said, he was sick," Jeffrey said.

"Sick," Big Mike said, nodding.

"Sick," Jeffrey repeated. Still, he pressed on.

Big Mike squinted. "We were all sick," he said.

"Some of us still are," Jeffrey said.

Big Mike breathed in. He breathed out slowly. "Son, I'm gonna tell you this. People were always making this big deal about the way Buddy rode. Or about Michael's looks. And then people were making this big deal about Buddy dying. But since I was your trainer for so long, I know that you were the real rider. You might not be number one in the ribbons all the time, but like Buddy always told you, you could handle the hard horses. You could steer a dirty gelding clean. You could burn a black mare white. I know I never told you that before, but I'm telling you now." He put his thumbs in his front belt loops.

Jeffrey nodded. "Thanks, but I'm still wondering why you didn't stop him. Michael told you about the rope, that he was planning to do it."

"It doesn't matter," Big Mike said, again, shifting from boot to boot.

"It matters to me."

"Let it go, Jeff."

"No," Jeffrey said.

I was feeling shifty, standing there, but Jeffrey grabbed my hand, so I stayed. I knew the hardest horse he had ever handled happened to be his father.

"You don't want to know the whole truth of it," Big Mike said.

"I do," Jeffrey said, making a fist with his hand.

"At first, I just ran away, stayed in hotels and stuff. Rumor at the shows was that I ran off with Liz' Mom. You know, Mrs. Rex, who owned all those grand prix horses. Lilly was her first name. I did sleep with her for a while. We hit it off at the shows for years, even when I was still with Sandra Lee. But as soon as I left Sandra Lee, Lilly wanted nothing to do with me. She was on to her next trainer."

"And...there's more, isn't there?"

Big Mike looked every which way. "Sandra Lee always knew I was with Lilly. She let me stay with her anyhow. Me leaving had to do with not wanting to mess up the rest of you, like I did with Buddy."

"That's bullshit," Jeffrey said, moving in closer.

I backed up into the doorway quietly.

Jeffrey grabbed Big Mike's shirt near the neck. "I want to hear it from you. I want to hear you admit it, that you knew about Buddy's plan, that you did nothing."

"Son, I knew about the rope. He wanted to join that band, and I couldn't let him. He was in the ribbons."

"Fuck. Fuck." Jeffrey hooked a hand around Big Mike's neck, holding it there.

Big Mike looked at the ground.

Jeffrey hit Big Mike in the cheek hard. He yelled, "The music was his fucking medication!"

Calmly, Big Mike wiped some blood on his sleeve.

Jeffrey punched him again, and he took it. Jeffrey pounded at his chest, and Big Mike took it. "You left me to clean up the whole fucking mess."

"Are you done yet?" Big Mike asked.

"Jeffrey, stop it. It's not going to bring Buddy back," I said from the doorway.

Heavily, Jeffrey breathed, his fist still clenched in a tight ball.

Big Mike's eyes spilled over, wetting his lips. "It was way, way wrong."

Jeffrey punched him one last time, in the gut.

This time, Big Mike punched him back. "You didn't know what it was like trying to run a farm, keep a crazy son in check, and all of that pressure to win!" Big Mike yelled.

"Buddy was not crazy," I said. "He was not. He was sick, but he was not crazy."

Jeffrey fell on the floor. He coughed, getting up. "The hell if I don't know what it's like. What do you think I'm feeling? I got two dead brothers, and I just cleaned up another dead mare. What I want to know is this – when is somebody else gonna clean up the dead bodies around here?"

I walked forward, grabbing Jeffrey's hand. "Ease up, brother, easy now," I said.

Jeffrey stared Big Mike down. They both had bloody lips.

Big Mike cried out, "I didn't think Buddy would do it."

"I think I'm the one going crazy now," Jeffrey said.

"You're not going crazy. You're the only one in this family who's kept his head screwed on straight. That's why I left. I couldn't face you all after what I'd done."

"You left me there, Dad. I had to hold up the whole goddamn farm."

Big Mike stiffly hugged Jeffrey tight, slapping his back. Then he hugged me with a solid grip. Holding his oxford sleeve against his bloody cheek, Big Mike said, "Jeffrey, you can take anything. You'll be the last Griffin standing."

"He needed you, Dad. We all needed you," Jeffrey whispered back, thin-lipped, taking the hug.

Big Mike backed off. "I know," he said. "But don't call me 'Dad.' It makes me feel old as hell."

Jeffrey looked at me and said, "Let's go."

I nodded, following him out the door.

In the truck, I said, "You know that's the best he'll ever do."

"I guess," Jeffrey said. "It's all out, so why do I feel like there are still no answers?"

"I'm hungry," I said.

"I'm tired," he said. "Damn tired."

And by the way he drove, carefully turning the wheel, I knew that he was still stiff from the fight.

"Mary, I just don't think I can clean up this mess."

"Me either. I guess the best we can do is just forget about it for a little while."

When we got back to the barn, it was pitch dark. We headed for the lounge. Jeffrey picked me up, lifting my small body onto his desk.

He leaned forward, kissing me.

I sat still, breathing hard.

He grabbed my arms, touched my head, sliding his fingers across my face. His hand moved, drifting to my sweaty neck.

"I can't do this," I said. "Let's face it, you're still married."

"I know," he said, slumping down, sitting on the floor. "Christ, Mare, I'm sorry."

I sank down with him, caving into the ground, knees buckling from the stress and joy and madness of it all.

Jeffrey tugged on one of my belt loops. "You're driving me crazy," he said.

"You want me to help with the night hay?" I asked.

"No, let 'em be. They're not starving. Stay here on the ground with me. Sleep with me here, with the mice."

"Okay," I said.

Curled up on the floor of the office, I said, "Jeffrey, I always thought it would be different. I thought we'd grow up together on the old farm. I thought you'd marry me, and we'd live there."

"It's so frustrating. My wife and I. We're fighting over money. She won't give in. I can't lose this farm too."

"I don't think you'll ever go through with it."

"Why do you say that?" Jeffrey kissed me softly. "Sorry, had to get one last one in."

"I say that because I know you. You're Jeffrey Griffin, and you always come back. You never disappear on anyone. You couldn't do it."

"You know what?" Jeffrey asked.

"What?"

"We waited way too long. But now there's no turning back," he said.

"How do you figure?"

"We Griffins are also winners. We never fall off. Well, almost never. If we do, we always come back for more, whether or not we are hurt." Jeffrey laughed, then his face grew serious. He ran a hand through his brown hair.

I laughed. "Tell me about it."

Jeffrey said, "You're still the only one that I trust."

"Scary."

"Yeah, scary. It's our secret," Jeffrey said, holding a hand over my mouth. Then my eyes, blinding me.

I pushed his hand away. "That's the thing. I don't want any more secrets," I said.

Jeffrey ran a hand along my wrecked wrist and whispered, "But the horses have ears too. They already know about the two of us."

"I can't," I mouthed.

An orange cat wandered into the lounge office.

"Another tomcat," Jeffrey said. "You should take that one home. He's no good at catching mice."

"I think I will," I said. "Did you name him yet?"

"Nah."

"I think I'll call him Buddy."

Six.

The more time I spent at the barn, the more I forgot about the life where I suffered in hospital rooms, the life where my brain had slipped away. I became part of the horses and the fields again. I loved being filthy and tough. It was in my genes and jeans. The smells and sounds reminded me of when Margene and I first swerved down the gravel drive at the original Griffin Farm, later sitting in the orange vinyl-cushioned chairs in the fly-infested lounge.

Before I even opened the lounge door, I heard the sounds of horse people talking about shows, rides, bridles, boots, husbands, wives, dust, hay, leather, chaps, and brushes. My lungs were immune to dirt. Every morning, Jeffrey leaned against the wall and said, "Howdy" without a grin. Jeffrey and I worked, sweated, froze, got filthy, built muscles, talked trainer talk, rode and rode more. I hugged many horses' necks, and I relearned how to lose them as well. And in having and losing and loving them all, the horses brought me back to life, back to breaking ice out of water buckets, back to walking long aisles, back to showing, riding, teaching, putting to use my study of motion. My hands and body saw some cold days. The skin got cracked, but hail or haze, the weather never stopped us.

If Jeffrey looked at me and nodded, his glasses tilting, that meant I rode the horse well. When he slipped on his deerskin gloves, it was time to get more horses ridden.

From the movement of creatures beyond my windows and walls, from each long blade of grass that hung on to its height, I learned to trust voices, real voices that came from a blink, a limp, an ear pinned back, the restlessness of twenty-five horses pawing at stall floors, telling me that a hard rain was coming. Horses brought me back to the wind, breathing in to test it. When I breathed out, the horses breathed out with me, hard enough to make lips quiver.

I was peaceful in my position of teaching lessons and riding. At horse shows, Jeffrey and I often stood next to each other, and when no one was looking, he'd reach an arm over, touching the back of my neck. Jeffrey wanted me to be able to ride as well, if not better, than he did, and he told me that. He had no ego problems, no hang-ups. And he never asked for credit. When one of his students rode well at a show, he smiled wide.

But there was something eating at me, something unfinished. Gus. I had to see the real Gus, to see if the music and the noise were still inside of me. I needed to face it, face him. I needed to see, to see if he was still there, inside and out.

And so I checked the band's schedule on the internet. They were playing in Scallycat that weekend. I told Jeffrey the whole plan.

"Whatever you need to do, Mare," he said, staring at his boots.

A few days later, I drove back to the Scallycat mountains, searching for Gus.

Seven.

Scallycat Civic Center.

There was no choice. I had to dance. When the bodies leaned, packed together tight, the squeeze of it held the human slant against the stage, and if I surrendered to the pressure, I could hang on to my brief life. I had to leap, punch, and kick for space. Held up by waves of heads and hands, bodies surfed the air, fighting to stay afloat. I nodded along to the drums, afraid that if I lost the rhythm, my neck might snap, and my head would roll away, a marble cast across the slick floor, my medicated brain joining the loose change left behind – a target for anyone's boot. In these pits, the enemy was slippery ground. The Devil was a broken lace, a lost shoe. Here, the dance depended on this – keep the shoes strapped and stay standing.

I had twelve braids in my black hair. I wore a black T-shirt and ripped, Welch Thrift jeans with a Harley ass patch, jeans so long they covered my shoes, dragging and swiping grime from the ground. As far as sweat went, I was dripping. As far as skin went, I was greasy. Marlboros, back pocket. Earrings, all ten, removed. Black combat boots tied tight for the war zone. Sober, I was no mosh pit virgin. When it came to slam dancing, I was a proud, mean whore. If anyone doubted these mosh pit credentials, then let them doubt Gandhi or Jesus. Amen.

The pit circled, a tornado of men and me fighting fist-to-fist-to-stomach-to-back-to-ground. I scowled, casting my limbs in a personal rage workout. Between the elbow of an Asian boy and the head of a shorter hippy, I tiptoed, straining to see Singerman Gus.

Eyes shut, he screeched. He shook his yellow hair. He strutted and fretted with his guitar across the stage. Like a puma. His blue eyes, during a rare moment when they were open, reminded me of deep dens, asphalt, black soles, and the lost and found zone of fields and gutters.

Hanging on a strange boy's bicep, I weaved, following his sweaty lead to row two. The bodies swayed like a great hammock. Any moment, that swing could turn, flipping us all over to another side. Then, I lost hold of the swing and fell. Clawing at pants and legs, I squirmed on oily ground, a belly-up beetle. They wouldn't even know I was missing until they found me in a comatose heap, left behind like a stolen, emptied wallet. Picturing headlines, I waited. Some shoe swiped at my nose, and I gave in to the face pain, waiting for another crush.

"Here," said a tall, fat one, saving me to my feet.

No time for thank yous. No Thomas to lead me, making the world change its light. No Magic Man. I made it to row one, but my nose bled, enough to seep through my finger cracks. The bodies parted open; blood was the only sight that made the sea of skin relax, letting me out.

Three bouncers followed me to the bathroom, which was nothing special and nothing clean. The fat boys poked their faces in and asked, "You need help, girl?"

I sopped my broken nose with paper towels.

Some paramedic said, "Let me see."

"I get these all the time," I said, proud and loud enough for them to leave me alone. *This will burn tomorrow.* Bloody me groaned. And my wrecked wrist felt wrong again but by then, I was used to my troubled bones.

I splashed my face with icy water and checked for my holy smokes. *Still there. Still smokin', Tomcat.*

I had to ease in on the side, flirt, and become a crowd dart, rewrapped inside strange, shadowy arms. The crowd stretched in a massive yawn, straining to open. Gus slowed his moves, and the bodies around me felt weaker; they were easier to bend. At last, the end was coming.

When Gus moved to the stage edge, his face was clown white. His guitar, a lost child, wailed. I imagined his fingers reaching to close around my neck, melting into a liquid choker. I felt the chilly choke. I could almost hear Thomas whisper, *Breathe, Shorty.*

"This song's about Easter," Gus bellowed. Even though the haze of lights must've blinded him, when he looked my way, I wondered if he saw me – small, barely breathing, bruised and bloody me. Just when I needed to yell, my throat wasn't working again. *Let me have sound. God, let him hear me.* The crowd pushed to make my silent body rise, then sink down, finding land.

Before the next song, Gus said, "This song is for your demons."

Dull wrist pain reminded me of the days when my skin was clear, unmarked from ink, scars, and holes, when I knew nothing of battles, the weapons of extremities, the white rooms, and the pits.

When the lights returned, I was glad to be small.

People wandered, searching for lost cash, watches, and weed. All around, clothes were shredded. Someone scurried beside me, a leather centipede.

Outside, I shivered, checking the traffic. When I found my pickup, I put on my army jacket and walked behind the concert hall, where blue vans waited, engines running.

I joined the groupies behind a fence of tape in a little caution congregation. First, I sat Indian style. Then, jumping jacks. Back down again, I stretched my legs under the caution tape. I waited. My teeth chattered. I took my braids out, using my hair as a scarf. The voices were muffled; I was half deaf.

Finally, Gus appeared, wearing black leather and a striped scarf.

Fans waved tickets, waiting for his autograph.

Signing his name, Gus looked past them into vacant space.

On the curb, I sat, arms around my knees. I searched my pockets for paper. Nothing.

Gus came closer.

I shivered, hiding and crouching there.

Marker ready, he turned to face me.

Reaching over the caution ropes, I stretched out an empty hand. I looked down at my wrecked wrist and said, "Go ahead. Hold it or break it."

Gus reached down, grabbing my hand. The grip was hard enough to hurt. When we shook, the tape wall stretched, cracked, and tore. Suddenly, it split. I started to jerk, to fall back, but he hung on. God, how he hung on. Around us, people fumbled and grabbed for a piece of CAUTION. But they didn't rush him; they kept their places behind an invisible fence.

Gus smiled and leaned in close. His shape, his skin, and the world turned from gray to pale yellow, moonlit.

Gripping his hand, I studied his form – long and lean, as quiet as a secret. Not a scream machine, but small and red-eyed like Thomas was when he was in the doghouse again.

Biting his lip, Gus whispered, "How you doing, Shorty?"

"Sore, but I made it out alive. How're you?" I whispered back.

He looked down, breathed in. He looked up, breathed out. "Tired…my voice is shot, but I'm learning to sign my name," he said, grinning.

"Good to know your name," I said, letting him go.

He shivered, nodding. "Happy Easter," he said, tucking a piece of yellow hair behind his ear. For another trembling, yellow-lit moment, he waved and said, "See ya, sister." Scratching his head, he shrugged and winked, vanishing into his tour bus, his sleek, crimson home.

And then the door reopened. Yellow hair. His real, open smile. He pushed through the crowd, walking toward me. "I don't know what to say, but you're in my mind, like really in there. Can't seem to shake you."

"No kidding," I said, laughing.

"Funny how things turn out. I'm alone now, for real. Been alone for a while. Been thinking about you, I admit. Probably been thinking about you for about ten years," he said, looking down, then back up, his blue eyes burning light. He shifted from boot to boot. "So I have a few days off. If you want, we could run around Scallycat together, eh little one? I mean, if you want to."

"I could show you around. My roots are here." I gave him my number.

"Maybe we could even drive out to the coast, see the ocean if there's time," he said. "I love the ocean."

"Time will tell," I said, smiling. "But I think there's a good shot we could make it happen, if you call soon enough."

Gus looked up. "Looks like a storm's coming."

I looked up. "When Thunderbird came down, lightning filled the sky!"

"I'm not afraid, Mary. Are you?"

"Nope. I kinda like the rush."

"The rush of light," he said, looking me in the eye.

"All yellow," I said.

Suddenly, it was our world.

With his long arms, Gus hugged me. Long, thin, solid arms. Light as wings.

I watched him walk away, his slow swagger.

Then he turned around and shouted, "See you soon. Thanks for coming!"

"No, thanks for playing," I said.

Gus nodded, slowly turning to leave. When he walked, his legs wobbled. Long, wiry sea legs.

Driving away, I searched for a hotel, turning his CD to Track Three. As the voice moaned through the speakers, I tapped my weak hand on the dash. I listened to the Rare Tracks album, the one that even the most devout fans barely knew. But I didn't sing along. I didn't even move my lips. Instead, I swallowed and stole his sound. I locked his lyrics inside, let him blend into bruised and broken me. I praised the medium tone, let the sound stone me, scrape me. I let him rise up through Track Three and become my Magic Man. I let him scream away the words, the letters, his name, my name. I let in his sound, his screams, his piracy. And then I screamed for all of the Big People to hear. I screamed and touched the black sole, letting the treasure go. *Breathe, Shorty.*

Down the highway, Gus' tunes moved into something living, and a feeling was reborn, a feeling that even I, sweet and bloody Mary, the camouflaged Shorty in Scallycat, could blink to make the whole world change shades. And in my aching dance, my messy ride, my grownup fight, this heave of life, these pits, if I hung on to one lingering handshake, one Easter touch, one grip was strong enough to pull me up, make me rise, and keep me standing. The whole way to the hotel, I kept listening. I kept hanging on to the sound and the grip, one grip strong enough to break the caution tape.

When I checked in to the hotel, Gus called and said, "Hey, just wanted to make sure it was really you. This number. I mean, you never know." He laughed into the phone.

"It's me." I laughed back. "Sorry about your luck."

"Aw, I'm glad it's you. So are we going to the ocean tomorrow, Shorty?"

"Looks that way."

"You know what, Mary? All this time, all these years, I had a feeling we'd have adventures someday. Can't wait to run around Scallycat with you. Maybe we can play Spin the Bottle again. Ha. Shit, I gotta run. Sound guy's calling, and that strange guy with the unicorn shirt, the singer from the headlining band, has been busting up my phone too. Geez, rock stars, we really are a pain in the ass, haha. I'll call you first thing tomorrow, k?"

"Aye," I whispered.

"Actually, I might even call you to say goodnight. Don't think I'm weird."

"I love that you're weird," I said.

"Good thing, ha. I love that you're weird too. Listen, I'm so glad you came. I always look for you. Why didn't I get back with you sooner?"

"Beats me," I said, chuckling. "Actually, you wouldn't want to know where I've been. It hasn't been pretty. I guess now's the right time."

"Maybe it hasn't been pretty, but you're pretty. For sure it is the right time. Damnit, I gotta go. Man, this traveling is wearing on me, but I'll see you tomorrow, and we'll see how this all shakes out. I have a feeling things are just right. Christ, I sound like an asshole. But I really do believe it, Mary."

"Me too," I said. "See you tomorrow, rocker." I hung up.

A minute later, Jeffrey called. His tone was dead serious when he said, "Mare, it's me."

Silence.

"Mare?"

"Yeah?"

"Sit down," Jeffrey stated.

"Okay, sitting," I said, shaking.

"Mare, they found him. I just talked to Margene. She's a mess. They found him."

"Found who?"

"The killer. Thomas' killer," he whispered. "They need you…to identify…the face."

Silence.

"Say something, Mare," Jeffrey said.

"Where is he then?"

"Up Northwest. They're holding him out there on other charges right now."

"Okay. I guess I'll wait here at the hotel, wait for them to call. Did you bring the horses in yet?" I asked him in a quiet voice.

"I think for a change I'll just let them be," he said.

"Looks like fair winds there?" I asked.

"Yes. Come home. Please. It's too much for you to handle all alone. I could go out there with you. Fuck, my eye's twitching again."

"I'm all right here. I've made some muscles. I may have broken my nose at a show last night though. Shit, I need the vet. I think I'll stay here in Scallycat awhile until they all start calling. These mountains calm me. Maybe I'll travel some, hit up the ocean, follow the music, follow the different fields, then head Northwest. I'm gonna ride this wind for a while."

"No matter what, Griffin Farm will always be here," he said, "when you get back."

"Take care of Buddy, the tomcat," I said.

"I will. That Gus better be good to you, or I'll fucking kill him, you know I will. He may be a rock star, but he's no Griffin. Mare, are you sure this is the right answer? You're a Griffin winner, and so am I. We always were. We always will be. Are you sure…about him?" Jeffrey asked softly, his voice cracking.

I breathed in. I breathed out. I looked out the window, gazing up, checking the sky, and all was crimson. In my head, I heard one more voice, a voice that was clear and true. *At last, Captain Tomcat, our fields are safe again.*

"Mare, are you still there?" Jeffrey cried out. "You love him, don't you," he stated.

"Jeffrey, I'm here, I'm here. I'm staying in Scallycat. Then I'll follow the music Northwest. I always liked the rain." *I spy a treasure, Shorty. Safe.* "I will see you, I will. We'll ride again when I get back."

"If you come back," he said. "Are you sure?"

"Everything's pointing this way…red sky at night, sailor's delight."

Record.

Made in the USA
Columbia, SC
22 February 2018